# EARTHSINGER CHRONICLES NOVELLAS

## THE COMPLETE COLLECTION

### L. PENELOPE

HEARTSPELL

# CONTENTS

## CODA OF STORM & SORROW
A Bonus Epilogue for Cry of Metal & Bone

## ECHOES OF ASH & TEARS
Earthsinger Novellas, Book 3

## ABOUT THE BOOK

A reluctant queen. A sheltered teen. A dangerous mage.

Their futures are intertwined—the paths they walk will ultimately determine the fate of their people. Seeds sown in the past will bear unexpected fruit, and what's come before could be the prologue to salvation. Delve deeper into the world of the Earthsinger Chronicles with these prequel novellas full of magic, adventure, destiny, and love.

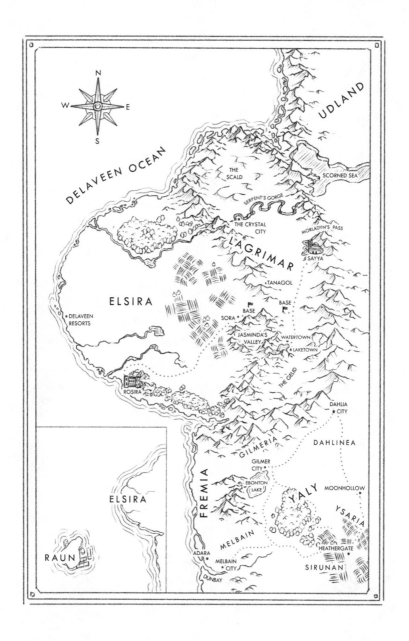

# DEAR READER

*Song of Blood & Stone* was the first novel I ever completed, as well as the first one I ever published, although it was never meant to be a novel. I told everyone, "I'm writing a novella!" because I still couldn't wrap my head around what it would take to write a full-length book. That initial draft clocked in at about 50,000 words, and my very patient editor pointed out all the places where expansion was not only suggested, but *highly* suggested. She was far too kind to tell me the book was barely sensible.

So as that novella turned into a novel, the urge to write something shorter in this world I'd created never left. I had the (somewhat random) notion that this series should include four novels and three novellas, and it stuck. I instantly knew what the first novella would be and had a vague idea that Jack and Darvyn's first meeting was a story he'd tell Jasminda some day. The other stories didn't come clearly into view until I had more of the main series under my belt.

I tossed around the idea of showing how Jasminda's parents met, but unlike her papa, her mama wasn't coming back and to show the two of them happy and young and in love and then go back to a present where she had passed away made me sad. That story will have to exist in our heads, friends.

Each tale presented here bridges the gap between the full-length entries in the series and shows where the characters have been so that where they're going will come into sharper focus.

I hope you enjoy!

# BREATH OF DUST & DAWN

## EARTHSINGER NOVELLAS, BOOK 1

**This novella begins after the events of *Song of Blood & Stone*—it's both an extended epilogue AND a prequel and is intended to be read after reading that book.**

For Jasminda ul-Sarifor, the war may be over, but her conflict is not. New, overwhelming duties leave her caught between two worlds but belonging to neither. She turns once more to Jack, hoping the bond that got them through the first battle is strong enough to weather a new storm.

For Jack, Jasminda's struggles hit close to home. To help her find her way, he entrusts her with a tale from his past when, after another war, a young Jack Alliaseen must also adjust to new responsibilities. But his take a lethal turn when prisoners of war start showing up dead on his watch. With the aid of a mysterious young man destined to change his life forever, Jack must save the lives of those under his protection before it's too late.

As his story unfolds, will Jack's memories help Jasminda conquer her present trials?

# CHAPTER ONE

The throne is a burden and a gift. From its height, we are closer
to the light that creates all, to the skies from which our blessed
Founders emerged. But from great altitudes we may also fall to
great depths. Take heed.

— *BOOK OF HER REIGN*, 19:93

Two weeks ago, Jasminda ul-Sarifor lay on a blood-soaked field,
slashes of harsh morning light burning her eyes, believing she
was about to die. Today, she sat on the floor of the Elsiran
palace's Blue Library, very much alive, and surrounded by a sea
of books.

The volumes she'd pulled from the shelves were stacked in
piles, with some rising over her head. Lining the walls were
rows and rows more on every topic imaginable. She would have
given anything for access to this much knowledge while
growing up on her family's isolated farm. The nearest town
hadn't had a library at all, and while she'd naively thought her
personal collection of books back home was vast, stepping into

any one of the palace's many libraries quickly disabused her of that idea.

Still, none of these books could tell her what she most wanted to know—what she needed to know. For not only had she *not* perished that morning two weeks past, but before noon struck, she had been made queen.

Queen Jasminda of Elsira.

The name fell off the lips of servants and citizens. "Rustic to Regal," a newspaper headline read. "Modest Farm Girl Turned Monarch," boasted another. And her personal favorite, "Once Wretched, Now Royal."

These same papers which had only days earlier lambasted her as a half-breed whore poised to destroy their Prince Regent, now lauded her as fresh blood to the royal line.

Jasminda sighed and closed the book in her hands more forcefully than she'd intended. The slam echoed across the room, and she winced. The book was old, its spine delicate, but a quick inspection proved that her frustration hadn't harmed it. She set *A Detailed Elsiran History, Volume III: The Iron War* on top of the stack nearest her and dropped her head.

Her Song alerted her to the library door whispering open on silent hinges. The power within sensed a change in the air and the presence of another. She held a brief hope that it was the Queen—the true queen, Oola, newly risen from half a millennia of magical sleep. Though the woman was now being called the Goddess Awoken since She was no longer the Queen Who Sleeps.

But a tiny, polite cough dashed Jasminda's hopes. The Goddess was not polite, and the crackling force of Her power preceded Her wherever She went. Had it been Her, Jasminda would have felt the tingles a full minute before the woman arrived.

No, the soft footfalls and deferential disapproval Jasminda

felt from the newcomer's emotions had nothing magical about them. She wiped her face clean of any hint of unrest or annoyance before turning.

"Your Majesty." The Elsiran woman standing in the doorway dipped into a low curtsey. "It is one o'clock. Is now still a good time for our meeting?"

The clock in the corner struck the hour just then. Nadette Gaviareel, event planner to the rich and important, was always perfectly punctual.

"Yes, yes, Nadette. Please sit down." Jasminda rose and picked her way through the spires of books to one of the large, polished tables. She sat heavily in a cushioned chair in a manner that was definitely not majestic.

Nadette approached, her slim, manicured fingers holding a large binder which she gently placed on the table before demurely floating into the seat beside her. "I heard from the palace matron that your office renovation is well underway. What a relief when it's finally complete. It will be so nice to have these meetings in a more appropriate venue."

Jasminda did not miss the soft rebuke in the woman's words. She was almost sure Nadette's gentle reproach wasn't directed at her specifically but rather at whomever couldn't make an office renovation happen instantaneously. Unless she thought such things could be done with Earthsong. For all Jasminda knew, maybe they could, but she certainly wouldn't be wasting her Song on wallpaper and carpeting.

"I like this library," she said. "I find it very relaxing."

Nadette sniffed politely and smiled. Everything the woman did was polite and proper. She was the perfect aristocrat. In her early thirties, her hair was a pale gold with just a hint of red. Her face was smooth and even, line-less, which meant her smiles were rarely ever genuine. And yet, Jasminda had sensed no true animosity coming from the woman. Astonishment and curiosity, certainly, with hints of exasperation. At this point that was all she could hope for.

"So, what decisions need to be made today?" Jasminda asked.

"Well, Your Majesty, almost everything."

Jasminda clenched her jaw to keep her mouth from flying open in dismay as Nadette continued. "The only thing you *have* decided is that the wedding ceremony will be according to the Elsiran custom and not Lagrimari."

"I'm not even sure what a Lagrimari ceremony would be, honestly, though I've heard they are several days long. We don't have that kind of time." She barely had time for this meeting, she really needed to be continuing her research before heading to no less than four events later that afternoon, but Nadette had been insistent and the others assigned to Jasminda's "transition team" had felt that the wedding plans were of utmost import. Oola had agreed.

When the magical border between Lagrimar and Elsira had fallen and Queen Oola had awoken, the long war between the two countries finally ended. Five hundred years of hostilities suddenly over. But the real work was just beginning, for Oola had determined that the two lands should become one, as they had been in antiquity. How could two peoples: the Elsirans with their ginger hair and freckled skin, and the Lagrimari with their dark curls and rich coloring truly live together? They'd been enemies for generations. And even though most Lagrimari had been stripped of their magic, some still had their Songs, and their beautiful power was decried as dangerous witchcraft by the Elsirans.

Jasminda, with her Elsiran mother and Lagrimari father had grown up in Elsira, outcast for her power and her skin. And Oola, instead of taking on her role as monarch, had abdicated, deciding on a whim that Jasminda should be queen. *Queen.* Her role completely independent of Jack, the former

Prince Regent and now king. Their positions unrelated to their upcoming wedding, as Oola didn't believe that marriage alone should make monarchs. It was an opinion Jasminda shared, but how the Goddess expected her to learn to be a good queen, unite a divided populace, rule with any sort of skill, *and* plan a wedding at the same time was beyond belief. It was absurd.

"I'm not familiar with Lagrimari culture," Nadette was saying. "A three-day ceremony would be rather taxing." She tapped her lips as her eyes brightened, in anticipation. "It would be quite the challenge. But we only have four weeks, so I agree, the Elsiran ceremony is best." Shaking her head with disappointment, she opened her binder. "You still haven't told me which color scheme you prefer, Your Majesty."

Jasminda eyed the rows of square color swatches placed evenly across the pages while panic swirled in her belly. If she couldn't choose a color scheme, how could she rule a nation? "Would it be possible for you to decide?"

Nadette's scandalized expression quickly blanked. She ducked her head for a moment and took a breath. Fortunately, Jasminda was spared from the courteous diatribe no doubt ready to spew from the woman's lips when the door opened again—this time with quite a bit more force—slamming against the wall and rattling some of the shelves.

Jasminda didn't need to turn to know who it was, only one person opened palace doors in that manner.

"Jasminda," Rozyl's stern voice sliced through the quiet. The Lagrimari woman spoke in her native tongue, a guttural language made even more harsh by her tone. She didn't bother with honorifics of any kind, and Jasminda was oddly grateful. "You need to call off your dogs."

Jasminda turned and smiled at Rozyl, who scowled back, but in a friendly way. Nadette sucked in a breath, probably at the scars. Rozyl's left side, from behind her ear to the base of her nose, was marred by claw marks.

"Bobcat," was all the woman had said when asked about them, and Jasminda hadn't pried further. But no Earthsinger must have been around to heal her since the scarring was so pronounced.

Rozyl's dark hair was closely shorn, and she wore a stiff pair of trousers with a billowy white blouse — Elsiran clothes, men's clothes at that, but worn much looser, the way the Lagrimari seemed to prefer.

"What dogs am I supposed to call off?" Jasminda responded.

Rozyl glared at Nadette and prowled across the room to sit on Jasminda's other side.

"The ones blocking the plan to rehouse the new influx of Lagrimari in the challengeball arena. There's a petition going around to preserve their sports field and instead set up another refugee camp up the coastline." She shook her head violently. "It's too far from town and too near the water. Autumn is upon us, and the winds will tear through those tents like a knife."

"Excuse me," Nadette said in Elsiran, her polite voice taking an edge of iron. "The new queen and I have a meeting scheduled. Her time is quite valuable, perhaps you can set up something for another time."

Rozyl peered around to glare at the woman. "If she's talking to me, she'd better watch her tone. I may not speak Elsiran, but I recognize a stuck up swine's daughter when I see one."

Jasminda took a deep breath. The language barrier was just one of many struggles to overcome in the unification. "Rozyl, Nadette and I had a one o'clock meeting scheduled."

Rozyl's eyebrows rose. "So did we. And, might I add, I should think the issues of the new Provisional Council would take precedence over your," she looked down at the fabric swatches in front of them on the table, "crafts party."

Jasminda agreed. The last time she'd spoken to Oola she'd said as much, but the Goddess had insisted that the wedding was a vital part of the unification efforts and needed to be attended to by Jasminda herself.

She turned to Nadette, whose prim glare at Rozyl was almost comical. Switching to Elsiran she said, "It appears as though I'm double-booked. Is there any way we could move this meeting?"

"A royal wedding cannot just be thrown together like that of a commoner's, Your Majesty. The timeline is already a challenge. There are craftspeople who will need every available moment to do their best work. Decorations, favors, clothing. Food and supplies to order, plans to make. This is a national event that will not only employ hundreds of workers but will capture the heart of the people after such dark times. The more you push back these decisions, the more it affects the workers. It isn't fair to have them be made to rush and throw things together at the last minute when they could have more time."

Chastened, Jasminda turned back to Rozyl. "Aren't these decisions the Provisional Council can make? There's a reason why we created one immediately after the Mantle fell."

"Yes, but you and the king are the heads. The Elsirans on the Council don't trust the Lagrimari or the translators. They want everything run by either you or Jack for verification."

"Oh, for Sovereign's sake." Jasminda rubbed her forehead. Pressure built behind her eyes.

Nadette gave a little cough. "Is she speaking of King Jaqros? Did I hear his name spoken in such a disrespectful manner?"

"What did she say?" Rozyl asked, leaning forward.

Jasminda groaned and shook her head. "I'm not translating an argument between the two of you." She repeated in both languages. "In fact," she said, standing, placing her hands flat on the table, "I'm not having an argument at all."

9

She looked wistfully at the stacks of books she'd been working through before her interruption. It was her fault she'd double-booked meetings. She was being pressured to hire a secretary who would manage her schedule, but the Lagrimari elders wanted the person to be a Lagrimari. Of course, there were only a tiny handful who could speak Elsiran, and none of them had any secretarial skills. Hiring a qualified Elsiran would have been a slap in the face to the elders, so she'd put it off, handling matters herself, on top of everything else.

Once again, she was being pulled in two directions. She had only ever lived in Elsira, but she looked Lagrimari so they had claimed her as their own, after a fashion. She spoke their language but didn't know their culture yet still felt it was her responsibility to help them integrate more fully into society. However, she was ruler of the Elsirans as well, and couldn't be seen to be preferential to either group.

Her head pounded and she felt like she was going to explode. Before she did, she needed to get out of here. The walls threatened to close in on her, and the two expectant, frustrated faces looking up at her caused her to panic.

"I'm sorry. I— I'll have reschedule you both." She spoke half the statement in one language and the other half in the other before fleeing the room. Not the most regal thing to do, but then, Jasminda most definitely did not feel like a queen.

# CHAPTER TWO

May your conviction in the Sovereign be as water running down the face of the mountain, etching grooves in its solid surface. Stronger than the granite, but impossible to hold in your hands.

*— BOOK OF HER REIGN*, 41:11

If Jasminda had had a secretary, she would have cancelled her afternoon commitments, but since she didn't even know how to do that, she was obliged to attend the hospital wing dedication and a youth talent exhibition. She was grateful at least that someone had thought to include a few Lagrimari children in the program at the last minute. The simple songs and wobbly dances of the boys and girls warmed her troubled heart. But not enough for her to want to brave the formal state dinner scheduled that evening.

No one would mind if she skipped out on the pomp and circumstance and hid in the royal suite instead, would they? But as she attempted to slip through the palace's wide, brightly lit hallways unnoticed, she realized it had been a futile attempt.

"Your Majesty," cried a steely haired butler who appeared, it seemed, out of a wall tapestry. "The dinner tonight honoring the Fremian ambassador is being held in the Sapphire Hall. Would you like me to escort you there?" He held out his arm.

Jasminda's shoulders settled into a dejected slump. "Yes, thank you, Rishard."

The little twinkle in his eyes made her feel a fraction better. She was making the effort to learn as many of the servants' names as possible. It was daunting but felt like a task she could accomplish given enough time and effort. The rest of her queenly responsibilities? She still wasn't certain.

Somehow, King Jaqros had managed to get out of the dinner, a fact she would be sure to needle him about when she saw him. After more than half a dozen courses of fine food and what Jasminda considered an appropriate amount of small talk with the guests, she finally was able to retreat into the solitude of the royal suite.

She sat in front of the sitting room's fireplace, the rest of the space in darkness. Though the palace had been outfitted with electricity some time in the past decade, the rooms were drafty, and the large fireplaces lent warmth to the cold stone floor and walls. Jasminda had been staring into space, wondering, not for the first time, how she could convince Oola to find another queen, when the warm scent she now associated with home enveloped her. Strong arms wrapped around her, and she tucked her head into Jack's chest.

She breathed in deeply and allowed the fear and uncertainty to melt away—at least for now. Jack must have sensed her mood, for he allowed them to sit in silence for a few minutes.

"You left me to manage the Fremian ambassador alone, Jack.

That was very unkind." She playfully jabbed his stomach with her elbow, meeting a wall of dense muscle.

"And for that I apologize. It was a military emergency."

She craned her neck around to find his amber eyes aglow, reflecting the firelight. "Military emergency?" she asked, brow raised.

"A small issue at the refugee camp." When she began to rise, he held her tighter. "Nothing big, not like last time." He referred to the incident in which an Elsiran soldier had shot a Lagrimari boy for using Earthsong. Jasminda's heart still raced when she thought about it.

"We've been enacting some additional training measures," Jack said, "to prevent something like that from happening again. Educating the men on Earthsong and Lagrimari cultural practices. Any soldier who interacts with a refugee will have to undergo the training, but one of the instructors was getting a bit...creative. I had to go and set things right."

And Jack no doubt knew exactly what to do and say to get his men to fall in line.

He shifted behind her. "Was the dinner that bad?"

She shook her head. "No, it was fine. The ambassador was lovely, it's just... I double-booked a meeting with Rozyl and Nadette this afternoon and then ran out on both." She drew back to meet his gaze. His lean face held no judgment. She smoothed down an unruly tuft of his ginger hair before sinking back into his arms.

"I'm not cut out for this, Jack. I can't manage a schedule, how can I help manage a nation? What was Oola thinking? I don't have any special skills. I was never a leader. I've never even been to school." Her chest felt heavy.

Jack squeezed her shoulder. "Well, I can tell you as someone who has trained with the most elite soldiers in the world, led an entire army, and attended the best private academies in this country, none of that makes the fear go away. It doesn't mean you'll always make the right decisions either. Every step of the way, I've felt just as unprepared and unqualified as you do, and yet you're the most natural leader I've ever seen."

She scoffed and pretended to push him away. He didn't budge. "You're being nice to me."

He tilted her head towards him. "No matter how much I love you, I would tell you if I thought there was any chance you would ruin our country or harm any person in it."

She swallowed, feeling the sincerity as his gaze held hers.

"There will be growing pains," he said gently. "When I first was put in charge of the army, I was only seventeen years old. And though it was something I'd trained nonstop for, I felt the pains, too. These times we're in, this unification... It's unprecedented. I know you're looking for answers in the library, but believe me, you won't find a book of instructions on how to do this job."

"But studying the history of former Prince Regents and other rulers around the world is sure to give me insights."

"Yes, insights, certainly. But you've studied history—didn't your mother teach you?"

She smiled at the thought of her late mother. "Yes. It was her favorite subject. And I was the only one interested, the twins never were." The pang at the thought of her lost family hit, same as always, but she was used to it. "Still, it's different to having a formal education."

Jack shrugged. "No other country in history has had to unite two peoples who have been at war with each other for generations. There's no precedent for this, we're in uncharted land. You won't find an answer in any book, we must navigate our way through this by faith."

"But the only things I've ever had to manage were the goats and the chickens back home." Now she wondered if the caretaker Jack had hired to maintain her family's land was doing a better job of that as well. "I don't think I deserve this faith," she whispered.

"Oola does. Otherwise She never would have made you queen. I remind myself of this when things get tough. They're calling her the Goddess Awoken for good reason. She knows things we don't."

"But I'm so scared of messing this up, Jack. How did you handle it? I mean, you were born a prince, but becoming the army's High Commander as a teenager? How did you do it?"

Jack settled back further into the couch, drawing Jasminda onto his lap. "Honestly, Darvyn helped me."

She perked up. "Darvyn? I can't wait to meet this mysterious Earthsinger." She'd heard so much about the Lagrimari man who was indirectly responsible for her meeting Jack. They'd thought he was dead, but Oola had assured them he lived and was even now on his way to the capital city.

"How did he help you? I don't understand how that's even possible."

"Ah, would you like a story, my love? Perhaps to take your mind off your unfortunate day?" Jack's golden eyes glittered with mirth. "I should warn you, it's filled with murder and mayhem."

She mock gasped, placing a hand against her heart. "I'm not sure my poor, delicate constitution could handle hearing talk of something so vile."

He raised his eyebrows. "That's a fair impersonation of Nadette."

She grinned.

Jack leaned his head back and pulled her in tighter to his chest.

"It was the autumn after the Seventh Breach. Only weeks after the Mantle had closed again. I had just been named High

Commander of the Army that spring, on my seventeenth birthday, and was still trying to find my footing in the new role. I knew it wouldn't be easy, but I hadn't expected it to be so...messy..."

3 MONTHS AFTER THE SEVENTH BREACH

A soft, mushy tomato whizzed by Jack's head. His quick reflexes were the only reason it didn't hit him square in the face. Still, some of the moist, red flesh rebounded off the wall to splatter his ear and shoulder.

Jack groaned and wiped the mess from his uniform. He stood at the front of the temple's sanctuary facing down the majority of the town of Sora's residents. The temple was the largest building in the county and served as the primary meeting place.

He held his hands up. "Throwing things is not going to help!" A murmur of disagreement washed over the gathered crowd, who had grown more and more unruly as the town meeting went on.

Constable Belliaros, a thick-waisted man with heavy mutton chops, had the good sense to stand a few paces away from Jack. He shouted over the din, "Let the High Commander speak. And stop throwing things! For Sovereign's sake!"

His smirk belied his words. The constable seemed to be enjoying the confusion.

Seeking to take back control of the situation, Jack projected authority into his voice. "I hear your concerns, but I'm simply here to ensure the army does its duty in keeping the peace in this area. I can take the issues you've raised to the Council and the Prince Regent, but the Lagrimari settlement for the former prisoners of war is here by the agreement of treaties going back to the Fifth Breach. Only the prince can order it moved." And his brother, Prince Alariq, would not do that, but Jack didn't voice this knowledge to the townsfolk.

A wiry woman spoke up from the back of the room. "We're only two kilometers away from that place. Those *grols* are just too close to our children and our livelihoods. I don't see why you can't move them to that settlement up north that's out of everyone's way."

"That's good land they're sitting on," another man shouted. "Tell the prince it should be auctioned off to a real Elsiran, not wasted on filthy enemy scum."

Three women from the Sisterhood sat quietly in the front row. The local priestess, a severe woman whose silver hair was still red at the temples, had her arms crossed. But none of the three Sisters spoke up in defense of the settlers. Maybe they understood what Jack had not before undertaking this fool's errand—there was little point in talking sensibly to insensible people. He should have listened to his mentor, General Larimel. This meeting was a bad idea.

The Lagrimari settlement, a desperate place called Baalingrove, was located near both the Eastern Base and the town of Sora, and Jack had wanted to improve relations between the three. Since the end of the war, tensions with settlers had been high, and there had been a few incidents with soldiers on leave making trouble in town as well. He'd thought an airing of grievances could lead to solutions, but this was turning into nothing but a complaint session about the presence of the Lagrimari.

While more citizens had their say, Jack's attention was caught by a group of teenage boys standing along the side wall, whispering and snickering with one another. They looked mischievous and carefree. Stains darkened the knees of their trousers and scuffs covered their worn boots. Jack suspected the only things they had to worry about were chores or being discovered carrying out some prank. The boys were his age, but they'd had proper childhoods while he'd had drills and duty. He wasn't sure he'd ever really been a child. None of these boys had armies to run. None of them were even *in* the army.

A wave of longing swept over him. If he hadn't been born into the Alliaseen family, son of the late Prince Regent, would he be like them, joking and fooling around with friends? Surreptitiously passing out rancid fruit to throw at the poor sod trying to lead a community meeting?

He swallowed away the wistful longing and raised his arms. The room grew fractionally quieter. "I promise I will take your concerns to the prince myself. Until then, we cannot have outbreaks of violence. I hold my soldiers to a high standard, but the citizens must do their part as well. We will not accept lawlessness in the Borderlands or anywhere else in Elsira. If someone commits a crime, soldier or citizen or settler, they will face our justice—full stop. Does everyone understand?"

This time, when he caught sight of the object launched in his direction, he moved even more quickly than before. A tomato was one thing, but the rotten egg that smashed into the wall behind him was just disrespectful.

# CHAPTER THREE

Tainted thoughts pollute the hands. Cleanse not only the skin,
but the mind before you undertake good works, lest you befoul
your virtue with a defiled heart.

— *BOOK OF HER REIGN*, 40:15

Jack's assistant, Sergeant Benn Ravel, was waiting in a four-
wheeler outside the temple, Sovereign bless him. He must have
known that Jack would want a quick getaway after that nightmare. Jack jumped into the passenger seat, and Benn gunned the
engine.

"Well, that was interesting," Benn said.

"If there's no angry mob chasing us back to base, I'd be
surprised."

Benn chuckled as they sped off into the night. Though Jack
ran an army, he hadn't yet learned to drive, and Benn had been
assigned to him several months before. He hadn't been sure
they'd get along—Benn was a longshoreman's son and had
grown up in Portside, quite a far cry from Jack's affluent

upbringing. But they had become fast friends and Benn, only two years older than Jack, always seemed to know when to talk and when to stay quiet.

The sergeant had quickly become indispensable and now, not only drove him but managed his schedule and provided a sounding board when Jack needed it.

By the time they reached the base, the stars had begun to pepper the sky. The squat gray, concrete structures of the Eastern base with its nearby mountains had been his home for the better part of ten years. Between stints in various private academies for specialized training, he'd laid his head here. And after the not-so-welcoming response of the enraged townspeople, he was grateful to be home.

He hopped out of the vehicle and straightened his uniform, hoping there were no produce stains hiding in places he couldn't see. That was all he needed when trying to be taken seriously by men twice his age and older: rotten egg clinging to the seat of his pants.

As soon as he entered the command center, salutes from the guards stationed at the entry greeted him. Jack was responsible for not only every man in the base and the few women on staff but every soldier in the Elsiran army. As the second son of the nation's late ruler, he took his responsibility seriously, even if he didn't quite feel equipped for the job.

He was just heading down the hall to his office when a voice called out from behind him.

"Commander Alliaseen, sir." Jack turned to find a baby-faced sergeant speedwalking his way. "There's been another incident at Baalingrove."

He took a deep breath. "Of course there has. What's happened now?"

"A settler was caught after curfew last night. This is not his first offense, so he's been brought into custody. He's currently in the brig."

"All right. So what's the problem? Hold him another night then release him with a warning."

The sergeant's gaze skittered nervously to the side. "Well, sir, you see... some of the settlers are protesting."

"Protesting what?" An ache was beginning behind Jack's eyes.

"The curfew. It appears this particular settler is stirring them up. At least that's what Old Zimm is saying."

Jack wanted to roll his eyes but held back. "Zimm's behind this?"

"Not sure, sir. But he's certainly front and center. Says he's trying to help keep the peace."

Zimm was an old settler, a leftover from the Sixth Breach, one of many who chose to stay rather than escape back to his birth country when the Mantle opened up again during the Seventh. The army often used him as a translator for the new Lagrimari settlers who hadn't yet grasped the Elsiran tongue. But something about his relentless helpfulness had always rubbed Jack the wrong way.

He fisted and unfisted his hands, then shook them out. "All right, I'll head over there in the morning to see what's what."

"Yes, sir," the sergeant said.

Jack could only hope the Lagrimari protestors didn't plan to weaponize fruit.

Early morning sun peeked over the eastern mountains as the wheels of the open-topped four-wheeler bumped over the dusty road. Farmland stretched out all around them, freshly harvested fields dotted with thickets of trees, painted in the golds and oranges of autumn. Rain had been scarce this past summer, and the damage left by the Seventh Breach could still be seen in some places in blackened craters marring the earth and groves of dead trees. Plus, the crop had been slightly below average, dampening the relief of peace and further increasing the tension of the locals.

Benn turned a corner and the trees lining the road thinned, leaving a clear view of the Lagrimari settlement known as Baalingrove. The sight of the community still shocked Jack, even after all these years. The poorest of Elsira couldn't compare to the destitution on display here. Shacks made of tin and wood, held together by hopes and dreams as much as nails and pitch, made up the place.

Instead of the orderly crisscrossing rows of Elsiran towns and cities, all the structures here had been built in the Lagrimari style, with a single road spiraling through the tiny town, alleys cutting between allowing access. As such, there was only one entry point, and this was currently blocked by about three dozen settlers chanting and waving blue strips of fabric.

Four Elsiran soldiers assigned to oversee and guard the settlement stood by their vehicles. Thank the Sovereign their weapons weren't drawn, but their relaxed stances belied the tension evident in their expressions.

Jack's vehicle pulled up alongside two others. On the far side of the lane, a larger Sisterhood truck was being unloaded by two young Sisters.

Generations ago, when the first Lagrimari prisoners of war had been trapped by the closing of the Mantle, the group had taken it upon themselves to care for them, seeing service to the poor as a way to honor the Elsiran goddess. Settlers could own no land, could not become full citizens, and had almost no employment avenues, so the food and supplies from the Sisterhood were vital.

Jack approached his men, who stood at attention and saluted. "Commander Alliaseen," said an acne-scarred sergeant, "I— I did not know you would be coming yourself."

"Yes, Sergeant. Bring me up to speed."

"The settlers have been shouting and carrying on for nearly two days now. At first just a handful, but their numbers are growing fast."

Jack regarded the men, who were mostly older Sixth Breachers. When the Seventh Breach had first begun and the Mantle opened, Jack assumed most of the existing settlers would go back to their country now that they had the chance. But none had. And only a small number of new Lagrimari had gotten stuck on this side when the magical barrier closed, marking the end of the Seventh.

As Jack approached the group, a middle-aged man, graying at the temples, stepped forward to meet him halfway. The protestors stopped their chanting—words which Jack hadn't been able to catch.

"Zimm," Jack said, greeting the man in the Lagrimari style with a hand to his forehead.

"Commander." Zimm grinned and executed a low bow. He was a heavy-boned fellow with a firm jaw and calculating eyes. "We are honored." He spoke in heavily accented Elsiran, his voice just a touch too loud.

Jack waited for the man to straighten. He supposed they must have acting troupes in Lagrimar; if so, Zimm would have been perfectly at home on a stage. All of his movements were made with a flourish, with an audience in mind. It put Jack on his guard.

"What is this about?" he asked.

Zimm swept his arm back towards the protestors. "We ask you to free our countryman from prison. And we ask for ending to curfew. Simple requests really. No trouble at all for you." He grinned. "The young man you hold is newcomer. He does not deserve to rot in jail for wanting to enjoy moonlight outside confines of this settlement."

Jack crossed his arms and rocked back on his heels. "And did this young man organize this? Tell you to protest?"

"Oh, no, no, no. We come together ourselves—we are loyal to our own, that is all. Without loyalty, what do we have?" He spread his arms apart. "Elsira is place of freedom, true? That is all we want, good sir. Same freedom as others." Zimm was all polite reasonableness, but Jack felt the deference was feigned. He'd seen men act in such ways with his father, bow and scrape before his face and scheme behind his back.

Jack kept his tone measured. "You understand that the war is still fresh in the minds of my people, right? They will need time to accept you."

"I am here over fifteen years, Commander." Zimm hunched over as if trying to make himself smaller. "We cause no trouble. Keep to ourselves. We just want peace."

The silent protestors watched the exchange from a few paces away. Beyond them, on what passed for the settlement's main street, a few more settlers had stopped to observe.

"You all could have returned home during the war, when the Breach was open. Why did you stay?"

Zimm's eyes darkened, the smile fell from his lips. "This time the True Father grows clever. Does not want anyone... how you say 'stick' here after the Breach closes?"

"Stuck? Yes."

"Ah, stuck. At end of war, all of us ordered back. But going back to Lagrimar is death sentence. Is very hard to be *stuck* in Elsira, true? But stuck here, better than stuck there. Understand?"

Jack nodded. "Yes, I think I do." He motioned toward the men watching the conversation. "I'm going to talk to them."

Jack had been working on learning the Lagrimari tongue for years. He had a knack for languages; he'd picked up Yalyish quickly, spoke both High and Scholarly Fremian fluently, and was passable in Artistic Fremian. However, Lagrimari was the most difficult language to learn on the continent, and he was still struggling. He knew of no Elsiran who had mastered the tongue, so he was especially determined to do so.

Zimm followed when Jack walked toward the men. Jack's unease hadn't quieted, but he sympathized with the plight faced by the Lagrimari.

"Settlers," Jack said in Lagrimari. "I ask for patience, please. I hear you. You want no curfew. Is not my decision. But I...I take your thoughts—"

"Concerns?" Zimm offered, in a low voice.

"Your concerns to my people and hope to find good solution."

He watched the faces. The few newer men seemed shocked to hear him speaking in their tongue, but he observed no hostility and even a few nods of approval. Daring to feel a twinge of hope, he stepped back.

Maybe they could do this, bridge the divide and find a way to keep the peace. Maybe under his watch, things could get better, and these men could have lives with more dignity than they'd been allowed so far.

The cautious optimism and glow of hope warmed him. That is until a bloodcurdling scream ripped out, echoing off the tin roofs. It was a woman's scream, and it was coming from the interior of the settlement.

A small group had already gathered in front of a shack just around the first bend of the spiraling road. Jack brushed by the settlers and paused in the open doorway.

The interior was a simple one-room design. A low bed hugged one wall. In the center of the room, a board propped up by short stacks of bricks comprised the table, which was low to the ground with one battered cushion next to it for sitting. Some shelving was nailed to one wall; the opposite wall featured a makeshift wood stove made from a metal barrel with a pipe rising from it and disappearing through the ceiling. Everything was neat and ruthlessly organized.

Aside from the meager furniture, the room was crowded with two people in it. One, a Sister, standing next to the table, shaking with fear, the other a prone Lagrimari man lying face-up on the ground. His eyes stared sightlessly upward. They would never see again.

Jack entered the shack and knelt at the body, checking the pulse just to be sure. Then he closed the man's eyes and said a brief prayer to help his spirit pass safely to the World After. The air in the tiny home was stuffy and smoke tinged; it clogged his nose and mouth.

He coughed a few times then rose and faced the Sister. She was in her mid-thirties, he guessed, her golden-red hair too short for a proper top knot. A chunk at the crown of her head had been wrangled into a little tuft that stuck up. She shook her head and clutched at her neck.

"Sister, what happened here?"

She looked at him as if seeing him for the first time. "I— I was passing out supplies. There was no answer at the door when I knocked, so I was just going to leave the food inside, but when I opened it... I found him just lying there." She pointed at the man, a Sixth Breacher maybe in his 50s or 60s.

"All right," Jack said, taking her elbow to lead her out. "There's a lot of smoke in here, let's get some fresh air."

"Everyone back!" he called out as they exited. "What's your name?" he asked the woman.

"I'm Sister Lorelle."

"Commander Alliaseen. Are you new here?" Jack hadn't recalled seeing her before and assumed she was a recent convert since all the Sisters he'd ever seen wore their hair long.

"Oh, no Commander. I've been tending to the settlers for the past ten years. Poor creatures. Such wretched lives." She shook her head, face crumpling.

Afraid she was going to break down into tears, Jack patted her arm awkwardly and then turned to find his men. He asked the pair of soldiers waiting nearby to make sure there was a safe perimeter around the home, not wanting a bunch of looky-loos either disturbing the body or breathing the fumes inside.

"Zimm." He motioned the translator closer. "Who is this man? Is this his home?"

Zimm peered through the doorway, his eyes going flinty for a moment before nodding. "That's Pensar ol-Lagrimar. He lives there—lived—there." He stared at the body. "He's definitely dead?"

"Yes."

"Hmph," was Zimm's reply. For such an expressive man, his response was uncharacteristically muted. There was no sorrow or regret in his response or tone. He turned to the other settlers, many craning for a look into the tiny home. "Pensar is dead," he announced in Lagrimari.

You could have heard a pebble fall into a bale of cotton. A few men crossed their arms. Several eyed Jack and the other two Elsiran soldiers. But not one man appeared upset or bothered in the least by this announcement.

"Not a popular fellow, this Pensar, I take it?" Jack asked.

Zimm stroked his chin and craned back around to look at the body. "You can say that."

The question of what caused the scream now answered to their satisfaction, the crowd began to disperse quietly. Jack wondered if they would go back to their protesting.

He turned back to Sister Lorelle, who still looked shaken. Thankfully, another Sister had appeared by her side and held her in a half-embrace. "When you entered, was the room smoky?" he asked.

Her eyes widened. "Yes, it was difficult to breathe."

Jack stepped back to peer at the top of the chimney, rising over the tin roof. "Perhaps the chimney became blocked somehow, and he didn't realize."

Sister Lorelle looked up as well. "A dangerous situation. A life can be snuffed out that way so easily. You just... fall asleep and never wake up." Her gaze was far away until she shuddered and looked down, quickly. "I've seen it happen before."

Jack examined the rusted pipe that had been salvaged and repurposed to create the chimney. All the shacks were built of scrap parts. "It's a wonder any of these homes are still standing."

"If chimney is blocked," Zimm said in a low voice, "I doubt it is accident." At Jack's questioning glance, he shrugged. "We use stoves all through year to cook and heat. Is autumn now, and nights are colder. Hard to block chimney this bad, with no warning, since we use every day. Besides, you think man who keeps house this tidy does not keep stove clean? Not clean... immaculate." He looked very proud of himself and his vocabulary.

Considering Zimm's words, Jack peered again at the interior of the shack. The man was right, everything on the shelves: a few plates, bowls and cups, a small mirror, some carved wood figurines, were all evenly spaced, arranged with either great care or great obsessiveness. Perhaps both.

The lingering smoke gave everything a dingy air, but the arrangement of possessions alone spoke of military precision and a man who would be incredibly clean.

"So you think this wasn't a simple accident? That would mean it's..." He turned back to the doorway to the dead man within.

Zimm spoke in Lagrimari and said a single word that sent chills through Jack's blood.

"Murder."

# CHAPTER FOUR

When walking with a stranger, the path to concord is built brick upon brick, word upon word, each utterance a paving stone along the way. The cracked foundation will lead to an unsteady gait.

— *BOOK OF HER REIGN*, 23:28

Jack spent the morning at Baalingrove questioning the settlers about the dead man, with Zimm's help. Pensar had been seen entering his home around sunset the night before and no one admitted to seeing him afterwards. Not a soul had heard anything unusual either. The man hadn't had any friends as far as Jack could tell, in fact, from the settlers' reactions, he seemed like something of an outcast.

When asked what kind of man he was, no one would say anything beyond vague statements like, "Better than some and worse than others, I suspect," or "A regular kind of man, I guess."

The interviews having turned up nothing, Jack had the body of the victim sent back to the base for examination. They didn't have the facilities or expertise for a true autopsy, but the army physician should at least be able to determine if the man died of natural causes or not. Then Jack could go back to worrying about other things.

On his way out, Zimm stopped Jack to inform him that the protests would begin again the next day, "Out of respect for the dead."

Unease about both the death and the protests followed Jack all the way back to the base. Once there, he told Benn he needed to head to the brig.

"Yes, sir," Benn replied. "Just remember the meeting with the Board of Generals is this afternoon."

Jack nodded heavily. "I'll be there." How could he not? After Jack's assumption of his new duties, Prince Alariq and the Elsiran Council that governed the land had seen fit to create a new advisory group for the High Commander, the Board of Generals. A ringing vote of confidence in Jack's leadership abilities. The lack of faith in him stung. He wasn't the youngest person to fill his role. It was common for the second son of the Prince Regent to start overseeing the army before his early twenties, but Alariq was a stickler for details. And backup plans. Jack tried to remind himself the doubt wasn't personal, even as he felt chastised for some unknown error he'd made.

So far, the meetings had been tenable. A bit condescending perhaps, but manageable. And helpful, though he'd never admit it aloud. So he needed to hurry and see this prisoner who had the settlers so riled up, so he could squash the protests as quickly as possible.

The base's small brig was located in a narrow building on the perimeter. Skylights illuminated the interior, cutting through the gloom cast by gray cement walls. Most of the high-use facilities on base had been converted to electric over the past decade, but the jail hadn't yet been outfitted.

Jack entered, receiving salutes from the guards. He went through the door separating the front from the holding area and slowly approached the lone prisoner in the far cell. A shadowy outline of a long-limbed figure lounged on a thin cot, hands behind his head, as if he hadn't a care in the world. As Jack drew nearer, the prisoner looked up. He was young, maybe two or three years older than Jack, with sharp cheekbones and a stern jaw. His eyes sparkled darkly, and though his face was serious, his eyes seemed to laugh constantly. Jack didn't like him at all.

There was no translator on base, so Jack hoped his Lagrimari was up to snuff. He didn't want to bring Zimm in given the man's agenda on this matter.

"What is your name?" he asked the settler. The young man popped up like a cat and approached the bars, eyes full of questions.

"I am Darvyn ol-Tahlyro. And you are?"

"High Commander Alliaseen."

Darvyn tilted his head and peered at him. "And you speak Lagrimari?"

"I...work close with Baalingrove many years. Working to..." Jack racked his brain unable to come up with the word for 'perfect' or 'master.' "...speak right."

Darvyn scrutinized him in the dim light. It was like the young man could see beneath his skin. "Strange. You should not be able to speak our language at all."

"Why?"

He shrugged. "It is for Singers. Those born with Songs at any rate." He narrowed his eyes. "Who are you again?"

"*My* questions," Jack said, tapping his chest, growing

annoyed and frustrated with his limited vocabulary. "Curfew—
you understand curfew?"

Darvyn move back to sit on the cot. "Yes, I understand."

"So, why are you... closing it?"

The prisoner squinted in confusion. *Shite.* Closing... that
wasn't the right word, but Jack's brain couldn't come up with
the correct one.

"Why ...break curfew?" Darvyn asked in halting Elsiran.

Jack's head jerked in surprise. "You speak Elsiran?"

The young man shrugged. "Probably as well as you speak
Lagrimari," he said, switching back to his native tongue.

"Lagrimari...more easy to understand...not speak." Jack
could gather the gist of what was said based on the words he
knew and the context. Elsiran, on the other hand, relied on
vocal tone and pitch to a much greater degree.

With a sigh, Jack switched to Elsiran. "You can understand
me?"

Darvyn nodded.

"So why break the curfew then? This is your third time."

"The third time I've been caught." Darvyn's eyebrows rose
suggestively as he responded in Lagrimari.

Jack looked sharply, not sure he'd heard correctly. "What is
so important to do between the hours of nine p.m. and dawn
that you can't be inside your bunk like the others?"

Darvyn sat up straighter. "Why should it matter?"

"What?"

"Freedom," Darvyn said, this time in Elsiran. "Not prisoners,
not now. Free. Want freedom."

Jack moved forward, gripping the bars. "The curfew helps
keep the peace among the local villagers and farmers. They
feel more comfortable knowing that the settlers aren't
roaming the countryside at all hours of the night. Do you
understand?"

Darvyn stood and approached Jack solemnly. "Not prisoners," he repeated in Elsiran. "Not children."

Jack understood the man's point, but the curfew had been agreed upon, voted into place by the Council for all the settlements that existed on the eastern border. The closest towns found this to be a decent compromise to the insult of having a settlement located near them and this was the way it had been for years.

"Is there something that you need to be doing at night?" he prodded. "Some specific reason you need an exemption?"

He wasn't sure Darvyn had understood, the young man just repeated, "Freedom. No curfew."

Jack threw up his hands. "Work together," he said in Lagrimari. "Compromise."

Darvyn held out both hands like weighing a scale. "Free. Not free. No compromise," he responded in Elsiran.

Jack switched back to Elsiran. "It's not something that I have the authority to change. Tensions with the villagers are too high right now, anyway." He shook his head. "Besides, I can't rescind the curfew—even if I wanted to."

He had to admit that Darvyn's reasoning was valid. They were cut off from their country with no communication through the Mantle while it was closed. And given that the majority of Sixth Breach settlers had remained after the Seventh Breach, when they could have returned, meant they held little loyalty to their homeland and the cruel dictator who ruled it.

"If you have to be out at night, can you at least not get caught?" Jack muttered under his breath.

To his surprise, Darvyn began laughing. The smell of burning metal tinged the air and the bars beneath Jack's hands suddenly grew hot. He stepped back, shaking his hands as the cell door popped open. Darvyn stood and approached, standing in the open doorway.

Jack's eyes grew so wide, they felt like they'd overtaken his face. He couldn't quite process what had just happened. With a shaking hand, he reached for his sidearm and drew, pointing it at Darvyn whose eyes glittered in the lantern light.

A ball of flame appeared between them, conjured out of nothing. Jack had a flashback to the Seventh Breach—he'd watched arcs of flame streak overhead to light up the countryside. His men had fired into the mass of soldiers attacking, and along with the bullets and shells they'd had to contend with a series of natural disasters that had destroyed their equipment and many lives.

Rumbling earthquakes sucked men into the ground. Ice storms spat sleet and hail in the middle of summer. The Elsirans had retaliated against the Earthsong attacks with the full might of their artillery and held the enemy off, but the fighting had been brutal.

"You still have your Song," Jack said with horror. He hadn't encountered any settlers who'd retained their Songs. The True Father, Lagrimar's immortal ruler, stole his peoples' magic, often when they were still children. Jack had heard that only one regiment in the Lagrimari army were Singers, and they were the ones responsible for all of the magical attacks.

The pistol in his hand grew too hot to touch; he dropped it with a curse. The prayer of the Queen Who Sleeps went through his mind. He'd been foolish to come and question the prisoner alone, now he would pay the price.

But Darvyn didn't attack. He just stared at Jack as if taking his measure.

"I'm not here to harm anyone," Darvyn said. "I have my own tasks to carry out. I think you will make a good leader, High Commander Alliaseen. But you are going to have to learn to think for yourself. And come to your own conclusions."

Darvyn stepped back into his cell and closed the door, then went to lay back down on the cot.

"W-what are you doing?" Jack stammered.

"What do you think would happen if I left now?" Darvyn's voice was even, almost uninterested.

Jack cringed to think of it. "Chaos. If my men knew there was a Singer here, there would be chaos." Darvyn's life would be in danger. The short, three-month war had nonetheless been brutal, and fear of Earthsong magic would spark a mob mentality. Darvyn would be attacked and it was quite likely the entire settlement would be as well.

"So you agree, it's better if they don't know."

Jack froze. "I should take your word that you're not here to harm anyone? That you won't use your magic against my men or the citizens nearby?"

Darvyn nestled deeper onto the cot's thin mattress. "I have been here for months, have I caused any trouble yet?"

A sick feeling overtook Jack at the thought of an Earthsinger in their midst for all that time. "I am responsible for the lives of thousands of soldiers and, by extension, many of the citizens in this region. You are a threat to them."

"I am responsible for lives as well, Commander." He craned his neck to look upside down at Jack. "Make the decision you must." Then he rolled over onto his side to face the wall, apparently ready for a nap.

Jack stood there for several minutes then picked up his gun and turned to walk away. It wasn't illegal to be an Earthsinger, and Darvyn had committed no capital offense. As edgy as the townsfolk were, alerting anyone to his presence could very well mean a death sentence for the young man, that is, if anyone could get close enough to kill him. It could also cause a riot and mean the loss of many more lives—mostly Lagrimari, however, some Elsirans would get caught up, no doubt. But keeping this secret could be just as bad. How could he trust a Lagrimari? One with a Song no less?

The guards on duty saluted Jack as he passed through the front of the jail building.

"Double the guards on this prisoner," he instructed on his way out. "And don't release him until word comes from me." He wasn't sure what else to do—what action would save the most lives?

He wished he could call his brother and ask for his advice. But Alariq had far larger issues on his sizable plate. The entire country, in fact. And he couldn't go running to him for help with every decision.

He thought of asking the Board of Generals or General Larimel, then decided against it. Anyone he told could take the decision from his hands by telling others, forcing an outcome Jack wasn't prepared to be responsible for.

He said another prayer to the Queen for guidance and trudged back to the command center.

# CHAPTER FIVE

So saith the Sovereign: I warned you to take heed, yet you listened not. Why is truth so difficult to hear and respect? What great power has the Lie that it overtakes the ear and heart so easily?

— *BOOK OF HER REIGN*, 43:8

Jack's meeting with the Board of Generals passed in a blur. He barely recalled the specifics of their recommendations or his responses—his mind was on the Earthsinger he'd left in the cell across the base. Tension churned in his gut as indecision battered him. Had he done the right thing? Had he put people in danger?

He avoided the mess hall, where he usually spent time in effort to maintain a rapport with the troops, and instead asked Benn to bring him a late lunch to his office. He needed quiet to think, without the constant reminders of the men whose lives were impacted by his decisions. If an earthquake pulled them all into the ground, or a flood drowned the base, it would be his fault.

As he was chewing over the problem, along with some very tough grouse patties, General Larimel blew into his office without knocking.

Jack had been eight years old when he first met Ambros Larimel. As a child, Jack had lived a cushy life in the palace, at least that's what most people believed, but after his father's death, he was shipped off to military school to begin his training.

Turning the boy into a soldier had been largely Larimel's task—the school's leaders had a healthy fear of the office of Prince Regent, having been at the mercy of Jack's father, Prince Edvard's, notorious rages. They had not yet grown used to the idea of Prince Alariq's far gentler nature and would not be sure for many years on which side of the temper divide Jack would land.

Larimel was a stern traditionalist who'd known no life but the army. He didn't treat Jack any different than the other boys, ignored his whining, leached out what little entitlement had seeped into the child's bones, and replaced it with iron. He was not a kind or warm man, being a soldier through and through, but he was fair-minded, tough as nails, and unbending in his loyalty to Elsira.

"Pleasant afternoon, General," Jack said, swallowing the last mouthful of slightly burnt coffee. He hated the stuff but had grown used to the vile taste since it was part of most soldiers' daily routines.

"Jack," Larimel said, folding himself into the chair opposite the desk and crossing his leg. Though Jack had known the man most of his life, the lack of use of his title rankled. Being a stickler for protocol, the general had always treated the previous High Commander with deference. Not addressing Jack correctly felt like a slap in the face.

But he didn't mention it. Instead he said, "To what do I owe the pleasure?"

"Your mind was elsewhere at the meeting today." The general's grim smile was tight. He was a leathered man, his gunmetal gray hair precisely cut, skin sun-toasted. "I don't think the others noticed, but I did. What's on your mind?"

Jack should have known he couldn't hide much from Larimel, the man knew him too well. But he wasn't ready to discuss the Darvyn situation yet. "The protests at the settlement," he replied, truthfully. "I've got to get a handle on this unrest before it spills out into something worse."

"So, what do you plan to do about those old *grols*?"

Jack's skin chilled at the use of the racial epithet. "Is this a personal curiosity or do you represent the Board?"

Larimel spread his arms. "Just here as a friend, Jack. To offer my wisdom and experience."

"I went down to the settlement yesterday to start a dialogue."

"*You* went?" Larimel's gray brows rose. "Why not send a representative?"

Jack sat up straighter. "I have a rapport with the men because of my time as a guard there. I think visiting in person and at least trying to speak in their own language will do a lot. It will show—"

"Honestly, I don't think that's the best use of your time. This base and its surrounding area isn't your only concern."

Under the desk Jack's knee bounced with annoyance. He stilled the movement when Larimel narrowed his eyes. "Of course, General. But this is the largest base in the country and the one with the most pressing issues. Solve them here and I can solve them elsewhere."

Larimel scoffed. "I don't think a bunch of whinging settlers could be called *pressing*."

"Tension with the townspeople is tight as a thread." Jack said with a rigid jaw. "I'm trying to avoid another riot. We've seen these kinds of situations get out of hand before."

"Certainly, son. My point is there are other people who could handle this. Assign someone to enforce order in the settlement and deal with the bullheaded farmers."

Jack shook his head. "It's not just about enforcing order. I want to listen to them. Understand their concerns." His conversation with Darvyn the night before played over in his mind. "The settlers aren't prisoners or children. They deserve to be heard."

"And what about this *grol* body in the infirmary? The poor sod stationed there has been raising quite a ruckus about it."

Jack bristled. "Really? How odd that he didn't use the chain of command if he had a gripe." He reined in his temper but seethed inside.

"This isn't about chain of command, young man. It's about basic decency. A *grol* dies, and you want to use army resources to determine the cause? All of this is a waste of time and energy." The general's face grew red.

"The settlers have protected status here. They fall under my watch. If there was foul play involved in the death of one of them—"

"Tell it to the constable." Larimel threw his hands up.

Jack stood, anger rising. "The county constable is not the appropriate party to deal with this. Settlers are under the oversight of the army. Their welfare, or lack thereof, falls to me. Now as to whether that *should* be the case or not..." He shrugged. "But I need to determine if this man was murdered."

"Murdered?" The disbelief on Larimel's face was almost comical. "And if he was?"

41

"Then I need to find out who did it."

A knock sounded at the door. "Come in!" Jack called.

Benn stood holding out a filthy, soot-covered bundle in his hands. "Sir, the inspection of the victim's chimney was completed. They pulled this out of the top of the pipe."

Jack walked over to pluck the bundle from his hand. It was a large swath of fabric, a bedsheet, if he wasn't mistaken, that had been crumpled and stuffed to plug the opening.

"How far down the pipe was it found?"

"Over half a meter."

"So about an arm's length."

Benn nodded. "And there were several ladders within close proximity of the victim's dwelling. Impossible to tell if they'd been disturbed."

"Thank you. Please take this into the meeting room. I want a closer look at it, maybe we can tell where it came from."

"Yes, sir." Benn spun away and departed.

Even without the physician examining the body, it was now clear that Pensar had been murdered. Jack stared sightlessly at the door thinking through all the implications of this kind of crime in the settlement.

"This isn't one of those tenthpiece detective novels you used to read as a child, son." Larimel spoke from directly behind him. "Don't confuse fiction with fact."

Jack fisted his hands. "I'm not playing out a childhood dream of being a detective. A man has been murdered. It stands to reason the murderer may strike again. So he needs to be found. Lives are at stake."

Larimel rounded on him, his face a storm of fury. "Someone offing *grols* is not—"

"And if they kill an Elsiran next? Would you be interested then?"

The general frowned. Jack set his jaw and held the door

open. "Thank you, as always, for your advice, General. But I need to do my duty and investigate this."

"And how, exactly, do you plan on doing that? You think they'll just tell you what you want to know?"

Jack firmed his lips into something that approached a pained smile. "Pleasant day, General."

The older man shook his head and walked out, muttering under his breath about young men and their foolishness.

Jack was left standing there with the general's words echoing in his head. Would the settlers talk to him? Or would the investigation end before it began? The men he'd spoken with that morning about the dead man had been less than forthcoming. And why *should* they talk to him? They had no reason to trust him. Beyond the Sisterhood, most Elsirans had never shown much care about the settlers. Jack couldn't expect that to change overnight.

But, if one of their own was involved, they might open up. True, Zimm had been alongside him to translate, but Jack had never had a good feeling about the man. He had influence amongst the settlers, but his reaction to the victim was troubling. Was he the reason no one had much of anything to say?

There was someone else who the settlers seemed to respect, at least enough to protest over. Someone who, unlike Zimm, seemed authentic, if maddening. What better way to keep an eye on Darvyn, and maybe begin to address his concerns, than bring him in to help in the investigation?

Jack wanted to brush aside the idea as too crazy. It was probably just as ill-conceived as the town meeting had been. But his hand tapped against his thigh in staccato as he latched onto the thought. Strange as it was, he couldn't let it go. He was certain no other High Commander would even consider something like this. That meant he shouldn't either.

Right?

❦

Darvyn sat in the cell on the cot, cross-legged, eyes closed. Jack stood outside the bars, trying to determine whether he was sleeping, lost to the world, or something else. Then the young man's eyes opened, slightly glazed, unseeing and staring into space. Slowly, he focused on Jack as whatever trance he was in fell away. He blinked a few times, then rose easily.

"Commander," he said, approaching the bars.

"Are you all right?"

"Right as the river."

Jack froze. He and Darvyn still each spoke in their own native languages, but Jack was certain he'd understood the words correctly.

Darvyn squinted. "Are *you* all right?"

An empty feeling opened up in his belly over the familiarity of the words. It was part longing for his long-absent mother, who had fled the country years ago, and part dawning understanding of some fundamental truth that still wasn't quite in focus...but felt big.

"It's just... That phrase, *right as the river*, is that something they say in Lagrimar often?"

"It's... not uncommon," Darvyn said, frowning in thought. "I think my mother used to say it."

Jack swallowed and took a step closer to the bars. "Mine too." The two stared at each other for a moment before Jack looked away.

The reality of that shared connection across countries, cultures, and languages solidified his decision, overriding the heavy doubts. He cleared his throat. "There has been a murder in Baalingrove. A man named Pensar ol-Lagrimar was killed yesterday."

Darvyn looked off to the side. "May he find serenity in the

World After." Another identical turn of phrase to that was used in Elsira as a blessing for the dead. How many more were there?

Jack's throat tightened as he determined to push forward. "I have to ask, did you kill him?"

If Darvyn was offended, he didn't show it. The young man merely raised his eyebrows and leaned against the bars.

"You've proven you can leave here at will," Jack said, motioning to the barred door. "Sovereign only knows what other powers you have and what they can do. You're the perfect culprit for this crime." He held his breath, awaiting the answer.

"Your logic is sound, Commander. And being locked up would give me the perfect alibi, would it not? But tell, me, how did the man die? Was he drowned in a sudden flood? Buried alive in mud or sand? Impaled by a falling icicle?"

Jack shook his head. "No, none of those things."

Darvyn shrugged exaggeratedly. "If an Earthsinger were to kill—a Singer of sound mind, not one of the army's wretched Wailers, mind you—if he could bring himself to take a life and snuff out part of the energy fueling Earthsong—wouldn't he chose a method that wouldn't leave a body? Or at least was undetectable as murder?"

Jack remained silent.

"You fear our power because you don't understand it. If you did, you'd know that when you feel the essence of the energy of life flowing through your veins, there's nothing more beautiful. There's nothing you want to protect more. Taking a life is very difficult for one whose Song is intact. So difficult it's virtually unheard of."

Curiosity about Earthsong filled him. "And the Wailers? They're the regiment of Earthsingers in the Lagrimari army, right?"

"They are controlled. Forced to do what they do." He shook his head grimly. "And they suffer greatly for it."

Jack took a deep breath and blew it out. He hadn't believed that Darvyn was the killer, but asking was prudent, considering what he was about to do. He didn't have Earthsong to judge lies from truth, all he had was his gut instinct. And even though the Board would crucify him if and when they found out, he was going to follow his gut.

He took the key ring from his belt and found the one to the cell.

"Commander?" Darvyn said, surprising lighting his face.

Jack opened the door and glared. "You are going to help me solve this."

Darvyn raised a brow. "You're investigating the murder yourself?"

"I am." Jack puffed out his chest, daring the other man to challenge him.

Darvyn's face gave little away, though the ghost of a smile danced on his lips. "So you believe I'm not the murderer?"

"I have no proof either way. But I need to keep a close eye on you."

"And if I *am* the murderer?" He had the nerve to let the smile loose.

Jack pursed his lips, already regretting his choice of action. He wasn't sure that he and Darvyn would get along well enough to work together. The Lagrimari man's flippant attitude chafed at him. "Then you'll do something to give yourself away."

"This is a strange plan, Commander."

"It's the best I can come up with. I can't keep you in here forever, I can't allow an Earthsinger to roam around unsupervised, and I can't tell anyone what you are. I'm rather stuck. But I think that you could help me figure this out. The men will talk to you, and you have insights into life in Baalingrove that no outsider could gain."

Darvyn studied him. "Let me ask you a question, Commander. Why are you doing this? Why investigate at all? I would not think Elsirans would care who murders one old Lagrimari man."

Jack tensed. "I've already been advised not to bother. But a man has been killed on my watch. He deserves justice at the very least, so the killer does not go on to do it again."

Darvyn was quiet for a long time, and Jack's restlessness grew. He did his best not to fidget under the young man's scrutiny. "All right. I will investigate with you. Because you seem to view us as human beings, and I have not seen another Elsiran do the same. And also because…"

"Because what?"

"Because you're going to need my help." Darvyn grinned.

Jack shook his head. This was definitely a bad idea.

# CHAPTER SIX

May the breath of the Sovereign be upon you, filling your lungs
with heavy air, weighing you down toward a dream-filled sleep.
May the expectation of Her awakening overflow your waking
hours and Her guidance guard your slumber.

— *BOOK OF HER REIGN,* 45:8

Jack fitted a pair of handcuffs on Darvyn, who merely whistled
as they were put on him.

"Please keep these on," Jack asked under his breath. "It will
make my men feel more comfortable."

Darvyn snorted and Jack hoped that meant he would agree.
"So where to first, Commander?"

"We have some evidence in the meeting room, a bedsheet
used to block Pensar's chimney."

"Block his chimney?"

"That's what appears to have killed him, the gas and smoke
buildup from the stove as he slept. I'd hoped our physician
would be able to tell more by examining the body, but I have a

suspicion he's going to do a less than thorough job." And it would be difficult to discipline the man for dragging his feet on such an assignment.

Darvyn grunted but said nothing further as they crossed the busy pathways back to the administrative building that housed Jack's office. Soldiers saluted Jack and glanced askance at the Lagrimari prisoner, but Darvyn kept the cuffs on in front of him, and no one dared ask the High Commander what he was up to.

Inside the meeting room, the bedsheet had been lain out across the large table. The two of them were alone, and Darvyn shook off the handcuffs with a flourish and pocketed them. Jack's jaw ticked, but he clamped it shut.

He brushed his hand across the sheet, coming away with soot on his fingertips. "Can you tell anything about this sheet, where it came from?"

Darvyn was quiet for a bit, rubbing the black residue together and sniffing at it. "Not with Earthsong. I can sense living things, natural phenomena, animals and plants, water and air, not dead things. I can tell that this fabric is far too fine to belong to a settler though."

Jack examined a fairly clean portion of the sheet. It wasn't of high quality, but definitely better stuff than the Lagrimari received. "You're right. Though it could have been stolen. It's hand sewn, with orderly stitches, but plenty of imperfections. If it had been mass produced, we might have been able to go to the general store and learn something more about who purchased it."

"Don't give up hope yet," Darvyn said, a crooked grin twisting his mouth. He held up a corner of fabric. Jack wasn't sure what the smile was for until the Lagrimari man moved his thumb. An embroidered monogram had been stitched into the sheet.

"M.M.," he read, skin rapidly cooling.

"You look as though you've seen a ghost, Commander."

Jack rubbed his forehead; he didn't have a headache yet, but he predicted one would soon appear. "Not a ghost exactly, more like a bad memory."

Darvyn's smile only grew wider. "Sounds interesting."

The next morning found Benn, Jack, and Darvyn in a four-wheeler, rumbling down a pitted country road. Jack hadn't been down this particular road in half a year, but there was a time when he would sneak off base after hours, steal one of the electricycles from the depot, and ride all over the county. Now, he stared at the passing countryside wistful for those stolen moments of freedom.

Benn handled the wheel nimbly, avoiding the deep holes that were reminders of the damage the countryside underwent during the war. One such pit refilled with dirt on its own as they passed. Jack's head whipped back to where Darvyn lounged, handcuffed in the backseat. Jack narrowed his eyes, and Darvyn merely shrugged. If Benn noticed anything amiss, he kept his peace about it.

The Borderlands farm they approached was owned by Eriq Maridall. It was a medium-sized plot of land, a twenty-minute drive from the base. When the lopsided farmhouse and barn came into view, Jack steeled his nerves. The last time he was here, he'd vowed never to return.

The place had seen better days, several slats were missing from the sides of both the faded red barn and the dingy, white-washed house. A spindly cow stood in a makeshift pen between the two structures.

They pulled to a stop in front of the house. The curtains in the front room were moving, and he knew he was being watched. Sure enough, not ten seconds later, the farmhouse door opened, and a teenage girl rushed out, brushing flour off her palms. Her flaming red hair was caught in a long, thick braid down her back.

"Jaqros," she said with a pout, placing her hands on her hips.

"Margritt," he said, straightening, feeling his face redden. "Is your pa around? I need to have a word with him."

"I haven't seen hide nor hair of you in over six months and suddenly you need to speak to Pa?" Her eyes widened. "Whaddya need to talk to him for?"

"This is official army business, Margritt. Not a personal matter."

The girl—

"Hold on," Jasminda said, pulling out of Jack's embrace to turn and face him. Was it her imagination or were his cheeks growing red? "Wait just a minute. Who is this Margritt Maridall?"

Saying the name out loud made her own eyes widen as something clicked in her mind. "And why is it that when you saw her initials on a *bedsheet* you knew exactly where to go?"

She scooted away from Jack, whose face was now the color of a turnip. "Had you seen that sheet before? And how many other monogrammed sheets would you recognize if they presented themselves to you?"

"It's just a story... I mean, history. Very-far-in-the-past history and that's not really the important part. I was just following the clues, you see. And I happened to... I mean, there weren't so many people with those initials in the area, so it was only logical to... You know. I mean, a *man* wouldn't embroider his initials and, well..."

Jack swallowed, loosening the button of the collar around his reddening neck. He looked so adorable, sputtering and flustered; his reaction dampened the sting of jealousy that had nipped her.

Still, she gave him the evil eye, evading when he went to grab her hand again. "I'm going to sit over here while you continue this story of yours." He'd had a life before he met her, of course, but she didn't have to be happy about it.

"Jasminda, my love—"

"Don't 'Jasminda, my love' me. Just continue." She waved her arm in a very queen-like manner from the other end of the couch, determined to let him squirm for just a bit longer.

Jack cleared his throat, looking pained. "Yes, well, the farmer. Since I didn't consider the likelihood of a sixteen-year-old girl murdering a grown man, it was he we'd gone to talk to anyway..."

Eriq Maridall was a tall, slim fellow with an unfortunate constellation of facial hair that never quite connected. His coveralls were filthy, and he had the disconcerting habit of leaving his mouth open all the time. Jack worried something might fly in there, if the man weren't careful. He emerged from the barn and stood next to the pen holding the underfed cow. Three barefoot children raced one another in the grassy field beyond. Once she realized Jack was not here for her, Margritt disappeared back into the house, pouting.

"Yeah, I hire *grols* from time to time," Maridall said in response to Jack's questioning. "They come cheap and work hard." He shrugged, eyeing Darvyn distrustfully.

"But the settlers aren't permitted to work—not for private individuals at any rate," Jack said. The treaty allowed that special government work programs could be created to employ the men, but those had never materialized.

Maridall spat tobacco juice onto the ground. "Got more work than I can handle, is all. Figured what's the harm in spreading it around. I don't rightly know which one Pensar was, though."

Darvyn tipped his head to the side. In Lagrimari he said, "He's lying. His body temperature is rising, and his pupils shrank."

Maridall's gaze darted to Darvyn and back. "What's this one here saying?"

Jack cleared his throat, his attention caught by the laundry lines with shirts, trousers, socks, and men's drawers, strung up behind the house. He turned back to Maridall. "How many men did you hire?"

"Round about half a dozen, I reckon."

"And how did they get out here? We're too far from the settlement to walk."

"I didn't ask them about their transportation or what they had for breakfast. They showed up and I put 'em to work."

"And you pay them?" Darvyn spoke up in Elsiran.

Maridall squinted and rubbed a hand on top of his scrubby hair. "That's the idea, yeah."

Darvyn shook his head almost imperceptibly. The farmer was lying again.

"How much did you pay them and how often?" Jack asked.

Maridall tensed. Jack could only imagine what Darvyn was sensing with his Song, but the farmer didn't want to answer that question, that much was clear.

"Well, see I'd told the mouthy one that they'd get their

money after harvest; that's when I get paid. Wasn't cheatin', just how it is."

"The mouthy one?" Jack asked.

"Yeah, you know. 'My pleasure, Master Maridall' and 'Pleasant morning, Master Maridall'," he said, bowing in a credible impersonation of Zimm.

"So the men understood that they wouldn't be paid for their work for weeks?"

Maridall scratched his head. "Well that's what I told 'em. Couldn't say if that's what they understood or not."

"They ask for their wages, true?" Darvyn asked.

Maridall cut his eyes at Darvyn and pursed his lips.

"They asked for their wages and then what happened?" Jack prompted.

"Well, when I told 'em what I'd already told 'em, some of the fellas got right distressed. Shouting and carrying on. I told my oldest boy to ride for town and bring back the constable before we had a full-blown riot on our hands."

Jack took a breath, rubbing his forehead. "So the settlers objected when you wouldn't pay them for the work they'd done and you called the constable?"

"Well, what was I supposed to do? Sovereign knows how those *grols* act when they get angry. I got children here. They coulda burned the whole place down. Constable Belliaros took the one that was carrying on so loud, and a Sisterhood truck came to get the rest." He looked dejectedly at the land around him. "Still got more work for 'em but can't get none to come back out here."

"I wonder why," Darvyn said under his breath in his own language.

Jack bit the inside of his lip, thoroughly disgusted by this man. "Where were you last night?"

Maridall drew himself up to his full height. "What you wanna know fer?"

Jack drew himself up as well and took a step forward. "Because I asked you."

The farmer deflated. "Here. Home. Ask my daughter or the boys. We was here listening to the news readers on the radiophonic."

Jack nodded. He'd have to confirm with Margritt... Then again, he could ask Benn to do it. That was a much better option. "I need to take a look at your laundry," he said, marching over to the clothes drying.

"What? Why is that?"

Jack was already inspecting the clothes, searching for anything with embroidered letters. Darvyn found it first, a woman's nightgown with 'MM' done in the same precise lettering.

"Are you missing any bedding, Master Maridall?"

The man scratched his head. "Couldn't rightly say. You'd need to take that up with Margritt."

Jack nodded, looking back at the house to find the girl in question peering at them through the back window.

"Benn!" Jack called out. His assistant had stayed with the vehicle and could use something to do.

Jack turned to Darvyn. "Any questions you want to ask him before we go?"

Darvyn stared at the farmer for a moment before breaking into a grin. "No. No questions," he said in Elsiran.

The smell of smoke scented the air, and Jack looked down to see a tiny flame floating at their feet. Maridall hadn't noticed it yet.

Jack grabbed Darvyn by his upper arms and pulled him close. "Stop that right now!" he growled into his ear.

When he looked down again the flame was gone. Maridall sniffed and looked around, eyes wild.

"Pleasant day to you, Master Maridall. May She bless your dreams," Jack said with a nod of his head.

"Yours as well," the man called out curtly, still searching for the source of the smoke. He looked up aghast at a stone-faced Darvyn before the Singer turned to stalk back around to the front of the house.

# CHAPTER SEVEN

It is no burden for those with plenty to spread their excess among those who lack. No law can be made against charity, no prohibition on forgiveness, no entreaty against discipline, and no restriction on honor, for these are the only precepts which can truly rule us.

*— BOOK OF HER REIGN, 48:5*

Jasminda toyed with the fringe of one of the couch's pillows, still sitting an arm's length from Jack. He looked miserable to have her so far away. "So about this Margritt character—" she began.

"Benn confirmed with her that a settler had been arrested, and the rest had gone with a Sister. Apparently, they'd always arrived in a Sisterhood truck as well. She also confirmed that she was missing a bedsheet from the laundry."

"Hmmm. And how is dear Margritt these days?" She kept her voice flat, her expression stern.

"I'm not entirely sure, I believe she's married with two children, or so I've heard. I don't really keep in touch with..." Jack narrowed his eyes, and she tried to keep her lips pressed together firmly to hold back a grin. "You're having a go at me?"

"Not at all. I'm just curious as to how many former paramours of yours will be featured in this little story." Her smile finally broke through.

He rose on a knee and moved toward her. She shrank back, pressing herself into the arm of the couch, challenging him to advance. "The local residents made every effort to make the soldiers stationed at the base feel welcome," he said.

She snorted. "I'm sure they did."

"But honestly, I can barely remember anyone before you." He drew closer.

"Oh, there were so many that it's a blur now? I see." She scrambled backward, but not very quickly or very adamantly. He wrapped an arm around her waist and drew her down beneath him.

"Not so very many, just unremarkable. But you I could never forget."

Jasminda had a retort planned but allowed him to silence her with a kiss. She did want to hear the end of the story, but it could wait for a minute or two.

Or more...

Not so very long later, he continued his tale.

Sora was the county's head town and consisted of a single, unpaved street with a post station, smithy, general store, temple, and magistrate's office, which held the constabulary that served the entire county. Towns like this were common in the Borderlands. Some didn't even have names. Sora, however, had been named after its founder, Colonel Nedriq Sora, who had been a hero during the Yalyish War two hundred years ago.

The county constable, Belliaros, must have been alerted to their arrival somehow. Maridall didn't own a telephone to alert the man, as far as Jack knew, but yet Belliaros met Jack out front of the building as the little investigative team piled out of their vehicle.

"Commander, a pleasure." The two touched palms, and Jack fought the urge to recoil from the man's cold skin.

"Constable," he replied. He wasn't looking forward to the interview, but it had to be done.

"You want this one arrested, eh?" Belliaros motioned to Darvyn. No longer cuffed, as he'd already served the penalty for breaking curfew, Darvyn stood, limbs loose, next to Jack.

"Not at all. Constable, this is Darvyn, he... has an interest here."

Belliaros rose his brows and led them into the small front room of the constabulary. The entire back of the space held the jail cells, which were currently empty.

Jack took the offered seat across the desk from Belliaros, while Darvyn chose to lean against the wall. "I need to ask you some questions about a settler you took into custody a few days ago."

The constable whipped out a pen knife and began cleaning out the crud from underneath his fingernails. "Oh yeah, a fella called Pensar or some such. He was trouble. Kept mouthing off. We were scared for our safety, isn't that right, Mud?"

Jack hadn't noticed the young deputy sitting in the far corner. He blended into the furniture, barely moving or breathing.

"Yes, sir," Mud said in a deep rumble.

"Had to give him a tune up if you know what I mean." Belliaros cracked a knuckle and had the nerve to wink in Jack's direction. From the corner of his eye, Jack saw Darvyn stiffen. Was it his imagination or did the air around them begin to warm?

Jack clenched his jaw. "How long was the settler in custody, and what was the charge?"

"He was here overnight, then I turned him loose. Had to wipe down the stalls—or rather Mud did. He's in training, you know. No charge filed. Just gave him a little time to cool off. He'll think twice about flapping his trap so disrespectful at an Elsiran from now on."

The wall of heat behind him grew. Jack looked over his shoulder and mouthed, "No fires."

Darvyn narrowed his eyes in response.

"Why all the questions about that old *grol?*" Belliaros chuckled.

"He is dead," Darvyn responded in Elsiran. "Murdered."

The constable froze for a few seconds, then began scraping at his nails again. "Hmph," was his only response.

Jack studied the constable. He was heavy boned and his bushy mutton chops covered loose jowls. He'd always seemed good natured, but Jack hadn't worked with him closely before. Could the man be a murderer?

"Where were you yesterday evening?"

Belliaros's eyes widened. He turned to Mud then back again and couldn't have appeared more incredulous than if Jack himself had begun using Earthsong in front of him. "Me? Where was *I?* Are you thinking that I did that old witch in?"

"I'm simply asking everyone who'd come into contact with him over the past few days. You can understand. The settlers are under the army's purview, and I need to cross all my t's, so to speak."

Belliaros sobered, giving Jack a suspicious glare. "After the town meeting, I came back here to finish up some paperwork."

He punctuated the statements by pointing the tiny knife at Jack.

Darvyn took a step forward. "Was anyone with you?"

"Now look here, you!" Belliaros turned, knife still extended, face red. Spittle flew from his lips. "I don't know who in Sovereign's name you think you are, but I'm the constable of this county and I don't have to answer—"

"Master ol-Tahlyro here is assisting me as a consultant to this investigation." Jack stood to block the constable's view of Darvyn. Who promptly stepped to the side again into the man's sightline.

"*Assisting* you?" Belliaros spat. He eyed Darvyn up and down obviously trying to figure out what type of assistance the young man could be providing.

Jack cleared his throat. "I'd like your response on the record, so there's no questions if the case is reviewed later."

Belliaros glared daggers at Darvyn. "No one was here with me. I don't need a babysitter to do my bloody job!"

That little knife was getting closer and closer to Jack's chest. In one swift movement, Jack grabbed the man's wrist and twisted, causing the pen knife to fall from his grip. Belliaros howled in pain.

Jack looked significantly at the knife then back at the constable. "Wouldn't want anyone to get hurt, would we?"

He let go, and Belliaros clamped his lips shut, holding his wrist.

"I thank you, Constable. I'll let you know if I have any further questions." Jack motioned to Darvyn, and they head for the door.

"Why are you bothering with this anyhow? You really think if someone murdered that *grol* it wasn't one of the other ones in the settlement?" Belliaros pointed at Darvyn. "Band of bloody savages within our borders," he muttered.

"Pleasant afternoon," Jack said between gritted teeth, before leaving the building.

Back at the vehicle, he whirled on Darvyn. "We agreed that you are not supposed to antagonize people. If you can't be helpful, you can go back to Baalingrove."

The young man seethed. "He lies. His—" He shook his head and switched from Elsiran to Lagrimari. "Alibi... His alibi is a lie. When he said he was here alone working, his voice dropped, and he began to sweat."

Jack looked back at the building they'd just emerged from. "You're sure?"

Darvyn crossed his arms. "Yes. He is probably the murderer."

"I don't think Earthsong told you that."

"It didn't need to. He's a pig. He hates us and would not hesitate to kill one of us."

Jack twisted his lips. "His views are...unfortunate. All too common, I know. But stuffing a chimney? That seems...roundabout. Plus, how would he have gotten the bedsheet?"

Darvyn shrugged. "He probably thought no one would find out and everyone would think it an accident. Or blame would fall to that idiot farmer."

Jack shook his head. "Belliaros is vile, but he's a man of the law. I don't think he would commit murder."

"That's naive, Commander."

Jack stiffened.

"Law men murder all the time in Lagrimar. All the time." Darvyn stared at the constabulary building.

Taking a deep breath, Jack refused to admit Darvyn's point. Society would fall apart if the men who had sworn to uphold it fell down on the job. He could allow for individual failings, outliers, but a systemic shirking of duty? It was madness.

An Elsiran constable, even a backwater one like this, had been trained and taken an oath to serve the Queen and the

Regent. And murderers were evil. He could admit that Belliaros was a bigot, that much was clear, but his cynicism wouldn't go so far as to let him think that Belliaros had broken his oath—at least not without more proof.

"Let's go back to Baalingrove and interview the rest of the settlers," he said. "One of them has to know more than they're saying."

Seated on a frayed cushion, Jack accepted the offered steaming brew of fragrant coffee from the old man's shaking hands. He and Darvyn had squeezed into the tiny shack along with its resident, a grim man called Ravar. They sat around a tiny, low table, though the two additional cushions had been procured from neighbors as Ravar only owned the one.

The cup in his hand was made from a cylindrical food tin, cleanly cut with its edge soldered to a rounded lip. The coffee was sweet and strong. Much better than what he got on base. He wondered where the Sisterhood sourced it.

Ravar eyed Jack warily from his place across the table.

"Thank you for speaking with me again," Jack said in Lagrimari. "I...hold questions about Pensar." He'd decided to interview everyone in the homes surrounding the dead man's. Hopefully this time he would get answers they hadn't given before.

The man's face scrunched like the sound of the dead man's name was a bad taste in his mouth. "I told you before. I saw him headed to his hut around sundown. Didn't see him afterwards or the next day at all."

"And no one, before now...disagrees with Pensar? Wants to harm him?" Jack asked.

Ravar squinted. "He is in the World After now. Eternal peace until the Time of Waking."

"Yes, but can you think of one who he argues against? Before now?" Jack thought he had the confusing grammar correct considering the lack of past tense in the language, but the old man just stared. Jack turned to Darvyn for help.

Darvyn merely watched Ravar pensively, apparently coming to a decision. He leaned forward to speak low. "I think it is time, uncle, for us to tell the Elsiran about the Scourge of the Sixth."

Jack knew that the term *uncle* was used as a means of respect among the Lagrimari, rather than denoting actual familial relationships, but he had no idea what Darvyn was talking about. "What is the Scourge of the Sixth?"

Ravar eyed Darvyn for a few moments before nodding. "Very well, if you trust this boy."

"I do," Darvyn replied, making Jack's brows jump in surprise.

"The Scourge of the Sixth," Ravar paused to spit onto the dirt ground, "is what we called Pensar ol-Lagrimar. He had risen to lieutenant very young and led a platoon of sixty men. Man had a cruel streak a gorge wide, which the True Father noticed and rewarded him for."

Ravar shifted on his cushion. "Early in the war, his entire platoon died under mysterious circumstances. Their bodies were found drained of their blood. The men were all harem-born—as many of us are—and the True Father may do with his sons what he likes; finding bloodless bodies isn't that unusual in and of itself, but an entire platoon's worth—it gave Pensar a certain reputation.

"After that, he got a promotion of sorts. He was no longer tasked with leading his own platoon, he would march with others and carry out the punishments on men who fell out of line. Marching out of formation?" He smacked his hand against the table. "Ten lashes. Caught after lights out?" *Smack.* "Ten lashes. Disobey an order?" *Smack.* "Ten lashes."

He grew quiet and sipped his coffee. Jack's stomach tightened, almost not wanting him to continue.

"Sometimes a whole squad would get flogged if he didn't like the way they performed in battle. Saw him give a man forty lashes for missing his shots when his rifle jammed."

Ravar's dark eyes were cloudy but his gaze met Jack's and held. "He was judge, jury, and executioner. His tool of choice was an eight-pronged whip and he wielded it with delight. You ask if any man in this settlement would have wanted to harm him. I can't think of a man here who didn't."

The aftertaste of coffee grew bitter on Jack's tongue. "But you lived here with him, peacefully, for sixteen years."

The man shrugged. "There are more of us than there are of him. He kept to himself and didn't cause trouble. All of us done things we weren't proud of. Surviving our army is a miracle in and of itself. Let him grow old among the green grass under the shade of the mountains, I said. Same as the rest of us." He drained his cup.

"No one would tell the Elsirans this," Darvyn said. "Everyone knew it would make them all suspects."

Jack nodded. "And so you really don't think any of the men killed him?" he asked in Elsiran.

"Not the way he died. If it had been a crime of passion, then yes. If it was rage simmering for decades finally heated to a boil. But that would have been violent. Bloody. This peaceful end, smoke and fumes and gases that make the lungs shut down?" Darvyn shook his head. "That is not the style of a man focused on retribution."

The air felt heavy; Darvyn might be right. They thanked Ravar and went to question the other settlers. When prodded by Darvyn's gentle voice, they all told Jack similar stories of the horrors that Pensar had enacted on his own men. Beatings and floggings. He'd crushed a man's fingers for missing at target practice. Shot his gun next to a young private's ears until the boy was permanently deaf. He was a man worthy of being murdered, but none here admitted to it, and Darvyn claimed they were all telling the truth.

By the end of the day, Jack was exhausted; he wanted to cleanse his eyes and ears and brain of the horrific stories he'd heard.

For the first time, he wondered if Larimel was right. Was this investigation really necessary? The settlers didn't seem to be afraid of the violence. None expressed worry for their safety with a murderer running around. Despite what Darvyn said, the most likely explanation was that one of their own had done this —perhaps with a cool, calculating wrath that had decided a peaceful death was punishment enough.

He dragged himself back to the outskirts of the community where his vehicle waited. There was other pressing business for him to attend to as High Commander. He'd spent an entire day on this hunt with little to show for it. Maybe he should hand it over to the constable after all.

However, the thought of actually doing so left him uneasy.

Benn sat throwing dice with a duo of soldiers who were meant to be guarding the settlement. All three popped up to attention when Jack approached, but he waved them off, declining to get angry at the lapse in protocol.

Two four-wheelers and two Sisterhood trucks were parked in the grass. One of the Sisterhood vehicles was still running. The back door was closed and none of the women were around unloading goods or distributing supplies. They must be in the community then. Sundown was rapidly approaching, and the women generally cleared out by then, as there was little in the way of lighting in the settlement and surrounding roads.

Jack looked again at the truck. No one was visible in the cab. "How long has that vehicle been running?" he asked.

The young lieutenant looked over and squinted. "I'm not sure, sir. I haven't seen the Sisters in at least half an hour. Maybe more."

They could have left the engine on accidentally. Running out of fuel would not be desirable out here at night. He approached the truck to turn the engine off, when he noticed the hose.

A beige tube had been attached to the vehicle's exhaust pipe and then funneled into the front window, the resulting gap had been sealed with what looked like a dark green tarp. Jack yanked open the door and the smell of fumes overtook him. He reached in and turned off the engine, then recoiled. Wedged into the space behind the two seats lay a Lagrimari man with a bloody gash on his head.

"Medic!" he called, then wrenched the driver's seat forward to get at the body. The other soldiers were there in an instant and helped draw the man out and lay him on the ground.

Darvyn appeared at Jack's side.

Benn kneeled next to the injured man. "We may be able to force the gas out of his lungs." He pressed on the man's chest. "I've seen it done with water when a sailor drowned."

"Try it, Benn," Jack said eagerly. But Darvyn brushed his shoulder. When Jack looked up, the Earthsinger was shaking his head.

"He has gone to the World After," he whispered.

Benn continued to push on the man's chest, doing an admirable job of trying to save his life.

Jack took a step back and regarded the truck, the hose, the tarp. It was clear the murderer had struck again.

# CHAPTER EIGHT

If you find cause to reproach the Sovereign, do not then expect to hear Her voice pierce the veil of dreams. If you find cause to reproach Her servants, be ready to bear the rebuke of all the slumberous and faithful.

— *BOOK OF HER REIGN,* 19:89

A crowd quickly gathered around the dead man. Settlers streamed down the narrow lane from the settlement, forming a circle of onlookers with Zimm and Darvyn out in front. Three Sisters pushed their way through, Sister Lorelle along with two older women.

"What's going on?" a short, apple-cheeked Sister with a salt and pepper top knot demanded. "What's happened to this poor fellow?" She shot a glance at the body and wrinkled her nose, whether in sympathy or disgust, Jack wasn't sure.

He turned to face her. "We're trying to figure that out, Sister…?"

"Amelynne, I'm the underpriestess for Baalingrove."

"Did you know this man?"

She peered at the body again, her eyes softer. "Vedan, his name was. Sixth Breacher. I've been delivering food and supplies to him and the rest of this lot for over fifteen years."

Jack pointed back to the truck and its hose. "Who is responsible for this vehicle?"

"All of us are responsible for the vehicles. We share duties in the Sisterhood," Sister Amelynne replied.

"Well, someone left the keys in the ignition."

"The keys always remain with the vehicles, Commander," Sister Lorelle spoke up. "We find that expectations predict actions, and we don't expect the men to steal."

Jack actually agreed with the philosophy, though he was sure someone like Larimel would call it naive optimism. "And who would have had access to the trucks?"

"We were delivering the rest of the shipment today," the third Sister, a tall and rangy woman said. "Some of the men helped us to unload, and then we went off to distribute the supplies. Anyone could have had access to the trucks, they've been here half the day."

"Well, this looks to be the second murder in as many days." Jack rubbed his tired eyes.

"B-but I thought that Pensar's death was an accident," Sister Lorelle said, voice shaky.

"It was probably meant to look that way, but someone purposefully blocked his chimney," Jack replied.

Amelynne rounded on him. "And what's being done to protect these men?" Fire singed her voice.

"Trust me, I'm taking these deaths very seriously. I've already ordered an increase in the guard to be posted here."

Zimm spoke up from several paces away. "Last thing we need are more soldiers here, Commander. We can watch out for ourselves."

"I'm afraid I can't do sit back and do nothing, Zimm. The Republic of Elsira is responsible for you."

"Can you make guarantee your soldiers will keep on outsides and not harass settlers in our own homes?"

Jack hadn't heard anything about that happening, but one look at the settlers muttering to themselves and looking with suspicion at Benn and the other soldiers standing nearby, and he realized how would he know? Who would they have complained to, the very soldiers harassing them? He would need to do better for these men.

He *would* do better for these men. "Fine. I'll order the soldiers will keep to the perimeter. But the first killing happened inside a man's home. You all will need to be careful."

Zimm nodded. "We watch out for each other." He looked at his fellows, who also nodded.

"All right then. Will you translate for me, Zimm? I want to be sure they hear this properly."

"Certainly, Commander."

Jack stepped forward. "I want to assure you that we are taking these deaths very seriously, and I am personally committed to seeing justice done here. If anyone has any other information to share, please come forward and let me know."

Blank, wary faces greeted them. He couldn't blame them.

"You think an outside person killed these men, Commander?" Sister Lorelle was pale as a sheet. "There's a murderer running around?"

"I don't know for sure, but it looks likely."

Darvyn appeared at his side, perturbed. "My money is on that constable," he muttered in Lagrimari.

Jack glared at him. "We have no proof," he answered in the same tongue.

"Pensar was universally hated, sure, but Vedan—he was mild-mannered and generous. Those of us newbies, the Seventh

Breachers, he took under his wing. Personally showed us the way of things here when some of the old timers couldn't be bothered. I think you'll hear much different opinions of him when you talk to the men. Already, their emotions are full of grief."

Jack ran a hand across his face. The motive for the crimes just got more complicated. "Could there be two murderers?" he asked half-heartedly.

"Would that be better?" Darvyn's mouth curled into a sneer.

"No, not better. Just easier." He led the young man away from the crowd, closer to his own four-wheeler and switched to Elsiran. "I know you see Belliaros and think he's a bigoted provincial lawman, but that doesn't make him a murderer." At Darvyn's dubious expression, he continued, "Let's assume he hates all Lagrimari—"

"Which he does."

"Is he killing them at random? Using such innovative means? It doesn't track."

"It doesn't track for you because you've blinded yourself, Commander." Darvyn's voice was hard. "You can't imagine one of your precious Elsirans stooping so low."

"I'm not blind to my peoples' prejudices."

"But you refuse to see their characters. Belliaros lied to you yesterday. And we still don't know why."

Darvyn stalked off, disappearing into the setting sun. He walked away from the settlement, and this close to curfew it was guaranteed he'd be out late. But Jack had a feeling that he wouldn't be caught this time.

"Commander?" a soft voice called. Jack jerked around to face Sister Lorelle and the taller Sister whose name he still hadn't caught.

"Yes? How can I help you?"

"I thought you might want to know," Sister Lorelle said, her gaze lowering, "some of the men had been taking day labor assignments with farmers in the countryside." She clasped her hands together and appeared contrite.

"Ah, yes. I spoke with Farmer Maridall earlier."

"Oh, well, good." She looked relieved. "I know that he'd had words with several of the men a few days back. The constable had been called at least once. I-I'm not saying that the altercation could have provoked a murder..." She twisted her hands in front of her.

Jack gentled his expression. "I spoke with Belliaros as well. We're looking at all angles of this—don't worry. I'm trying to be as thorough as possible."

Sister Lorelle firmed her lips into a thin line. "The constable and Maridall also came here the day after that incident to try and convince some of the men to come back and work the farm."

This Jack hadn't heard. "But he wasn't paying them, right?"

She raised a shoulder. "I think he was trying to negotiate. Zimm was translating, but he was angry. None of the men went back with them to work except for poor Vedan."

"Which day was this?"

"Seventhday last." The day before Pensar was killed.

Jack peered back at the still-gathered settlers, searching for Zimm in the growing gloom. It seemed he'd have to ask the man some more questions. His limbs were heavy, not anticipating the conversation. "Thank you, Sister."

She nodded and began to turn away.

"Oh, Sister. How were the men getting out there? To Maridall's farm?"

"I would drive them. Being stuck here with not much to do

is bad for their morale, so I took it upon myself to shepherd them. All men need purpose. They were like my baby birds, and I had to push them out of the nest."

"But you know, by law, they're not allowed to work," Jack said, frowning.

Her timid demeanor hardened just a fraction. "It's not technically work if they aren't getting paid, is it?" He snorted, and she smiled grimly. "I know the law, Commander. But sometimes the right thing to do and the legal thing to do aren't the same."

Jack stilled with unease. Without the law guiding them, how was society supposed to function? And coming from a devotee of the Queen, it just seemed wrong. "Is that part of the Queen's teachings?"

A thoughtful look crossed her face. "'The disciple may ask, what of the law? Laws writ by men contain all the flaws of man. The sun needs no law but to shine.'"

"*Book of Her Reign*, 19:2," whispered the second Sister, citing the quoted passage from the Queen's holy book.

Jack was a follower of the Queen, as nearly all Elsirans were, but he didn't always find comfort in the pages of Her holy messages. Passages attributed to Her were confusing, sometimes contradictory, and rarely elucidated the issue he was facing. But he could never tell that to a Sister; they would merely point him in the direction of the nearest temple and tell him to pray for the Queen Who Sleeps to bless his dreams.

Even if She did show up tonight after a lifetime of silence, it would be quite a while until Jack slept.

He wished the women well, waited respectfully as they bowed deeply before turning away. Now he just needed to speak with Zimm.

The Lagrimari man stood in the middle of a group of men, just around the first bend in the settlement's narrow path, engaged in a hushed conversation. His face broke into a grin when Jack arrived.

"A word please?" Jack said, and pulled the translator off to the side, out of earshot. "You never mentioned that Maridall and Belliaros came to the settlement to recruit more workers after Pensar was arrested."

"I didn't? Well, they are scum." He spat on the ground, cursing them in the Lagrimari way. "They exploit us, think us too stupid to know better."

Jack sighed. "What did they say?"

Zimm shrugged in an exaggerated manner. "Who can remember? The men already agree not to work for those who don't pay fair. So it does not matter what words are spoken."

Jack crossed his arms, regarding the Lagrimari man's calculatedly guileless expression. He rewound the conversation trying to pinpoint what exactly had given him the feeling that Zimm was hiding something. "Did you tell the other settlers what Maridall said? The ones who don't understand Elsiran?"

"They are not stupid men, Commander. Farmer shows up, they know what he wants." Zimm sniffed.

Jack clenched his jaw and counted to five, anger building at the man's evasion. "But did you tell them?"

Zimm spread his arms wide. "Why tell my people lies? Constable says he arrest us and send us to labor camps if we 'break verbal contract.'" He put the words in air quotes. "Lagrimari cannot hold contracts in this land, verbal or otherwise. We need no more lies, so I tell none."

He confirmed the fear that Jack had held about the man— Zimm would only interpret the things he wanted to, likely in the manner he wanted to.

Jack shook his head. "So, the only one who went back to work at the farm was Vedan?"

Zimm rolled his eyes. "Vedan is good sort, but not so bright, eh? Says he needs no money since townsfolk do not sell to us and Sisterhood provides what we need. But he wants to work and feel like man—does not care that scheming Elsiran pig will not pay. No offense, Commander."

Jack waved it off. "Did him breaking ranks and working again make the rest of the men angry?"

A corner of Zimm's mouth kicked up. "Vedan is his own man. Does what he wants. We have... difference of opinion on this matter."

"So, you didn't mind his lack of loyalty?"

"Why would I?"

"'Without loyalty, what do you have?'" Jack parroted Zimm's own words from the day before. The settler's gaze sharpened to the point of a blade. "By agreeing to work, Vedan was tacitly endorsing the unfair treatment. What if others here had felt the same way? Wouldn't that have lessened your position in seeking equality and rights?"

Zimm's nostrils flared and his eyes turned hard. Finally the man's mask of helpful friendliness cracked, revealing an authentic emotion not designed to curry favor or elicit a sense of complacency.

"You think this enough to kill for?" Zimm asked, his voice cutting. Jack had never thought Zimm was who he pretended to be, but now he had his first glimpses of proof.

"It's my job to find out. I appreciate you talking with me, Zimm."

"Pleasant evening, Commander," he replied cheerily, the mask snapping back into place scarily fast.

"Pleasant evening." But the deepening mystery occurring in Baalingrove was anything but.

# CHAPTER NINE

Whispering words spoken by the weak are a chain of paper, too easily shredded under the vacillations of the heart. But vows spoken faithfully are iron shackles and may not be torn asunder.

— *BOOK OF HER REIGN,* 41:10

The next morning, Benn and Jack pulled up to the settlement again. In the morning light, all was quiet with smoke billowing from the various chimneys. Jack hoped none of them were clogged.

The Sisterhood trucks were nowhere to be seen, but Jack verified the presence of the additional soldiers he'd assigned walking the perimeter of the community. The nearest man saluted as Jack exited the vehicle.

He stood for a moment, realizing that without the settlers gathered outside, he didn't know how to find anyone. Fortunately, Darvyn came down the road at that moment, munching on an apple.

"Are you here for me, Commander?"

"Yes, how did you know?"

Darvyn shrugged and tossed the apple core in a wide arc. It disappeared behind a tree. That was apparently the only answer he was going to give.

"I want you to come with me to question Belliaros again."

Darvyn's eyebrows climbed.

"There are no clear suspects," Jack said, "so I think everyone is worth looking at twice."

To Jack's relief, the young man didn't appear prone to gloating. He got into the four-wheeler and they were off.

Unfortunately, when they arrived at the constabulary, the young deputy whose name badge read "Mud"—a name Jack had previously thought was a nickname—informed them in a rumbling, muted voice that the constable was not in.

"Where is he?" Jack asked.

The deputy, somewhere close to Darvyn's age, looked uneasy. His eyes shifted around, and he scratched his head. "I can't say, Commander. I can't rightly say. He should be in by this afternoon."

"Can't say or won't say?" Darvyn stood up straight and pinned the deputy with a glare.

Mud's gaze went back and forth from Darvyn to Jack, obviously scared. "W-well, that is, I..."

"Maybe if I turn you into goat, you remember?" Darvyn asked, grinning maniacally. "Or toad? Easy enough to do." He cracked his knuckles and Mud gulped, his hands beginning to shake.

Jack wanted to chastise Darvyn for threatening to use his Song to scare the Elsiran, but he also wanted to locate Belliaros as quickly as possible. And he was almost certain Earthsong couldn't turn a man into a goat. He hoped. He monitored the door to make sure no one else would come in and witness the unconventional interrogation.

Then Jack leaned forward, coaxing Mud to lean forward as well. "Listen, I can't really control what he does, and he's a bit of a loose cannon here. I think the best thing for you to do is just let us know where the constable is. We won't tell him you told us, if that's what you're worried about."

Mud paled, eyeing Darvyn worriedly.

"Who are you more afraid of, Belliaros or..." Jack nodded towards Darvyn, who had conjured a tiny flicker of flame that hovered over his palm.

As much as Jack hated the use of Earthsong to intimidate, he was entertained by the performance. And for some strange reason, he was confident that Darvyn wouldn't really harm anyone with his power.

The Singer could have conjured up any number of things, done all manner of destruction, but he was showing restraint. The action told Jack a lot about his character.

"F-fine. He's at Mayor Qoral's house. Right around the corner from the temple."

Jack shook his head. "Why didn't he want anyone to know he was there?"

"Because the mayor's down at the capital for a conference. And only Mistress Qoral is left home."

Understanding dawned. Darvyn's flame died as he fisted his hand.

"Well, Mud, thank you for your help." Jack bowed slightly at the flustered deputy and left with Darvyn right behind him.

The mayor's house was a two-story clapboard with black shutters. It was one of the largest homes in the town and easy enough to find. Jack's knock was answered by a pretty house-maid, who stared at him with wide eyes.

He feared her eyes may become stuck in such an enlarged state when she looked at Darvyn. Her surprise was almost comical.

"Pleasant morning, Miss, I'm High Commander Jaqros—"

"I know who you are." She giggled. "The Girls' Circle calls you Commander Cute." She bit her lip as if shocked she had made such a statement, and then began giggling again. Jack's face reddened, the collar of his shirt felt suddenly tight.

"Commander Cute," Darvyn said, a grin in his voice. Jack didn't bother to turn around and check.

"Well, then, um—is Mistress Qoral available?"

With even rounder eyes than before, the maid turned as if to check if her mistress were behind her at that moment. "No, sir. She's…indisposed."

"I see." Jack peered into the bright foyer behind her. "And is Constable Belliaros 'indisposed' as well?"

The maid blushed and looked away.

"Do not worry," Darvyn announced. "I do not understand this word, in-dee-spose, but I will find the constable." Then he slipped past the young woman, whose eyes now were truly in danger of some sort of irreparable strain and disappeared into the house.

"If you'll excuse me." Jack bowed, before following Darvyn as the maid sputtered.

The Lagrimari man was quick on his feet. He was already at the top of the steps by the time Jack entered. Jack took the stairs two at a time and stopped short in the hallway at the sight of an enraged, shirtless Belliaros bounding out of a door at the end of the hall. Darvyn was nowhere to be seen.

"Constable," Jack said with a polite nod. "Might I have a word?"

"Th-th- that *grol*... H-he just... It's indecent!"

Jack moved past him to peek in the bedroom to find Darvyn turned politely to face the wall as Mistress Qoral slipped a robe on.

Belliaros's bare chest, complete with massive belly and copious hair was distracting. "Would you like a moment to compose yourself, Constable? We can meet in the parlor in, say, five minutes?"

Jack grinned as Belliaros grumbled and returned to the room to fetch his shirt. Ten minutes later, all four were seated in the parlor, Jack and Darvyn on a couch, the constable and the mayor's wife in armchairs facing them.

"I have additional questions about the murdered settler. The night Pensar was murdered, you were...?" Jack prompted.

Belliaros rolled his eyes. "Here, I was here, all right. Qoral had just headed for the capital, and I came over."

"And how long did you stay?"

Belliaros glared.

Mistress Qoral, a forty-something woman with angular features that would be considered more handsome than beautiful, spoke up. "He left before dawn." Her voice was clipped, but she didn't hesitate to look him in the eye. Darvyn, she ignored.

"And you wouldn't be lying about that?" Jack asked.

She waved a hand. "Ask my staff. My maid and my cook saw him leave."

Jack shifted. "And are they not used to lying for you, Mistress?" He was trying to remain as polite as possible given the situation.

"I ran into Old Lem outside," Belliaros huffed, exasperated. "Out on his milk route. Told him I was suffering from a bout of insomnia and headed in to work early. And Timm what runs the stables will tell you the pony was there all night. I wouldn'ta had a way out to that settlement if I wanted."

Jack looked to Darvyn who after a pregnant pause, nodded. "They tell the truth."

"This would have been easier if you would have told me this from the get go," Jack said.

Belliaros pouted like a petulant child. "Weren't nobody's business what I get up to in my own time."

Jack shook his head.

"Will you—" Mistress Qoral cleared her throat. "Will you tell my husband?" Her voice fluttered. Jack sensed she was a no-nonsense woman, so either this was an act or she was genuinely scared.

"I have no reason to share details of this investigation with the mayor."

With great difficulty, she shifted her gaze to Darvyn. He responded with an insouciant grin but remained silent.

"Well then," Jack said, rising after the moment had stretched on a bit too long. "We won't bother you any further. Thank you for your cooperation."

The mayor's wife led them to the door herself and slammed it soundly when they left.

"Now what?" Darvyn asked.

Now what indeed? Their best suspect had an alibi. Jack wasn't sure what to do.

# CHAPTER TEN

From the beginning, you heard, and saw, and touched that which was put before you by our Sovereign, and still you did not understand. When eyes close to the blinding light of day, they may open to the wisdom found in sleep.

— *BOOK OF HER REIGN,* 62:1

Jasminda started when the clock struck midnight. How had it gotten so late? Jack shifted behind her. The sneaky thing had managed to coax her back into his arms at some point during his story.

She yawned and stretched. "Commander Cute?" she asked turning to him, eyebrow raised.

Jack groaned. "There was a time when the gossip columns had a competition to see which of them could come up with the worst, most embarrassing nickname for me."

"Oh, really?" She leaned forward. "What were the others?"

Jack shook his head. "It's late. We can continue this tomorrow—"

"Oh, no you don't. I need to know what happens next. And don't think I won't look up those nicknames."

A pained look crossed Jack's face. "I'm sure you will."

She pressed a palm to his cheek. "I won't if it bothers you." Her voice was sincere.

"Oh, that's not it. It's just..." He took a deep breath.

"What?"

"I'm not sure you'll like how this story ends."

She tucked her arm through his and leaned her head on his shoulder. "It ended up bringing you to me, so no matter what happens, I can hold onto that."

He squeezed her shoulder before continuing.

The door to Jack's office crashed open and General Larimel stood in the entryway.

"Do come in," Jack said under his breath.

Darvyn sat in the chair in front of the desk helping to review the notes of the case. They had been going over the facts from every angle, trying to discover what they'd missed.

In the doorway, Larimel looked like an angry boar ready to rampage. Smoke practically poured from his nostrils. His face was red to the tips of his ears.

"Commander!"

At least he'd used his title. "Pleasant morning to you, General. Do you know Master ol-Tahlyro?" He pointed to Darvyn.

Larimel barely spared the Lagrimari man a glance. He entered the room and slammed the door shut.

"What is the meaning of this? It's entirely inappropriate for you to entertain this kind of person in your office."

"This kind of person?" Jack tilted his head to the side.

"And I've had reports that you've been towing him all around the countryside while you work on this fool's errand of an investigation." Larimel's arm slashed through the air.

Reports. So someone didn't like what Jack was up to and thought tattling to the general was the solution.

"I assure you, General, I've had to tow Darvyn nowhere. He's perfectly capable of walking under his own power."

Larimel's face reddened. "You know what I'm saying, boy. And questioning the constable? As if a man sworn to uphold the laws of this land would murder a *grol*?"

Jack held a hand up. "I may be young, but I am the High Commander of the Elsiran army, and I expect you to address me as such, General."

A gasp flew from the man's lips and his eyes rounded comically. Larimel pointed his finger at Jack. "I was the one who checked on you when you were a snot-nosed tot new to the academy."

"And I am grateful. But you think I'm still that child. And I'm not. I've been training for this responsibility for nearly ten years and it is mine. Like it or not. Whether *anyone* likes it or not. The only one who can remove me from my position is the Prince Regent, and my brother has shown no signs of doing so. And *while* I am in this position, I will conduct this investigation into those under my charge in the way I see fit."

Larimel stood frozen for a few moments before sputtering, "The Board is here for a reason. You've yet to consult us on this."

"I haven't yet felt that consulting you would have any benefit."

"Well, maybe the Prince Regent needs to know about this." He crossed his arms.

"Feel free to inform him. If I thought for a moment he would remove me from duty, I'd tell him myself."

That seemed to surprise him. "You don't want to be the High Commander?"

"Wouldn't have been my first choice. But it is my duty, and so long as I'm in this position, I will do my best. Now, if you are no longer happy on the Board of Generals, I would be delighted to accept your resignation and transfer you to a placement more in line with your desires."

They stood staring at one another, Jack perfectly calm and Larimel anything but. Finally the general turned and stalked out of Jack's office.

The door slammed shut again leaving Jack equally satisfied and sorrowful. It was true, Larimel had been there for him throughout his training and career. But now he questioned whether the man's advice had ever been truly sound. He scrubbed a hand across his face. The loss of his mentor stung. He'd never thought the general would turn from advocate to adversary.

He sat back at his desk and faced Darvyn. "Did you catch all of that?"

"You all spoke so quickly, but I understood the emotions." Darvyn scrutinized Jack carefully. What could he see? What did Earthsong say about Jack's state of mind? He desperately wanted to know but wouldn't allow himself to ask.

Darvyn cleared his throat. "When I got the assignment to join the army, I had a mentor—Turwig—who was opposed to the plan. It was difficult to disappoint someone so instrumental in making you the person you are. Difficult to discover that maybe they weren't the person you thought they were after all. Better to have no heroes. Better not to be one."

He hung his head, and it didn't take Earthsong for Jack to sense something more going on there. A deeper story. A deeper level of pain.

Jack nodded, leaning back in his chair. "Yes. You're right. What do you mean you were assigned to join the army?"

At first he thought Darvyn was not going to answer, but the young man spoke slowly. "I work as part of a group dedicated to overthrowing the True Father. I was sent to close the breach in the Mantle."

Jack looked up, shocked. "What? How? And did you?"

"It's closed isn't it?" His expression was wry.

Jack looked around, half expecting reality to have shifted on its axis just as much as he was internally. "You can just... just close it?"

"It is not a simple task. But the breaches have never simply closed on their own. The spell responsible for their opening must be located and destroyed."

The invisible, magical barrier separating Elsira from Lagrimar had been breached by the True Father only seven times in five centuries, but the seven breach wars had left deep national scars on both sides. Sometimes the conflict lasted only a few months. The Fifth Breach lingered for seventy long years. No one in Elsira had ever understood how the rifts in the Mantle began or ended, so the idea that the young man before him was responsible for ending the war left Jack gob smacked.

"So, you found the spell and destroyed it, closing the breach? And then you got stuck here?"

Darvyn nodded, something sad melting in his eyes.

Jack sat up straight. The shift in his regard for Darvyn had already begun but settled into a deep respect. "Well, I thank you. On behalf of Elsira. The Seventh Breach was the shortest on record. You saved many lives."

Darvyn had a faraway look in his eyes. "Not enough." He shook off the hold of whatever emotion had gripped him. "At any rate, we've established that Pensar and Vedan were most likely killed by the same person."

Jack had so many more questions about the bombshell Darvyn had just dropped. But it seemed obvious that the moment of sharing was over. The war was long done, but this case was still unsolved. "The murderer was someone with knowledge of suffocation using smoke and exhaust."

"And someone with knowledge of automobiles. That in and of itself should exonerate any Lagrimari."

Jack frowned. "You may not have them in Lagrimar, but the Sixth Breachers have had ample opportunity to learn about vehicles. I don't think we should clear anyone based on that."

Darvyn pursed his lips but, after a moment, nodded in agreement.

Jack looked down at his notes, scribbled on a large yellow pad. "A bedsheet from Maridall's laundry line was used in the first murder."

"And the tarp used in Vedan's murder? Do we know its source?"

"The tarp is one sold at the general store in Sora. Just about every home in town has at least one. They're helpful during the rainy season."

Darvyn looked out the window, tapping his finger on the arm of the chair. "So the killer must have had knowledge of vehicles *and* access to the Maridall farm."

"As well as motive and opportunity," Jack said. "The Scourge of the Sixth and a well-liked man willing to work for no money." He pushed away from the desk in frustration. "We must be missing something."

"The Queen says, 'That which is often missed is usually the thing in front of you that moves the least'."

"Is that from the *Book of Her Reign*?"

Darvyn squinted in confusion. "I do not know that book."

"Well, what book were you quoting?"

"I was quoting the Queen."

"Yes, but... from what source?"

Darvyn frowned, speaking slowly, as if to a child. "From the things She has said."

Jack threw his hands up. "Never mind." He turned to the window and looked out on the ugly, gray buildings of the base. If he couldn't find justice for two men living under his protection, then what exactly was he doing? Why was he the High Commander? Just because he was the second son and it was his birthright?

He wished the words of the Queen would help him in this situation.

A small black and white bird fluttered down to perch on the window ledge.

Jack sat back.

Looked at Darvyn.

Then raced to his bookshelf. There was always a *Book of Her Reign* around. Sure enough he found one and flipped to chapter 19.

"'The disciple may ask, what of the law? Laws writ by men contain all the flaws of man. The sun needs no law but to shine.'" He looked up at Darvyn, eyes wide, then continued reading. "'At night, it dies its little death to be reborn the next day. The trees need no law but to birth leaves, nurture their short-long lives, and lose them in an endless cycle of life and death. For no law is higher than the law of death. The World After is the ultimate master that must be obeyed.'"

He slammed the book shut.

Darvyn stared, blinking. But a growing awareness rippled through Jack like a gentle breeze. "No law is higher than the law of death," he repeated in a whisper.

A feverish excitement stole over him. "In Lagrimar, what do you say when you learn of a death?"

"May they find serenity in the World After," Darvyn replied.

"Exactly. We say the same thing. It's a blessing for the dead who have found their final peace."

Darvyn nodded, his brow furrowed.

Jack tapped the book in his hand, staring at its leather cover, sightlessly. "I think I know who the murderer is. We need to get everyone together."

"Why?" Darvyn asked, eyes wide.

"Because that's what good detectives do."

Darvyn looked perplexed but shrugged. "If you say so."

# CHAPTER ELEVEN

Favored is the woman who, when she learns of the deeds and teachings of our Sovereign, keeps them in her heart and lets their enlightenment bleed into the rest of her body and thus into the world. For she is the Sovereign's daughter, and her time is ever at hand.

— *BOOK OF HER REIGN,* 66:1

Jack stood in a narrow alcove of the base's administration building, hand tapping against his thigh in a rapid tattoo. Around the corner and down the hall, the people he'd called together for this meeting were gathering.

He steeled his nerves, working to combat the buzzing swarm taking wing in his belly. Footsteps approached, and Benn rounded the corner.

"Is everyone here?" Jack asked.

"Yes, everyone you asked for."

"All right then." He straightened his brown uniform jacket. "I guess it's time to begin." Benn looked like he wanted to say something but then changed his mind.

Jack hadn't been lying when he told Darvyn he thought he knew who the killer was. But the idea of accusing an innocent person rankled. He had to be sure.

He paused just outside the meeting room to shore up his veneer of authority. This was his duty, and he would do it well, Sovereign willing.

Stepping inside, he found Constable Belliaros seated at the head of the long table, a petulant expression twisting his face. He'd brought along Deputy Mud, who stood in the corner behind him, arms folded like a silent sentry.

Next were three women from the Sisterhood: Sister Amelynne, Sister Lorelle, and Priestess Syllenne, the head of the Sora temple. All sat placidly in a row, the pictures of serenity.

Across the table from them were the Lagrimari contingent: Zimm and Darvyn. That left the other head of the table to Jack. He lowered himself into his chair and folded his hands in front of him, willing the riot in his midsection to quiet. He focused on making his voice stable and commanding. "Thank you all for responding to my request to meet. I appreciate your attention to this matter."

Priestess Syllenne raised a brow, eyes fierce but voice honeyed. "It's our pleasure. What can we do for you, Commander?"

"Priestess," Jack said, "while you are certainly welcome here, I know you must have many duties to attend to. It was not my intention to take you away from them."

"This incident has greatly discomfited my sisters, and I must see to their well-being," she replied simply.

Jack nodded and took a deep, steadying breath. "The tragic murders that have taken place in Baalingrove are deeply disturbing. I think we should all be able to agree that no matter who the victims are, having a murderer on the loose in the area cannot be tolerated."

The Sisters and Lagrimari nodded, while the constables remained straight faced. "This has been a strange investigation," Jack continued. "These settlers who over the past fifteen years have lived quiet, peaceful lives—" The constable snorted and everyone else gave him the evil eye.

Jack cleared his throat. "Men, who asked nothing but to try and eke out a living in our land, deserve justice. And it is my responsibility to supply it. The investigation provided a number of suspects, but I believe only one is our culprit."

He straightened his shoulders. "Constable Belliaros, you have an unmitigated hatred of the Lagrimari."

The man sputtered. "Hatred? I don't hate them, I just would rather they go back to where they came from."

When both Darvyn and Zimm went to retort, Jack held up a hand. "But your alibi during the time of the first murder checks out, and you were seen in Sora during the time of the second murder."

Belliaros sat back looking smug. "Did you really think I would kill a *grol?*"

Jack stared, unblinking, until the man began to squirm. Then he turned to Zimm. "The Scourge of the Sixth was hated by virtually every man in the settlement. But you, Zimm, may be the only one there with reason to murder Vedan—a man who showed disloyalty and could have harmed your fight for improved rights."

Zimm's mouth firmed; his eyes narrowed. "You accuse me, Commander?"

Jack looked at the man for a moment, then to Darvyn frowning beside him. "No." He then held up his copy of the *Book of Her Reign* that he'd placed on the table earlier. "I think that the Queen herself has given us the answer to this mystery."

His gaze moved to Sister Amelynne.

Her jaw dropped. "You can't possibly think it was *me* who murdered those poor men! I've dedicated my life to caring for the indigent. I would never—"

"No, Sister, I don't believe it was you. We did some checking, and you were seen at the temple all day on the day Pensar was killed."

Amelynne leaned back, still appearing shaken.

"Both men were killed in similar manners—the blocked chimney and car exhaust fumes produce a nearly identical effect." He turned to Sister Lorelle. "You said you've seen this manner of death before, is that right?"

Sister Lorelle blinked. "Me? Yes. As a matter of fact, my father died in such an accident. A bird's nest had clogged the chimney's flue over the summer. When he lit the fire for the first time that autumn and fell asleep, he just...never woke up."

Jack leaned forward, gripping his hands tight. "Did you know the gases from the truck exhaust were the same kind as are built up in the chimney?"

Her eyes were open and guileless. "It stands to reason they would function in a similar manner, though I'm no scientist."

Goosebumps popped up on his skin. He didn't want to be right, but he didn't think he was wrong. "Did you kill the settlers, Pensar and Vedan, Sister Lorelle?"

The woman's shoulders went back. Her brows climbed higher on her forehead. "What reason could I possibly have for killing those men?"

"I don't know." Jack shook his head sadly. "That is the part I cannot figure out. But the scripture you quoted after we found Vedan's body, it stayed with me. '*Laws writ by men contain all the flaws of man.*' You believe that the law of the Queen is higher than man's law."

Her eyes shifted, quickly taking in those gathered. "Yes. The

Queen's wisdom is greater than that of men."

"And you were intimately familiar with the manner of death. I don't believe you wanted to cause these men pain—the gash in Vedan's head notwithstanding. But I do believe that you are responsible for their deaths." Jack sat back, holding his breath.

The Sister remained quiet, her face a mask. There was no fear in her expression, nor guilt, at least none that he could see. But Darvyn leaned forward, deep lines cutting into his face. "You did kill them, didn't you?" he whispered in Lagrimari.

He turned to Jack and nodded. In Elsiran, he said, "It is her."

Sister Lorelle whipped her head around to stare at him, all serenity gone from her expression. Deep outrage shone through, and her fists clenched on the table.

The priestess placed a hand over hers. "Lorelle?"

Sister Lorelle relaxed immediately, deflating like a balloon stuck with a pin. Her shoulders slumped and she stared down at her hands. When she spoke, her voice was hushed. "They will have peace in the World After until the Time of Waking. Isn't that a better fate than their wretched lives here?"

Sister Ameylnne gasped. "What are you saying?"

Sister Lorelle looked up again at the Lagrimari men. "Those poor men were being vilified and hated by this community. All they wanted to do was work honestly, hold jobs that were fulfilling to them, and do their best. They just weren't given the chance."

It took Jack a moment to find his voice. "Then why kill them?"

Her eyes were feverish when she turned to him. "So they would flourish in the World After." She spoke as if the answer was obvious.

"Their lives here were so full of struggle and indignity. Working for men who scorn them, if they're allowed to work at all. When I got to know them, I found so much compassion for them. They're like lambs really, so docile and powerless. They needed guidance, a shepherd to show them the way."

Her short, choppy attempt at a topknot fell askew as she spoke. "In the World After, they can be who they were meant to be: free men. I simply hastened them on their path. It's what the Queen would want." She nodded repeatedly, and Jack wasn't sure if it was madness or just misguided passion he was seeing.

"And *you* know what the Queen wants?" Darvyn asked through a clenched jaw.

She regarded him serenely. "I have spent my life serving Her, even before I joined the Sisterhood, so yes, I know."

Darvyn snorted. "I spend my life serving Her, too." His eyes flashed dangerously, and Jack was afraid something was going to go up in flame soon.

"Do you understand that what you did was wrong, my sister?" the priestess asked slowly.

Lorelle flinched. "Wrong for men, perhaps. But Her will is paramount." Whether she was deranged or not, her apparent zeal had made no room for remorse.

Priestess Syllenne sat back, lips pursed and eyes downcast. Sister Amelynne hung her head and the constable's jaw hung open.

"Why that way, with smoke and fumes?" Zimm asked, sorrow etched into his face.

"'May the breath of the Sovereign be upon you, filling your lungs with heavy air, weighing you down toward a dream-filled sleep,'" she said, quoting scripture. "Father died painlessly in his sleep. It was peaceful and calm, his physician assured me. I gave them good deaths. In sleep they are closer to the Queen. I sent them to the World After with more peace and dignity than they were given in life.

"With Pensar it was simple, I stuffed the sheet I'd taken from the farm where they worked into his chimney. That farmer should never have had the poor man arrested." She looked accusingly at Belliaros. "And I asked Vedan to come help me unload the truck, he was always so helpful." A small smile played upon her lips.

"But he wouldn't stay in the truck once I placed the hose in. I had to knock him unconscious, though I hated to do it." She shook her head.

Weariness and regret weighed down Jack's bones. "You are not the one who gets to judge. Not even the Queen is the arbiter of life and death. The World After decides who is to join them."

"In the Time of Waking they will be reborn better," Lorelle said, leaning forward with a disturbing light in her eyes. "They will be reborn as free Elsirans and will never know suffering or strife again."

The priestess's face could be described as stern on a normal day, but now it looked like had been etched from stone. She stared down at her hands for a moment, and when she raised her head, her eyes shone with unshed tears. "Constable Belliaros, I think it's time to take our sister into your custody."

"Yes, Priestess," the man said, rising and pulling out his handcuffs. He looked reluctant to cuff the woman, but she rose gracefully and held her arms out.

"The Queen has my reward," she said. "She knows I've done no wrong."

The priestess stood as well and soon all around the table were on their feet. "You *have* done wrong, my sister. But I still wish for Her to bless your dreams and show you the error of your ways."

Sister Lorelle's expression lost its certainty for a moment. She frowned at Priestess Syllenne with confusion. "No, sister. When I dream of Her, She will thank me."

Belliaros shook his head and led the murderer away, his steps heavy and hers light as air.

# CHAPTER TWELVE

The vine that produces the sweetest fruit shall be known throughout the vineyard. Many grow, and many yield, but they will still be forgotten. Strive to bring forth food that nourishes and sustains and melts like honey on the tongue.

— *BOOK OF HER REIGN,* 40:7

The fire had burned down to embers in the fireplace, and Jasminda watched the glow with sadness. "What happened to her?"

Jack sighed deeply and didn't answer for a long moment. "She was tried in an Elsiran court and acquitted."

Jasminda sat up sharply, spinning to face him. "What?"

Pain creased Jack's face. "They could not convince the tribunal that her actions met the standard of malice for a murder conviction. But I was able to successfully petition the Council that the murder of settlers should be considered a war crime. Another trial was held in the army's court, and the judge convicted her and sentenced her to live out her days in a mental hospital."

Jasminda's body softened; she rested her head on Jack's shoulder. "Lorelle claimed she saw the settlers as men, but she didn't. She really thought of them as children who she needed to save from themselves. I don't know whether that makes her crazy or not."

He rubbed his hand up and down her arm. "Darvyn wasn't convinced either, but it was really the only way to get her away from society."

"And the settlers?"

"They took it all in stride. A few murders didn't rise to the level of a crisis for the Lagrimari." Jack's voice was wry. "Darvyn and I met regularly for the next few months, practicing our language skills with one another. And then one day, he disappeared. I thought maybe another murderer had sprung up, perhaps a copycat, but then I remembered Darvyn was an Earthsinger. He could handle himself. We searched for him to no avail."

His fingers began fidgeting with the sleeve of Jasminda's dress. "I'd always wondered what happened to him. If I'd ever seen him again. Six weeks ago he reappeared, and you know the rest."

Jasminda nodded. Darvyn had arrived out of the blue to warn Jack that the Mantle would be destroyed soon, releasing the True Father on the world. He'd led Jack through a crack in the Mantle, disguised him using Earthsong, and then been lost again, pushing Jack into Jasminda's path. Now the Mantle was gone forever, and the two warring countries were coming together as one. Something that seemed to be an impossible task.

"So, somehow you and he became unlikely friends and allies," she mused. "But you each had your own agendas, right?"

"Darvyn was certainly there for a reason. Now that I know he was a Keeper of the Promise and was here working toward the downfall of the True Father, it makes more sense. But even when our only shared goal was to find a murderer, we were able to find common ground."

"Common ground," she repeated. "That's the key to this whole thing, isn't it?"

He rested his head on hers. "I think so. I was able to look at things through his eyes, and I think he was able to look at things through mine."

Jasminda grimaced. She could admit, she hadn't tried very hard to see things through Nadette's eyes. But as queen, she would have to consider how decisions affected everyone, those she agreed with and those she didn't. She was queen of everyone and owed it to them to find something to relate to in everyone's struggle.

She vowed to try again with Nadette. For if Jack and Darvyn could find common ground after being on opposite sides of a war, she could figure out how to smooth things over with one overly enthusiastic event planner.

The next morning, Jasminda sat at her usual table in the Blue Library and greeted her guest. "Nadette, thank you for meeting with me again. I want to apologize for my behavior yesterday."

Instead of the sanctimonious smile Jasminda expected, the woman nodded in understanding. A small smile crept onto her face. "This must all be overwhelming for you, Your Majesty. And I'm sorry to add to your burden. I do understand that your priority is the physical needs of those coming here, fleeing that awful land. I just want you to see that while you think the wedding frivolous, it supports the emotional needs of both Elsirans and Lagrimari."

The woman's fingers ran across the cover of the enormous binder on the table before them. "Think of how inspiring it will be for the Lagrimari, who have spent a lifetime under the thumb of brutality, to witness someone who they think of as one of their own marry in a grand celebration. Such a thing must be honored. It will unify both peoples and help us learn to live with one another, which is what we need."

Jasminda was surprised and deservedly chastened. "You're right, Nadette. I didn't... That's very astute of you. It's an excellent point."

Nadette appeared surprised at the praise.

"Please show me your swatch book again and let's make those decisions. And perhaps the scale of the event can be just a touch less opulent, if only to save the craftsmen some worry and hassle."

Nadette smiled warmly and heaved open the binder.

Outside the window, the sun shone brightly on a beautiful day. Though she couldn't see it from the palace, somewhere out there Lagrimari children who had never known full bellies were receiving regular meals.

Her next meeting was with Rozyl to work on the plan to rehouse the refugees temporarily, and talks were already underway for the building of new housing, new villages and settlements—not shantytowns this time, but real towns—to accommodate them all. Jasminda would somehow manage to find her way as queen and help both people, because it was her duty, her privilege, and her purpose.

"I like the pale green," she said, pointing out a shade that reminded her of springtime.

"That's a wonderful choice, Your Majesty."

The story continues in *Whispers of Shadow & Flame (Earthsinger Chronicles, Book 2)*.

# HUSH OF STORM & SORROW

EARTHSINGER NOVELLAS, BOOK 2

**This novella is intended to be read after *Whispers of Shadow & Flame*.**

While battling a vicious winter storm, Roshon ol-Sarifor, along with his father and twin brother are kidnapped and thrust on a journey that takes them far from home—leaving his sister Jasminda believing them dead. Their captors claim that the Queen Who Sleeps is behind their abduction—She wants them to reclaim a magical object hidden in a deadly part of the ocean. But a violent encounter with a gang of pirates forces the ol-Sarifors to seek refuge on a smuggler's ship, where Roshon meets a girl unlike any he's encountered before.

Ani Summerhawk never met a risk she didn't take. But with a price on her head, she and her older brother need to make a quick getaway from a deal gone bad. Every ship in the sea is seeking the reward for returning her to a ruthless captain who believes she's his property. But when her brother agrees to transport three passengers to a dangerous destination, Ani's heart is put on the line for the first time.

The two families battle a treacherous sea, greedy sailors, and a powerful mage as they struggle to retrieve and secure the ancient artifact. And the attraction between a high-spirited girl and a cautious boy comes to a head when they discover that their biggest fight just might be with each other.

**Set two years before the events of** *Song of Blood & Stone*, **this action-packed novella answers the question of what happened to Jasminda's family and sets the stage for the events in** *Cry of Metal & Bone (Earthsinger Chronicles, book 3).*

# CHAPTER ONE

Fear is not a pillar of our art, but it is the substance out of which the wheel is formed. Master it or submit to it and you will travel two very different paths.

— DAIPUNA: THE ART OF COMBAT

*Two Years Before the Fall of the Mantle*

"Varten!" Roshon's voice rose with his growing panic, echoing throughout the dark cave as he called for his twin brother. Next to him, Papa held the lantern high. The glossy walls sparkled in the flickering light, and shadows leaped about in a war dance, closing in on them.

"Varten!" Papa shouted. Sweat beaded on his forehead as he quickened his pace. The air inside was close and warm, unlike the frigid temperature outside, but Roshon's blood still held a chill. He raced to follow his father, stumbling over the uneven surface of the cave floor.

The strap of his bag bit into his arm as the various items they'd purchased in town weighed him down. Roshon readjusted the bag and kept moving, struggling to find his footing. They'd been returning to their valley home, crossing the mountain that separated them from the tiny Elsiran Borderlands town where they bought whatever they couldn't make or grow, when Varten had disappeared from the trail. Though his brother had a penchant for mischief, he wouldn't have run off without telling anyone, not here with a storm threatening. And not so near the mountain caves Papa had long ago forbidden them to enter.

Papa had visibly shuddered before entering this one, his Earthsong magic having tracked Varten this far. Even now, his breathing was labored and he appeared to be in pain. Something about these caves affected Earthsingers, his father and sister included, differently than it did everyone else. The lantern light barely pierced the gloom, and though Roshon had no magic, he didn't like being down there, either.

They turned a corner in the tunnel they were searching to find that the space widened into a vast chamber. Papa sniffed and lowered the lantern to illuminate the cave floor. A hollow feeling opened in Roshon's gut when the weak light showed dark droplets on the strangely glossy surface.

Was that blood?

"Varten!" they both screamed.

It was getting harder to hold the terror at bay. If something happened to his twin, would Roshon know? Would he sense it? He didn't feel anything different inside and once again cursed the fact that he had been born without magic.

Mama's face filled his vision for a moment, and he froze,

shaking. He couldn't lose his brother, too. And their sister was waiting for them at home. Jasminda never went to town unless absolutely necessary, not that he blamed her. But how could he face her if something happened to Varten?

"Papa, can't you try to track him again?"

The older man pursed his lips and gave Roshon a heavy look. Using Earthsong in the caves was different for him somehow, more difficult maybe. Papa kneeled and touched the drops on the ground with the tip of his finger. The liquid shone dark red against his skin.

Roshon held his breath. Varten wasn't just missing; he was *bleeding*. Injured and lost in the darkness in this snarl of unnavigable tunnels and caverns.

"Take this." Papa handed him the lantern. Roshon gripped the handle hard enough to bruise his palm as Papa closed his eyes.

If Jasminda were here, she could at least help Papa find Varten. They could link their power together and enhance it, using that strange connection to Earthsong that joined their inner Songs with the energy of every living thing. But she had stayed behind, electing to watch the farm and avoid the three-day journey to town and back. And Roshon was useless, helplessly watching his father concentrate to perform the silent magic of an Earthsong spell.

Papa gasped, clutched his chest, and fell onto his hands and knees. Roshon was immediately by his side, grabbing his arm. "What's wrong? What's happened?"

After a few huffs, Papa's breathing steadied. "I think I found him. There's another way out. Just through there." He pointed, though Roshon saw nothing but darkness in that direction. Still, relief washed over him as Papa stood and led the way through the cave to a narrow tunnel.

"Is he all right?" Roshon asked.

"Yes," Papa replied but didn't elaborate.

"Are *you* all right?"

"These caves . . ." He looked around warily and hastened his steps.

At fifteen, Roshon was far too old to be afraid of the dark, and he wasn't . . . usually. But when his strong and fearless father was this on edge, well, he made sure not to fall behind the man's quick pace. There were plenty of things Roshon *was* afraid of, and losing another family member was high on the list. Should he have kept a closer eye on his twin? He *was* the elder brother, if only by a quarter of an hour, and he'd always tried to keep Varten's flighty ways in check. What should he have done differently to stop this from happening?

They moved quietly through the tunnels, Papa's unease seeping more and more into Roshon. There was no trail of blood, though, so perhaps the injury was not severe. Finally, the temperature began to drop and the sound of wind whipped against the rocks. The light, cold and anemic, brightened as they approached the exit.

Outside, they emerged into a heavy flurry of snow. When they'd entered the mountain, soft, fat flakes had been falling, but the surprise storm was growing.

Roshon looked up to find that they'd exited farther down the mountain than they'd entered, having lost ground somewhere inside. Now, once they found Varten, they'd have to fight the snow to get home. And Papa had said he felt Varten, so that meant they *would* find him.

The foothills had been spared the threat of the storm, which only raged on the mountain, and they descended into the crisp autumn day.

"Should we call for him?" Roshon asked, voice low. Papa shook his head, on alert, and Roshon wished he could sense whatever his father was sensing.

"Where is he?" Roshon whispered, searching the surrounding area but seeing nothing but a barely there path that led to a small grove of elms and oaks.

Papa squinted up into the red-gold mass of leaves still decorating the trees before them. He held up his arm to stop Roshon from moving any farther.

"Go back up the mountain," he said, emphasizing his words with a push to Roshon's chest. "Run!"

Roshon stumbled backward, then gulped, but before he could turn around and follow Papa's command, a whizzing sound flew by his ear and his neck exploded in pain. He reached for the wound. Something long and sharp protruded from his body. That was strange. So was the warm, red liquid coating his hand. He tried to look at Papa, to ask him what was happening, but his eyes weren't working properly. Neither was his tongue.

Before everything went black, he thought of Varten and wondered if he'd ever see his brother again.

# CHAPTER TWO

As you progress in daipuna, the scales of human armor will fall away, no longer needed. Protection and aggression, first seemingly at odds, are revealed to be the same. Both useless under the shadows of the eight pillars.

— DAIPUNA: THE ART OF COMBAT

Ani Summerhawk bounced on her toes. The anticipation of negotiations always made her giddy. Her brother, Tai, shot her a dark look, and she struggled to wrangle her excitement. Still, she couldn't stop the tapping of her foot as the shadowy figures of four men approached.

The warehouse serving as their meeting place was lit with overhead bulbs that cast pools of light every twenty paces or so. The rest of the space was in shadow with the bulk of the crates and boxes forming an obstacle course of sorts. If things went wrong, there were plenty of places to hide, and she'd already scoped out the quickest paths to the two exits. Her exhilaration ratcheted up a notch, and she felt as if she were vibrating out of her skin.

"If you can't behave . . ." Tai began, speaking out the side of his mouth.

"Don't try to police me," Ani said through clenched teeth. "I'm not a child."

Tai snorted, and Ani replied with an elbow to his arm. Now fifteen, she had been a part of their father's smuggling operation since before she could walk. Father had taken her out with him on his runs and had never once expected her to stand quietly at his side during a negotiation. Then again, Tai did things a bit differently than Father had, and it was probably for the best. Maybe if Father had been more like Tai he'd still be alive.

She gritted her teeth and stilled the constant movement of her limbs, determined to try things her brother's way. The interior of the warehouse smelled of mildew and mothballs. Mik, Tai's first mate and best friend, had found it for them in a seedier section of the already-seedy docks of Portside. He'd stayed behind on the ship to ready it for a speedy departure. The men who stepped into the nearest cone of light were fellow Raunians, so Mik's preparedness would likely come in handy.

"Bor," Tai said, addressing the largest of the men. "You're looking well."

Ani held back a snicker. This Bor fellow resembled the creature his name sounded like. Squat and meaty, with a piggish nose and deep-set eyes, he was just about the ugliest Raunian she'd ever seen. His hair was dyed the same blue as Tai's and Ani's, but Bor had done his in vertical stripes, alternating with its natural black, which lent him a deranged appearance.

Unsurprisingly, he had no marriage markings tattooed on his face. Aside from his *siokka*, or family crest, along with his captain's and taxpayer's tattoos, he bore five horizontal lines on his left cheekbone. He'd served five years of hard labor. Not a man to be trifled with.

"What's this exclusive haul you've brought me here to see, Summerhawk?" Bor crossed his heavy arms.

Tai leaned against a crate, which towered several handspans above his head. His pose was casual and carefree, but only to those who didn't know him. Ani could see that beneath his cool exterior he was on alert. Bor's reputation as a hard bargainer had been well-earned. The presence of the three large men behind him hinted at exactly how he liked to negotiate. If they were going to make any money on this deal, and leave with their lives and limbs intact, they had to be vigilant.

Her finger itched for the hidden knife sheathed down her back. Tai had several weapons concealed on him, as well, and both were proficient in their usage. Tai was probably hoping it wouldn't come to that, but Ani loved a good dustup. She hadn't seen much fighting action since she'd started traveling with her brother; working with Father had been much more exciting.

"Narwhal ivory," Tai said, answering Bor's question after a pause for dramatic effect. "These tusks were sacrificed by the Relamendor clan after they lost the Fifty-First Great Ocean War."

"And how did you come by them?"

"I have a good relationship with the chief of the victorious clan, the Diogenedes narwhals. We traded."

Bor sniffed. "Narwhals aren't trustworthy. You expect me to believe they'd trade the spoils of war to you? Those could be stingray barbs for all I know."

Tai shrugged, looking like the most nonchalant person in the world. Ani held back a smirk. She slowly moved her hand behind her, ready to grip her blade if necessary. Bor was trying to appear aloof, but his eyes sparkled with interest he couldn't completely hide.

"They're only dishonest with people they don't like," Tai replied, grinning. "I assure you, the ivory has been authenticated. And there are a great many in Fremia who would pay handsomely for thirty crates of rare narwhal tusk."

Bor raised his eyebrows. "Thirty crates?"

Tai scratched his chin. "Aye."

"And your price?"

"Twenty thousand Elsiran pieces."

Bor and his three companions burst into laughter. Tai laughed, as well, but it was shallow, and his eyes remained hard.

Ani cracked a smile but not for the same reason as everyone else. A flash of an image had crossed her vision: Bor's face, confused, as if he'd just made a deal he didn't quite like and wasn't sure how he'd been bested. These tiny premonitions came to her from time to time. The visions might come true within minutes, days, or even years. Given that she never planned to see Bor again, she hoped this one meant that Tai was about to turn a hefty profit.

"That's seaway robbery, and you know it," Bor snarled.

Tai shrugged again. "That's the price. If you don't want it, I know an Udlander who won't scoff at it."

"He also won't be able to move the merchandise, Summerhawk. How could you trust an Udlander?" Bor grumbled.

"I'm just a simple sailor."

"You're a smuggler, and we both know there's nothing simple about it. I'll pay eight thousand pieces and not a copper more."

Tai sent Ani a sidelong glance. The corners of her mouth lifted.

"Well, then I'm very sorry, but we don't have a deal." He straightened and made a big show of brushing off his trousers. Ani retrieved the knife from her sheath and twirled it around her fingers. It had been a gift from Father and was perfectly weighted for her hand. Tai's eyes narrowed at her almost imperceptibly, but she was just having a bit of fun. None of the men had even looked at her twice, not thinking her a threat.

Tai walked around the back of the sample crate they'd brought and levered it onto the rolling dolly. She knew just how heavy it was, but he made it look effortless. Another thing Father had taught them: make everything appear easy. A good negotiator is a blank slate—no emotions, no challenges, no problems. A deal was just a deal you could take or leave, as far as the other party was concerned.

They were halfway to the exit when Bor spoke up. "How about another offer for you, Summerhawk?" A counter had been expected. It was all a part of the bargaining process, after all, but something about Bor's tone made the hair on the back of Ani's neck stand up.

"And what's that?" Tai called without looking back.

"You take my price and I don't tell Noa about his apprentice being here with you instead of on his ship, as contracted."

Tai whipped around, anger flashing in his eyes. He didn't even look at Ani before his own blade was out, ready in his hands. The four men chuckled, and a sick feeling hit Ani's gut. She'd been itching for a fight, but something wasn't right here. The fact that these men knew about her mother's deal for her meant a bounty had gone up. They'd known it was a possibility when she hadn't shown up for her apprenticeship but hadn't thought that Mother would go so far. That's the last time Ani would underestimate the woman's ruthlessness. The price of the cargo Tai possessed was nothing in comparison to the benefits of being in both Noa's and Mother's good graces. Besides, Noa would pay handsomely for the retrieval of his property—her.

"Ani, go. Now," Tai said from the side of his mouth.

"You can't take them all alone," she replied. Bor's three friends were tall, though none as wide as their leader. Their builds were similar to Tai's, lean and ropy from living on boats most of their lives.

"As your captain, that's an order," he hissed.

"And as my brother?" she asked, not taking her eyes off their adversaries.

Tai growled low in his throat as the men approached. Between them lay a jumble of boxes and crates, leaving no clear shot for any of her blades.

She was a member of her brother's crew and should really obey his order, but she was also a Summerhawk. Ani shook her head and planted her feet. "Raunian women don't run. We fight," she said through gritted teeth.

"You're fifteen, Ani. Not a woman yet, not by any stretch of the imagination."

Anger burned inside her at his statement. Though she hadn't come of age, she was old enough to be an apprentice, to accept a future mate if challenged. She'd mastered twenty-five levels of daipuna, the Raunian martial art. She was definitely old enough to fight with her brother against a crew of thugs who thought they could intimidate them.

"Father trained me. And he was the best brawler to ever board a ship."

"The odds aren't good, Ani," Tai pleaded, a note of desperation in his voice.

"Leaving now would be dishonorable." She gripped her blade tighter as Bor and his men came closer.

Tai let out a sound of frustration. Then he whipped his head toward her and did the unthinkable: he turned around and ran.

Ani had no choice but to chase after him. Two against four were bad odds, but one against four in these conditions was suicide. Footsteps clattered behind them as they raced out of the warehouse, down a narrow alley, and into the flow of heavy Portside traffic.

"You son of a mud licker," Ani called after him as he nimbly wound his way around the horses, wagons, autos, and pedestrians clogging the crumbling streets.

She wasn't so much dashing away from the thugs as she was pursuing Tai, who she planned to give a good pummeling when this was over, even if he was seven years her senior. Running from a fight was what had ruined their father's reputation. The Summerhawk name would never regain its former respect if they didn't stand up for themselves.

She dodged a uniformed Fremian sailor and a gaggle of Elsiran street urchins as she raced down the street. Tai was going to get a big piece of her mind when this was over.

# CHAPTER THREE

Honor is not a pillar of our art, yet it comprises the pegs which hold the spokes of the wheel in place. To practice without honor is to breathe with no air.

— DAIPUNA: THE ART OF COMBAT

For a moment, Roshon feared his eyes were sealed shut. He tried to open them for the third time and finally succeeded, wincing as the light above him shattered his head. He quickly squeezed them closed again. When the pain had dulled enough for him to venture to open his lids again, he squinted, trying to bring clarity to his blurred vision.

A briny smell met his nose, and a groan sounded next to him. His head was heavy as a sack of rocks. With great effort, he turned to find a face identical to his staring back at him.

"Varten." The word was a soft rasp. Cotton coated the inside of his mouth, and he smacked his tongue against his lips to clear it away. His twin's amber eyes glinted in the harsh light. "What happened?" Roshon asked. He and his brother were lying on the ground side by side.

A pair of sturdy black shoes strode into view between them. He tilted his head up and caught the swish of a dark-blue skirt before the pain had him slumping down again.

"They're waking up, Sister Myreen," a melodic voice said above him.

"Thank you, dear. Let's move them." This voice was older and gruffer and came from somewhere out of sight.

The black shoes walked away, once more revealing Varten, who was struggling to sit up. Roshon felt as if he were swimming underwater while wearing a winter coat. His limbs were unusually heavy, and he had little control over them.

Footsteps sounded behind him, and then he was being hauled up by two—no, three—pairs of hands. Someone grabbed his ankles, there was a great deal of huffing and puffing as they carried him what seemed like a short distance and placed him on a hard chair.

Roshon's vision was clearing rapidly, and he took in the features of the woman who had stepped into his line of vision. She was older, perhaps Papa's age, her dark auburn hair streaked with gray and bound tightly in a topknot. Eyes of deep honey regarded him shrewdly, making him feel like a cow prepared for the slaughter.

Three other women joined the first, though they all stood slightly behind her, making him think they were subordinates. They seemed so serene with their hands clasped together in front of them. All four women wore identical blue dresses and wore their hair in the same severe style. They were women of the Sisterhood.

After a moment, they stopped staring and dragged Varten into the chair next to Roshon's. The seats had been placed in a circle of light, outside of which the space was too dark to make out.

Papa shuffled into view, walking under his own power but still needing to be supported by one of the Sisters, a much younger one with carrot-colored hair. He settled roughly in the chair on Roshon's left and regarded the boys. "Are you all right?"

Roshon nodded.

"I'm fine, Papa," Varten said.

Papa then turned his attention to the four women. "Sister, why have you brought us here? And where are we?"

The one Roshon had pegged as the leader stepped closer. She was not the eldest woman present, but she carried herself a bit taller than the rest. "Dansig ol-Sarifor, the Queen Who Sleeps has need of you."

Papa's head dropped, and he let out a loud sigh. From the corner of his eye, Roshon saw Varten shift forward awkwardly. Roshon was barely able to sit upright in the chair, but in a few minutes he figured he would be able to move more freely.

He turned his head slightly, and Varten shot him a questioning look. Roshon shrugged. Papa had talked of having the Dream of the Queen in his youth and of his reverence for the Elsiran deity who was said to have been sleeping for five hundred years, but Roshon wasn't sure what to make of it all. Varten, however, looked a bit green.

"You've kidnapped me and my sons on the Queen's order?" Papa asked, his voice rough.

"No," the Sister said. "Your children have no part in this. The Queen did not mention them. But we needed a way to draw you out."

Shock sparked inside Roshon, and Papa tensed, a rare display of anger glinting in his eyes. "By using my children?

Leading my son away and kidnapping us is no way to honor Her. Where. Are. We?"

"Rosira," the Sister said.

Roshon gasped. The capital city of Elsira was hundreds of kilometers away from their home in the eastern mountains.

"You can't be serious," Papa said, incredulous. "How long has it been since we were taken?"

"About eight hours. The sleeping darts were quite powerful. That was my idea, not the Queen's, though I have no doubt She would approve. She was very clear in Her Dream to me. She needs you for an important mission. You are to journey across the Delaveen Ocean and retrieve a magical object hidden deep in the sea in a place called the Narrows. The object is called the death stone, and it is of the utmost import."

Papa's face contorted as a series of emotions played across them: disbelief, confusion, regret. "And you could not approach me in a civilized manner to carry this message? You had to hurt my boys? Take us by force?"

The woman brushed off his aggravation with a wave of her hand. "I could not take the chance that you would refuse or waste time with arguments. She made it very clear that time was of the essence."

Papa groaned and ran a hand through his dark, coiled hair. He shook his head and stared at the ground, thinking. Was he seriously considering this bizarre request?

Yes, the Queen was supposed to be powerful, and Papa, Jasminda, and Varten were all believers—Mama had been, too—but Roshon tended to have more faith in things he could see with his own eyes. And he'd never dreamed of Her.

Varten's mouth was agape, hanging on every word the Sister said. The women of the Sisterhood pledged their lives to serve the Queen Who Sleeps. Mama had been a member before she met Papa, but her order had done nothing to help her after she married a dreaded Lagrimari. As a result, Roshon had never felt very kindly toward the group. Why was Varten so enthralled? Roshon looked to the woman again, disturbed to see a manic gleam to her eyes.

"The Queen has entrusted me with this. It's the first Dream I've had in over thirty years of Her service. I have vowed to not let Her down."

"You will not, Sister," Papa said, his voice low. "It is I who will disappoint Her. In your zeal to carry out Her request, there is much you did not consider. I cannot very well leave my sons —here in Rosira, no less—and go on such a mission. It is bad enough that my daughter is home alone with no idea what has become of us. The twins are only fifteen, and whatever journey you propose is out of the question for them. I simply cannot do it. There must be someone else."

The Sister's eyes flashed as Papa finished speaking. Her face contorted until it was almost unrecognizable. She shook her head so hard that her topknot slipped out of its band a bit. "That is not acceptable. The children can be sent back. I knew we should have left them on the mountainside." The last part she said under her breath. Her movements had grown jerky, and the three women behind her looked at one another with alarm.

Papa held his hands up as if to calm a wild animal. He turned his attention to the other women present, seeking reason among them. "Surely you can understand my position."

The three Sisters merely dropped their heads, deferring to their leader. Roshon's heart sank. Was that what faith looked like? Blind obedience to an unhinged personality?

He flexed his legs subtly, hoping he'd regained full control by now. They just may need to run from these crazy women.

"Unless you plan to prevent us from leaving," Papa said, "we need to find a way back across the country to our home now."

He moved to stand, and the elder Sister braced herself as if for impact. "She warned me of this, you know. She told me that when you refused, I should remind you of the favor you begged of Her nearly twenty years ago and how She granted your request. If nothing else, you owe Her a debt. Woe be unto you to reject the request of our blessed Queen."

Her eyes lit with triumph as Papa's face fell. He blinked slowly, and when his eyes opened, they were filled with defeat. Roshon wanted to shake him and demand to know why he was relenting.

"I want to go, too, Papa," Varten said.

Roshon's attention darted to his brother, whose chin was tilted up somewhat defiantly.

"No." Papa's voice brooked no opposition. Never once had he changed his mind when that voice was used. No cajoling could persuade their otherwise amiable father to do something he had set his mind against. It was pointless to try.

Papa turned back to the Sister. "If I do this, you must escort my sons back to our home. You owe us that after dragging us all here."

The woman's eyes shone with the inner fire that Roshon feared was madness as she nodded in agreement.

Papa turned to them. "I'm sorry, boys. I must do this. I'll need you to tell Jasminda what has happened."

Roshon shook his head. "You will have to explain it to me first. I don't understand."

"The *Queen* has made a request specifically of Papa," Varten said plainly.

"So?"

His brother's eyes widened. "*So* you cannot ignore that sort of thing."

Roshon shrugged. "What sort of mission is this? How long will it take? And why didn't She visit Papa Herself? She's done it before! Why do we owe Her anything?"

The four women gasped at his blasphemy and made the sign of the Sovereign, placing a hand over their hearts and tapping their chests three times. Papa rose somewhat unsteadily and came to kneel at Roshon's side. "Even if you cannot believe in the Queen's power, believe that I am indebted to Her. At the end of the day, that is the truth. The debt I owe Her brought me here, to Elsira, to your mother, and to you. The time has come for me to repay Her. That is all. A man pays his debts."

"That is the mark of a man," Roshon muttered under his breath, repeating the words his father often said. His head sank heavy on his shoulders with the knowledge that nothing could be done about this.

When he looked up, his eyes were brimming with tears. He was already motherless, and now he was soon to be fatherless, at least for a short time, if not forever. This mission was bound to be dangerous; Papa might never return.

For the first time, Roshon wished for the Dream of the Queen so he could talk to Her himself and tell Her just what he thought of Her meddling in his family's life.

# CHAPTER FOUR

When meeting an opponent on the challenge ground, gather yourself, remember who you are, for without identity there can be no victory.

— DAIPUNA: THE ART OF COMBAT

The woman who had kidnapped them was called Sister Myreen. Once Roshon and his family had recovered enough to walk reliably, she led them up a set of creaking, wooden stairs and into a marble-tiled vestibule.

"Where are we?" Varten asked, craning his neck to look around. Two hallways branched out from where they stood, one with white walls and white ceiling, the other a darker corridor of paneled wood.

Sister Myreen started them down the wood-lined hall, the other three women at the rear.

"This is the Southern temple," replied a youthful voice

behind them. The youngest-looking, orange-haired Sister was about their age and apple cheeked, and she kept fluttering her eyes at Varten. Roshon held in a snort.

"Keep your voices down," Sister Myreen grumbled.

At the end of the other hall, Roshon caught a glimpse of the main auditorium, where people were lying on sleeping pallets and blankets they had brought to the temple in the hope of having the Dream of the Queen—the same sort of dream that had started this crazy nightmare he was trapped in.

He wasn't even sure he believed the Dream was real. For all he knew, Papa had just had a regular dream all those years ago and so did everyone else. No one had ever actually *seen* the Queen Who Sleeps in these dreams. They just heard Her voice and felt Her presence, then awoke with renewed purpose and vigor, which they attributed to their goddess. He couldn't really explain his father's belief, but Sister Myreen's psychotic kidnapping plot didn't speak well to what interactions with this deity were like.

The dim hallway led to a side door that opened onto a narrow alley bordering the temple. There, the three other Sisters whispered their good-byes. Only Myreen was to accompany them wherever it was they were going. Varten winked at the youngest Sister, who blushed and ducked her head as the door closed. Roshon rolled his eyes. Leave it to Varten to flirt with one of the people who'd kidnapped him.

They emerged in the late-afternoon sun, and the glare reignited the headache the sleeping drug had created. Myreen led them to the mouth of the alley and onto a busy, urban street. He had never been to a city before, much less the capital. The tiny town where they bought supplies—known only by its post station code—was the largest civilization he'd experienced until now. This place made the town look like a collection of twigs.

Shiny autos, the likes of which he'd only seen in magazines, rolled down the narrow street. Horse-drawn carriages also peppered the pavement, but the autos were far more prevalent. Tall columns made of wood towered overhead, wires running from each column to the buildings lining the road. Electricity. He'd read about that, too, but hadn't seen it in action. He also had never seen streets so packed with people before. Actually, he'd never even seen so many people in one place before.

Folks turned to stare at Papa as they walked. He was the only Lagrimari in sight—the only non-Elsiran, in fact. Not so different from the no-name town, then. Roshon stared back, sneering at anyone who dared to look askance at his father.

Papa and Jasminda always had to endure scrutiny, whispers, and snubs whenever they left the safety of their isolated farm. Though Roshon looked every bit as Elsiran as everyone else here, he felt the slights personally. No one could choose how they looked, and it ate at him that his family was treated as they were.

With dark hair and eyes, and a skin tone he'd always envied, Roshon's father and sister were easily recognizable as Lagrimari. The Seventh Breach had only ended three years ago, the latest battle in a centuries-old war between Elsira and Lagrimar. Papa had fought in the Sixth Breach nearly twenty years before and had been stranded on this side of the Mantle when the magical border had closed again. Eventually, the prisoners of war had been released to make their way as best they could without the benefit of citizenship and with the constant suspicion of the populace, but somehow Mama had seen past all that. She'd fallen in love, and it hadn't mattered to her what Papa had looked like or that he had possessed magic.

Their family already had been torn apart by Mama's death, and now Papa was about to leave, too. And on some mysterious errand given by some mysterious Queen who may or may not even exist, no less. Roshon gritted his teeth and kicked at the curb as they walked.

Sister Myreen drew them to a stop before an iron gate that spanned the width of the street. Three soldiers stood outside a tiny wood structure. Rifles were slung casually across their shoulders, but their postures grew rigid when they caught sight of Papa.

"They're with me," Sister Myreen bit out, pointing at his family.

"How did this one get out of Portside in the first place?" a soldier who did not seem much older than Roshon asked. "Do you have papers?"

She narrowed her gaze on the soldier. "Sisterhood business. Step aside, young man."

He grudgingly moved to allow them through the gate, and Roshon glared at him. "What's this gate for?" Roshon asked.

"To separate Portside from the rest of the city. Keeps the ruffians out," the man responded.

Roshon raised an eyebrow at Varten, who frowned. This soldier was far scruffier than Papa. Even after walking for hours, being drugged, kidnapped, and transported across the country, their father's pants still held their crease and his hair was neat and well-kept. Neither twin had inherited nor learned the skill of keeping their appearance as impeccable as their father did.

"So people aren't allowed to move freely about the city?" Varten asked.

"Of course not. The port is full of riffraff from all over the world." The soldier's gaze fixed on Papa. "They need papers to cross from the Portside neighborhood into Rosira proper. That's just the way it is."

Again Roshon looked at his brother, and this time a thread of panic worked its way through him. If Papa was going on the

Queen's mission, how would he ever get back? He had no papers. Though he'd lived in this country for decades, he was a former prisoner of war. He wasn't an Elsiran citizen and had few rights here. This journey wasn't just dangerous. It could mean that even if Papa survived, they might never see him again.

As if sensing their distress, Papa put his arms around both of them and pulled them closer. "Don't worry so much," he said in Lagrimari. "You know I have a few tricks up my sleeves to get around this sort of bureaucracy."

Varten grinned, but Roshon was unconvinced. Papa's Earthsong could calm tense situations, but there were limits and Roshon didn't like the odds.

"Where are we going?" Varten asked once they were a block away from the gate.

The neighborhood had changed drastically after just a minute of walking. The streets were not kept up as well, trash littered the gutters, and a foul odor had increased dramatically. Along with Elsiran people, the "riffraff" the soldiers spoke of was evident. Hair colors ranging from yellow to black, and everything in between, topped the heads of the people around him. Skin colors, clothes, and styles varied, as well. Roshon felt more comfortable here than he had on the other side of the gate. Here they could blend in better.

"We're going to get your father passage on a ship, and then I'll take you back home," Sister Myreen said amiably. Now that she was getting what she wanted, she was almost tolerable. Her mood was much improved over what it had been, and her sanity appeared mostly restored. It was a miracle.

"When you get back to Jasminda, I want you all to take care of one another," Papa said to the twins. "She'll worry, and I don't want any of you to."

Roshon shook his head. There was no way they weren't

going to worry as long as he was on this mission—Jasminda most of all.

"Sister Myreen," Papa called, but whatever he was about to say was lost as a man with blue hair raced by. Dark, swirling tattoos decorated his forehead and chin. A similarly blue-haired girl with a tattooed chin was fast on his heels. They leaped over some debris at the corner and nearly crashed into Roshon.

He jumped back out of her way, and the girl winked at him before tearing down an alley. On their heels was another man of the same race, but this one's hair was a sickly green color. As the girl sped past the blue-haired man, the green-haired one reached forward and snagged the collar of the first man's shirt. With a blindingly fast move of his elbow, the blue-haired man shook off his pursuer and put on a burst of speed.

Something dropped to the ground, torn from around the blue-haired man's neck, but neither man noticed as the chase continued. Three more men appeared—two running full-out and the other, who was the largest of them, bringing up the rear.

Roshon darted forward to retrieve the object that had fallen. Hanging from a cord was a pouch made of a strange material he'd never seen before. It was as supple and strong as leather but scaly like fish skin.

The first four men continued into the alley, but the large one hair, whose hair was striped black and blue, skidded to a stop and glared at Roshon. "Give that here," he growled in accented Elsiran.

Roshan's fist tightened around it. "I don't think this belongs to you."

"That ain't your business. Give it to me before I break your scrawny neck."

Roshon put his hand behind his back and stared the man in his beady, mean, little eyes. His leathery face was a maze of dark lines, both swirling and straight. They lent him a feral quality, punctuated by the snarl he let out as he rounded on Roshon.

Papa stepped forward, his voice quiet and calming. "We don't want any trouble."

Roshon felt the energy of his father's power brushing across his skin—an Earthsong spell to calm the large man's temper. The energy cooled Roshon's ire, as well.

"Then don't give it," the large stranger said. "Tell this one here to give me that pouch, and quick."

Just then the first blue-haired man and the girl came back from around the corner and stopped, taking in the scene.

"Bor!" the man yelled. "Leave them alone. It's me you want."

The fat man, Bor, turned around. "I don't have any need for you." He pointed a thick finger at the girl. "It's her who'll fetch a pretty price once I turn her in. And I think you'll see the benefit in negotiating with me to get your birthstone back."

He made to snatch the pouch from Roshon, who was too fast and skittered away. Unfortunately, he moved right in the path of one of Bor's cronies. The other three men had surrounded their small group during the exchange.

Sister Myreen let out a huff of frustration and crossed her arms. She mumbled something that sounded like, "Bloody savages," but Roshon couldn't be sure.

Varten stood close on his right side and Papa on his left. Tension radiated through the air, seemingly immune to Papa's calming influence.

Then the girl stepped forward. The man she'd been running with looked pained, but she grinned broadly, twirling a knife around her fingertips with great skill.

Roshon clutched the pouch tighter and waited for her to speak.

# CHAPTER FIVE

If your heart knows peace and beats with purity, then no matter how bloody the battle, your body will unavoidably follow the heart's lead.

— DAIPUNA: THE ART OF COMBAT

Ani liked the mettle of the Elsiran boy holding Tai's birthstone. She'd always thought of Elsirans as coddled weaklings with their ridiculous ginger hair and tendency for freckles. But this one was sturdier than most and had a set to his jaw and a gleam in his eyes that she approved of. Plus, he hadn't cowered before Bor in the slightest.

Behind her, Tai exhaled loudly, his exasperation obvious. She ignored him. This was about her, after all.

"What's the rate on my head?" she called out, still speaking in Elsiran.

"The price?" Bor asked stupidly.

She rolled her eyes. "Yeah. How much does Noa want for me? I'd like to know how valuable I am. Who knows? Maybe I could use the bounty." She shrugged.

Bor shot a puzzled look to his companions. "Five thousand runas," he said finally.

Her eyebrows shot up. "Five thousand?" She tossed a look over her shoulder to her brother. "Not bad. He must really be mad."

"Mother is no doubt sponsoring the bounty," Tai murmured.

That was probably true, but Ani was pleased to know she was considered such an asset.

"How about a deal?" she asked, motioning behind her back to her brother using their secret hand signals. From the corner of her eye, she saw Tai shift. Bor was standing just in front of the Elsiran boy. When the man's gaze moved toward Tai, Ani twirled her knife and tossed it in the air to catch it by its blade. This brought Bor's focus back to her. She didn't want anyone seeing exactly what Tai was doing. Sleight of hand was important in these delicate negations.

"What kind of deal?" Bor asked.

Good. She'd been counting on his greed to work to her advantage.

"I turn myself in to you, and we split the bounty." She grinned, sort of like the way she did before digging into a delicious meal.

Some instinctual part of Bor's brain must have recognized the malice in her smile, and he shrank back just a little. Now Tai was almost in position.

Ani turned her attention to the boy holding her brother's pouch. "What do *you* think? Should I collect my own bounty?"

"That certainly would be unexpected," he said wryly.

Ani grinned. "I hate being predictable," she said before tossing her knife into the air again. This time it was to mask the unsheathing of the narrow blades concealed along her wrists. She flicked them expertly at two of Bor's men and caught the other knife nimbly. With a clear line of sight and the men distracted, she hit her targets easily. They clutched their legs in unison, felled by the thin knives dipped in a fast-acting paralyzing toxin made from selakki ink.

While she was dealing with the first two men, Tai had managed to take down the third with another toxin-covered blade. That left only Bor standing. Ani sheathed her bow knife at her back and approached slowly, her empty hands fully visible to Bor.

The man sputtered and looked around at his fallen men, then pulled a pistol from his waistband and grabbed the Elsiran boy, pointing the gun at his head. "Don't move or I'll kill him."

The boy's twin, who Ani hadn't noticed before, cried out. The man with them, who had the coloring of the Summ-Yalyish people, tensed and tightly curled his fists at his sides. The Sister standing next to them closed her eyes and brought her hands together before her as if in prayer. They certainly were a strange group.

As much as Ani hated being predictable, she hated other people being predictable even more. She stopped moving, hands still up. Tai appeared by her side, his hands raised, as well.

"Tell this boy to give me the pouch," Bor said through gritted teeth.

"What pouch?" the boy asked. He brought empty hands in front of him, turning them over as proof.

Bor looked down and jerked him closer.

"Roshon," the man next to him said, his voice admonishing.

"I don't have a pouch, Papa. Look." He wiggled his fingers as if to prove his point.

The man was the Elsiran twins' father? Ani searched for a

resemblance and finally found it in the shapes of their faces. Well, that was unexpected, too.

Ani spotted the second twin easing something into his pocket. They must have handed off the pouch at some point during the confusion. Ani nudged Tai. He grunted, which could mean he'd seen the handoff or could be that she nudged a little too hard. It was difficult to tell with Tai.

"No one's going anywhere until I get that pouch," Bor said.

A Raunian's birthstone was precious to them, and she felt her own pouch warm against her chest with her stone inside. It had been given to her the day of her birth and was to be sent back to the sea on the day she died. The stones were a gift from Myr, the Raunian god, and to lose it or have it stolen meant eternal separation from the divine. Stealing a birthstone was one of the most dishonorable acts a Raunian could commit. It was akin to stealing a soul.

Ani didn't think her brother would sell her out under that sort of blackmail, but she herself would do anything to get her brother's birthstone back. He may not care about his immortal soul, but she did.

Bor cocked the hammer of the pistol and pressed it more firmly against the boy's—Roshon's—head. To his credit, he appeared more annoyed than afraid.

Tai was working his jaw from side to side. Ani grinned, eager to see the look on Bor's face when he discovered the last surprise that Father had taught them. The Summerhawk name may not mean much anymore, but before falling into disgrace, Father had never been bested in a negotiation. Not even one as tense as this.

"No, I think that we'll be going to our ship and you'll be staying here for a while," Tai said.

A number of things happened at once. Tai spat, sending the thin blade he'd lodged between his teeth and gums forward toward Bor. The Sister's eyes flew open, revealing a universe of crazy in her haunted gaze. "For the Sovereign," she screamed, then leaped onto Bor, grabbing the arm that held the pistol.

Roshon stumbled out of Bor's grip as Tai's blade hit its mark. Bor fell backward, the Sister on top of him, still grabbing at his arm when a deafening *boom* shattered the air.

Roshon hit the ground on his hands and knees.

Bor groaned before his body went slack.

The Sister rolled onto her side, and the boys' father dropped to her side to check on her, but no doctor would be able to repair the gaping hole in her head. The bullet had struck just under her chin.

Ani's breath heaved, her jaw hanging open in shock. There was such a thing as too much unpredictability. She ran a shaking hand through her short, cropped hair. The expression on Bor's face was one of surprise. It was the same look he'd had in her premonition.

Roshon rose on unsteady legs, his brother assisting him. He was visibly pale and shaken now. Probably a delayed reaction. It was obviously the first time he'd had a gun pointed at him. Ani was about to offer him some sage advice for the next time when pounding footsteps approached.

Tai craned his neck and then turned to her, his lips set in a line. "Bor must have contacted the men from his ship. There are about a dozen headed this way."

Ani looked over and, sure enough, a sea of green and blue heads were disrupting traffic and would be on them shortly.

"Time to go," Tai announced. He held his hand out to the twin who carried the birthstone. The boy dropped it into Tai's outstretched palm. "Trouble's coming. Best get to safety."

"Better come with us!" Ani grabbed Roshon's hand and pulled, dragging him along as she took off running.

"What are you doing? Let go!" Roshon bellowed, trying to wrench his hand from her grasp.

"Look to the left!" she shouted. She gave him a moment to observe the uniformed men headed their way. "Portside militia. Trust me, you do *not* want to stick around and be questioned by these guys. Neither does your dad. Is he Yalyish?"

"Lagrimari."

Ani raised her eyebrows. She'd never met a Lagrimari. "Even worse. The militias hate magic."

Roshon's father and brother were already on her heels, apparently having seen the wisdom in fleeing.

"Where are we going?" Roshon asked.

"My brother's ship. Technically it's independent land and the militias have no authority. And the *Hekili* has never been boarded by an enemy. It's the safest place for us right now."

"Who are you anyway?" His hand in hers was warm. After his initial struggle, he now held on tightly, even when he didn't need to. Something about that made Ani's grin grow wider.

"My name is Ani Summerhawk, that's my brother Tai. Nice to meet you." She shook the hand she was holding once, and they kept running, darting through the crowded streets to where Tai's boat was docked with both Bor's men and the corrupt militia on their tails.

# CHAPTER SIX

Before stepping up to a challenge, it is wise to know when to advance and when to retreat. Withdrawal is as important a strategy as standing one's ground.

— DAIPUNA: THE ART OF COMBAT

Roshon could not get the image of Sister Myreen's lifeless eyes staring into nowhere out of his mind. Blood had pooled beneath her head, her hair mixing with it as if it was bleeding its own deep color onto the pavement. He didn't have the time or lung capacity to vomit at the moment, as he was still running for his life, but as soon as he slowed down, his twisting, rioting stomach was going to revolt.

He had no love for the crazy Sister who'd kidnapped his family, but seeing her cut down in the middle of the street like an animal had been terrible. And it was all because of her own foolishness. He tripped over a loose stone, nearly plowing into a middle-aged woman pulling a hand cart. Only Ani's firm grip on his arm kept him steady.

The people they passed didn't seem as shocked to have this motley crew racing by them as he would have expected. Even the woman he'd nearly knocked down had barely given him more than a cursory glance. No, these folk were minding their own business, ignoring anything that didn't directly affect them. Wasn't that how he'd always imagined life to be in a city?

Tai was in the lead as they sprinted to the crowded docks. The stone under their feet was pockmarked and heavily worn. The port itself boasted a wide array of vessels: sailing ships, steam-powered behemoths, sleek crafts shaped like bullets with round windows all along the sides, and more. He only got a glimpse before Tai hurtled onto a steep ramp leading to the strangest ship he'd seen yet.

The body sat high off the water on three legs that disappeared beneath the dark-blue ocean. And it was covered in . . . The closest description he could come up with was scales. Yes, plates like gigantic fish scales armored the entire hull. On the top level, the scales were lighter, more reflective, iridescent even.

"Mik!" Tai yelled as Roshon and the others followed him up the metal grate leading to the ship's deck. "Please tell me we're ready to go!"

Ani hung back until Papa had his feet on the deck, then began turning a crank that speedily withdrew the ramp. "Welcome to the *Hekili*," she said, grinning. "Come on." She disappeared into a dark passageway. Roshon looked at his brother and father, both staring back at him with wide eyes, and then went after her.

A narrow metal staircase led up to the bridge, a glass-enclosed space with seating for four. Tai stood in front of the instrument panel, furiously turning dials and switches, while the man beside him—taller and wider with a thick, green beard —muttered under his breath in Raunian.

Ani lounged in the seat behind the captain's chair, swiveling back and forth. The bearded man looked up when Roshon and his family entered, raising a black eyebrow. "Hey Mik, these are our stowaways, Roshon, second Roshon, and their dad."

"This is Varten," Papa said, pointing to Roshon's twin, "and my name is Dansig."

"And we're not stowaways," Roshon added.

"Mik!" Tai yelled. He was seated now and pulling on two handles that, judging by the effort he was putting in, were heavy. Then the ship was in motion, pulling back from the dock with alarming speed.

Mik dropped his bulk into the co-captain's chair and began adjusting settings on the panel. The ship jerked again, and the abrupt motion sent everyone else sprawling. Papa flew into the back of Mik's chair while Roshon and Varten dropped to the floor.

Ani peeked over the side of her chair. "Sorry about that. We're kind of in a hurry."

Roshon thought it best he stay on the floor, especially as their speed increased and the ship made a sharp turn, making his stomach complain even more.

Tai began barking commands to Mik in their native tongue. Ani righted herself in her seat and faced forward. Roshon was almost afraid to ask but couldn't help himself. "What's going on now?"

She looked down at him, a huge grin on her face. "We're going into burn mode. You're gonna wanna see this!"

She pulled back a panel next to her seat to reveal a mirror. Roshon sat up as other panels around the room opened on their own, reflecting an image from somewhere else into the first panel. Suddenly, the back of the ship was visible, with the city of

Rosira shrinking in the distance. The ship's wake frothed behind them white and foamy, and then . . .

Roshon wasn't sure he could believe his eyes. "Is . . . is the water *on fire?*" Orange flames mixed with the churning ocean in a trail behind them.

"Technically, the salt in the water is on fire." Ani kept talking, explaining something about shocking systems and hydrogen, but the ship had an even greater burst of speed that made Roshon's ears pop. His stomach lurched again, and he barely kept its contents down. Varten wasn't so lucky. He was retching on the floor next to the chair their father had made his way into.

The motion of their acceleration was like nothing Roshon had ever experienced. His eyes watered and teeth chattered. He didn't want to imagine how fast they were going, but through the thickness that had invaded his ears, he heard Ani cackle with delight.

Then, blessedly, it was over. The ship slowed and Roshon's ears cleared. When he opened his eyes, Ani was dangling a silver bucket in front of him. He took it gratefully and promptly emptied the contents of his stomach.

"Thank you for your assistance back there," Papa said, clasping his hands before him. Varten had cleaned up his mess, and now both twins were seated on a bench that folded down from the side wall of the ship's bridge.

Tai swiveled around to face them. Beyond him, the endless blue of the ocean was visible with no land in sight. Roshon wished Jasminda could see it. None of them had ever been farther from home than the small, nameless town where they bought supplies.

"I'm sorry that you all were caught up in this," Tai said. "I had no idea it would get that heated. And I thank you all for your help." He grasped the pouch around his neck. "Our birthstones are precious to us. They link our souls to Myr, our god, and to lose one means a kind of spiritual death. But even more precious to me is my sister's life and freedom." He gave his sister a look of tenderness mixed with exasperation. "I fear I am in your debt."

Papa shook his head. "No need. It was a strange circumstance in which we found ourselves. Is it possible to head to another port? I need to get a message to my daughter as soon as I can. She doesn't know where we are, and we're already overdue at home. She's probably beside herself with fear as we speak."

A shudder went through Roshon just thinking of it. Jasminda was capable, and bossy as the day was long, but she was all alone back home. What must that be like?

"We should be able to stop in the north at one of the resort ports." Tai turned and retrieved a thick, leather-bound journal from a compartment below the instrument panel. It looked like an atlas of some kind.

"Tai," Ani said, warning in her voice. She had donned a strange headset that covered her eyes and had a long tube snaking out of it that attached back to the wall.

Her brother looked up from the book. "What is it?"

"We've got company," she said.

"Let me see." He grabbed the headset from her outstretched hands and peered into it. Then he let out what sounded like a Raunian curse.

Varten looked at Roshon with wide eyes.

"Two ships," Tai said, tossing his sister the headset again and turning back to the controls. "They're coming up fast."

"Can we do another burn?" Ani asked.

"Not this soon after the last one."

"We'll have to evade, before they—" A boom sounded, shaking the ship. Ani nearly fell from her seat.

"—get into firing range," Tai finished, shaking his head.

Ani leaped to her feet.

"Is this ship armed?" Roshon asked.

"After a fashion," Tai said. "You all know how to shoot?" The three of them nodded. "Ani, will you handle it?"

"Already on it." She raced out of the bridge as if her feet were on fire. "Are you coming?" she shouted back from somewhere in the hall.

Roshon, Varten, and their father jumped up and followed her to a storage hatch in the corridor. She pulled out two rifles. Roshon took them from her, and she grabbed out two more from the compartment, which seemed to have an endless supply. They were fully automatic, and she began tossing out loaded, detachable magazines. Varten whistled. This was quite a bit more firepower than the shotgun and pistol they had at home.

"These were from a bad batch of merch," Ani said as she showed them how to insert the magazine. "The guns work just fine, but the scopes on top are faulty. Some kind of ensorcelled Yalyish foolishness that never seems to work right. Our buyer wouldn't take them so we decided to keep them. Come on."

They went down a level to a small space lit only by glowing spots on the floor. She hit a switch on the wall, and two panels slid away to reveal gun ports with ledges for balancing a weapon.

"Looks like there used to be built-in guns there," Roshon observed, noting how the scratches and drill holes indicated something had been removed.

"Yeah. Used to be. But the big ports in Fremia outlawed them on all but military ships. We had to take them out." She twisted her face to show how she felt about that decision just as the water before them exploded in a spray of foam, some of which came inside the gun port.

"They're getting closer. You two set up here." She motioned to Varten and Papa. "We're going up higher." She nudged Roshon and ran back up the staircase, returning them to the bridge level. She spun a hatch in the ceiling and climbed through.

Roshon watched her legs disappearing through the hatch with dismay, then hung the rifle from his shoulder, jumped up, and pulled himself through after her. They were outside now, on the roof of the bridge.

Ani fiddled with a panel of controls she'd uncovered and a clear, glass shield rose from the floor. In front of it, two posts also emerged. Once the shield was in place, Ani leaned over one of the posts, balancing her rifle on it to fit through a small hole in the glass.

"What are you waiting for?" she shouted over the noise and force of the wind as the ship moved at a fast clip.

"Aren't we exposed out here?" he yelled. He was surprised he was able to balance as well as he could, given their speed.

"Bulletproof." She pointed to the shield.

He doubted that any sort of glass could be bulletproof, but there was little he could do but get his weapon ready.

Looking beyond the *Hekili*'s wake with his naked eye, he could barely see the pursuing ships. She'd said the rifles' scopes were faulty, but he clicked open the iris anyway and took a look through it. Immediately, two massive ships came into view, both with cannons attached to their fronts. He focused the scope on the ship to the right and watched as the cannon was loaded by a large Raunian man. The man stepped back. Several seconds passed before an explosion burst in the water, just a few paces off the back of the *Hekili*. Water splashed into the shield from the spray.

"Sacred Sovereign!" he cried, the force of the explosion pushing him back. He took his stance again, peered through the scope, and aimed at the man who was beginning to reload the cannon. Roshon took a deep breath and pulled the trigger.

"I got one!" he said, surprised when the man went down, grabbing his thigh. Papa had ensured they were all proficient with the weapons in the house, but Roshon had never shot a human being before. The man wasn't dead, though he was bleeding profusely. Roshon had aimed for the torso but was secretly glad he'd been off.

"Your scope works?" Ani asked.

"Guess mine's not faulty." He shrugged.

Static rippled from a speaker somewhere, and Tai's voice rang out. "Keep them away from their cannons. We're almost ready for another salt burn."

As Roshon peered through the scope, another man went down, a bullet in his shoulder. Ani was firing, apparently not needing a scope to see that far away. Roshon focused his fire on the deck near the feet of their pursuers, keeping them from loading and firing the cannons. He didn't want to shoot another person if he didn't absolutely have to.

"All right, inside! Now!" Tai screamed.

Knowing what was coming, Roshon dove for the hatch and scrambled back down.

"Burn mode in three, two, one."

He was lying on the ground in the dim hallway when the world around him fell apart and his ears popped again. Luckily, there wasn't anything left in his belly to vomit.

# CHAPTER SEVEN

Our art is solitary, though we practice with others. When you train your body in daipuna, you also train your spirit, and a strong spirit is both the individual and the collective. The ocean exists within a single drop of water.

— DAIPUNA: THE ART OF COMBAT

Ani had been born on a ship. That was back when things had been good between her mother and father—maybe for the last time since Mother had returned to the island when Ani was barely out of nappies. After that, Ani and Tai split their time between land and sea. The open waters with their father and his ever-decreasing band of loyal smugglers, and the island with their mother as she outwitted those older and supposedly wiser, wheedling and scheming her way into more and more power.

Ani had learned as much as she could stand to from her mother. Both her parents had exposed her to traders and scholars, warriors and holy men, the corrupt and the corruptible, and even at the age of fifteen, she'd been privy to many tall tales at ports all over the world. But Dansig ol-Sarifor's tale of kidnapping was still one of the stranger stories she'd heard.

"So they got Varten first?" Ani asked. The twin in question had a cut over his eye. He looked down, appearing guilty.

"I heard a woman calling for help," he said. "I was ahead on the trail, and she sounded so bad. So I went over to check without waiting for Roshon and Papa. And then someone shot me with a dart, I think."

"We went off to find him, and they led us through the caves before shooting us, as well," Roshon grumbled.

"I think they underestimated how difficult it would be to transport three bodies from where we were on the trail," Dansig added. "That's why they used Varten to lead us back down to the foothills." He shook his head.

Ani wouldn't soon forget the deranged look in the Sister's eye as she'd jumped onto Bor, screaming. Who knew what other schemes or craziness she'd gotten into in the name of her goddess? Ani was glad that Myr didn't inspire such madness. The Raunian god delivered calm seas or strong winds according some plan of His own design, and other than creating His people and the marine life that kept their society running, and accepting their souls after death, He mostly stayed out of everyone's way.

Tai looked up from his nautical charts, a grim expression on his face. "If we turn back now and head for any mainland port, we risk being caught by Bor's cronies. Their ships have advanced tracking technology, and while we're faster in short bursts, they can definitely catch up if we turn around."

"Plus, a message went out to all Raunian vessels in range," Mik added gruffly. "The bounty has been raised." He gave Ani an apologetic head tilt. "Ten thousand runas."

Ani whistled. Tai cursed.

"Every ship in the eastern seas will be after us now," Tai said, rubbing his face.

Dansig's head hung heavy, probably with worry for his daughter. Though Ani had her own troubles, she felt for the girl. How would it feel being left behind like that, not knowing what had happened to her loved ones?

"Once we get into the main Raunian shipping channels, we can find a messenger to send word to Rosira," she offered. "My friend Machen might be able to do it. He and his family have a big network. Then it's just a matter of locating someone there who can take your message to your daughter."

Dansig looked dubious, but given the situation, sighed and acknowledged that it was too dangerous to turn back now. Roshon was scowling, but seeing as that was so close to his natural facial expression, she wasn't quite sure if he was upset or not. After a few moments where the only sound was the whirring of the thermoelectric engine, the older man spoke. "How far is it to the Narrows?"

Ani froze and so did Tai, mid-drink from his canteen. "Why would you want to go to the Okkapu?" Ani asked.

Dansig's brow furrowed.

"The place you call the Narrows," Ani explained, "its true name is the Okkapu, and it's not a place for men who want to live."

Roshon appeared alarmed at her words, but his father just stroked his chin. "She never does anything by half measures, does She?" he muttered. "You've heard of the Queen Who Sleeps, I trust?"

Ani nodded, and Mik grunted from the co-pilot's seat.

"Elsirans keep the body of their goddess in the palace and believe She walks their dreams, right?" Tai asked.

"Not just Elsirans. She visits the dreams of Lagrimari, as

well. I was once a member of the Keepers of the Promise, the rebel group inside Lagrimar fighting for freedom from the True Father. There were some of us who'd had the Dream of the Queen. We believed She was guiding us toward our eventual victory."

Dansig took a deep breath, as if relaying this was taking a lot out of him. "Nearly twenty years ago, during the Sixth Breach, the Queen visited my dreams, and I made a request of Her. I was . . . disillusioned with the Keepers and their methods, but there was no way out, neither of the organization nor of the country. However, She knew a path. She led me through a crack in the Mantle, one of the earlier ones that had formed. I crossed into Elsira and lived in the mountains for some time while the war raged. After every breach closed, there were always those stuck on the other side, I just had to wait it out. My plan, such as it was, was to blend with them. Live among them, away from Lagrimar and away from the Keepers. I had no idea I'd meet Eminette and everything would change for me, that I'd have a life, a family." He looked at his sons with pride and love.

Ani swallowed, her throat growing thick. Her father had done a lot for her, but he'd never looked at her that way.

Dansig continued. "When She agreed to tell me where I could find a place to slip through the Mantle, She warned that I would be in her debt. It is one I must pay, and that requires going to the Okkapu, as you say."

Silence descended until Tai finally spoke. "What is it you hope to find there?"

"An artifact of some kind. It's a magical object the Sister called the death stone. I don't know much of it, but I recall years ago there was talk of a Singer who had found another stone . . . There are objects like these in the world that hold different purposes, different powers. This one, I don't know what it does, but it's probable that a need has arisen for whatever magic it holds. It was lost generations ago and must be found. The Queen does everything for a reason. Even helping me."

Ani pursed her lips. "How does She expect you to find it? Only the foolish or desperate attempt to sail the Okkapu. The waters are rough, storms plague it, and there are jagged rock formations jutting all throughout the area. They say it was once a beautiful island and that its people built enormous statues of their kings. This sort of thing displeased Myr, as there was no statue of Him, so He sank the island. Now the tops of those statues are the only thing left, peeking out of the water to rip apart ships and men."

"Don't forget the band of selakki who use it as a hunting ground," Mik added, his voice rumbling. "The place is dangerous in about a dozen different ways."

"What are selakki?" Varten asked.

"Fish," Mik said, evidently believing this to be a complete answer.

"They're gigantic sea creatures, their scales cover our ships and their bones are strong as iron," Ani added. "They hunt us and we hunt them, and much of Raunian life depends on them. But they're . . . not creatures we want to cross." She actually shivered. There wasn't much in this world that scared her, but the vicious fish, as Mik called them, were on the list. A memory tried to push its way through her consciousness, one of pain and sorrow and fear, but she beat it back, determined not to dwell on those dark days.

Dansig nodded. "I can't, in good conscience, ask you to endanger yourselves for me. Is there a smaller boat or even a raft on this vessel that I could take? If you bring us as close as you're able to this area I could go the rest of the way alone."

Tai winced. "Even if there were, have you ever free dived before? There have been many eager to seek the rumored treasure that sank with the island. The best divers in Raun have tried to explore the depths and only a few have survived to tell the tale."

"I doubt an Earthsinger has tried before," Dansig said.

"And how would your magic help you?" Ani asked.

Dansig turned his dark gaze on her. His eyes were kind, his face gentle. The things that were said about the Lagrimari were terrible and painted them as wayward savages creating storms with their magic everywhere they went. But Ani had never believed tall tales.

"I can sing a spell to bring me air underwater, to light the dark depths of the ocean, whatever is needed to find what I seek."

Ani scrunched her nose, trying to picture such things. She would have thought he was making it up as if just then, a cloud hadn't formed over the perfectly sunny day, shading them all. Just one cloud, and only over their ship, moving at the same speed as they were.

Tai looked up in shock, then turned to Ani for confirmation that she was seeing it, too. She was. "Unexpected," she whispered, grinning with approval.

"Even with the aid of your magic," Tai said, "if you say this object was purposely thrown there so it would never be retrieved, then they did a good job. When Myr sunk the island, He did it thoroughly. Artifacts have washed up on some of the uninhabited smaller islands nearby, leading folks to think that the Okkapu held untold treasure, and many Raunians have gone to search, but mostly what they have to show for it are damaged or destroyed ships. No one has ever retrieved a single item from the depths."

Dansig dropped his head. "I understand the risks. Truly, I do. But I owe a debt, so I must try. And the sooner I do this, the sooner I can go home. *We* can go home." He put an arm around each of his sons and pulled them tighter. The boys looked somewhat embarrassed at the display of affection from their father, but they allowed it.

Ani looked away. The man was brave but foolish—two of Ani's favorite qualities in a person. In that, he reminded her of Father. What would she give to go on one more adventure with him? One more journey, no matter how dangerous. No matter if he'd never hugged her like Dansig had hugged his children or praised her for any reason, regardless of how hard she tried to please him. He'd understood her in a different way. He'd known how she was built. As Tai liked to remind her, they were a little too much alike. Then again, Tai was going back on a negotiated deal to save her from an unfortunate apprenticeship, and while it was noble, it was also a little too close to what Father had done to earn disgrace.

Tai was a good captain and a great smuggler, but he took after their mother: orderly, organized, and ruthless when needed. Ani and Father were risk-takers. They loved the sea because they loved danger, and neither of them had ever met a fight they didn't want to be a part of.

Fighting the Okkapu was the biggest adventure yet, and as much as it scared her, she'd never turned down a challenge before. Being captain had made Tai cautious, so had dealing with the aftermath of Father's betrayal. Still, Dansig and his family needed help, and saving Tai's birthstone when they didn't have to, at some risk to themselves . . . Well, it put the Summerhawks in their debt.

"Noa would never look for us there," she offered. "You know how scared he is of that place after it took his last ship."

Tai shot her a look that said he knew exactly what she was doing.

"Who's Noa? Is he the one looking for you?" Roshon asked, perking up.

"Yeah, my mother promised me to him as an apprentice, but

Tai had other ideas. Now I'm a fugitive, and Noa has a bounty out on me. Ten thousand runas. Not bad." She really was impressed with the rate.

"Why a bounty for an apprentice?" Varten asked. "Can't he just find another one?"

Ani shrugged. "The contract was broken. In Raun, contracts are king. I mean, the king is king, of course, but the contract is a close second."

"Like the queen?" Roshon asked, his mouth turned up in an almost smile that made Ani's heart rate speed.

"No queens in Raun," she said with a wink. He reddened and looked away.

"Why break the contract?" Varten asked Tai.

Ani turned to her brother, waiting for an explanation. His actions had disrupted his trade and made them the target of a crew of smugglers and pirates feared across the ocean. "Yes, dear brother. Why kidnap your own sister to save her from an apprenticeship with a very prestigious captain in a piracy operation that was well respected among our people?" She blinked rapidly, affecting an innocent expression.

Tai's lips curled in a snarl. He wasn't amused and turned to Varten. "The man that holds my sister's contract is a shark, bloodthirsty and brutal. I know for a fact that he intends to challenge for her. I've seen the damage he leaves in his wake and cannot in good conscience allow her to marry a scoundrel such as Noa."

"Marry?" Roshon yelped.

Ani shrugged again. "Not until I'm of age. After my apprenticeship would be when I'd have to lose my freedom, and that's only *if* I best Noa in the challenge."

"You would," Tai said. "You have too much pride to do anything but, and Noa is an idiot."

Ani's shoulders sank. He was right. This would all be so easy if she could throw the challenge, lose on purpose, and not be seen as a decent match. But Ani never could. Not since Father had sullied the Summerhawk name. She'd rather keep her honor and be saddled with a man she hated than maintain her freedom in a shameful way.

She turned back to their guests. "So you see, Tai had to resort to desperate measures to save me."

"How long will you have to be on the run?" Roshon asked.

"Until Noa stops chasing or someone buys my contract from him. Or if I accept another challenger." Though that was unlikely. Noa was too powerful for any other Raunian to risk trying to take what Noa thought of as his. And it wasn't like Ani was a prize on the marriage mart.

"The king can also intervene," Tai said.

Ani snorted. "But she won't."

"She?" Varten asked at the same time Roshon said, "The king is a woman?"

Tai nodded grimly. "In Raun, kings can be male or female, and the current king is definitely a woman."

"Yeah," Ani said, standing to stretch her back. "She's our mother."

# CHAPTER EIGHT

The ability to distinguish truth from lies and reality from illusions will always serve you well. If a practitioner does not conquer the lures of the world, no matter how far they progress in the art, they will never become a master.

— DAIPUNA: THE ART OF COMBAT

Noa Whiteel plucked the message from the courier's shaking hand, scowling before the boy ran away. The little urchins always wanted a tip, and he was in no mood for charity. The door to his office closed with a slam, and he scowled.

The message was from one of the informants he had stationed at ports and in crews around the world. Ani and her treacherous brother had been chased out of Rosira, and their ship, the *Hekili*, was last seen heading west northwest. Odd. He'd have thought they would have sailed back to Raun to beg the mercy of their vicious mother and possibly negotiate a change in his contract. But they must know that King Pia never changed her mind. So where were they going?

Some abandoned island maybe? Doubling back and sailing north to Udland?

No, they wouldn't find safe harbor there among the Icemen. And if they planned to head to the far west and hide out in the Lincee Isles, then their route was off. They'd hit the Okkapu first and navigating that quagmire would be foolish.

Noa squinted at the message.

He recalled the last state dinner he'd attended with King Pia and how he'd drunkenly declared that he would never be so reckless or greedy as to set sail through that cursed section of the sea again. Ani had laughed at him—she laughed at everything, the insouciant child—and all but call him a coward. He was no coward. He'd lost his diesel clipper in that crash, and two or three crewmen besides. The ship was no great loss. It had been noisy and inefficient like everything not built by Raunians. But the fact that he could afford the costly fuel and upkeep had been a point of pride.

The look of derision on Ani's face as she had mocked him still made his blood churn. Oh yes, he would teach her a thing or two about respect when she was his. After three years of his particular attention during her training, the girl would be as pliable as the leather of a whipping cord. All that fire and flame would be doused. He couldn't wait.

He crumpled the message and sat at his desk, shouting for his second-in-command. Noa had put the bounty out on his apprentice at the king's suggestion, but he'd been land-side for several weeks. It would be quite a bit cheaper to simply give chase and collect his property himself. Why pay others when he was perfectly capable? He'd take the *Rialoko*, the fastest ship in his fleet, and catch up to the ancient *Hekili* in a matter of days. Once he had his apprentice, he'd deal with her irreverent brother. The Summerhawks needed to learn to honor their agreements.

The door to his office opened and a strange man entered. Not his second but a foreigner, green eyes glowing from a pale face. His white-blond hair was thin and wispy, appearing as if it wanted to escape his scalp. Yalyish, if Noa wasn't mistaken.

"Noa Whiteel?" the man asked.

He rose to face the newcomer. "Who are you? What do you want?"

The man slowly walked over, never taking his eyes from Noa's. His smooth face had an ageless quality to it, but a weariness in his eyes belied his youth. He could be anywhere from twenty-five to fifty. "I wish to hire you."

Noa waved him off. "I don't take on passengers personally. You can see one of my under-captains if you'd like to hire a fishing vessel or go for a sightseeing cruise. How did you get in here, anyway?"

The man shook his head. "It's not a cruise I seek. And I need a man with *your* particular skill set."

Anger grew within him at the man's persistence. "I run a large operation and am not available to ferry around foreigners."

"Not even for fifty thousand runas?"

Noa froze, reassessing the man in a moment. He wore a thick red cloak, inappropriate for the tropical Raunian weather, but the wealthiest men were often the most peculiar. "And where, exactly, do you want me to take you for fifty thousand runas?"

"The Narrows. I seek something within its waters. And I believe something you seek will be there, as well."

Noa gave a cold smile. Now this was a negotiation that would go his way.

# CHAPTER NINE

Conflict is its own art form. On the eight pillars rests the daipuna artist's ideal for management of inharmony. All, whether benevolent or tyrant, must choose their path and walk in its way.

— DAIPUNA: THE ART OF COMBAT

For the first time in his life, Roshon had his own bedroom. Sure, the cabin aboard the *Hekili* was small—there wasn't even enough space to spread his arms all the way out before touching both walls—but it was blessedly private. Just a narrow bed, a little table next to it, and some pegs on the wall for clothes. But he wouldn't have to listen to Varten's snores as he had every other night of his life.

He barely slept at all the first night. The second and third weren't much better. It was a week before he was able to get a decent rest. The evenings were just so quiet, with nothing but the hum of the engines and the gentle swaying of the ship as it sliced through the waves. Not much at all to distract his mind from dwelling on what would happen to Papa, what would happen to them all as each day brought them closer to the Okkapu. He wished he could talk his father out of the foolish mission, but the man would not be dissuaded.

At least Tai hadn't fully agreed to sail the dangerous waters. He'd consented to go as close as was safe and then reassess. It was a hedge, but one Roshon was mightily grateful for.

Varten spent much of each day on the bridge with Mik and Tai, learning how the ship worked. Roshon's brother had always had an interest in mechanical things, tinkering with them and pulling them apart to see how they functioned. But this was the first opportunity he'd had to study an engine up close and in person, not merely in books.

The ship was optimized for a small crew and could function for short stretches with as few as two people. Though apparently, when Tai and Ani's father had been the captain, he'd had a team of half a dozen. So Ani bustled about, taking up the slack. She had an aversion to idleness, both hers and anyone else's, and quickly roped Roshon into helping with her duties. Keeping busy at least kept his mind off what lay ahead, if only for a few minutes at a time.

"So are you Tai's apprentice now, instead of Noa's?" he asked one day, swabbing the deck while Ani hung precariously from the side of the ship, recalibrating the plates of sun-absorbing selakki scales. The engine was powered by the sun's energy so at least they didn't have to worry about fuel.

"Not officially, but I do all the duties of an apprentice. I'm hoping to make captain before I'm eighteen."

"That seems young."

She just shrugged, hanging from one hand and one foot

while she held a wrench in the other hand. "Life happens while you're waiting to grow old," she said.

He frowned. What did that even mean? "So tell me more about the Okkapu."

"Why? So you can worry about it?"

He bristled. "So I can prepare."

"Why not just deal with it as it comes? You can't prepare for everything."

He paused in his mopping. "But you can for some things. So why shouldn't you?"

"How exactly are you planning to prepare for the Okkapu?"

"I don't know yet. That's why I'm asking you."

She tilted her head back, laughing so hard that, for a moment, he thought she might fall. It would serve her right. "You don't take anything seriously, do you?" he muttered, dipping the mop back in the soapy bucket.

"Not when I can help it. What difference does it really make? You can think and worry and plan all you want, but things go sideways all the time. I'd think you'd know that given how you ended up here."

"Sure, unexpected things happen, but strategizing before jumping into the unknown is just good sense." He huffed in exasperation. "Running around like you don't have a care in the world isn't the way to live a long life."

"Why live a long life if it's miserable?" she shot back, swaying from her perch and jumping to land next to him on the deck. "Accept the danger. Accept that you don't have control. You aren't always going to be safe and warm on your farm in the middle of nowhere." With each statement, she stepped closer until she was right in front of him, staring up.

He gritted his teeth. "You don't know anything about me and my life."

"Poor little Roshon, tucked away in your little valley where you can't hear mean people saying mean things about your strange family." She tilted her head, mocking him. "Elsirans are jerks, small-minded little bigots, but the world is hard. You need to toughen up."

"You don't think I'm tough?"

She looked thoughtful for a moment, actually considering. He found himself holding his breath under her scrutiny. "Actually, I think you are. You stood strong as a stonefish with that gun pointed at you. I've seen grown men piss their pants for less." Her dark eyes were glittering jewels as she stared at him. "So why can't you do that now?"

He recalled how his knees had shaken at the feel of the meaty arm across his chest, the cold metal of the pistol pressed into his head. He'd tried not to let it show, but pissing his pants had been a very near thing. Swallowing, he forced the emotion and the memory away. "Because going into danger now is a choice. And I'm not a reckless hellion . . . unlike some people."

She blinked, and he thought he saw a flash of hurt in her eyes. But that couldn't be right. She was the one chiding him. This girl had nerves of steel. He knew he'd imagined the expression because a brilliant smile overtook her face. "More fun that way."

He turned back to his mop. "Not everything is supposed to be fun." Jasminda would laugh and call him an old man. *Prickly as a porcupine*, she'd say and tweak his ear. *You're being disagreeable just because.* And he was. He could admit it to himself if not anyone else.

But Ani obviously had a few screws loose. She'd been raised by pirates, and it showed. She didn't even have enough sense to consider her own well-being. "Don't you care that every ship at sea is hunting you, trying to take you off to eventually marry some gangster?"

She didn't answer for a long time, and he turned back to find her still as a stone, watching the water. "You think I don't care?" Her voice was small, all its usual humor and teasing gone.

"I . . . I don't—" he stammered, taken aback by the abrupt change.

"Some girls entertain their first challenge at thirteen—girls from *respectable* families. But even before Father . . . betrayed us, there wasn't anyone calling. Mother already had a place in the Cabinet, and everyone knew she'd be the next king. Captains should have been lining up, seeking me for an apprentice, trying to curry favor with my family, but still nothing." She turned slowly, her face placid. "Women can have power in Raun. We can be whatever we want to be. But all I've ever wanted is my own ship. Captain Ani Summerhawk. And the only way to get my mark—" she pointed to her forehead, which was empty of the tattoos that Tai bore "—is as an apprentice. And that can only happen with a contract signed by my mother. Noa was the only one who came offering. That's why she accepted the deal over Tai's objections."

"Why not apprentice with Tai?"

"He's barred until he clears Father's debts. So my options are limited. No apprenticeship, no license. No license, no tattoo. No tattoo, no ship." She shook her head.

"You still have a choice."

She shrugged.

"And you'd apprentice with him, knowing he is cruel and wants to marry you, just to get your own ship?"

"He's got plenty of them. And if I'm sailing, I wouldn't have to see him that much anyway. Mother always said the only reason she and Father lasted so long was because he was never home." She gave a little snort.

A fist tightened around Roshon's chest to think Ani valued herself so little. Accepting a miserable partnership just so she could have a chance at her dream? "Could you wait until Tai clears the debt? Or wait for someone else? You don't know that no one else will offer."

"Not since Mother signed the contract. Besides, once Noa let it be known he was interested, anyone else who might have been would never cross him. He's too powerful. Mother knew that. Tai will try to outrun fate for as long as he can, but we both know where I'll end up."

The resignation in her voice gutted him. So did the pain in her eyes. He had been wrong. She wasn't made of steel. She was made up of the same stuff they all were: beating hearts and pulpy, tender pieces, trying not to fall apart.

He swallowed, realizing that he'd almost reached for her. To comfort her? She certainly didn't want that from him.

Toughen up.

He hated that she was right. "What's this challenge? What does it entail?"

She sucked in a deep breath and visibly shook off the melancholy. Motion started in her limbs again and the fidgeting ball of energy he'd met in Rosira quickly returned. "The challenge is a game, a fight, a contest of strength and strategy. We use daipuna—it's our martial art." She cracked her neck and turned to face him. "In Raun, marriages are true partnerships. Men need capable wives. Good partners who will bear strong and intelligent children. Savvy negotiators who will make advantageous deals. It's the man's job to challenge a woman he believes can best him both mentally and physically."

"Wait . . . What? How can you best any man physically? No offense, but you're tiny."

"I've been training in daipuna since I was three years old. I've mastered twenty-five levels."

His only warning was a flash of her teeth, and then Roshon was flat on his back, looking up at the clouds passing overhead. "What just happened?"

Ani stood above him, hands on her hips, grinning. "Daipuna is different for women and men. We learn how to compensate for smaller size and strength differences. Pressure points, leverage, the art of surprise." She stuck a hand out to him, and he took it gratefully. "But a male challenger still needs to last a full round in order to be considered a suitable husband." Her voice was wry.

Roshon dusted himself off. "Sounds like there are a lot of rules."

"Oh, definitely. Challenges must be held within three days of issue. They can be rejected by the challenged or her guardian if she's not of age." She ticked off with her fingers. "Girls as young as twelve can be challenged for. A parent can accept for a child, but it can be overruled if the girl accepts a more desirable challenge."

"So if this Noa finds you, you could still reject him?"

"Since my mother is still my guardian and she approves, I could only reject if I accept another challenge, one I feel is worthier."

Roshon was still working to get the breath back in his lungs after her takedown. "Someone better in daipuna?"

"Maybe. Really just someone better in every way possible. Then I'd have to beat him."

"Just seems unfair."

"Well how do they do it in Elsira?" She crossed her arms and leaned against the wall.

His face heated. "I . . . I think you just . . . find someone you fancy and then you talk to them. Court them. Learn if the two of you are a good fit. Then at some point, if you both like each other, you just decide to get married."

Ani mulled this over. "But how can you be sure they're right? How do you know they have the proper values and will be a good partner and have your back in a fight?"

"A fight? Who do you plan on fighting?"

"Who knows?" She spread her arms out. "Negotiations go bad all the time."

Roshon stared, eyes wide. "And that's how you *want* to live? Running from gunfire and smuggling in ports around the world?"

"That's my life. The strongest and fastest wins." She rolled her eyes. "One day, I'm sure you'll find some simpering ginger girl with nonsensical freckles who's as afraid of her own shadow as you are and you two can be blissfully happy planting apple seeds on your farm."

Roshon sputtered. "I'm not afraid of my shadow."

"You're afraid of everything, Roshon. Why is that? Why are you so scared?"

"Why are you so reckless and annoying?"

She clamped her jaw shut. "Well, at least if we crash in the Okkapu I won't have to deal with you anymore." She turned on her heel and stomped away.

"I'm sure you'd love to die in a shipwreck. You'd probably think it was exciting!" He stood fuming on the deck until her footsteps returned.

"Get inside. Your skin is starting to burn." Then she marched away again.

His cheeks did feel hot and tight, but he'd stay out there as long as he wanted, just to spite her. There was nothing wrong with being cautious. Caution would have saved them a lot of heartache. Varten didn't have to chase after every voice crying for help, and Papa was usually far more sensible than to run off based on the instructions of some supposed goddess. For Sovereign's sake, if Mama had been more careful, she wouldn't have climbed that ladder in the barn by herself, and she wouldn't have fallen . . . alone.

No, he was perfectly fine being cautious, and if certain

people didn't appreciate it, well, he didn't care much. And if his skin burned, it was his skin, after all. It wasn't anyone else's problem.

He sat on the deck of the *Hekili* gazing out at the churning ocean surrounding them. There was no land in sight, nothing solid to plant his feet on. The water was so vast, so infinite it made him feel small. Small and alone.

# CHAPTER TEN

Winnowing peace out of chaos is the goal of our training. For if you can find the calm within, then the storm becomes an illusion.

— DAIPUNA: THE ART OF COMBAT

The rain started sometime in the middle of the night on their tenth day aboard the *Hekili*. Roshon awoke to a sound like the plink of pebbles in the pond back home as raindrops struck the ship. His sleep had been light, the conflict with Ani still reverberating within him, keeping him from true rest.

But as he blinked up at the ceiling, dimly visible by the low light embedded in the floor of his cabin, the storm intensified, beating against the hard scales. When the ship listed heavily to one side, he rose and ran out into the hallway, not wanting to be so boxed in. He imagined water piercing the hull and flooding the tiny room. The narrow hallway wasn't much bigger, but he didn't feel as confined.

He stood outside the door, chest heaving until he noticed Ani at the entrance of the sleeping quarters. She banged on a wall panel until it creaked open. She looked over at him and did a double take, mouth agape. That was when he realized he was bare from the waist up. He ducked back into his room and grabbed the discarded shirt Tai had loaned him. He threw it on before returning to the hall.

When he did, her face was normal again but her expression wary.

"What's going on?" he asked.

"Storm." Her tone made him wince, underscoring the stupidity of the question. She adjusted something within the panel, then slammed it closed and moved toward the stairwell. Knowing he'd be unable to get back to sleep, he followed her silently up to where Mik was manning the bridge.

The only thing visible through the wall of windows was the orange glow of the ship's headlamps. They barely cut through the gloom a few paces before them, but they illuminated the angry waves well enough.

"Is this the Okkapu?" Roshon asked, the sheets of rain blowing sideways in the harsh wind.

"We're still a day away," Mik grumbled. "Storm came out of nowhere."

The ship listed left as if in response, throwing Roshon off-balance. He stumbled into Ani's side, mashing his chest against her arm.

"Sorry," he said, trying to regain his footing. She merely glared at him.

Mik's thick fingers tensed on the steering levers, and the floor became level again.

When Tai and Papa appeared on the bridge, Roshon's

growing agitation calmed somewhat. Everyone was here except Varten, though he could sleep through an earthquake.

Tai took over the steering, sliding into his seat smoothly. "Mik, I need you to check the stabilizer tanks. We're getting a lot of roll, and something feels off."

"Those salt burns in quick succession could have accelerated the corrosion," Mik said.

"Right. Better take a patch kit."

Mik nodded and hustled off.

"Something feel strange to you, Dansig?" Tai asked, still focused on the instrument panel.

Papa settled heavily into the seat behind the co-captain's chair, rubbing his eyes. "Not anything I can put my finger on, but yes."

Tai nodded as if this confirmed something for him.

"What could be strange about the storm?" Roshon asked.

His father appeared weary. "For one, it rose without warning. Far too intensely. I've been keeping track of weather changes the entire trip and didn't feel any hint of a disturbance all day."

"And that's unusual?"

"Storms don't just pop into existence out of nowhere. Unless . . ." He looked away, obviously troubled, tapping his fingers on the arm rest.

"Unless what?" Ani asked, standing next to her usual chair.

"Unless it's not natural," Papa finished.

Roshon gaped. "You mean, like, created with Earthsong?"

"Something like that."

"Well that complicates things," Tai muttered.

"Unexpected," Ani said under her breath. She finally sat, then opened up the mirrored panels and put on the headset. Only her mouth was visible, and she was talking to herself silently.

Roshon watched her lips move, entranced. He couldn't tell

what she was saying. It might not even have been in Elsiran, which they'd all been speaking as a courtesy to him and his family. Something in his chest tightened, and he tore his gaze away. Through the front window, the waves seemed even more irate, fizzy caps like white smoke battering them.

Once again there was nothing he could do but watch. He was useless here. He couldn't sense the storm or help with the ship. When he turned to go, the ship canted sharply and a loud *boom* sounded. Both Tai and Ani cursed in unison. Roshon grabbed on to the back of her chair, barely keeping himself upright.

"That wasn't a wave," Tai said ominously.

"No," Ani agreed, "it was a cannon."

A red light began to flash on the ceiling in time with the sound of an alarm. "We've been hit," she yelled. "Lower aft cargo hold."

"What's in there?" Tai asked.

"The narwhal ivory."

Tai groaned. "Seal it off."

"Aye," Ani answered, then jumped up to take Mik's seat. She expertly maneuvered around the instrument panel, which still looked impossibly complex to Roshon.

"How close are they?" Tai asked.

"Not close. Must be long-range cannons. I couldn't even see them."

Roshon sat in her abandoned chair and put the headset on. It seemed to work similarly to the scope on the rifle he'd used before, but it was somehow more rudimentary. Whereas the visual in the scope had perfect clarity, this was grainier and harder to make out. He pulled the gear off his head and then rushed off the bridge and toward the storage compartment where Ani had returned the guns.

Once he'd retrieved one, he flipped open the rear gun hatch, the same one his father and brother had used, and positioned the rifle. He looked through the scope. Cold air and spray hit him through the small opening, but he ignored it. Flicking the dials on the side of the weapon, he entered a mode that let him see in the dark. More ensorcellment from the Yalyish mages who had created the device.

Ani and Tai hadn't known much about how it functioned—both had claimed it didn't work at all—but Roshon was able to see just fine. And as he adjusted knobs he hadn't used before, he was able to see farther and farther.

A lighted indicator at the bottom of the image ticked off. Could it really be zooming in two kilometers? Two and a half? Three?

The night was a solid wall of black, with churning waves and sheets of rain to boot, but through the magic or science of the scope, a large ship came into view, its deck lit up in glowing blue. It was of Raunian design, with the same gigantic fish scales covering its surface, but it must have been twenty or thirty times larger than the *Hekili*. Huge cannons dotted the side.

"There's a giant warship!" he yelled. "A dozen cannons on its side. Three kilometers away."

"Probably the *Siomarra*. It's one of Noa's." Ani's voice came from behind him, and Roshon startled.

"He's following us?"

"It's one of his fleet, but he might not even be on it." She must have turned back toward the bridge because her voice was farther away when she screamed, "Evasive maneuvers!"

Roshon kept his eye pressed against the viewfinder, monitoring what he could of the ship. Unlike the ones that had chased them from Rosira, this deck was empty. Everything must be happening inside. There was no way the rifle, even if it could shoot that far, would do any damage to the behemoth of a ship or its hidden crew. As he watched, two of the cannon barrels shifted slightly.

"Noa wants you alive, right?" he asked.

"Last I checked." Ani was right behind him again, speaking in his ear to be heard without shouting over the crashing waves.

"I think they're about to shoot again."

"Let me see." He moved aside, and she looked through the scope, then cursed. "Why do these things only work for you? I can't see anything."

He took over again, her scent filling his nostrils. It wasn't perfumed or cloying, mostly a mix of the green soap stocked on board, breezy and grassy with her own unique sweetness mixed in. He inhaled deeply and tried to focus. She was standing too close, as if her proximity would help her see something through the scope his eye covered.

One of the cannons shuddered, and its mouth flashed with an orange flame. Smoke poured out as the missile fired. "Incoming!" he cried.

The ship jerked as Tai changed direction just before the explosion. Roshon wrenched his face back as the floor shook beneath him. It felt like the cannon had missed them; the rattling crash wasn't nearly as intense as before. He wiped sweat from his brow, and his heart hammered like crazy. Ani had disappeared.

The ship put on a burst of speed, racing through the choppy waters. Mik thumped up the stairs from below, wiping his hands on a towel as he passed before going up to the bridge. As the *Hekili* drew away, Roshon checked the scope once more, this time finding the battleship fading into nothingness. He decided to keep the rifle available in case it became necessary again and slung it over his shoulder.

When he reentered the bridge, Papa's eyes were squeezed

tight and his hands were in fists. Beads of sweat popped out on his brow.

"What's he doing?" Roshon asked.

"He said he could try to calm the storm with his Song," Ani replied.

Roshon clenched his jaw. "Be careful not to drain yourself, Papa." He wasn't sure if he'd been heard, but Papa's knuckles seemed to loosen a fraction.

Tai swiveled around. "Thanks, Roshon. That was a big help."

"I . . . I didn't really do anything," he stammered.

"You had the idea to use the scope. Gave us valuable intel. It's much appreciated."

Roshon blinked, unsure what to do with the praise.

"Now we just need to survive this storm." Tai turned back around to face the windows displaying the force of what they faced.

From the corner of his eye, he saw Ani watching him, assessing. He didn't move, didn't look in her direction, but he wondered what she saw.

# CHAPTER ELEVEN

The practice of tandem combat, wherein teams of two or more face each other, requires pillar five—force—to be in ultimate alignment. It should not even be attempted by those who have not progressed at least to level sixty.

— DAIPUNA: THE ART OF COMBAT

Since Father had died, Tai ran the *Hekili* with a minimal crew, which was just fine with Ani as she hadn't much liked her father's men anyway. Disloyal louts, the lot of them. But on nights like this when there were a thousand little repairs to be made after an attack they'd suffered, she was grateful for a few extra sets of hands. Roshon and Varten both held qualities she appreciated: a willingness to work and the ability to follow directions. They were tall and strong, as well, which also came in handy.

The last task that needed attending to was to check the

remaining lower storage rooms. Mik had already taken care of the hull breach, but the old pipes running along the walls of the storage areas tended to leak when the ship was jarred. They had needed to be replaced months ago, but it was a pricey repair. The deal they'd traveled to Rosira for would have gone a long way toward helping with the cost; without it, they'd just have to keep mending them.

"There's a gauge that's supposed to report the integrity of the transfer pipes, but it's blown so we have to do manual checks," she explained to Roshon as they walked down the narrow corridor. She spun the wheel to the storage area's door and pushed it open. Water rushed out over her feet.

Roshon cursed, but it was just as she expected. The water was about knee-high, having risen over the steps to the sunken room, and a thick pipe, wider around than she was and which ran from the port anti-roll tank to the starboard one, was leaking from a large crack in its side.

"Are we taking on water?" Roshon asked, panic filling his voice.

"No. The crack was likely from the impact of the cannon. We just have to seal it and get the water out of here."

"So we're not going to sink?"

She chuckled. "Not today."

The sealing kit was at the top of a high shelf running around the room. Roshon was able to haul it down easily, saving her the trouble of climbing up to get the thing. She retrieved a can of sealant and a few sheets of patch made from an inner layer of selakki skin that sat beneath the creature's scales.

"You pump. I'll patch." She pointed to the handle of the pump they'd installed, which would dispatch the excess water.

Ani took out the fire sparker to heat the sealant can and got to work on the crack. The foul-smelling goop had to be melted then applied without creating any bubbles. Then she could spread the patch sheet on top. The pipe was covered with patches already, and while they would hold, the integrity of the material had been compromised. Expensive or not, they'd have to replace the thing at the next port they hit.

A few paces away, Roshon worked the pump, pulling and pushing the heavy lever that forced the water around their legs back into the ocean. She knew from experience just how much effort it took and was momentarily distracted by the wet shirt clinging to his chest as he strained against the force of the machine. It brought her back to the moment in the hallway when he'd come out of his bunk shirtless. Myr's grace, she'd thought her eyes were going to fall out of her head. Farm life certainly agreed with him. She'd seen plenty of shirtless boys before—Raun was a tropical island, after all—without ever giving it a second thought. But she'd had *dozens* of thoughts about those few moments in that hallway. And the number was steadily rising.

She flinched as hot sealant dripped onto her fingers, and she refocused on the task at hand. The water soaking her boots and trousers was icy, but an inner warmth rose within her.

By the time she finished the patch, the water on the floor was gone, leaving only small puddles that were of little concern. "Good job," she said, dropping the tools back into the kit.

Roshon looked truly surprised at the praise, and a pang squeezed her chest. "Happy to help," he replied.

"Hey," she said, when he turned to leave. "I'm sorry about . . . whatever it was we were fighting over. Friends?" She stuck out her hands, palms facing him in the way Elsirans greeted each other.

He stared at her for a beat before nodding. "Friends," he said and pressed his palms to hers. His calluses rubbed against her own, even though his hands dwarfed hers.

They stayed like that for a long moment. She tore her gaze

away from his fingers and up to his amber eyes, which shimmered like molten gold. The bluish lighting of the room gave him an otherworldly glow. One of her rare premonitions hit her then: those eyes laughing, full of joy, looking at her.

She swallowed and drew her hands back, shivering slightly. "I'm glad," she forced herself to say. "There's not enough room around here for bad feelings."

Roshon nodded, looking at his own palms as if something about them surprised him. Ani lingered, noting his reaction and searching his face for that expression she saw in the . . . vision or whatever it was. She'd never seen him quite so happy, but knew one day she would.

The storm petered out just before a dawn that rose cloudless and serene. The ship had been battered, but it was nothing they couldn't fix, for which Ani thanked Myr.

After expending his magic in doing what he could to dampen the storm's impact, Dansig had returned to his room for some much-needed rest, and Mik was manning the bridge while Tai and Varten did additional system checks in the engine room.

Ani was bone weary, ready to collapse into her bed, but Roshon claimed he wasn't tired. Then he proceeded to drop into the chair his father had vacated and fall almost immediately asleep. With a sigh, Ani took the co-captain's chair.

"You need rest, too, little tigerfish."

She snorted at Mik's endearment. "I'm all right." She appreciated that he didn't respond to the obvious lie. As long as the oversized, ginger knucklehead behind her was here, she'd stay, too. There wasn't much point in investigating why. Something about his gentle breathing, his presence even while sleeping, soothed the restlessness within her.

They crossed a sea so placid, it looked like a mirror reflecting the rising sun. Mik was quiet as always, and Ani felt herself drifting into a place that wasn't quite sleep but wasn't quite awake, either.

When she blinked her eyes, the sun was higher in the sky. Mik was checking the navigation charts, and she peered over his shoulder at her brother's neat handwriting, which covered the sides of the hand-drawn pages. A captain's charts were traced during their apprenticeship, each man or woman copying from their master's. It was the best way to familiarize themselves with the vast seas that would be their homes for the rest of their lives.

"We're close," she noted, comparing the page before them with the coordinates.

Mik just grunted.

"Do you think Tai is going to make Dansig row into the Okkapu alone?"

He put the leather-bound book away. "You know he won't."

"I know he doesn't like the odds," she said. "And I know that while he's grateful they saved his birthstone, he won't risk our lives for it."

Well, he may risk his own. Hers, not so much. Tai had always been overly protective.

And look what it's costing him.

Mik stroked his bushy, green beard. "Said he feels like he's supposed to help them. Like it's Myr's design." He shrugged. "Intuition. The path is the way, and it looks like this is ours."

Intuition had certainly gotten them out of plenty of scrapes, and a captain should never discount it. She was about to ask about the forecast when one of the alert lights on the panel flashed blue. Ani broke into a wide grin and gave a great whoop.

Roshon sat up in his seat, looking around wildly. "What happened?"

"It's Machen! He's hailing us!"

Mik chuckled. "Better go see what he wants."

"Come on." She motioned to Roshon. "You're gonna wanna see this."

He followed her, rubbing his eyes as they climbed down the stairs and onto the deck. Ani rushed over to the rail and leaned over the side, waving at the water. She cupped her hands around her mouth and gave a melodic, "Ooh, ooooh. Ooh, ooooh." It was the greeting she and Machen Teledonius had shared since she was a girl and he was just a calf.

Roshon leaned over next to her, staring at the sea. "What are you . . . ? Oh . . ."

The pod of dolphins came into view, leaping through the waves, moving faster than the ship. They were a half dozen strong, but two broke off to swim alongside the *Hekili*. She recognized Machen immediately. The second dolphin was his brother Braloch, identifiable by the unique pattern of bite scars on the side of his mouth.

Her friend reached the side of the ship and leaped up to splash her. She laughed and wiped her face with her hand. "Roshon, meet Machen. Machen, this is Roshon. He's our stowaway."

Roshon shook his wet head grumpily. "*This* is Machen?"

Ani peered at him for a moment, noting his confusion. "Who did you think he'd be?" Then she turned back to her friend. "Where have you all been? We're on an adventure."

*We know,* Machen replied in the whistling, clicking vocalizations of the dolphin tongue. *We've heard all about it. The warship that was chasing you was fierce. They nearly got you.*

She shrugged. "Noa doesn't want to sink us—well, he doesn't

want to sink *me*. But he wouldn't mind incapacitating the *Hekili* just to stick it to Tai. There's no love lost there."

*It's not just Noa. He's taken on a client, one who is paying him a small fortune to search the Okkapu for something called the death stone.*

Ani froze. "Are you serious?" Dolphin pods had a system of communication that was faster than a land-side telephone. They were the best messengers, and the biggest gossips, on the seas.

"You speak dolphin?" Roshon asked, incredulous.

"Of course I speak dolphin," she answered without looking. "Along with four other languages. Well, humans can't actually *speak* it, but we can understand. So was Noa on the *Siomarra?*" she asked Machen.

*No, they're taking his new cruiser, the* Rialoko. *He sent the warship ahead with a foreign crew and some kind of squallmaker. But he's only a day behind you, burning salt fast.*

Her mind raced with this new information. A squallmaker? It was one of those Yalyish ensorcellments that was incredibly unreliable. It was only used by foreign sailors and pirates who wanted an advantage over Raunian sea superiority. They were rare and expensive. She hadn't encountered one before, but such a thing could definitely have created the storm that had thrashed them. Noa was serious about getting her back.

*One more thing,* Machen added. *The Orarinas were seen north-northwest of here, traveling in this direction. Not sure who will get here first, Noa or them, so you all had better be careful.*

The odds of success for this mission were getting worse and worse all the time.

Roshon put a hand on her arm. "You just turned pale," he said. "What's wrong? What's he saying?"

She swallowed and looked over at him, her eyes feeling too wide and dried out. "Noa's on his way. He's got a client who wants the same death stone your father does. And remember that band of selakki that hunt at the Okkapu?"

He nodded.

"They're called the Orarinas, and they're headed this way, as well." A weight dropped into her belly, and she vibrated with tension.

Roshon squeezed her gently, and his touch felt like a lifeline. "Unexpected?" he offered softly, and a laugh bubbled up from inside her.

"Look, I know you think I'm just an irresponsible, impulsive daredevil who doesn't care about my own safety—"

"Ani, I never said that. I never thought that." He truly looked appalled at the suggestion.

"Y-you said I was—"

"Brave. What I meant to say is that you're brave. You're probably the bravest person I've ever met."

Her throat felt clogged, thick, as though all her emotions were welling there. He was looking at her so closely, almost if he could see inside her. She looked away again and took a deep breath. "Well, I'm scared out of my mind right now. Any chance your father will give this up? I know he owes a debt, but does he have to pay with his life?"

Roshon dropped his hand, leaving her arm cold. "I doubt he'll turn back, but he won't want to put you all in any more danger. Of that I'm sure."

A series of concerned tones sounded from Machen. She turned to him and plastered on a smile to hide her fear. "Do you have any idea why Noa's client wants this death stone so much?"

Machen angled his body in a way that communicated his worry for her. He knew how much she hated selakki. *No, but I can ask around. Do you know anything more about it? What does it do?*

"It's a magical object that someone hid here hundreds of

years ago, probably for a good reason," she said. "That's all we know."

The dolphin looked thoughtful. *I'll do some checking and let you know.*

"Thanks, Machen. Be careful. And tell your auntie I said hello. How's the new calf?"

*They're doing great. We're rendezvousing with the nursery pod in a few weeks. I'll tell her. And then he was gone.*

She took a step closer to Roshon, brushing his arm with hers as the pod of dolphins disappeared into the distance.

"Do you think the Queen Who Sleeps knew that someone else was coming after this thing?" he asked.

"Can't be a coincidence. It's been here for centuries, and all of a sudden, everyone wants it."

"Yeah," he said, sounding miserable.

"Yeah," she echoed. Even if they could persuade his father not to go after it, would that be any better? Letting Noa and whoever was paying him get their hands on this thing was bound to be trouble.

"We have to get it first," she whispered.

Roshon nodded, looking defeated. "Get it, keep it, live long enough to get it back to Elsira."

An adventure, indeed.

# CHAPTER TWELVE

From Level 259: Lie on the ground, face up. Bend arms so that elbows are on the ground, fists up. Bend legs so that knees point to the sky. Send power to both elbows, and using your inner strength, push your body from the ground. With practice of not less than three years, your elbows will harden to the strength of selakki bones.

— DAIPUNA: THE ART OF COMBAT

Roshon's nerves weren't improved by Ani's jitters as she waited for her friend to return. He was at least relieved she wouldn't find out how jealous he'd been of Machen before meeting him. She'd mentioned his name several times over the course of the journey, so finding out this friend she'd spoken of so fondly was a dolphin made something settle within him.

Unfortunately, nothing seemed to settle Ani.

"I need to spar," she said, walking around in circles in the mess hall shaking out her limbs.

They'd just finished dinner. Every meal aboard the ship was exactly the same: salted dried fish and seaweed. He shouldn't complain. Except for the fact that the inside of his mouth tasted like a fish tank all the time, it wasn't that bad.

Varten stood at the tiny sink, taking his turn to wash the few dishes they'd dirtied. The others had remained on the bridge.

"Would sparring help you calm down?" Roshon asked. He'd never understand how one person could have so much energy.

"I am calm," Ani said too loudly, then winced. "Tai or Mik usually go a few rounds with me, but they're busy not crashing the ship." She turned in a circle, arms and legs vibrating. Then she stopped, narrowing her eyes at him. "You wanna give it a go?"

Roshon's brows rose to his hairline. "Me? Umm . . ."

"I'll do it," Varten offered, grinning broadly. He slung the towel over his shoulder and leaned back against the cabinet.

Roshon shot him a murderous look that just made his smile grow broader. "No, I'll do it. She asked me, so I'd better. Don't you have something you need to do somewhere else?"

"Not really." Varten settled into a chair and propped up his feet. "This should be very entertaining."

Roshon tried to remember that he loved his brother, but right at this moment, he wanted to toss the ingrate overboard. Ani, however, wasn't even trying to contain her exuberance. She bounced up and down on the tips of her toes, clapping her hands. "Let's move the tables out of the way. We need open space."

They slid the heavy furniture to the sides of the room, after which Varten reseated himself for the impending show. Ani began preparing by cracking every part of her body: first her neck, then her back, arms, fingers. It sounded like fireworks sparking from her joints. Roshon stood mostly still, unsure of what he'd gotten himself into.

"So does it matter that I don't know what I'm doing at all?" he asked.

"Don't worry. I'll show you what you need to know." Ani's grin did not reassure him.

She motioned him forward so they stood face-to-face. She was at least a head shorter and a fraction of his weight, but he knew better than to believe this would be anything but embarrassing for him. However, he certainly didn't want Varten in his place, wrestling or boxing or whatever it was they were about to do.

She cleared her throat and took a deep breath, the restless motion of her body calming as if a switch had been thrown. It was truly remarkable. "Imagine a wheel with eight spokes." Her voice was solid and steady. "These are the pillars of daipuna. The first pillar is space—awareness of your surroundings. Where are you? What direction are you facing? How is the wind blowing? The first Raunians learned seafaring from Myr Himself, and these were the questions they always needed to be able to answer in order to take a journey and return home."

She closed her eyes and stood ramrod straight with her hands at her sides. "Close your eyes and stand like this, like the mast of a sailing ship, and feel your surroundings."

Roshon began to close his eyes but hesitated. The only time he'd seen Ani this still was when Machen had given her the bad news about the selakki and Noa following them. Otherwise, she was always in constant motion, pulsating with a volatile energy that had little outlet. Seeing her peaceful and calm was almost eerie. Her features were slack and relaxed. Her chest rose and fell with her breathing, placid as the sea.

She stood like that for so long he was half-afraid she'd fallen asleep. Then she cracked open one eye and found him looking. "You weren't doing it," she accused.

"I was."

"No, you weren't."

"He wasn't," Varten offered helpfully. "He was just staring at you the whole time."

Roshon shot him a death glare, and Varten cackled, throwing back his head. Ani looked annoyed at both of them.

She let out a huff before continuing. "The second pillar is breath. To control yourself you must control your breathing. There are hundreds of breathing exercises to master, but most come back to managing your speed. Breathe in slowly for a count of eight, hold for a count of eight, then breathe out just as slowly."

She demonstrated for him, lifting her hands to her chin on her inhales and lowering them down on the exhales. He matched her movements, breathing deeply, then releasing it with a loud *whoosh* the way she did.

"That's it. The wheel is a cycle that goes around and around, all the elements working together. You earn a level of mastery in one pillar, then move to the next and the next until you arrive back at the beginning and go further. The levels are infinite. The greatest masters have achieved upward of nine hundred levels for each of the eight pillars. This is your level one."

She walked around him, watching him breathe. He felt silly doing it, but even after just a minute or two, the constant tension that had been weighing him down felt lighter. He was also starting to feel light-headed and was grateful when she stopped in front of him again.

"The third pillar is form. It encompasses the movements necessary to turn the wheel. Watch me." She bent her arms and raised them parallel to the ground until they were at chest height. Then her knees bent and her body was a flow of moving parts gracefully rippling through various positions that obviously required both strength and flexibility. If this was level one, then he had no hope. Thankfully, she didn't expect him to match the motions and moved on quickly.

"Four is foundation. Ground your feet like a mountain below the sea." She approached and tapped each of his legs. "Five is focus. You cannot become distracted. Your entire being must concentrate on your actions in that moment. Six is force. Form and focus are nothing without follow-through and the power to make it a reality."

She executed a complicated spinning move, ending with the flick of her fingers against his sternum that pushed him pack two paces. He wobbled and just barely kept his balance. Pain bloomed on his chest from where she'd hit him, but it quickly faded. He swallowed and returned to his initial position across from her.

"Seven and eight work together. They are the past and the future. You can learn much about your opponent from watching them, both what they've done and what they plan to do." She went into the same impressive spin, but this time when her fingers reached for him, he stepped out of the way.

Ani grinned broadly. "Watching where someone starts their form, at what point they apply their force, and what their style of movement is are all important. We each have individual ways of practicing daipuna. Pillar eight requires you predict a future action based on your observations."

She danced around him some more, kicking and punching, connecting but without any force behind the movements. He knew she could easily knock him off his feet and hurt him quite badly, so he was grateful she was holding back.

"Endurance comes from a combination of the eight; the wheel working as one creates power. A strong foundation to stay standing. A steadying breath prepares the muscles and eases pain. Use your space, plus your knowledge of past and future, to avoid the blows you can. Focus on your opponent and work to reroute their force. Here." She took his arm and straightened it. "Try to punch me."

"Are you sure?" He'd been doing a fairly good job of concentrating on her lesson, but her hand on his arm was a distraction.

She raised an eyebrow as if to say, *Are you serious?* He gave himself a mental shake. Though he had been raised never to hit women, he had to acknowledge that the Raunian culture was different. To take it easy on her would be an insult. His head understood, but his heart was lagging behind. He gritted his teeth and fisted his hand.

"Hard as you can." She released him and took a step back.

He shook his head and then drew back his fist and propelled it forward. She somehow used the momentum of his punch to flip him over, sending him slamming into the ground on his back, her foot on his chest, his fist in her hand.

"Leverage is force. Momentum uses past and future." She let him go and danced backward. He struggled to his feet. "Again?" Her expression was so hopeful.

Varten was snickering softly, his shoulders moving up and down, but Roshon didn't care. His back smarted, as did his pride, but at the same time, he found it exhilarating. Having this thin slip of a girl best him made him unaccountably proud. He wished he could be this good at something. Plus, he was happy that her bravado was at least somewhat well-earned.

He nodded at her eager face. "Again."

By the end of their sparring session, even though she'd gone easy on him, Roshon had bruises in places he'd never considered before. They'd spun, kicked, punched, flipped, and slapped for over an hour. Now he was covered in sweat and ready for a hot shower and a soft bed.

"You keep that up and one day you may even be able to stay

on your feet for a full round," she said as he hobbled toward the bathroom.

"How long is a round?"

"Four minutes." She chuckled, then disappeared into her bunk.

He groaned and nearly collapsed, thankful she wasn't there to see it.

# CHAPTER THIRTEEN

From Level 522: Practice this every day for one or two years and you will gain the strength to uproot a tree from its roots and break its trunk. At that point you may think you have gained mastery, however, this is only the first step.

— DAIPUNA: THE ART OF COMBAT

The next morning, Ani awoke refreshed thanks to the sparring session with Roshon. And her mood improved even more when Machen returned early, his brother Braloch in tow. They'd located an elder in a nearby pod that was friendly with his group of juveniles. Dolphins had long clan memories with tales passed down through the generations, and the elder recalled a story so strange that many had stopped telling it. Ani suspected it might be added back into the rotation given current events.

The elder had said that in the time of the Forty-Fourth Great Ocean War, which would have been about five hundred years ago, a ship sailed to the Okkapu from the east. This vessel wasn't full of greedy treasure seekers with more avarice than sense; it was of Elsiran build and manned by experienced sailors. The crew survived the area's legendary storms nearly unscathed.

Apparently, the dolphin ancestors had watched the ship move so smoothly through the tempest, it could only have been done with magical aid. Then the crew used a catapult to shoot an object deep into the water. With the additional force, it sank far faster than it should have, as if it wanted to be hidden. The ship turned around and left before the Orarinas were even aware of its presence. Many sea creatures believed that Myr had taken it easy on the humans because they were giving something to the ocean, not seeking to take.

A pod of juvenile dolphins had gone to investigate the object where it lay deep in the ocean, and found a bloodred stone. They reported that it had exuded *wrongness,* creating feelings of fear and pain. The one soul brave enough to touch it had convulsed before falling unconscious. When he awoke, he babbled nonsensically for days. He'd eventually recovered, but after that, word spread quickly, and all—even the selakki—avoided the resting place of the stone.

The story of how it came to be in the ocean may have fallen by the wayside, but the location remained legendary. Occasionally, a young male, headstrong and foolish and seeking to prove his mettle, would ignore the warnings and attempt to retrieve the stone. If they touched it, they suffered the same fate as the first dolphin and were overcome by a strange madness that lingered for days or sometimes weeks.

"Do you know where it is?" Ani asked.

Machen was grave as he answered yes.

Ani considered. "I won't ask you to help us. I know you're honor bound to protect the ocean and all its contents, but can you at least point us in the right direction?" For as friendly as dolphins could be to people they liked, they could not help a human find or steal anything belonging to the sea, even if it had originated above water. Their culture prohibited it.

*I will take you there,* he said. *This death stone disturbs the sea. It is not like the other things humans seek. It has caused much pain and suffering. If the humans want it back, you should take it. Myr would be glad to be rid of it.*

"Thank you. You are a true friend," Ani told Machen. "We have to hurry. Noa is on our tail and gaining speed."

Ani raced to the bridge to relay the message to Tai, and he set a course in the southwesterly direction Machen had indicated. He and Braloch swam just off the port bow, keeping pace with the ship.

There was no specific border that marked the Okkapu. The edges of the legendary region seemed to shift and change with the water itself. Tai's charts marked the general area where the ancient island had sunk, but navigational instruments malfunctioned the closer one got, making precision impossible. The unlucky would realize they'd gone too far when a sudden squall erupted out of nowhere or they slammed into a hidden rock formation lurking beneath the water.

Ani and Tai were the only ones on the bridge—the others getting some much-needed rest—when the color of the water shifted before their eyes. She herself was running on fumes, having had a few naps, but overall remained too keyed up to do more. Now, she blinked, wondering if the lack of sleep was making her see things. The dark blue of the waves shifted to a light green, clear as an emerald. The ocean should definitely not be that color.

An indicator on the panel lit up. This was the sensor tuned to certain dolphin frequencies. Machen was whistling a hurried warning that made the light flash red. Not a trill of greeting, this one was for danger. Tai engaged the ship alarm and within a minute Mik rushed in.

"What is it?" He looked wild-eyed while Ani flipped through the sensors, verifying what her gut was telling her. Her skin turned cold. "Selakki. One-point-four kilometers."

Mik visibly paled before running off. There was a flurry of movement at the door, and she caught sight of Roshon racing away, as well. Ani followed him out and found him fiddling with the latch to the rifle cabinet.

"Don't bother with that," she advised. "Selakki scales are impervious to bullets. Their bodies are almost impossible to pierce without high-grade ballistics like the cannon that got us the other day. Barring that, it takes twenty to thirty men to bring one down."

"So how do you usually fight them?" he asked, breathing hard.

"Usually we run. If we can't do that, the next best thing is to trap them in the nets and try to subdue them."

"Subdue them?"

"And *then* we run. Besides, even if we could kill one, it's illegal if we're not harvesting."

He gaped, obviously not understanding, but the way of the sea was sacred. Selakki were enemies of a kind, but Raunian life depended on them. Humans were not a favorite meal of the giant creatures, but they all lived in a painful cycle of conflict and tremulous peace.

The whine of the net motors sounded as Mik unfurled their only defense. Ani kneeled at the cabinet next to the guns to retrieve a harpoon launcher. Attached to the base of the long spear was a thinly packed net. Its webbing was like spider silk but strong as steel.

"When they swim close, the ship's nets can catch them. But usually they're too smart for that and we have to shoot the nets out. This edge—" she pointed to the spearpoint "—can hook onto the side of a scale. It won't penetrate it, but it'll keep the net in place until we soothe them. Hopefully." She eyed the device with trepidation.

Her only big shipwreck was nearly eight years ago now and had been on the first *Hekili*. The selakki had come out of nowhere, bearing down upon them without warning. There had only been two of the beasts, and they'd been juveniles at that. But the nets hadn't held and the chant hadn't worked. The ship was smashed to pieces, and Ani and Father floated in the open sea for four days before Machen's pod had come along and rescued them.

She shivered, recalling the sensation of cold seeping into her bones. The unrelenting sun beating down on her head, and the pain as her stomach convulsed with hunger. She rubbed her lips together now, remembering how blistered they'd become. Tai had been land-side on Raun with Mother. Somehow she and Father had survived, but it had been a near thing.

Fear shook her bones as she gripped the harpoon launcher tightly.

"You said soothe them? What does that mean?" Roshon had grabbed a second harpoon launcher from the cabinet and was fingering the fragile-looking strands of netting.

"They respond instinctively to certain acoustic patterns, a specific kind of harmonic blend. We have a recording that we use, but it's only effective a small percentage of the time."

A low vibration began to hum around the ship, and Ani's heart nearly stopped. She closed her eyes and gathered her courage. Roshon had called her brave, but all she could feel was the crash of a barbed tail against the ghost of a ship, the panic as water slipped over her head, Father's hand in hers as he pulled her onto the wreckage where they had been trapped for days.

The ship shook again. "That's their call. Too low for human

ears." Her voice was a whisper she wasn't certain Roshon could hear.

The growing, restless waves tossed the ship from side to side. How many of them were there? And what could they do? No one knew the true size of the Orarina clan as the older and larger selakki swam alone and didn't often attack. Even one fully mature creature could destroy the ship with a flick of its tail.

No, their only hope was for a small hunting party, an offshoot of the main clan. She prayed to Myr it was merely one or two juveniles who were still susceptible to the chant that mimicked the one their mothers used to put them to sleep. It sounded like a mesh of voices in beautiful, aching harmony that would soothe even the most savage beast.

"Should you start playing the recording now? Since they're close?"

She shook her head. "Unless they're immobile in the nets, the chant just riles them up."

The ship listed and continued to shake. Tai's voice rang out on the intercom. "Looks like three of them. Midsize juveniles."

Ani's heart sank. She nearly dropped the harpoon launcher. "Three is too many."

Roshon took the weapon from her hands, and she looked up with surprise. "Show me how to use it."

He looked scared but determined, with a glint in his eye that reminded her of the first time she'd seen him. She nodded mutely and turned to lead him toward the stairs. They passed his father, who was on his way to the bridge.

"I'll see what I can do to calm them with Earthsong," Dansig said.

Once outside on the deck, Ani realized there was no clear view of the selakki. "We'll have to go up to the gun deck."

They went back inside and climbed up through the hatch.

She engaged the clear shield, if only to protect them from a bit of wind and water, and scanned the area. Cutting through the ocean behind them, the jagged spikes of a selakki spine jutted out of the water.

The midsize juveniles, as Tai had called them, were about three-quarters the length of the ship itself. Ani suppressed a shudder as the beast undulated and its barbed tail flipped out of the water behind it. She spotted the second one to the right, but the third wasn't visible until another impact rolled through the ship.

It was already on the other side of them and had just slammed into the *Hekili*. The hatch was still open, and alarms rang from the damage indicators. A hit like that might not breach, but it could certainly shake a few things loose.

"Got it!" Mik shouted through the speaker.

Ani ran to the starboard side and looked down. Sure enough, the netting sparkled silver around the beast that had just hit them.

"Unexpected," she whispered. The debilitating fear that had gripped her body melted a fraction. Maybe they *could* do this. "Now that we've got one, the other two will be more careful," she yelled to Roshon to be heard over the angry ocean. "They'll try to hit us from below so we should aim to get them as they're diving."

It was exactly what Father had told her before the ship had broken apart in pieces underneath them.

Roshon held his own harpoon launcher and watched as she positioned and aimed hers. They were gunpowder operated with the distance and power needed to catch a creature within half a cable length. Ani held her breath, centered the selakki in her sights, and fired. The pointed arrow of the harpoon sailed through the air, now dim with the approaching dusk. It fell into the water with a splash, just as the creature's tail disappeared. A miss. She didn't even bother unfurling the net, just cursed and pressed the button to reel the tip back in.

Varten appeared beside his brother, and the two of them examined the launcher.

"Point, shoot, then release the net with that button there," Ani directed.

The twins shared a wordless conversation before Roshon handed his brother the weapon. Ani focused on catching the line as it was sucked back into the launcher but looked up when Varten hooted.

"Got it!" he yelled.

She gaped at his prowess and turned, wide-eyed, to Roshon. "He's the better shot," Roshon admitted, lifting a shoulder.

"Two down!" she shouted into the hatch. She didn't have eyes on the third one and expected the ship to jump from a blow from below, but it didn't come.

"Dansig says he's holding the third one. I'm going to start the recording," Tai announced, voice staticky through the speaker.

Ani wondered at the fact that the Lagrimari man could handle an entire beast on his own, but she was glad for it. The two they'd captured were wriggling wildly in the nets, teeth snapping, as they tried to tear their bonds.

"That wasn't too bad," Roshon said.

She didn't have the heart to tell him that the nets were actually the easy part. Eventually, if the creatures weren't subdued, they'd be able to get through. Seaspider webs were strong, built to protect their young from predators like this one, but they weren't impossible to destroy.

Ani motioned for the twins to plug their ears, and they did. A moment later, the chant began playing full blast from the intercom. Additional speakers placed around the ship broadcast and amplified the sound. No one had ever been able to record a real selakki mother cooing to her child in this manner, but divers had heard it and created the recordings to mimic it. Every ship that sailed this far west carried a copy if they wanted any hope of surviving.

The chant was hypnotic, a repetitive blend of voices in a chorus so pure and beautiful it was little wonder the sounds could soothe the raging monsters. But, as expected, before they were calmed, they were angered. The giant fish caught in the ship's net began to buck and shake, rattling the entire vessel down to its struts.

The one Varten had captured was batting the waves in its agitation, seeking to be free of its bindings and away from the sound.

"How long does it take for them to calm down?" Roshon asked.

"It depends. Can take as long as an hour, sometimes less. As long as the nets hold, we should be okay. Once they're completely motionless, we can cut them free and leave. They'll be out for a few hours." She'd never seen it happen before, though, and hoped what she'd learned was actually true.

They waited, watching as the protesting creatures slowly calmed, their movements quieting until they were little more than twitches. The sun set as the chant went on and on, soothing even the humans and draining the tension from Ani's limbs. Her breath was steady. They'd all sat down to wait, checking on the selakki every few minutes to monitor their condition.

They were almost there, the fish sinking into unconsciousness, when the chant began to skip and stutter. Ani popped up and sped over to the hatch. Once she was through it, she raced to the doorway of the bridge. "What happened?"

"The phonograph canister cracked." Tai's voice was low and monotone. They both stared at the phonograph player, which was built into the wall of the room. "It was fine and then it just cracked out of nowhere."

"Uh, you guys?" Varten called from above. "I think they're waking up."

"We just need a few more minutes!" Ani could hardly think, the panic returned so quickly.

Tai let out a string of soft curses with no real heat behind them. They looked at each other, Ani hoping her big brother had some secret plan up his sleeve. Myr knew they should have a backup recording, but they were so expensive. Only one group made them so they could charge what they wanted. Plus, the chances of the chant working were so small that nobody bothered.

Roshon appeared in the doorway.

"Canister broke," she told him.

"Can you start over from the beginning?" he asked.

Ani shook her head and pointed at the thin cylinder sitting in the player. A wide crack ran through the deeper grooves on which the sound had been recorded. It was useless now. Subtle tremors began to shake the ship as the selakki became more agitated.

"Can we repair it?" Roshon looked as if he was holding back panic by a thread.

"Can't we just sing the song?" Varten asked from behind his brother.

Everyone turned to stare at him. "Sing it?" Ani asked, incredulous.

"It would require a range of tones in perfect harmony," Tai said.

"Well, do you have any better ideas?" Varten raised his brows.

Ani shook off her confusion and started really considering his idea. "Tai has a terrible voice." Her brother snorted but didn't disagree. "Mik might be able to, and I can try, but we're not enough."

"We can help," Roshon added.

"There aren't any words, it's just . . . sounds." She couldn't believe this might be a real option.

He nodded impatiently. "We've just been listening to it for a half hour. I think we'll be okay."

The ship rumbled again as the selakki attached to it grew more restless, breaking free of the trance.

"We need to hurry," Tai said.

Mik appeared in the doorway. "Status?"

"Warm up your vocal chords."

The big man frowned in confusion as Tai placed the intercom microphone on the instrument panel. Varten explained the plan to him, and they all gathered around the main console. Dansig sat behind the co-captain's chair, his eyes closed in concentration, still controlling the third selakki. Sweat popped on his brow, and Ani hustled into place before the microphone, trembling with nerves.

"If we do this wrong, they'll just get angrier," she warned.

Mik shot her a dark look. "So get it right!"

She cleared her throat and began the first notes of the chant. Her soprano lilted over the phonetic sounds, trying to match the recording. Mik's bass filled in the bottom, matching her phrasing in harmony. Roshon's strong tenor came in and then Varten, wrapping around his brother's voice to give the additional harmonics the recording had produced.

It wasn't perfect, but after a somewhat wobbly start, they found their footing, repeating the chant over and over, the balance of voices growing stronger.

Tears formed in Ani's eyes and she closed them, living inside the chant. The musicality of the sound vibrating within her. She'd always found it beautiful, and recreating it slowly began to shrink the ball of fear that had taken up residence within her.

From somewhere close by she heard Tai's whisper, "It's working. Keep going."

They kept at it as the beasts' thrashing ceased and they fell into unconsciousness. Only after Tai left to release the net and returned to steer the ship away did they dare to stop.

# CHAPTER FOURTEEN

The line between foolishness and bravery is not always clear.
When making a determination, take into account motive and
cost. Our art can inspire bravery; the fool is often selfish.

— DAIPUNA: THE ART OF COMBAT

Roshon lay on the gun deck, staring up at the vivid night's sky.
For now it was clear, but he wondered if this was the calm
before the storm. The stars didn't look the same here on the
open water. He'd noticed it before, but now he actually took the
time to examine the differences. Back home, Jasminda had tried
to teach him about the constellations, but he'd never paid attention. She knew more about the shapes and names of celestial
bodies than he did. He hoped he made it back to tell her all
about how the sky touched the edges of the ocean out here, and
without the mountains to block them, the stars filled his entire
vision. He wished he could enjoy it more.

After a week and a half on board, the smooth motion of the ship had finally grown comforting, but he was all too aware that they were traveling into even more danger. Machen and Braloch had returned, having wisely fled the selakki attack. They'd reported that Noa had gained more ground; he was now only a few hours behind them.

Roshon had hoped the selakki would awaken to torment the captain and maybe slow him down, but Machen told Ani he doubted they would have had much trouble with the creatures. Apparently, Noa's client was some kind of powerful mage who had been assisting them in making such good time by magical means.

Part of the reason Roshon was looking at the sky instead of the ocean was to avoid thinking about the protrusions of rock jutting out of the water. So far, Tai had steered them through expertly, but Roshon still didn't want to see or even think about what could happen. The glimpses he'd gotten of the jagged fingers of stone they'd been sailing through were enough to feed his nightmares for the rest of his life. Which may turn out to be short, indeed.

He heard Ani coming through the hatch, recognizable because of her light feet. Roshon sat up as she took a seat beside him.

"Making big plans on how we're going to get through this?" she asked with a weary grin.

"No, I've given up on it. You were right. It's impossible to plan for everything. Somehow I just have to . . ." He shrugged.

"Yeah. It's not always great being right. A plan might be nice." She chuckled.

"I'm really sorry you got caught up in all of this with us."

She looked at him askance. "I'm sorry *your* family got caught up with *us*. None of us chose this, but the path is the way. We can't do anything else but follow it, no matter where it goes."

Roshon nodded. If that's what she'd been trying to say all this time, then he finally understood.

"I came to tell you your dad's down on the deck. Machen says we'll be there soon."

They sat silently for a few more moments, and then, by wordless agreement, they stood and climbed down to face what was next.

Papa stood at the railing looking tired. Roshon figured he must have either exhausted or nearly exhausted his Song calming that selakki. Bags and dark smudges ringed his eyes, and his hair was actually disheveled. He needed rest and time they didn't have to recover.

"Will your dolphin friend be able to lead me down there?" He stroked his chin, looking contemplatively at the dark waters.

Ani eyed him from beneath her lashes. "Yes, he's willing. Though he can only help so much. All the dolphins who've touched the stone have had very strong negative reactions. He can't afford to be out of commission for days."

Papa nodded and held out a pair of gloves he'd gotten from somewhere on the ship. "Hopefully, these will help protect me from having the same response."

Worry churned in Roshon's belly. "This is crazy, Papa. Are you really going through with this?"

Weary eyes of the darkest brown turned to him. "What choice do I have, son?" His voice was determined, resigned.

Roshon closed his eyes and grabbed his pounding head. A different chant was taking up residence in his skull, one that rang with doom. He didn't know how to swim, but he'd much rather go into the ocean than have his father do so, Song or not.

"You said something about a bubble of air," he said. "What if you gave that to me? I could go down instead. I could—"

"We are not debating this," Papa cut in. "It's my risk to take.

My Song is weakened but not completely drained. I have the best chance of surviving such a deep dive."

Next to them, Ani was uncharacteristically still. The intercom crackled to life with Tai's voice. "Machen is signaling. He's coming back around."

Ani leaned over the railing. In the dark, the dolphin's round nose was barely visible as it breached the water. He gave a series of bleats and chirps that Roshon still didn't understand how it was possible to decipher.

"We're here," Ani translated. She pointed to a narrow column of rock coming from the water. It resembled the tip of a spear if you squinted. "This statue broke and shifted sometime within the last hundred years or so and brought the stone closer to the surface. Follow this and you'll find it, but it's still nearly two hundred fifty meters down."

Behind them, Tai and Varten emerged from the stairwell. "That's deeper than the professional divers go," Tai said.

Ani nodded. "It would be a record dive." The two of them shared a glance, and Tai's eyes narrowed at whatever he saw on his sister's face. When she turned to Roshon, her face was blank of all expression. He grew suspicious.

"Listen, Dansig," Tai started.

"How far behind us are our pursuers?" Papa asked, ignoring him.

"At last check, less than an hour. Navigating the obstacles here may slow them down."

Papa nodded. "But let's assume it doesn't. How long will such a dive take?"

Tai looked to Ani. "I've never gone that far down," she said. "Machen and I have done about sixty meters, usually at one meter per second."

Papa took a deep breath. "Just over four minutes down."

"And then you have to get back up," Ani reminded him.

Roshon grabbed his father's arm. "And you still have to find the stone down there. In the pitch-dark."

Papa nodded. "I understand." His voice was patient, and he squeezed Roshon gently.

"The water's cold," Tai warned. He looked over at Ani again and gave a short nod, communicating something between them. "Let's go get you fitted with a swimming suit."

They disappeared into the stairwell. As soon as they were gone, Ani dropped to sit on the deck and began removing her shoes.

"So he's really going to do this?" Varten whispered.

Roshon nodded grimly. "Ani, what are you doing?"

She had removed her trousers and was taking off her shirt. Varten gaped as she revealed her undergarments, strips of tight, stretchy-looking fabric. Roshon's jaw dropped, and he quickly covered his brother's eyes.

"You're looking," Varten complained.

"That's different."

"Why?"

He jerked his brother around so that he faced the opposite direction. Varten snickered, but stayed put. When Roshon looked again, Ani was still sitting there in her underclothes, doing some kind of deep-breathing exercise. Machen splashed around, calling out something high-pitched. Ani slipped on a pair of tight-fitting gloves she'd produced from the pocket of her trousers, popped up, and slung a leg over the railing.

"Wait, wait a minute. What are you doing?" Roshon asked. Varten turned back around, and Roshon was too distracted to stop him.

"Your father is a sweet man, but he's never so much as floated in the ocean. I've been diving since before I could walk. I've never gone quite that deep before, but—"

"The deepest you've gone is sixty meters, right?"

"Approximately."

Both twins snorted in disbelief. "And now you're going to go four times deeper?" they said in unison.

Ani looked back and forth between them and broke into a grin. "I've been waiting for you two to do something like that."

"This isn't funny," Roshon said.

She sobered. "You have to admit, I stand a better chance than he does. Machen will lead me down. I'll just hold on to him, find the stone, and come back up. Easy peasy."

"No, not easy peasy." Roshon stiffened.

"If your dad's magic isn't depleted yet, it must be nearly so. He slept almost a day after the storm. I don't know how it works, but keeping a selakki calm must be extremely hard. I don't think he's being honest with us about how much he has left."

Roshon had the same feeling, but knew Papa would only say exactly how much he wanted to. "I could go instead."

"You have tons of diving experience, do you?" She shook her head. "We're wasting time. Noa will be here soon. This is the only thing that makes sense." She swung her other leg over the railing until she was sitting with her back to him. She sucked in another deep, slow breath while undoing the band of her wristwatch.

"Here, time me." She offered it to him.

"What?"

"The longest I've held my breath is nine minutes."

"Really?" Varten said, obviously impressed. Roshon elbowed him in the stomach.

"I'm very good." She beamed.

*Four minutes down and back, and time to find the stone.* Roshon swallowed, his stomach a beehive of nerves. "I still wish you wouldn't."

Her expression was sad for a moment. His hand closed over

hers to take the watch, and he could feel her shivering. Her fear was obvious now, shining through her bravado. With his free hand, he covered hers and held tightly for a moment before releasing her.

The door to the stairwell opened, and Tai's voice could be heard as he approached.

"Tell your dad I'm sorry I stole his shine," she said hurriedly. Then she closed her eyes and slipped off the edge of the boat into the water.

🐚

*Four minutes.*

"She should have reached it by now, right?" Roshon asked, pacing the narrow walkway of the deck.

Tai leaned against the side of the ship, arms crossed, foot tapping. He stared straight ahead, unseeing. A few paces away, Papa fumed silently, his expression a storm cloud.

"Save your Song in case she needs it when she comes up," was all Tai said after Ani had disappeared beneath the waves. He'd known she was going to do it and hadn't tried to stop her. Though, Roshon had to admit, it was very difficult to stop Ani from doing anything she'd set her mind to.

"If she wasn't so determined to captain her own ship, she'd be one of the best divers Raun has ever had." Tai spoke softly, mostly to himself. "She's already unofficially beat several standing records. She just doesn't want anyone to know."

What must it be like trying to keep someone like Ani alive? She was braver than she had any right to be, sacrificing herself for something that wasn't even her cause.

"Why?" Roshon asked him, so much wrapped up in the question.

"The path is the way," he answered. "And this is ours."

Roshon shook his head and kept pacing.

*Seven minutes.*

A dolphin fin peeked up through the water. Tai had positioned a light on the railing so they could see Ani and Machen return. Braloch had stayed behind to pass along messages, for all the good he was doing.

"Has he said anything?" Roshon asked.

Tai shook his head. "He'll let us know if something goes wrong."

Roshon huffed and sank into a crouch.

Periodically, the dolphin would disappear for long stretches and then resurface with a squeak. Roshon understood it meant no change.

This time, though, his squeaks were longer and faster. Roshon straightened, looking over at Tai.

He looked pale. "She's having a hard time finding it. The statue falling moved it more than they'd thought."

Roshon thought he may vomit.

*Eight minutes.*

Was it possible to pace a hole in the floor? It felt like hours had passed instead of mere minutes. His worry had morphed into anger then regret then fear again.

*Nine minutes.*

When she'd said she'd held her breath for nine minutes, did

she mean nine exactly or a few seconds more? He desperately wished he'd asked more questions as the second hand ticked on. They all stood restlessly at the edge of the railing. Braloch had been gone for a long time. So long that the collective worry they all shared bled into the very air. Mik was calling out over the intercom for updates, and Varten went to shout up the stairs that nothing had changed.

Roshon couldn't breathe. It felt as though his own chest were being squeezed by the pressure of the ocean. Air seeped from his lungs. His brain went fuzzy. The ticking of the watch mocked him. And there was still no sign of Ani or the dolphins.

Tai muttered something in his native language and began kicking off his shoes. "I'm going in after her."

Varten came to whisper in Roshon's ear. "What do we do if something happens to Tai?" They needed two people to operate the ship. He didn't answer but knew in his heart that they would all drown here trying to save them before they left without either Tai or Ani.

A stripped-down Tai had just put a tattooed leg over the railing when the surface of the water burst with a splash. The two dolphins had somehow carried an unconscious Ani to the surface. They buoyed her with their heads, pushing her up out of the ocean. Tai dropped into the water and hauled her up around her waist, then lifted her. Roshon and Varten each grabbed an arm and pulled her onto the deck.

Her short, blue hair was plastered to her head. Papa knelt beside her and placed a hand on her forehead before closing his eyes.

Tai leaped down from the rail, dripping and shivering. Time slowed as they all watched Papa focus his power on Ani's limp body. Varten at least had the presence of mind to grab towels, covering Tai's shoulders and draping one over Ani's form.

Papa opened his eyes and drew in a staggered breath. He

turned her on her side and then sat back, nearly collapsing. After a long beat, Ani convulsed and began coughing up water. Tai tapped her on the back as she gasped for breath.

Wheezing, she struggled to a seated position, then grabbed her birthstone pouch. She turned her head to Papa and nodded, clutching the tiny bag in her gloved hand.

She'd found it.

# CHAPTER FIFTEEN

When practicing, beware of the following ways in which you may damage your spirit: gluttony, nonessential fear, a surfeit joy, talking too much, excessive sweat, copious weeping, immoderate sociability, prolonged sadness, very deep sorrow.

— DAIPUNA: THE ART OF COMBAT

The pressure in Ani's ears began to recede as she lay on the deck of the ship swaddled in towels, slowly filling her lungs with air. The pain and foggy-headedness of the dive were fading as oxygen and warmth returned to her body. A light haze still surrounded her vision, but it, too, was beginning to clear.

Her memory of the dive was spotty at first, but slowly came into focus. It had been cold, colder than anything she remembered experiencing before, and dark as pitch below the surface of the water. A true diver would have a supply of bioluminescent powder in little vials to take down with them, but Tai didn't carry anything like that on the *Hekili*, so she'd gone down blind.

She'd held on to Machen's fin the way she'd done a hundred times before, but this time the pressure of the depth had seemed as if it wanted to crush her bones. She hadn't been worried about holding her breath—it was just a few minutes down—but once there, Machen had made sounds of distress. The shifting of the giant statue had created hundreds of small rocks, a sea of rubble with the stone they sought buried within.

He could only tell her that the death stone was in the pile; he couldn't help her search. So she'd wasted precious minutes digging through the detritus blindly, holding up each stone that felt close to the size Dansig had indicated and waiting for Machen's confirmation.

Braloch came down periodically to monitor their progress. Since Ani couldn't speak, she just nodded or shook her head in response, relying on their superior vision to see her in these dark waters. Finally, she touched a stone that was different from the rest. Even through her gloves she could feel its heft and smoothness. Not like a stone formation carved by men or a broken off piece of rubble, but something else entirely.

Machen's tone was hushed as he confirmed the discovery. She'd gripped it, and then dizziness hit her. Deciding it was best not to risk dropping it, she placed the stone in her birthstone pouch, stretching it out somewhat. Then she'd grabbed on to Machen's fin once more as he took off for the surface.

She didn't remember falling unconscious, nor the dolphin brothers working together to balance her as they brought her to the surface. A violent shiver overtook her as she lay on the deck of the ship, enjoying the feeling of air entering and exiting her lungs.

"Come on, let us help you up," Tai said, crouching over her.

She shook her head. "Just another minute or two," she

rasped. "It won't hurt anything. I'd rather walk under my own power."

Tai blew out a breath and stood. His footsteps retreated into the stairwell. He knew how she hated to feel helpless, and she really was all right, just bone weary with a chill that had seeped into her marrow. Roshon sat next to her, brow furrowed, stroking her hair. It felt so good she wished he'd never stop. She leaned into his hand, hoping to communicate her desire for him to do this for the rest of time without actually having to speak again. The effort had drained her.

Roshon's face was close, peering at her with those golden eyes as if searching for something he could fix. She wasn't broken, just tired and cold, though warmth suffused her from where his palm touched her. His face wasn't quite close enough to kiss, but she wondered how his lips would feel. Soft but firm, and just the right pressure. It would be her first kiss, and she wanted it with him. The thought made her eyes flutter open. Perhaps she could steal a kiss and blame it on her lightheadedness. The idea took shape in her mind and caught hold of her will. She leaned up into his frown and brushed her lips against his.

He froze, eyes wide. She recalled that you were supposed to close your eyes when kissing, but she liked looking at him too much. There was a strange and fizzy feeling inside her that had nothing to do with the lack of oxygen and everything to do with his closeness. The way his often-suspicious gaze took in everything. The steady timbre of his voice. The sound of his rare laugh.

His lips were less than a breath away, and she wanted to feel them again, imagined opening her mouth and inviting him in, when a strangled shout rang out. She turned to find Roshon's father on his knees convulsing, in the grip of an attack of some kind. His eyes rolled back in his head, and his body shook with a seizure. Strange words flew from his lips in a language she had never heard before. She struggled to get up, but Roshon was already at his side.

"Papa? Varten!" he called, and his brother raced down the stairs to reach them. They positioned themselves on either side of their father as he continued to shake and gibber incoherently.

Ani's hand went to her pouch, which once again held only her birthstone. Her heart seized. She crawled over to Dansig, ignoring her own pain. She didn't know when he'd removed the death stone from her pouch—maybe after he'd expended his Song healing her—but he held it now in his ungloved hand, fingers tight around the red, gemlike ball.

Roshon saw what she did, and together they pried his fingers from the stone, even as he tried to bang his head against the side of the ship. Once they'd freed him from it, the seizure stopped, his body stilled, and his shouting quieted. Varten held his father's limp form. Then they all looked at Ani, the stone resting in her bare palm.

"No!" Roshon shouted, reaching for it, but she rolled away, avoiding him. It was just a weight in her hand, smooth and perhaps warmer than it should be. She experienced no ill effects, no body shakes or strange thoughts. No voices or tremors. Not for the first time, she wondered what its true power was.

"Maybe it only affects Earthsingers," Varten whispered.

But if there was a chance it could harm either of the twins, she wasn't willing to risk it. She peeled off one of her towels and wrapped up the stone. "No one else touches it, all right?"

They both nodded. Dansig moaned but was still out cold. Ani took a deep breath, exhaustion creeping through her very bones.

"Are you ready to go to your room now?" Roshon asked. She nodded, her head far too heavy for her body.

She allowed Roshon to help her to her feet while she cradled the bundle with the death stone in it with one arm and clung to him with the other. They entered the stairwell when a *crack* sounded, and the hairs on the back of her neck and arms rose. A brilliant flash of bluish-white light blinded her. When it was gone, all the electricity of the ship had died. The engine stopped, and the lights cut out. All was silent except for the murmur of Tai's and Mik's voices on the level above them.

Ani and Roshon froze where they stood.

# CHAPTER SIXTEEN

Surprise is an art to itself. It weaves a net of pillars seven and
eight, using your expectations of the future against you.

— DAIPUNA: THE ART OF COMBAT

Rapid bleating sounded from the water. A sliver of moonlight
was all that allowed Roshon to see, though his vision was hazy
in the sudden darkness. Ani stumbled back out to the deck and
leaned over the ship's railing. Machen was raising a fuss,
splashing and carrying on in a way that sounded frantic to
Roshon's ears.

"He says that Noa's here." Her face was obscured in the
dimness, but her voice was hollow.

"So that lightning that hit us from out of nowhere . . . ?"

"Probably Yalyish magic."

Orange light bloomed from the direction of the stairwell

and Tai was there, clothed and dry, holding a lantern, his face tense. "Noa?" he asked.

"Looks that way," Ani said.

"You'd better get down to the panic hole."

Roshon took a step back as Ani got into Tai's face, staring up at him with anger. "I am not hiding in that gross little cubby. What good will it do? They'll search the ship and probably tear the whole thing apart in the process. The path is the way, and this one is mine."

"They could search for a dozen years and never find the secret room, Ani. Father made sure of it. And made use of it more than once. You are my responsibility, and I won't see your life ruined because you're stubborn." A vein throbbed in Tai's forehead. "Now go and seal yourself inside."

The lantern he held bobbed up and down, the flame flickering as he gestured, but Ani wasn't backing down. Roshon almost wished she wasn't so brave, or so dead set on facing whatever came her way.

As the siblings continued to argue, Roshon peered out across the ocean. The night was just as calm and peaceful as ever, maybe more so due to the lack of electricity on board the *Hekili*. But a rustling sound soon pierced the quiet.

"Shh." Roshon held up a hand to the bickering duo, who ignored him. "Shut up, you two. I hear something."

They paused and listened, each cocking their head to the side as if they were having as difficult a time as Roshon in identifying the sound. The low, wheezing whir, like machinery spinning up, came from somewhere overhead.

The three craned their necks, staring out into the endless black. Tai held up the lantern, but nothing was visible. Nothing until a rope dropped down from above. A second rope tumbled down, then a third. Tai held the lantern even higher, but its range wasn't strong enough to illuminate the origin of the thick lines of twisted fiber.

Then a click sounded, and they were flooded in a harsh glare nearly as bright as daytime. Roshon blinked to adjust his eyes, then stared up in shock. The hull of a giant ship at least four times as tall as the *Hekili* had drawn up alongside them silently. Its sides were covered in dark selakki scales, marking it as Raunian.

"The stone?" Tai whispered. Ani stared up at the ship for a moment longer before disappearing into the stairwell. No doubt going to hide the stone somewhere.

Mik arrived on deck a few moments later, looking up in awe at the craft that had arrived so suddenly. Papa was awake now and stood with Varten's aid. A kind of fear Roshon had never known before flooded his bloodstream with ice. The ropes shook, and then the *Hekili* was being boarded by enemies.

For the first time ever.

Blue and green-haired Raunians slid down from high above to fill the deck. More men and women dropped onto the roof above the bridge, the thuds of their boots echoed off the hard-scaled surface.

Ani, dressed but still sopping wet, reappeared beside Roshon as a final man slid down the rope. By the way she and Tai stared daggers at him, Roshon would bet his farm that this was Noa. As tall as Tai but leaner, the man had a litheness that bordered on feline. He looked around, appearing very satisfied with himself as Tai snarled.

Noa snapped a command in Raunian, and a scratchy hand smelling strongly of fish clamped over Roshon's mouth as someone held his arms. Another person patted down his clothing in a search for weapons. Thick fingers pried his jaw apart, checking under his tongue and in his cheeks. He thought this was overkill until the newcomers pulled several blades from the mouths of both Tai and Mik. Roshon couldn't believe he'd forgotten Tai's trick on the streets of Rosira, but obviously, Noa had been prepared.

The captain had tattoos fully covering half his face, the dark lines showing his impressive credentials. He was about Tai's age, and though Roshon couldn't remember the explanation of all the symbols, at least some of them indicated which waterways the man had permission to use tax-free, along with the size of his fleet.

"Ani Summerhawk." He approached her with a sly grin.

"Noa Whiteel," she growled. Then her face blanked before she flashed him a heart-stopping smile dripping with malevolence. "We weren't expecting visitors. Sorry, I can't offer you any refreshments." Her arms were restrained by a green-haired female sailor who was obviously struggling to keep hold of her. Ani stamped on the woman's foot, and she yowled but didn't release her. Another woman crouched down to immobilize her legs.

Noa let out a deep chuckle, then replied in Raunian. His tone sounded completely unbothered and dripped with condescension. He swept an arm toward one of the ropes, where a robed figure stuttered down inexpertly. The man was pale with blond hair—not Raunian or Elsiran. He wore a thick red robe ill-suited for the balmy weather. Roshon couldn't tell his age— older than Tai but younger than Papa—though his lineless face was at odds with the ancient weight of his watery blue eyes. This had to be the mage.

He'd brought some kind of small contraption with him and had it wedged under an arm. Now he straightened and held the thing out with both hands. It was a bulky object about the size of a dinner plate but thick as dictionary, with gears and dials sticking up in the center of it. Noa spoke again, and Ani translated to Elsiran.

"He says this is Master Effram, who paid handsomely to be brought to the Okkapu."

Noa raised a brow and looked at Roshon and Varten for the first time. Then, in a very patronizing manner, he continued in Elsiran. "You see, the instruments on the *Rialoko* interfered with his machinery, so we will be borrowing the *Hekili* for a short while until he's completed his task. I trust the crew will accommodate us. Will this ship do, Master Effram?"

The mage didn't pay any mind to Noa or the rest of them. He was wholly focused on his gadget, adjusting dials and switches and muttering to himself in a foreign tongue.

Noa sighed, as if put off by the man's rudeness. "In the meantime, let's retire belowdecks for a long-overdue conversation." He smiled at Tai, then motioned his men to begin hauling them away.

# CHAPTER SEVENTEEN

When attacked by an enemy, my body is the fire that shapes my art.

When attacked by a friend, my mind is the water that purifies.

— DAIPUNA: THE ART OF COMBAT

Ani stumbled down the steps into the large storage room that she and Roshon had pumped and patched a few days ago. The adrenaline flowing through her warred against the exhaustion of the dive, making her feel especially rash and fearless. She sobered some at the wariness on the faces of Roshon and his family, but anger was a powerful motivator and she had plenty to spare.

"While my associate is searching for . . . whatever it is he's looking for," Noa said, waving his hand as if it were inconsequential, "I think that we should have a little talk." He'd switched back to speaking in Raunian, though maybe it was for the best that Roshon could not understand. It would be bad enough having to leave, and that's obviously where this was headed.

"I must admit, Ani, I was somewhat offended you would deny the gracious invitation to become my apprentice. But how long did you really think that would last?"

Now she could see what Tai had warned her of over and over again. Noa Whiteel was successful and handsome, with a charming manner and urbane ways. Those qualities had been enough to impress her mother, and while Ani had never fallen under his spell, she hadn't had Tai's strong negative reaction to him, either. But now that she really paid attention, the casual cruelty in his gaze was obvious. The way his dark eyes flashed with a feral intensity that all the fancy manners in the world couldn't hide for long. A chill went through her that had nothing to do with the dive.

Tai struggled against the two men pinning his arms together, anger making his face turn colors. "She has a much brighter future ahead than working with you, Whiteel."

Noa snorted, barely glancing at Tai. Instead, he approached Ani, swaggering until he was uncomfortably close. She considered spitting at him. She hadn't mastered blade-spitting, but she could hock phlegm with the best of them. But a voice in her mind, one that sounded suspiciously like Roshon, warned her against it. Noa wouldn't think twice about slapping her, or worse, and that would just make Tai even angrier. And feel even guiltier. With great difficulty, she buried the urge to lash out.

"As soon as my client is done, you're coming with me," Noa cooed at her, his hot breath fanning her cheek, making her recoil. "My contract for your apprenticeship is valid and signed by your mother, so no more stalling. I've gone to quite a bit of expense to catch up with you." He sighed dramatically. "Squallmakers aren't cheap, you know. Neither is rerouting my ships. But a deal is a deal, as they say." He spun away gracefully, as if performing onstage. He had about as much sincerity as an actor playing a role.

The sour feeling in her belly grew as she thought about what her life would be like married to this man. She didn't know when he planned to challenge for her, though likely soon to get ahead of any other potentials. As if there would be any. Then as soon as she turned eighteen, they would be wed. It's funny how Tai's harping on it hadn't left an impression, but now the thought of simply enduring that future sliced a wound in her heart.

Raunians married for many reasons: often for business or family affiliations, sometimes for love. She'd never thought much about it before, but suddenly, now that her options were few and her time had run out, she regretted not taking it more seriously.

"The question becomes, what to do with your brother and his crew? You certainly have collected a strange mix of folks, Summerhawk," Noa said, addressing Tai. "A middle-aged man and two identical ginger oafs. But I suppose with your reputation, you'd have to scrape the bottom of the barrel for employees." His grin was wide and mean.

Tai fumed silently, jerking against his captors and getting a kick in the shin in response.

"Don't touch him!" Ani yelled, struggling to free her feet and retaliate against one of the women holding her.

A malevolent expression twisted Noa's handsome face. Ani stilled. Would he challenge Tai to a duel over the broken contract? It was within his right, and she highly doubted Noa had any honor where dueling was concerned.

"If her mother wasn't the king, would she be so valuable to you, Whiteel?"

The voice was Roshon's. Noa paused, wearing a comical expression of confusion as he turned. Ani was just as surprised but hoped she hid it better.

"Likely not," he answered in Elsiran. "But one cannot choose one's parents. A strong alliance with the king is beneficial to me for many reasons. Calling her my mother-in-law will be useful, as well." He returned to Ani's side, Tai thankfully forgotten, and stroked her cheek with one long finger. Ani's stomach churned.

"Too bad you won't be able to," Varten said. Their voices were the same, but Ani could still tell them apart easily. Everyone in the room stared at the twin, whose eyes widened under the scrutiny. "He won't," he reiterated.

"And why is that?" Noa asked coolly.

Varten and Roshon exchanged a look that could only be twinspeak. Ani just knew that they could communicate entire paragraphs in one of those glances they shared.

"Well," Roshon picked up, "don't the laws of the challenge state that it must be performed within three days of issue?"

Noa was annoyed. "Yes, but I have not issued my challenge yet. And I am well aware of the laws of my own nation."

Roshon leaned away from the man holding him, as if straining to reach Noa. "Well, you see, I *have* issued a challenge for Ani."

Her heart stopped. Noa grew very still, focusing all his attention on Roshon for the first time.

"And when was this challenge issued?" Noa growled.

A smug grin spread over Roshon's face. "Just now."

Noa's nostrils flared, but that was his only movement until he spun around and grabbed Ani's chin forcefully. "This may be amusing to you, but you know you cannot accept. It is your right and responsibility to turn down challengers who are beneath you. This pasty, ginger Elsiran could not possibly last for a whole round against you." He spat the words out like bilge water.

Ani stared directly into his shadowed eyes, forcing herself to meet his gaze and threw her shoulders back. "I accept his challenge and am confident that Roshon is an apt adversary."

Noa stared at her for a long time, as if searching for the answer to some question. His lip curled, and he finally released her. She was certain she'd have bruises tomorrow from his unforgiving grip.

"Very well. We have some time to kill while Master Effram pursues his search. Besides, this will be good entertainment for my crew." Noa brushed his hands on his trousers as if touching her had dirtied him. "However, the king notwithstanding, we all know you cannot trust a Summerhawk. Your mother believes your honor to be unimpeachable, but I'm not so certain." His dark eyes flashed as he faced her. "So to prove there are no hard feelings, and that I'm invested in ensuring you end up with the most deserving suitor, if at any point I believe you are holding back against him and not using your estimable talent—" Noa produced a switchblade and sauntered over to where Roshon stood "—I'll slit his throat."

The bubble of joy inside Ani flickered and died. "W-what?"

"I'd prefer it to be your brother—" he glared at Tai "—but murdering the king's son is frowned upon. Some nameless, discarded Elsiran, however . . ." He shrugged.

"He has a name," she snapped. "And how would you know if I'm taking it easy anyway?"

"You've reached the twenty-fifth level of daipuna. As someone who's reached level sixty-eight, I can tell what levels you're using. If you were to, say, hold at a five or a ten just so he could last an entire round, well, that wouldn't be fair, would it? Fair to you, I mean, to be saddled with such an incompetent husband."

Ani swallowed. While a few days ago it had been nothing to claim that she wouldn't have thrown the challenge to avoid marriage to Noa, today the thought of Roshon losing made her question everything. Would she cheat to ensure he lasted long enough for the match to count?

"You're not exactly an impartial judge," she spat.

He tapped his lips. "Very well. I will create a tribunal. Two judges from my crew, and one from yours. As Tai cannot be trusted, Mik will do. You're a seventy-two, are you not?"

"Seventy-five," Mik said. Four men were restraining him. Noa really should have brought ropes for this.

Noa frowned. "Among three people, you should be able to agree on whether or not she pulls her punches, should you not?"

Mik didn't answer, turning his head away instead. Ani looked to Roshon, whose glare could have cut Noa to ribbons. She wanted to tell him to take back the challenge and not risk himself. She wasn't sure if Noa would make good on his threat, but given Tai's stricken expression, it was clear her brother thought so. However, Roshon wasn't backing down, and she wouldn't shame him by questioning him in front of all these people.

"Fine," Roshon said. "I accept your terms." His brother's and father's eyes were wide, but neither said a word.

Noa raised a brow at Ani, who nodded once and said, "No holding back."

"This should be interesting, indeed," Noa said, looking very pleased with himself.

# CHAPTER EIGHTEEN

From Level 64: Punch, applying greater and greater force to the center of the target. Every day, strike one hundred blows in this manner and the connection of force and form will gain another degree of clarity.

— DAIPUNA: THE ART OF COMBAT

It was dawn, and Roshon had spent an uncomfortable night sleeping on the floor of the storage room, watched over by crew members from the *Rialoko*. Noa had magnanimously decided that a good night's rest was necessary for the challengers to be at their best. Ani had been allowed to sleep in a bunk, though, and he doubted her back and legs were as sore as his were.

He hadn't had much of a chance to talk to his father. When they'd tried speaking in Lagrimari, the guards barked at them to keep quiet, threatening with menacing fists. But that morning, a sense of calm washed over him, accompanied by the buzzy, fizzing sensation of his father's power. Reassurance that Papa wasn't mad at him bloomed. Well, at least not *too* mad.

The feeling that had propelled him to challenge for Ani, that little spark of bravery within him, was still burning, but it was being battered by a gale of fear. An hour of practice on the fundamentals of daipuna was nothing compared to her years of training. Still, if he'd just let her be taken away, he wasn't sure he could have forgiven himself.

No breakfast was given to the *Hekili's* crew, though Noa's people chomped on their fish jerky and dried seaweed while they cleared space in the storage room where the challenge was to take place.

Tai had slept elsewhere and arrived with a black eye, hands tied in front of him and bracketed by four brawny sailors. They released him inside the storage room, and he approached Roshon solemnly. "I am in your debt, Roshon ol-Sarifor," he said, bowing his head.

"Only if I make it through." His voice wavered.

Tai peered at him. "You don't have to stay on your feet the entire time, but if you get knocked down, you must rise before the count of four or you forfeit."

Roshon nodded.

"Do you believe you can make it?"

Roshon swallowed. Did he? He'd known the rules when he'd made the challenge, and even though the odds were slim, it wasn't impossible. "The path is the way, and this is mine."

Tai grinned. "If Myr wills it, all things are possible."

Then the men in the doorway parted, revealing Noa with Ani trailing behind. Roshon half expected her to have a black eye, as well, but she looked as perfect as ever. Perhaps a bit surlier than normal. She caught his eye, and his heart stuttered at the depth of emotion he found there. She was afraid for him.

He gave her a wink and tried for a smile, adopting some of

her bravado. It felt weak on his lips but was apparently enough to reassure her.

Four minutes. Get knocked down, but don't stay down.

He'd have to avoid being struck unconscious by one of Ani's powerful kicks. She was small and fast, and managed to pack a lot of power into her diminutive limbs. He was bigger and stronger, but slower and unskilled. And he'd already been set flat on his ass by her more times than he could count. But he'd gotten back up, hadn't he?

The "tribunal" took their seats on three crates set up at the front of the room. Annoyed was the only way to describe Mik's expression. He crossed his arms and stared straight ahead. The two men Noa had chosen flanked him, one with a shaved head covered in tattoos and the other with a mix of green and blue braids halfway down his back. As for Noa, he'd dressed for the occasion in a black suit coat, brushed to perfection, with shiny boots. They weren't the normal Raunian style but a fancier kind more suitable for land than sea.

A cushioned seat had been brought in. It must have been from the *Rialoko* because there wasn't anything like that on board the *Hekili*. As soon as he'd settled into the chair, the room quieted. A dozen of his crew were present as spectators. When all eyes were firmly on him—this man was a peacock of the highest order and obviously craved attention—Noa produced a small hourglass from his inner coat pocket.

"This will time the round," he announced. "Once I turn the glass, the match begins."

Ani's disposition had already transformed into one of fight-readiness. She cracked her neck, back, and just about everything else before falling still. They faced each other on opposite sides of the loose sparring square delineated by boxes and crates. Impressed as he was by the change in her demeanor, he had to create a similar transformation within himself if he had any chance of lasting the full four minutes.

He ran through the pillars of daipuna, repeating them again and again as he took inventory of his body: space, breath, form, foundation, focus, force, past, future. He could do this.

Space. *I'm in the storage room, facing west.*

Breath. He began the slow-breathing exercise she'd taught him.

Form. That one stymied him. Ani had tried teaching him the simple level-one positions, but that was the part he remained weakest at.

Foundation. He planted his feet and bent his knees slightly so as not to lock them out.

Focus was easy. He'd never had a problem with that. Unlike Varten, Roshon wasn't easily distracted and could sit for hours reading, studying, thinking.

Force, he'd have to see about. He was strong, but the idea of using his strength against Ani was still very difficult.

Past and future? Well, he was about to find out because Noa turned the hourglass with a great flourish and placed it on the crate next to him.

With only a gleam in her eye as warning, Ani launched herself forward. She executed the same spinning move she'd done in their training session, and he slid out of the way just in time. She danced and spun around him with dizzying speed, hitting him with punches and slaps that stole the wind from his lungs.

"Come on, Ani, that's a thirteen at best," Noa called out.

Roshon didn't spare a look at the judges. Ani's grimace was enough to tell him the statement was true. He braced himself for her next onslaught, knowing it would be more intense. He dodged a blow to his face only to catch one in his gut that had him bending over. He could feel her coming up from behind him, and then her leg hammered down on his back and he was on his knees, vision blurry. He wobbled, fighting his way back to a standing position. A blur of motion in his periphery announced her next move. He tried to dodge but ended up with an arm hacking his chest.

"Thirty seconds," Noa announced.

Roshon groaned. Blood coated the inside of his mouth. He moved to the edge of the sparring box and worked on evasion for the next few seconds. Ani gave him a moment to recover as she shook out her arms, then sped toward him before Noa could complain.

Roshon planted his feet, creating a strong foundation when Ani looked like she was going to slam into him. At the last second, he pushed forward and tackled her, using his height and weight as an advantage and bringing her to the floor, hard. Her chest rose and fell beneath him. He craned his neck to look at her face, finding her smiling. Then she gave him a headbutt and slipped out from underneath.

When he rose to his feet, pride shone in her eyes. She looked . . . happy. In that deranged, somewhat suicidal way of hers. Her forehead was bleeding along with her lip, but she was grinning like a maniac. Something inside him loosened. Some intrinsic level of restraint had bound him even though he'd known it wasn't necessary or helpful. He wasn't beating her up by using his strength; he was proving that he found her worthy. And he did.

Her superior skill meant he probably wouldn't break her. And if by chance he did, Papa was there to fix her up. After that, it was as if his hobbles had been removed. He wasn't going to be a master of form anytime soon and his head was ringing so bad he couldn't tell up from down, much less north from south, but he wasn't a coddled child. He'd pulled a garden plow when they'd lost their donkey to old age, hauled lumber to patch the barn, carried a lame goat on his shoulders, and a thousand other things. It wasn't a pillar, but it would have to do.

When Ani whirled around him, climbed on his back, and tried to put him in a sleeper hold, he broke out of it by elbowing her, hard, in the belly. She sputtered and gripped him harder, until he rolled to the ground, pinning her. She slid out again, but before she could crawl away, he dragged her back by an ankle, dodging a kick by her other foot and wrapping his arms around her in a bear hug.

"Innovative," Noa said dryly.

"Two minutes," Varten called out.

Roshon was breathing heavily. He was slow compared to Ani and couldn't avoid her flurries of motion. But she had a style that he'd picked up on. The planner in him focused on past and future, avoiding some of her favorite moves and using her frenetic momentum against her.

He punched out, clipping her in the jaw and snapping her head back. Each time he connected, he had to battle the urge to help her, fight against the sickness in his gut that was the automatic response when she was in pain.

The gleam in her eye spurred him on. They were both bleeding, but she was obviously enjoying this. He wished he could say the same, but he'd lasted this long. He just needed to keep it up.

He took a running start toward her, then feinted right and spun around, catching her around her middle and lifting her kicking form into the air. She executed some kind of vision-blurring spin that resulted in him being kicked in the head, and then she once again had him in a sleeper. He rolled over, taking her with him, and smashed her down. She jumped up. He rose more slowly only to meet a kick to the ribs. He wobbled on his feet and withstood even more abuse, imagining his foundation as strong and solid.

They circled each other, and he wiped blood from his eyes. She winked at him. Despite it all, impossibly, his cheeks heated.

"When we're married," she said, grinning while fighting for breath, "we can spar every day."

He shook his head and rushed her again, grabbing, missing, and receiving nothing but punches in return. She tried to flip him, but he caught her. His arms wrapped around her middle again, her back to his chest. He lifted her off the ground and twisted to avoid being kicked in the knees. Then he pressed a kiss to the back of her neck, and she stilled. When he tossed her away, she landed on her feet, eyes wide.

"When we're married," he choked out, "I hope you'll take it easier on me."

In his peripheral vision, Varten was waving and jumping, only to be restrained by one of Noa's men. Did that mean time was up? Roshon had blood in his ears and wasn't sure if they were working properly. Ani was far enough away that he chanced a glance at the hourglass, but Noa was no longer in his throne-like seat. He'd approached the edge of the sparring box wearing a dangerous smile.

A glint of something shiny flashed between the man's lips, and then Roshon was falling backward, almost in slow motion. He didn't even feel it when he hit the ground.

# CHAPTER NINETEEN

Defeating your opponent is not merely the work of one match or challenge or sparring session. It is a lifelong goal, for you will face many opponents, not the least of whom is yourself.

— DAIPUNA: THE ART OF COMBAT

"You mud-licking bastard!" Ani screamed. She was still riled up from the fight, and the sight of Noa spitting a paralyzing blade at her future husband put her over the edge.

"Four, three, two, one. And that's time," Noa said calmly. "A pity he couldn't hold out. He was really doing rather well."

"He *did* make it through the round," she said, breath heaving. "You poisoned him."

"Did anyone see me poison him?"

"Yes!" Varten, Tai, and Dansig said in unison.

"Anyone impartial?"

"Who here is impartial?" Ani demanded. "I saw you, and it's my future we're talking about."

"You are sadly addled from the match. You blood is still high. You don't know what you saw. Let's ask the tribunal."

Noa's two men denied seeing anything.

"Mik?" Ani asked, hopeful.

"His back was to me. I . . ." He trailed off. "I'm sure he did, but I didn't see."

Ani nodded. The truth was all she wanted. Even if he had been a witness, it wouldn't have done any good. She glared at Noa. "The challenge was fair until you intervened."

"Hmm," Noa said, a finger to his chin. "Well, the king is the one who adjudicates challenge disputes. Let's all go to Raun and see what she has to say." He grinned wildly while Ani fumed.

"It was valid," she said through gritted teeth. "I won fair and square, trying my hardest, and he lasted the full round." She tossed her chin up, unwilling to be swayed. If Mother had to be brought into this, then so be it. Noa the snake was so smug, but she'd figure something out.

Dansig knelt by Roshon, who was beginning to rouse.

"If I bladed him, where's the blade?" Noa was the picture of innocence, holding his arms out.

She'd seen the flash of metal, but Dansig patted his son down and didn't find anything. Maybe Noa had used something that couldn't be traced. She'd heard of substances that dissolved when hitting the bloodstream. Who knew what his money could buy? The best evidence was Roshon lying on the ground, having fallen out without her ever touching him.

He looked up at her then, eyes still glassy before they focused on her. Something she saw in them shook her right down to the marrow. It was if a blow from a cannon had landed straight in her midsection; she rocked backward under the force of what she found in his gaze.

Her skin was hot, her breaths coming out short, she wasn't certain that could stand upright any longer. That look was everything every story about princes and knights promised—something she had never dared hope for and even now couldn't put into words. But with it, a connection between the two of them locked into place. An invisible chain linked them together across the short distance.

Her heart felt full, threatening to burst. He had fought for her and gave it his all. He was going to be her husband one day and she found herself jittery with anticipation. The rightness of it zipped along the bond between them, filling her with warmth and muting the blaring of her injuries.

The corners of his lips rose and she thought of the vision she'd had of him smiling at her, his eyes alight. Was it about to come true?

Just then, Master Effram raced into the room, still carrying that contraption of his with all those dials and switches. His expression was pinched, but to his credit, he entered a space filled mostly with large sailors and didn't bat an eye. He marched up to Noa appearing peeved. "I have been searching for the past twelve hours. The instrumentation shows the death stone is nearby, but it . . ." The box in his hands began beeping and whirring.

Effram frowned, adjusting it, while Noa looked bored. With his head down staring at his device, the Yalyish man paced the room. He walked by her and stopped in front of Dansig and Roshon.

"One of you has touched it," he said, gaping at them.

Dansig stilled under the scrutiny, and though Effram spoke in Yalyish, Ani had a feeling that the man understood the gist of the accusation.

"You've touched the death stone," Effram said, awe taking over his voice.

Ani spoke up in Elsiran. "What is a death stone, and what makes you think he's touched it?"

Effram switched languages smoothly. "My amalgamations don't lie." He brought the machine closer to Roshon, then swung it over to Dansig and froze. "It's you. You've had contact with it. Where is it? It doesn't appear to be on the ship. Did you hide it?"

Dansig steeled his features into a cold mask. "I don't have any idea what you're talking about." Ani had never heard him speak quite so forcefully. She'd grown used to his easygoing manner.

Varten helped Roshon rise, and they stood on either side of their father. At first, Roshon hunched over, hand around his middle in obvious pain, but over the course of a few seconds, he drew up straighter. The pain from Ani's own wounds lessened remarkably, accompanied by a tingling sensation. She'd never felt Earthsong before, but it wasn't entirely unpleasant.

Dansig and his sons were far more physically imposing than the scrawny Yalyish man who looked as if he didn't spend much time out of doors. But Effram didn't appear intimidated in any way. He stared at the family facing him and sighed. "Very well. I don't have the equipment I need to get the truth out of you here. You'll have to come with me."

"I'm not going anywhere," Papa said, voice brooking no opposition. "Anywhere but home."

Effram turned to Noa. "Have your men collect him, will you?"

Noa lounged back into his throne chair. "Listen, mage. You hired me to bring you to this accursed part of the sea. That's what I was paid for, and that's what I've done. Kidnapping sailors, as potentially entertaining as it sounds, would require a not insignificant additional fee."

Effram snorted and narrowed his eyes. "I'll not be bled dry

by you, Whiteel. You've been paid more than fairly." He eyed Dansig and the twins again, then set his device at his feet and produced a large compass from his robe. "Very well, then. You three are coming with me."

Effram stood only a few paces from them. Ani approached on quiet feet, not liking the Yalyish man's demeanor. He was a little too sure of himself for comfort. She wasn't familiar with the extent of the magic he wielded, but she didn't have a good feeling about it.

"You will tell us all how you found the death stone and where you've hidden it," Effram said, turning the dial of the compass.

"I've already told you that I don't know what you're talking about," Dansig replied.

"And I can hear the lie in your voice. You are not the only one who can manipulate Earthsong, *grol*."

Dansig stiffened. Ani crept up behind the mage, standing close as the man finished his compass adjustments.

"We will simply have to take this discussion back to my Board of Directors." He thrust the device in front of him, pointing it toward the family, and began speaking words in a strange language Ani didn't recognize.

Under her feet, the floor began to shake. The rumbling grew very quickly until the crates themselves, some full of weighty merchandise, jittered and slid across the floor.

Later, she would remember a bright light and a sound so loud it took days for her hearing to come back all the way. Locking eyes with Roshon and reaching for him. Seeing him scream out her name. He hadn't been that far away.

Then light followed by darkness.

Tai told her that Effram's compass had exploded. Weeks later, when she'd gotten a good look at the storage room, it certainly looked like a bomb had gone off there. Craters had opened up in the floor and in the ceiling, like a giant sphere had come into existence and eaten away everything in its path. A chunk had been taken from the pipe she'd patched, quickly flooding the room. Tai and Mik had needed to seal the space off completely to keep the ship from sinking.

She'd awoken in her bunk, woozy and cold. She'd sat up and tried to rub her eyes, only to discover she couldn't. A bandage covered what remained of her right arm. Her hand and much of her forearm were gone, sliced clean and flat as if from the world's sharpest knife. A surgeon would later have to round it into a stub that could be fitted with a prosthetic.

The damage in the storage room had been similarly precise. Not ragged and chaotic, but clean, circular cuts out of the floor and ceiling. Impossible, and yet all too real.

As for Effram, Roshon, Varten, and Dansig . . . they were gone.

Tai said they had to be dead, that nothing could have survived being in the center of that explosion. He remembered it vividly in a way she didn't, but Ani was equally certain they were alive. Yalyish magic was responsible, she was sure of it. Tai didn't think their magic was worth much, though, and he pointed to the rifle scopes as evidence. Whichever ones had worked for Roshon and his family still wouldn't work for any of them.

But Ani knew she was right even if no one else believed her. That premonition she'd had of Roshon smiling at her, joy evident on his face, hadn't come true yet. And her visions always came true sooner or later.

Roshon was going to be her husband someday. Of that, she was positive. His disappearance was unexpected, but it wasn't permanent.

# CHAPTER TWENTY

The evidence of mastery is found just as often in defeat as in victory. For what practitioner who had never lost a battle can claim true expertise?

— DAIPUNA: THE ART OF COMBAT

Ani and Tai stood under the twisting arches of bone that made up the Summer Palace. The name had been given to the seat of power of the tiny, tropical island of Raun by an outsider generations ago. The Raunians had found it funny so they kept calling it that. The palace had no walls, no real structure other than the one created from the elaborately decorated remains of a giant fish, some ancient ancestor to the selakki whose rib cage was as large as a house.

Bleached bone arches carved with the same symbols their people tattooed on themselves stood on a patch of ground at the edge of the island. Behind it, the waters of Pirate's Bay lapped gently. Many Raunian locations had adopted the names foreigners had given them.

King Pia sat on the throne, a hideous creation constructed of whale bones and decorated with shark teeth. It looked like an uncomfortable seat, and Ani's mother was an uncomfortable woman. Her heavily tattooed face was prematurely lined, her expression pinched as she regarded her children.

Beside Ani, Tai's head was high. He'd told her once that whenever he was called to the Summer Palace, he focused on the endless blue of the water behind the throne and not the thing itself, nor its occupant. Ani's shoulders were squared, the constant pain of her missing limb helping her to focus on the present moment and not on the past.

Attendants lined the space. There were no courtiers, just normal folk appealing to the king to confirm contract negotiations and settle disputes. Though some here were, no doubt, in attendance to see what would come of the notorious Summerhawks in a showdown with their mother.

"Captain Tai Summerhawk," the king said in a sonorous voice, "you are accused of removing Ani Summerhawk from her lawful contract with Captain Noa Whiteel. What say you to this charge?"

Tai's voice was clear as he answered. "Guilty."

Ani's shoulders jerked involuntarily.

"Very well," the king said, her eyes hard. "I sentence you to two years of hard labor in the western hunting grounds. You will lose ownership of your ship for the term of your incarceration. It will reside with your second-in-command, Mik Autumngrass, until your release."

Mik stood on Tai's other side, eyes glassy as he nodded in recognition.

The king's steely gaze slid over to Ani. A rod of iron shot through her spine to be watched so carefully by her mother. "As for you, Ani Summerhawk, you claim a challenge made and solidified to a foreigner."

"Yes, I am spoken for."

"However, as this party has abandoned you, is presumed dead, and clearly is not here to sign a marriage contract, I cannot in good conscience approve the match."

Ani's jaw clenched. "He did not abandon me, and he is not dead. He and his family were kidnapped by foreign mages."

Tai stiffened beside her, but they'd had this argument before. He thought she was delusional, but she didn't care. Her mother waved away her protest. "Be that as it may, the contract is unsigned and as such, is unratified. Any further claim on you is allowed."

The king's gaze shot to Noa, who stood with several members of his crew among the other court attendants. He stepped forward and bowed respectfully. "I make no further claim for Ani Summerhawk. I have no need of a one-handed apprentice or a disfigured wife."

Murmurs rippled through the audience. Tai's entire body was a taut wire as he held himself in check. Ani just smiled. Her fingers itched for her blade. She was learning how to do everything with her nondominant hand, including twirl her knife.

"Very well. Is anyone else here willing to enter into a contract with this young woman as an apprentice?"

Mik stepped forward. "I am." His freshly tattooed captain's mark blazed on his forehead. He could have made captain years ago, but he preferred serving as second for Tai. However, he'd undergone the final test in preparation to take over Tai's ship and for her. Tears stung her eyes as she held her breath, waiting for her mother's response.

King Pia's nostrils flared. "It is deemed acceptable. We will ratify the contract at this afternoon's signing ceremony."

Relief flowed through Ani's body. She looked over at Mik,

struggling to hold in her emotions. Then two members of the Security Force stepped forward to meet Tai. He didn't protest as they shackled his wrists and started to lead him away.

"Wait!" Ani cried, wrapping her arms around him.

"It's only two years," he said thickly. "Study hard during that time and I bet you'll make captain earlier than expected."

She smiled through her quickly building tears.

"And the other thing . . . The stone?" he whispered.

"You were right," she said. "Father's hiding place can't be found."

He nodded. "Keep it there. Don't forget Mother will be scrutinizing you closely. She'll take any excuse to deny your captainship. But we'll find a way to get the stone back where it belongs when I return."

She nodded, and the guards dragged him away. Only then did Ani let the tears fall, still holding her head high as Noa and the other vultures observed her.

When court finally ended, she didn't spare a glance for her mother. Instead, she followed Mik through the narrow streets of Raun to the dock where the *Hekili* was being repaired. It would be seaworthy again in a few short weeks.

In the bay, a pod of dolphins swam in circles. Machen had sent word of a connect with some highly sought-after merchandise down in the southern archipelago. That would be their first destination. They'd function just as they had before, doing business while Mother's watchdogs paid close attention to her training.

She planned to make captain faster than anyone ever had. She'd show Noa what a one-handed girl could accomplish. And she would use every contact she had, and create those she needed, to find Roshon and his family. The path was the way, and this one was hers.

# EPILOGUE

Progress in daipuna is made step by step, day by day, year by
year. It is not the provenance of the impatient or vainglorious.
It is the art of a lifetime.

— DAIPUNA: THE ART OF COMBAT

Roshon awoke to a harsh, blinding light searing his eyes. He
tried to sit up but couldn't, and discovered he was strapped to a
bed. Only his neck was mobile. He turned to find beds on either
side of him, all occupied. He was in some type of hospital ward.

Pain jabbed at his limbs, and his head felt foggy, as if it were
full of cotton. He groaned and struggled to free himself from
the wide straps holding him down.

A figure in white loomed over him, mouth and nose covered
by some kind of mask. The person held up a large needle filled
with red liquid. Roshon screamed as the needle stabbed his arm.

Later, he awoke with Papa peering down at him. He was in a different place, on a different bed, arms and legs free to move. He sat up clumsily to find Varten on another bed next to him.

"How was it today?" Papa asked.

Roshon rubbed at his arms, remembering the needle but not much else. He blinked slowly, trying to clear his slow-moving mind.

"Memory loss is a side effect of the newest experiments. Don't worry, son, it will come back shortly."

Roshon shivered. Papa's voice was as calm as ever, but an unfamiliar thread of anger was laced through it. He took Roshon's hand, bumping him with one of the strange bracelets affixed to the man's wrists. Those were for . . . something to do with magic. His father's magic.

The sensation of moving through a heavy mist began to recede, and Roshon took stock of his surroundings. Bars ringed the room in which they sat. Three beds lined the space. A sink was bolted to the wall. A toilet stood in the corner.

This was a prison.

"What happened to us?" His voice was thick and sounded far away.

Varten and Papa shared a look. Maybe he always asked this question, but for the life of him, he couldn't remember. He closed his eyes and saw a girl's face shining in the darkness. No, two girls. Two very different girls. One had wild black hair and a smile on her face. He knew her. She was his sister. Where was she? The other girl had blue hair, eyes full of trouble, and a mischievous grin.

"Ani," he whispered, somehow knowing it was her name. But who was she? And why did she feel important?

"Where are we?" he asked, rubbing his eyes.

"Far from home," Papa said, soft and sad.

"Will we ever get back?" His brain was starting to clear. He was just on the edge of an important memory.

Papa squeezed his hand, and his face grew tense. "The Queen owes *me* a debt now. So yes, son. One day we will go home."

The story continues in *Cry of Metal & Bone (Earthsinger Chronicles, Book 3).*

# CODA OF STORM & SORROW

## A BONUS EPILOGUE FOR CRY OF METAL & BONE

The special, bonus epilogue to *Cry of Metal & Bone* features Ani and Roshon's reunion, which happens after the events of that novel.

# CHAPTER ONE

Ani Summerhawk stood leaning against the rail of her ship, the *Rapskala*, an icy wind brushing against her face. She wasn't looking at the dark waters the hydrofoils sliced through, nor was she considering the formidable, rocky coastline to the east —mostly because her eyes were closed. Ani was remembering. Or trying to at any rate.

The fingers of her left hand tightened around the railing as a soft sheen of sea spray grazed her knuckles. The split hook prosthetic attached to her right arm rested at her side. Some part of her mind made a note to oil it tonight—the contraption was not of Raunian design and unfortunately did not hold up well against the corrosive salt water which was her life. But even this practical concern paled in comparison to the joy she sought in the past. It was on a deck like this that she'd had her first kiss.

That moment was etched forever in her mind and had often brought comfort over the past years when such a commodity was in short supply. But the memory she sought was more elusive, just a flash of an image that had never really happened in the first place.

The premonitions that had occasionally plagued her as a child had grown more rare over the years. Now that she was eighteen, there was only one that had yet to come true: the vision of a smiling face looking upon her with joy, eyes laughing. Roshon's face. As quickly as she brought the image into focus behind her eyelids, it was gone again. Water through the fingertips.

Her crewmate Ena's footsteps sounded softly behind her. Ani had been out here for too long, she acknowledged. She didn't need to worry much about the ship's progress; her second, Leo Silverray, had the controls, and he was nearly as good a pilot as she was.

"I've finished the alterations," Ena said, shaking Ani from her musings and causing her to turn around. Ena held up a dress—one of her own dresses—freshly cut down to fit Ani's significantly shorter height. Neither of them had been overly blessed in the chest department, so not much change was needed there. The delicate fabric was blue-green and shimmery, apparently the height of fashion back on Raun, though Ani hadn't been keeping up.

"It's beautiful. I'm so sorry Ena that you had to do this. I've already included extra in your salary to cover."

The willowy young woman shook her head. She blinked heavy-lidded sloe eyes, which some who trained with them had thought made her look unintelligent. Ani had known better and had scooped Ena up to round out her tiny crew as soon as she'd passed the captain's exam.

"There's no need," Ena said. "Dresses are one thing I have plenty of." Her voice was wry. Her wealthy family had not been keen on her pursuing a life on the sea.

Ani ran her fingers across the bodice before taking it from

Ena. The good thing about her double hook was the dexterity it allowed. She had excellent control of the device and wasn't afraid of it catching or snagging on the thin material like some of her other prosthetics would have. The gown's shifting colors reminded her of the shallow waters outside Pirate's Bay back home.

"Well, I'm very grateful nonetheless. Dressing to impress isn't my strong suit. Do you think he'll—" She cut herself off with a shake of her head and continued admiring the gown. Though she'd quickly become friends with Ena, who was only a year older than her, Ani was still the captain. She couldn't burden her crew with all her insecurities. It was bad enough Ena had felt the need to alter this dress for her in the first place —something Ani would never have asked of her.

But her crewmate smiled warmly. "I think he will be entranced by you in this, or in your regular clothes, or perhaps nothing at all." Ani's cheeks heated. "Besides," Ena continued, "he's never seen you in any finery, yet he still challenged for you."

"Over two years ago," Ani muttered.

"Do you really think the time apart will have changed his mind?"

She had nothing to say to that. In the two weeks since she'd received her brother Tai's message that Roshon and his family had been found alive and were now back home in Elsira, Ani had done little else but wonder and worry.

Not like she hadn't spent the previous two and a half years doing the same. But before it had been a muted thing. She'd had her training to focus on, studying her hardest and exceeding every expectation in her apprenticeship to dominate the captain's exam. She was the youngest captain ever to have earned the rank in a mere two years. She'd crammed three years worth of training into that time, aided by the fact that she'd spent the previous sixteen observing everything her father and brother did. All while being hounded by the spies her mother sent to watch and keep her in line. And keep her from investigating what really had happened to Roshon, his brother, and father when they disappeared from Tai's ship.

An ache pounded down her right arm. Phantom pain still assailed her, a ghostly haunting from the hand she'd lost, but she ignored it and gathered the dress close to her. She was about to go belowdeck to her quarters and try it on when a familiar high-pitched squeaking rang out from the water.

"Machen?" she cried, spinning around and leaning over the railing. Her best friend was there, lifting himself out of the water with his back flukes to greet her. The clicks and pops of the dolphin language filled her with a familiar warmth.

*How did the delivery in north Udland go?* His tone held a hint of smugness, which she honestly could have done without.

"Fine." Beside her, Ena remained silent. Bless her. Machen did the dolphin equivalent of raising an eyebrow: he rolled to one side and flapped a flipper.

"All right, all right, it was a disaster. I should have listened to you. There, I said it. Are you happy?"

*What happened?* The true concern in his manner leeched away a bit of her annoyance, but she still would rather not revisit the situation. Fortunately, Ena spoke up.

"A freak ice storm, though it's supposed to be too early in the season." She shrugged. "We were stuck for ten days in the frozen bay until the ice chipper was able to get us out."

Ani groaned and dropped her head. Machen chuffed in a dolphin laugh. "It's not funny! I was supposed to be back in Raun to meet Tai when he got out of prison. Not stuck in half a cable length of ice. How do the Udlanders stand it up there?" She shivered as the memory of the frigid winds raced across her skin.

*If only someone had told you not to take on that particular delivery.*

She shook her head and made a rude gesture with her left hand, causing more chuffing. "Go ahead, laugh it up!" she shouted over her shoulder as she turned away.

*Wait! I have news. Something you'll want to hear.*

She turned back around. "What is it?"

*We ran into one of the maternal pods who were just up from the south. There's a hydroponic mugwort dealer in Fremia who's asked for you specifically. Apparently, she heard about the run you made to the peninsula last month and thinks you're the perfect person to get her merchandise down to the Equatorial Isles.*

Ani tilted her head, considering. Fremian mugwort was highly sought after in the south for its psychotropic properties, but it was also highly illegal, hence the need to smuggle it. This would be a good haul. Lucrative.

"You know I have to go to Rosira. Roshon is back."

Machen bleated out acknowledgment. *I know. But I'm not sure how long she will wait considering the merchandise she's sitting on.*

She looked past him to where the rest of his pod was cavorting less than a click away. She'd only been a captain for a few short months and was eager to solidify her reputation. The Summerhawk name had been tarnished by her father, and in some eyes by her brother's actions as well. Many had underestimated her or written her off completely, especially once she'd lost her hand. This haul had the potential to be legendary, like the Floodhammer crew's slusium steel trade or the Autumnrivers gang's carnivorous manatee run.

Ena's expression was placid as usual. Her crew got a percentage of each haul on top of their normal salaries. She didn't owe them a say in her decisions, but she liked to get their opinions.

"There will always be another deal," Ena said magnanimously. "But you only have one betrothed. Whom you haven't seen in years."

"Think Leo will feel the same?"

Ena's long face pinched and frowned. Yeah, that's what Ani thought, too. But at the end of the day, it was her decision. She'd been waiting for years to see the boy who had fought for the right to marry her. They were only two days away from the Rosiran port. Going to Fremia and doing this run would keep her away for weeks, possibly longer.

She leaned back over the edge to where Machen was swimming in circles. "I need to see him. If the job is still available after that, I'll take it. But I can't go now."

Machen chirped and clicked his response. *Do you want us to go ahead and tell Roshon when to expect you?*

A brilliant smile crossed Ani's face, and the vision she'd been struggling to grasp came into focus in her mind: Roshon, joyously smiling at her. That promise, along with everything wrapped up in their betrothal, was like a lure dragged in front of a hunting dog. She chased it just as hard as she'd chased her captain's mark. She would see him again and he would smile at her like that and all would be right with the world. They would marry and sail the seas together on the *Rapskala* and life would be sweet.

"Tell him I'm coming, Machen. Tell him wild *selakki* couldn't keep me away!" She gripped the dress still in her hand tighter. Nerves raced in her belly along with joy. Anticipation. She could barely take a full breath because of it. There was no way she could focus on a job before she'd set eyes on him again.

Once they were together again, everything would fall into place.

# CHAPTER TWO

Roshon ol-Sarifor paced the uneven cobblestones of the docks. Sunset streaked across the horizon, blinding him when he walked out of the shade of a hulking steamer ship. It was one of only a few moored here in a port that should be much busier than it was. No Raunian vessels had arrived since Tai's ship, the *Hekili,* left two weeks ago.

A small fishing boat bobbed in the distance, but Roshon's constant scanning of the water did not make the ship he longed to see pop into existence. He wasn't even sure what Ani's ship would look like. He assumed it would be similar to her brother's but had no idea of the various types of crafts the Raunians used. All he knew was that she was on her way.

*The Rapskala arrives at sunset.* That was what the dolphin message had relayed. Roshon didn't even know how the dolphins managed to leave messages at the Rosiran port—were there others here who understood their strange language?

Nerves overtook him as his thoughts wandered. His palms were clammy and cold. The heavily starched collar of his shirt itched his neck, and the thick, fashionable boots that had materialized in his closet pinched his toes. But all of his discomfort froze when he caught a new glint on the horizon.

It was long minutes before the flash resolved itself into a ship, limned by the harsh oranges and reds of sunset. As it drew nearer, Roshon's nervous energy filtered away leaving him motionless, solid, and still as a statue as his future drew near.

The strange, reflective scales of *selakki* skin covered a ship slightly smaller than the *Hekili*. It was of a similar design, a hydrofoil with the body balanced on several thin platforms which glided atop the waves. Roshon's unpracticed eye could not tell if the ship was old or new, but it was beautiful.

His legs regained feeling when it became clear the vessel would be finding its berth a bit farther to the south than where he stood. He moved down the dock in that direction, not watching where he was going, bumping into people, and being roundly cursed for it. With absentminded apologies, he continued on his way until he arrived at the ship and stood on the wooden jetty running alongside it. The anchor dropped and the craft's foils lowered until they disappeared below the dark waters.

A Raunian man with short-cropped hair—black, with no dye in it—appeared on the deck and began cranking out the ramp which led to the jetty. Roshon stopped short. *Was* this Ani's ship? The Raunian embargo meant it had to be, but he hadn't expected . . . Well, it stood to reason that she'd have a crew. He swallowed and watched the man, who looked to be in his early twenties, turn the crank. Nerves flooded him again with more force than before, locking him into place.

And then a short figure raced out on the deck and leapt onto the ramp which wasn't even all the way down yet. The cranking man shouted, but Ani disregarded him and jumped the narrow distance onto the wooden pier. A brilliant smile shone on her face when she spotted Roshon, and his breathing stopped.

The dying sunlight behind her gave her an otherworldly glow. She wore a dress that looked like it was made of the sea itself. It had short sleeves and left her midriff bare, scandalous in Elsira, but likely common in tropical Raun. To Roshon, she was a creature of myth, like some kind of water sprite. His jaw was open, but he couldn't form words. Couldn't bring motion into his calcified limbs.

When he made no move toward her, Ani's step faltered. The smile she wore dimmed as uncertainty crept across her features. She approached more slowly, the enthusiasm of a moment ago fizzling out, but Roshon still couldn't move.

"Hi," he said, when she was an arm's length away.

"Hi," she responded, looking up at him through her eyelashes. On someone else it would be coquettish, but on her it was simply caution. That realization made his heart clench. He took a step forward on shaking legs when someone rushed past him and wrapped Ani in a hug.

Varten swung her around and whooped, making her laugh until he put her down. He'd come out of nowhere and a tickle of jealousy crossed Roshon's skin, but then his twin looked at him over his shoulder with a pointed glare. As if to say, *That's how you greet someone you haven't seen in years.*

His brother gently pushed Ani into Roshon until they crashed together, and he had no choice but to put his arms around her. His embrace was a bit more cautious than Varten's, and Ani didn't yell or whoop, she just sank into him. She smelled of salt and that green soap that he'd missed so much. Her scent was sunshine and cold nights and hope. He never wanted to let her go.

Eventually, reluctantly, he did. Tears shone in her eyes when she looked up at him.

She blinked them away and then cocked her head to the side. "Did you grow?"

A small smile cracked his lips. "I think you might have shrunk."

She was searching him very carefully, looking for something in his face. Maybe some evidence that he was the same person she'd known before. Before capture and imprisonment, before torture and the endless experiments and the despair that had nearly crushed him into dust.

He wished he could reassure her, but he wasn't sure himself.

"I'll have you know that I'm at least two centimeters taller than when you last saw me."

Roshon pulled back and eyed her dubiously. Her short hair was a vibrant blue, and perhaps she had grown a bit. Her face was a little less round, her eyes a little more flinty. He reached for her hand and paused, looking down. Attached to her right arm was a wooden prosthetic, a finely carved hand with articulated fingers. He held it and ran his thumb over the smooth, polished surface. The color matched her skin tone, and the straps that held it in place disappeared underneath the bodice of her dress.

Her eyes were wary, but he brought both hands to his lips and kissed them both. She relaxed a fraction before pulling away. Behind her, the man from the crank and a tall, graceful woman with a long green braid climbed down the ramp.

Ani saw where he was looking and turned. "This is my crew. Ena and Leo meet Roshon, my betrothed."

Ena's smile hovered just beyond her lips. She looked as if a strong wind might blow her away. Leo's expression was pleasant, though his eyes danced in a way that put Roshon on guard. His sleeveless shirt ostentatiously showed off well-muscled arms. He crossed them in front of him, leaning against the jetty's railing.

"Not quite betrothed though," Leo said, amiably.

Roshon tensed. "What?" He felt Varten shift beside him and knew his twin's hackles were up as well.

Ani grimaced. "Technically," she said, glaring at Leo before turning back to Roshon, "the contract was never signed seeing as how you and your family were . . . unable to do so."

"So what does that mean?"

"It means until the contract is signed, there's no engagement." Leo looked apologetic as he spoke, but there was a definite combative vibe coming from him.

Roshon squared his shoulders. "It's just a piece of paper, right?"

"We Raunians take our contracts seriously." Leo's eyes glittered.

Ani grabbed the base of her prosthetic and squeezed, as if the thing hurt her. Tai had told them how she'd lost her hand the day Roshon, Varten, and Papa had been captured while on the *Hekili*. Whatever magic had spirited them away from the ship had also taken her hand with them when she reached out for him. So then whatever pain she'd endured due to the injury was indirectly because of him.

"Are you all right?" he said, speaking low.

"I'm fine."

He peered into her dark eyes, but now she wasn't looking at him. She tapped her fingers against the wood below her right elbow. "Do you want me to sign it now?" he asked.

"Do you *want* to sign it?"

"What does that mean?"

She looked up at him and then at their audience. Varten cleared his throat and stepped around Roshon. "Will you show me around your ship? Is it thermoelectric?" He, Ena, and Leo disappeared back up the ramp, leaving the two of them alone on the pier.

"I mean," Ani said, "that once it's signed, that's it. No backing out. A Raunian contract is like a law."

Roshon took a step back. "You want to back out?"

Her brows descended, and she huffed. "Do *you* want to back out?"

"You can't just answer questions with questions." He threw up his hands. "What is it that you want to do, Ani? Just tell me. I'll do whatever you want."

"It's not just about what I want. We both have to want it." Her words were quiet, spoken to the ground. Very uncharacteristic of her.

A wave of panic swept over him, causing his breathing to stutter. This wasn't going at all how he'd pictured it. Was she looking for a way out? Had she come here to break things off? Maybe she'd found someone else, someone stronger and more viable. He looked up to where Leo had disappeared.

He sighed, a weight falling upon his shoulders. She had a good life. She was literally living her dream—captaining her own smuggling vessel. What could he add to that? He still woke in the middle of the night coated in sweat, feeling the echoes of needles puncturing his skin and foreign doctors observing him with calculating gazes.

"We can give it a few days," he said, watching her reaction carefully.

She peered up at him, eyes wide. "A few days?"

"I mean, there's no rush, right?" He wasn't breathing, then, maybe neither was she. Ani blinked a few times, then looked back at her ship.

"After all, you just got here," he continued.

"Yeah, what's a couple of days?" she said, tonelessly.

Roshon felt as heavy as the anchor they'd just dropped into the water. He was sinking, falling into the dark and the cold until he was submerged in a place he knew well. A place he hadn't wanted to ever go again.

# CHAPTER THREE

Ani regarded the table setting before her with trepidation. All these utensils . . . why did they need so many utensils? The beautifully carved wooden hand attached to her right arm mocked her. It had been a rare gift from her mother a few months into her training. At a cursory glance, it was hard to tell that the hand was not real, but unlike her split hook, she could not use this one for anything. It was almost entirely decorative.

Vanity had her put it on just before they docked in the Rosiran port. She'd reasoned that it matched the dress better, but if she was being truly honest, she had to admit the wooden hand looked better than the hooks and was less likely to horrify Roshon and his family. Though just at this moment, why she'd been so eager to impress him was a mystery.

He sat on her left side in a dining hall inside the Elsiran palace. Ena was on her right with Varten next to her. Leo had elected to stay behind on the *Rapskala*, grumbling under his breath about Elsiran toffs.

In the corner, a four-piece string ensemble played somber music. Three massive U-shaped tables took up most of the room, half-full of aristocrats and whomever else attended these sorts of things. The king and queen were not present; Roshon had apologized and promised he'd introduce her to his sister tomorrow.

Servants busied themselves clearing away the soup bowls from the first course of what was likely to be many. Since her amputation, Ani had grown quite adept at using her left hand— she never wanted to be dependent on her prosthetic if she could help it—but Raunian food did not require such a wide array of eating implements. The highly polished silver knife and fork winked at her as the smell of roasted meat filling the air promised that they would be expected to be used shortly.

She turned to Roshon, trying to swallow her apprehension. "So is this how dinner is every night?"

He scowled at the room in general. "A lot of people live in the palace and enjoy this sort of thing. Varten and Papa and I usually eat in our apartment, but I thought you might like to at least see how the other half lives." His expression transformed into a rueful half smile; Ani's chest clenched, drinking it in.

A young waiter approached Roshon from behind and bent to speak in a low voice. "Excuse me, Prince Roshon, you'd requested the fish for the main course for your party? You'd like to to replace the pork?"

"Yes, exactly. Thank you."

The man bowed sharply before scurrying away. Ani raised a brow. "*Prince* Roshon?"

He grimaced, shrugging. "I guess since our sister is the queen, it's been decided that we're princes. We don't seem to get a say in the matter."

"Is that so? Don't they realize you know more about chickens and goats than crowns and balls?"

He rubbed his palms against his thighs as if trying to warm them, evidence of his discomfort, but the sight was oddly soothing to her. She remembered this about him and wanted to grab his hand. But she held hack.

When the main entrée arrived, it was a tender grilled swordfish. She stared as platters of roast pork were distributed to the other guests.

"You said it was you favorite," Roshon rumbled into her ear.

"How did you remember that?"

"I remember everything you said. I had a long time to think about it."

She paused, fork raised, and swallowed. "Thank you," she said, holding his gaze. His golden eyes glittered with sincerity.

The fish's tender flesh was easy to separate using only one hand, and the first bite practically dissolved on her tongue. She closed her eyes and moaned. She felt Roshon's eyes on her as she enjoyed her meal.

After dinner, everyone retired to a large, adjoining parlor filled with seating areas and small tables for gaming. Ena and Varten rushed to claim an open zatraz table, while Roshon and Ani hovered near the entrance. He seemed unsure of where to go.

A group of younger people were seated in a conversation area. Several waved Roshon over and he reluctantly moved forward. He grabbed her wooden hand and Ani tensed, but he made no reaction.

"Your Grace," a girl in a deep gold gown said, once they'd arrived. "There's room to sit here." She patted the cushion next to her, which didn't appear to have more than two handsbreadths of space available. Ani's eyes narrowed and her fist clenched.

Roshon led Ani to the seat and motioned for her to sit. She did so as gracefully as possible, which wasn't all that graceful, to be honest. The girl in gold's smile turned brittle. She shifted over slightly to make more room.

"This is Ani Summerhawk," Roshon said, "my fi—," he paused, blinking. "My friend."

Something within her froze. He wasn't wrong, with the contract unsigned and all, however, that hadn't stopped her from claiming him as her fiancé for all these years. But she couldn't show her hurt or weakness before this school of barracudas. If they tasted blood in the water, they would attack.

Roshon perched on the arm of the couch as introductions were made, his leg brushing against Ani's. She shifted slightly to press more firmly against him, and he didn't move away.

"That is quite a unique gown, Miss Ani," a girl in jade green remarked. Ani had already forgotten everyone's name. "Are you not chilly with so much of yourself . . . exposed?"

Giggles sounded from the girls of the group, while the boys ogled her.

"It's fortunate that the palace is kept at such an agreeable temperature," Ani responded, sunnily. Ena's gorgeous gown *was* somewhat out of place in a land where skin was apparently not meant to ever see the sun. But she didn't care.

"I think it's probably the most beautiful dress I've ever seen," Roshon remarked softly.

The other girls looked like they'd sucked on prunes for a moment before roundly agreeing.

"Oh yes, I've never seen fabric like that before."

"It's quite stunning and fashion forward."

Ani sat up straight, keeping her shoulder back as conversation moved on to other topics. Part of her wished she'd stayed behind on the *Rapskala,* but she'd piss in the mud and call it butter before she'd let anyone intimidate her—even if she didn't truly belong.

"So, Miss Ani, what does your family do?" a round-faced young man asked.

"My brother is newly released from prison and my mother is the king of Raun."

She reveled in the shocked expressions surrounding her. "I am a ship's captain and lead my own smuggling operation. In fact, I have a haul coming up that promises to be very exciting. It will take us to the Equatorial Isles, which are quite balmy at this time of year. Perfect for my *unique* wardrobe." She looked the girl in green in the eye and smiled viciously.

Roshon jerked, his leg losing contact with hers. "You've accepted a job? When?"

"After I leave here," she tilted her head to watch his expression swiftly blank, masking the glimpse of shock. Though he betrayed no emotion, his face seemed unusually pale.

Ani blinked, tuning out the inane chatter from the others as something like guilt gnawed at her. She stood suddenly. "Show me the gardens?" She wasn't sure she could stand this oppressive room one moment longer.

He nodded and rose, and they left amidst a chorus of goodbyes, which he ignored. As they walked out of the parlor, Ani caught Ena's eye. Her crewmate smiled hopefully, but Ani could not return it. Everything seemed to be falling to pieces in front of her.

Roshon led them down a short hallway and through a set of glass, double doors, with a walled garden beyond. "This is my favorite spot in the palace. No one ever seems to come here, and there are flowers you don't see anywhere else."

The night air was crisp and refreshing. As she stifled a shiver, Roshon's jacket came around her shoulders. She grabbed the lapel and inhaled the warm scent of him, murmuring her thanks. He motioned to a bench in the center of the space, ringed with leafy greenery, still vivid and bright this late in the season. They sat together in silence for a long moment.

"How long had you planned on staying in Rosira?" he asked.

"I'm not sure. I was just alerted of this job yesterday. I haven't accepted it yet, though."

"Was this just a pit stop?"

She clutched his jacket tighter around her, though she was no longer cold. "I can't stay forever, you know. I have to work, my ship and my crew—we need to be moving."

Roshon swallowed and leaned forward heavily to rest his elbows on his knees. "I guess I didn't think much about the logistics."

"You mean when you challenged for me?"

He shrugged. "Or over the past couple of years."

They hadn't talked about prison. Honestly, they hadn't had the time, but now it seemed that those years were more of a ghost between them than anything else. She didn't want to ask him to relive the awful things she suspected he'd gone through, but she wanted him to know that she was here to listen, if he needed it. She just didn't know how to say the words. Her throat ached with things unsaid.

"There's plenty of room. Aboard the *Rapskala*, that is. She was built for a crew of eight." Ani held her breath, waiting for his response.

"I just got home," he whispered. "I'm relearning everything, even how my family works. We're all together again. I just can't leave immediately."

She lay her cheek against the shoulder of his jacket, breathing in his scent. Though she sat right next to him, an ocean and a continent might as well still separate them. He was brooding in that worrywart way of his, and she found herself shocked to be doing something similar. She was no longer certain that the vision she'd seen of him smiling at her with joy would ever come true.

A shadow passed before the doors leading back in to the palace. A figure stood there for a moment then the doors opened, and Varten galloped in with Ena gliding behind him. Varten came to a stop before them, blinking rapidly before a grin transformed his face.

"We're starting a game of Bone Shanks and we need two more."

"From what I understand, it's basically an Elsiran version of Hammers and Thunder," Ena added. "Only their dice have eight sides. I think you'd enjoy it." Her knowing gaze seemed to focus on the space between Ani and Roshon, visibly small but growing with every breath.

"Sounds like fun," Ani said, with extra brightness in her voice. She stood, removing his jacket and dumping it into his lap before following Ena back into the palace.

She did not look behind her to see if Roshon was coming or not. She told herself she truly didn't care either way.

# CHAPTER FOUR

Roshon had no desire to play any games or socialize with the palace rats in the parlor. He wanted to be with Ani, but she had walked away, and his feet wouldn't move to follow. Not back into that nest of vipers. She could handle them better than he could at any rate, why should he even bother?

Varten left him alone for about an hour, which he spent pacing the paved paths in the small, walled garden. But all too soon he felt his twin at his back again, concern wafting from him like a foul odor.

"Go away."

Varten stepped up to his side, solemn. "What did you do to mess things up with her?"

"*Me*? What makes you think it was me?"

"Because I know you, and I know how you are. You never say two words when you could say one, and you and Ani were always at each other's throats. It doesn't take a genius to see that two people as stubborn as you all might trip over your own feet."

Roshon vibrated with the tension that had been running

through him all evening. He did not want to release the lid on all his frustration, venting it onto his brother, who was only trying to help. So he slumped down to the ground, leaning his back against the wall. Varten slid next to him and produced a silver flask from his pocket.

"Where'd you get that from?"

"One of the sycophants."

Roshon snorted. The aristocratic set that had taken to following the "princes" around loved nothing more than giving compliments and gifts . . . except maybe receiving them. And gossiping about one another. Or trading insults. Their birthday wasn't for another month, meaning they couldn't purchase alcohol until then, but they hardly needed to buy anything anymore.

Varten took a swig then passed the flask to his brother. The smooth, heady liquid lit his throat afire for long seconds before resolving into a tingling warmth that quickly spread through his limbs.

"What is this?"

"No idea." Varten took the flask back for another drink. "So what are you going to do now?"

Roshon blew out a breath. "What can I do? She's the captain of her own ship. She needs to be on the seas. That's who she is."

"And who are you?"

"I thought you said you knew me?"

Varten nudged his shoulder a little too hard. "Yeah, I do. And I know what you're too stubborn or afraid to see."

"Which is?"

"We've been back what, two and a half weeks? And Ani is here. She dropped everything and came to Rosira immediately after she got her brother's message. Why do you think she did that?"

"She came back before she knew how much I changed." At

his brother's blank look, he shook his head. "She has options now. What happened back then was . . . an emergency. Our engagement was to get her out of a bad situation. I'm sure she came back, took one look at me, and realized she could do better." He snatched the flask back and took another, longer swig, relishing in the way it made the simmering heat within him cool a bit.

"I think you mean she took one look at you and never took her eyes off you." Laughter filtered through Varten's voice, but his expression was grim. "You just weren't paying attention."

"I'm the only one she knows here," Roshon grumbled and kept drinking.

After they'd finished the flask, Varten went off to bed, and Roshon found himself wandering the halls of the palace on wobbly legs. He wasn't sure exactly where he was—he and Varten had been exploring the palace for weeks, but it was so big and twisty and turny. He'd lost his jacket somewhere. He went to loosen the tie constricting his throat, only to find that it was already gone.

Heat radiated from his body; he needed to cool off. He found a door leading to an interior courtyard with rows of balconies ringing above it. A rock garden decorated the center with frothy bushes planted along the perimeter and ivy laden trellises climbing up the walls. Moonlight filtered down, making the space feel otherworldly.

Belatedly he noticed a figure standing on a balcony one story above him, an apparition in a sleeveless shirt and trousers. She looked a lot like Ani, with the pale moonlight making her blue hair glow. Through bleary eyes he had to admit that he'd never seen a more beautiful girl. None of the rich debutantes fawning over him could compare to the young woman he still, desperately, wanted to marry, but wouldn't get to now.

She was in profile, and something on her face glittered like a jewel. There must be diamonds on her skin—leave it to Ani to do something like that. But when she swiped at her cheek and they disappeared, he realized he was wrong.

Was she crying? That wasn't right. His eyes were a little clouded, his mind fuzzy, but he couldn't just let Ani cry. She was fierce and strong and a little scary. Of course, she was also soft and caring and smelled like dreams and home. He was going to find out what had made her cry and then stop it. That was a good plan.

He stumbled once or twice on the gravel as he approached the balcony but managed to stay upright. The trellis attached to the palace's smooth walls looked sturdy enough. Roshon was a good climber; this should be easy.

He grabbed hold of the wooden planks, which creaked as their moorings strained. A bright light spilled over the side of the balcony, shining into his eyes.

"Hey!" he cried out, shading them. "Watch where you point that."

"Roshon?" Ani sounded surprised. She moved the flashlight's beam away. "I thought you were a robber."

Did someone rob her? Is that why she was upset? He pulled at the trellis again and started to climb, determined to root out the scoundrel.

"What are you doing?"

"You're crying," he said, focused on his task. Placing one hand over the other wasn't quite as straightforward as it should have been—he was almost certain his feet were finding footholds, but progress was slow. His head spun violently, and he paused to let it settle before continuing.

"I don't think you can climb that," she said, alarm in her voice.

"S'okay, I'm a good climber. I used to pick the apples from the highest branches." His legs were bent, and he realized he only needed to straighten them, and he would be able to reach the balcony. He smiled in victory. Though the stone railing was further away than he'd thought. It was a short jump—he just needed to wait for the dizziness to subside before he attempted it.

Ani was there, leaning over, peering at him, her brows lowered. He swayed toward her, and she held her arm out. One was shorter than the other, but the reason why didn't quite penetrate his murky thoughts.

He released his hold on the trellis and leapt. Except the stone balcony shifted just out of reach. Was that magic at work? Maybe someone was playing a prank on him. Varten probably, but he didn't have any magic. Roshon was in midair for a long moment, staring into Ani's pretty, dark eyes as they grew horrified and then the flew away.

Someone screamed as he fell and then he was on his back, staring up at the moon, while itchy branches and leaves irritated his head. Ani threw her legs over the railing and jumped down to land like a cat beside him.

"Neat trick," he said, trying to sit up.

"You idiot!" she cried. "Are you broken?"

"I don't think so," he moaned and gave up on lifting his torso, instead rolling over and getting a face-full of bush. A strong hand pulled at his arm and partially dragged him away. Then he was lying on the ground, gravel biting into his back, staring up at Ani as she frowned down at him.

"What were you trying to do?" she asked.

"Stop you from crying."

"Are you drunk?"

"No." Again, he tried to sit up, but the world swam, and he decided that laying down might just be the thing to do. "I barely had any, Varten was hogging the flask."

Ani sighed deeply and sat cross-legged next to him. "You

can't go around climbing trellises whilst drunk and expect to keep all your faculties."

"I don't have any faculties." A deep melancholy washed over him. "I don't have anything, really. Not really a prince. The farm is forever away, and Papa doesn't want to go back there, anyway. We're all here together, and I've never been to a city before. Never thought I'd get to see Rosira. My sister's the queen, did you know that? And she's busy, but she makes time for us. She's so strong." He was babbling but he couldn't find the off switch to his mouth. "You're so strong. You'd like her, do you like her? Do you still like me? I think I *am* broken. I think they broke me there. In that cell."

Finally, his mouth stopped. Tears streaked Ani's cheeks. He hadn't stopped her from crying at all. In fact, she seemed to be crying more now than before.

He reached up to stroke her cheek and was awed by the feeling of her skin. "Your cheek is velvet. And something else . . ." He couldn't think of the word.

She cracked a watery smile. "We should get you drunk more often."

"I'm not drunk. You're perfect. You should go and do your job and be a great captain and not be saddled with me. Broken."

His hand dropped. He closed his eyes against the brightness of the moon on her skin. Luminous. That was the word he was looking for.

She sniffed. "I should have thought more about what being back here would mean to you. Of what you've been through. Your family. Seeing your sister again after all this time. Of course you don't want to leave right away. I understand."

Something was stroking his hair, massaging his scalp, and he didn't want it to ever stop.

"I don't want to stay forever," he said. "I know you're important and have things you want to do. I don't want to hold you back from that. Never." His eyes were still closed, and his tongue felt heavy. He wasn't sure if the words were coming out right, but the hand stroking his head continued.

"Sleepy," he mumbled as his body began to shut down.

"It's okay. You can sleep. I'm not going anywhere."

# CHAPTER FIVE

Dawn found Ani back on the balcony of the guest suite, absently twirling her knife across her knuckles. A palace worker in a pressed suit had found her and Roshon in the courtyard in the wee hours and had been scandalized by the prince's state of dishevelment. The man had hustled the barely awake young royal off to his chambers, leaving Ani to return to her rooms. But sleep avoided her just as it had all night.

Her patience lasted until the scent of fried meats wafted over from the breakfast tray of some nearby room. Taking that as her cue that the palace was sufficiently awake, she headed out. When a passing servant refused to tell her where the princes' apartments were, she channeled the authoritative posture of her mother and glared at him.

"W-wait here, miss," the man said, quivering under the strength of her stare.

She preened at her terrifyingness until the servant returned with a kind-looking, gray-haired man in tow. "Hello Miss Ani, I'm Usher, the royal valet. I'll lead you to the princes."

"Thank you, Usher."

The effort it took to be imperious was draining after such an emotional day and night. She followed the valet soundlessly through the snaking halls of the palace until they arrived at a gilded door.

Usher bowed and then left with a warm smile. It took Ani several minutes before she was ready to knock. Disappointment stroked her senses when Varten opened the door, red-eyed and rumpled, looking hungover.

"How is he?" she asked, tapping her foot.

"He's in the bath." Varten stepped aside to let her in. His hair was wet, like he'd just emerged from there as well.

"Is it okay if I wait for him?"

"Of course." He led her to the sitting room, which was double the size of the one in her own excessively large suite.

The twins' balcony looked over a wide lawn which ended with a view of the city and the ocean beyond. Her beloved ocean. It would wait for her, even if the prospective job would not.

"Are you nervous?" Varten asked, sitting in the chair next to her.

"Hmm? Why?"

"Because you're fidgeting."

She looked down to find her feet practically dancing a jig and then noticed she'd forgotten to attach her prosthetic. She often went without it on the ship unless she needed an extra limb to repair something or adjust some of the more finicky instrumentation. But people tended to react to the stump of her arm with disgust. Especially those who hadn't seen it before.

Varten was looking at her oddly, not at her arm but her face, his head tilted. She couldn't quite read his expression. It was one she hadn't seen on his brother either.

She was about to ask him what he was thinking when Roshon came out, stumbling to a halt at the entrance to the bathroom. He wore only a pair of loose-fitting pajama pants and no shirt. Water droplets still covered the surface of his chest.

Her mouth went dry.

"Well, I'm off to the kitchens to see about breakfast," Varten announced, hopping from his seat and swiftly vacating the room. Ani barely noticed him leave.

"Hi," she said, standing to face Roshon.

"Hi," he said, still in the doorway.

"So we should probably talk, right?"

"Of course, let me . . . I'll go get dressed."

Her lips quirked. "I mean, don't feel like you have to dress for *me*." Her face heated, and she looked away to hide her smile.

When she turned to face him again, Roshon was completely red from his face to his neck and down his firm chest. She wasn't sure what had happened during his time in captivity—she'd imagined starvation and torture, but he still looked strong and capable. A pang of longing hit her so hard it almost took her breath away.

She sat on the couch, hard, and blinked up at him. He seemed unsure of whether to go or not, so she patted the cushion next to her. Roshon slowly approached and sat, a little too far away for her liking. She slid closer until they were thigh to thigh. He was on her right side, and she froze as he looked at the stub of her arm.

"Did it hurt very much?" His voice was soft.

She looked down and shrugged. "I was unconscious for a long time. After that, not so much. It aches though sometimes still. A phantom pain that I've heard never quite goes away. But it's not so bad." She forced a smile.

"I don't imagine anything like that would ever stop you, Ani."

Her heart warmed and expanded at least one size.

"Can I . . . I mean do you mind if I . . . ?" His fingers hovered over her arm. She nodded, then shivered as his fingertips stroked down from the crease of her elbow to the rounded end the surgeons had created.

"The magic sliced it clean," she whispered. "It had to be reshaped so I could wear a prosthetic." Her golden-bronze skin contrasted with his paler hand, though the freckles dotting every inch of him were nearly her shade.

He skimmed across the scar tissue there, its sensation just a dull echo, and then stroked up her arm. When he reached her shoulder, she tilted her head, giving him more access. Then he skated across her collarbones and slid up her neck to finally bury his hand in her hair.

Bursts of pleasure ricocheted from the path his fingers had taken, pinging across her body and through it. She squeezed her legs together, conscious of the ball of need growing there, the heat and desire that was slowly being unleashed.

Her eyes closed involuntarily, but she felt his breath fanning her cheeks, hovering over her lips. She moved forward, as if pulled by an invisible tether, until their lips touched. His breath was minty like tooth powder as his soft lips pressed down on hers. She moaned, opening her mouth to taste him, remembering their only other kiss. It had fueled her dreams and imagination these past years. She'd often wondered if she had made more of it in her mind because of the distance and the loneliness, but no, this kiss was equally earth shattering. Her memory had not lied.

Her world fractured into pieces all over again as their kiss deepened. The beating of her heart was the propeller of a motor, spinning up faster and faster. Her thighs burned, wanting to wrap around him. Her skin was searing hot and hungry for his touch.

She grabbed at him, squeezing the back of his neck to pull him closer to her. How much closer could he get? It wasn't enough. She pulled, tightening her grip until he shifted, and then somehow she was on top of him. Straddling his legs and pressing every part of hers that could reach against every part of him.

She pulled away to caress the planes of his chest, admiring the taut skin, the dips and curves of his pecs and abs. Squeezing her legs against his, she rolled her pelvis, gasping as she came into alignment with his hardness. His lips moved to her jaw, her ear, her neck. He stole her ability to think and breathe, leaving only one sense functioning properly.

When she tugged at his hair, he leaned back. They both struggled for breath, chests heaving, lips kiss-swollen. His eyes sparked with fire and she was consumed. In their depths, she was awestruck. Something almost mythical lurked there.

It brought to mind stars at night on the ocean, how they stretched from horizon to horizon and were like a totally different creation than when watching them on land. She was lost in them until he dove back to her, a starving man attacking his meal. She tilted her head as he devoured her neck, closing her eyes again as stars burst behind her lids.

Roshon was everywhere, surrounding her, engulfing her. They rocked together through layers of fabric, but she felt every pulse as if nothing separated them. The heat within her grew and she chased sensation. Clinging to it, unwilling for it to pass through her fingers.

Vaguely, she heard a door open somewhere in the suite. She pressed herself against Roshon once more, vibrating from the building fury within, then froze, momentarily paralyzed as an explosion of pleasure washed out her senses. She gasped into his hair, shuddering with the aftershocks as his arms tightened around her, holding her in place. If not for them she might have fallen. Slid right off his legs and onto the floor and then below.

Down through the marble and wood and rock, all the way to the core of the earth.

Her eyes were squeezed shut, and she marveled at her own body. How could it produce such sensations? Especially fully clothed? And how soon could she do that again?

Suddenly Roshon stiffened. She shifted to regard his expression and then turned slowly to look over her shoulder.

Roshon's voice was strained. "Papa, you remember Ani."

Dansig ol-Sarifor raised his brows and smiled. "Of course."

Ani gave a little wave and then buried her face in Roshon's shoulder, embarrassment, almost, but not quite, dampening her delight.

# CHAPTER SIX

Roshon headed to the docks for the second time in two days, but this time the nervous energy bubbling within wasn't from the anticipation of seeing Ani again, because she was by his side. They strode hand in hand through the crowded port, Ani thrumming with the energy that always beat a rhythm beneath her skin. This afternoon he found it infectious. He was almost giddy, a thought which made him stumble. Giddy was not a feeling he could ever recall having before.

But as they crossed the cobblestones, his skin was a balloon filled with hope, and his feet barely touched the ground. They arrived at the jetty where the *Rapskala* was anchored to find Ena on the deck. She waved as they approached, then called over her shoulder and the other crew member, Leo, appeared. The Raunian man eyed them warily as they climbed the ramp, but even that couldn't dim Roshon's shine.

Ani squeezed his hand, beaming like the sun. "She's a class C hydrofoil, and I bought her on captain's credit, though I've almost paid it off." She tugged him forward to give him a tour of the ship, proudly listing its various qualities, both good and bad.

"The roll tanks were updated before I got her," she said glee-fully, "so even though it's smaller than the *Hekili*, you'll find the pitch and roll far less noticeable."

"She's a beauty Ani, she really is." Admiration for both Ani and her accomplishments filled him.

She stopped, looking up at him, a slow smile spreading across her face. "You mean it?"

"Of course, I do. I—" He looked around, noting the little touches that he suspected she was responsible for. "I think this will be a great place to live."

She turned away quickly before he could get a beat on her expression. "I've got something else to show you."

He followed her through the narrow halls, only letting go of his hand to climb the ladder between levels until they arrived at the bridge. Through the wide glass window, Portside spread out before them. Behind the instrument panel were the captain's and co-captain's chairs, and behind those two more seats. The one directly behind the captain's chair looked to have been refurbished—it didn't hold the creases that the others did, and the material looked new. Had she done that for him?

Footsteps sounded behind him. Roshon spun around to face Ena and Leo, who carried a round tube in his hands.

"Captain," he said, handing it over to Ani. She squeezed the tube between her arm and her body, unscrewed the cap, and pulled a rolled paper from before tossing the empty tube onto a chair. With a flick of her wrist, a scroll unfurled, revealing tight Raunian text.

"What is that?" Roshon asked.

"It's our contract—our betrothal agreement." She pointed with her hooks—an amazing contraption that Roshon was fascinated by—to the bottom. "By Myr's grace, I got my mother to sign it after I got my captain's mark. She was dead set against it, but finally relented after a bit of negotiation."

Ena sniffed and Leo coughed suddenly, both holding back laughter. There was a story there, Roshon sensed.

"Anyway," Ani continued, shooting a quelling look at her crew. "When you're ready to sign, it will be here. I just wanted you to see it. And of course, signing doesn't mean we have to get married today or next week or next month. We can take as long as we want. There isn't a rush."

She began the laborious process of rolling it up again one-handed. Neither of her crew members offered to help, and Roshon knew that Ani would ask for assistance if she needed it.

His breath caught.

She *would* ask for help if she needed. She wasn't filled with false pride—her bravado came from confidence and skill. If she changed her mind or had second thoughts, she was very much able to articulate them and act on them. Ani wouldn't let herself be saddled with an incompetent, useless husband who would only hold her back. She'd never let herself be held back from anything she really wanted to do.

The scroll slowly disappeared back into its roll, but he placed a hand on her arm to stop her. She looked up, a question in her gaze.

"Do you have a pen?"

She froze. Blinked. Sucked in a ragged breath.

Leo produced a pen from somewhere on his person and held it out. When Roshon turned to grab it, the man looked at him and nodded, then stepped back. Ena smiled, and it seemed to fill the room. It was infectious, and Roshon felt it catch hold within him as he gently removed the scroll from Ani's grip.

He shook it out once more and pressed it up against the wall to add his looping signature to it. Then he handed the pen to Ani and held the scroll while she carefully applied her name. Her writing was jagged, but still impressive given the use of her nondominant hand.

Something bubbled inside his chest, spreading through him, and shooting to his head, making him a little dizzy. That balloon feeling was back, like his body was filled with helium gas and he might shoot up into the clouds if someone didn't hold him down.

He held his marriage contract in one hand and turned to the woman he wanted to spend the rest of his life with. This ship or one like it would be his home.

The joy building within him lifted him until he felt he really was floating. His body felt distant, somehow detached. He smiled, and the action was both unfamiliar and a deep relief.

Ani's eyes widened again, growing rounder and rounder. An answering smile crept onto her face.

"There it is," she whispered.

"What?" he asked, laughing.

"My vision."

He didn't get the chance to ask anything else because she launched herself into his arms. She attached herself to him like a monkey, peppering his face with kisses and laughter and love. He held on tight to his future wife, knowing he'd never let go.

Roshon, Ani & Varten return in *Requiem of Silence (Earthsinger Chronicles, Book 4)*.

# ECHOES OF ASH & TEARS

## EARTHSINGER NOVELLAS, BOOK 3

**This novella is intended to be read after *Cry of Metal & Bone*.**

Brought to live among the Cavefolk as an infant, Mooriah has long sought to secure her place in the clan and lose her outsider status. She's a powerful blood mage, and when the chieftain's son asks for help securing the safety of the clan, she agrees. But though she's long been drawn to the warrior, any relationship between the two is forbidden. The arrival of a mysterious stranger with a tempting offer tests her loyalties, and when betrayal looms, will Mooriah's secrets and hidden power put the future she's dreamed of—and her adopted home—in jeopardy?

# CHAPTER ONE

Shield of Strength: To harden the body and mind against attack from within or without.

Add equal parts ground bitterleaf, blue ginger, and silent barbshell. Also have the ingredients for the Cleansing of Scales on hand in case a bony shell appears on the recipient's skin.

— WISDOM OF THE FOLK

With a steady drumbeat pumping in his veins, Ember wiped the sweat from his brow and regarded his opponent. The man across from him in the brawling circle, Divot, breathed heavily, but no other evidence of strain tensed his broad features. Ceremonial paint ran in rivulets down his neck and chest mixed with his sweat, but his eyes were bright. His waistcloth, however, was no longer pristine, but dingy with dirt. Evidence of the fierceness of the match so far. Ember grinned. This would be a good bout.

The two challengers circled one another, stepping lightly. The glow of firerocks illuminated the large cave, nearly all the way to its high ceiling and the tiny circle of daylight barely visible above. They were deep in the interior of the Mountain Mother, on neutral territory belonging to no clan. Whispers rising from the surrounding crowd reminded Ember of their presence, but he pushed the observers from his mind. He needed to stay focused to win this match—the blade of his father's intense scrutiny threatened to pierce his skin. Not only was his own honor on the line, but that of the Night Snow clan as well.

Ember and Divot were well matched as warriors. And though the other man had a few knots of height on him and was a bit broader about the chest and shoulders, Ember had been training nearly since birth. If not formally, then informally as a result of his brother's constant attempts to best him.

He rushed the larger man, grabbing him around the waist and sweeping his legs from underneath him, using well-prac-ticed technique to bring him to the ground. Grappling elimi-nated Divot's height advantage and longer arm-reach. The men wrestled, Ember trying to get his opponent into a submission hold, but Divot evaded and executed an impressive reversal, throwing Ember on his back. While Divot applied his weight to Ember's bent knee, attempting to press him further into the ground and pin him, Ember's other leg was free for a sweeping kick to the head. It knocked Divot back to allow Ember to escape the hold.

He jumped to his feet while Divot rose slowly. When the man faced him, a shiver of revulsion rippled through Ember. The kick had split Divot's lip; he spat blood onto the sand underfoot.

Ember's stomach roiled. He'd eaten no breakfast that morn-ing, for this reason. Shame brought the noise of the crowd rushing to his ears. The scent of sweat and blood and dirt assaulted him, shattering his concentration. With the aid of a lifetime of practice, he clamped down an unforgiving manacle on his body's reactions and his emotions.

A Cavefolk could not hate the sight of blood. It was absurd.

He steeled himself, not looking at the man's red-tinged smile, instead staring aggressively into his eyes before ramming his shoulder into Divot's chest. Soon they were caught in a clinch, arms locked together as they directed knee and elbow strikes. This close, the coppery scent of blood filled Ember's nostrils. It tickled his gag reflex and caused his gorge to rise. All involuntary reactions he had long ago learned to smother with ruthless desperation. But wrangling his body under control distracted him for a fraction of an eye-blink. Long enough to fall victim to a knee directed at his ribs. The breath flew from Ember's body. Divot took him to the ground hard, their momentum moving them right out of the sparring circle and into the spectators.

Cries of feminine shock and pain rang out. Hands pushed at him, and Ember rose to his feet. A chime sounded, indicating the end of the first round. Divot had recovered quickly and now stood in the circle, wearing a smug, ruby grin. Ember glared, his pulse racing in his ears, as the man laughed. Pushing him into the spectators was a sign of disrespect. He turned to see what damage had been wrought.

Several women were righting themselves, brushing dirt from their waistcloths, but one was still sprawled on the ground. She had taken the brunt of the force of him crashing into her and was a petite creature, with hair like midnight cascading down her back, loosed from the tight braid in which she usually kept it. If her skin tone hadn't identified her, the hair would have—clan women kept their heads shaved, preferring instead to decorate their bare scalps with paint as a sign of beauty. The hair of the unclanned was kept long, never cut until their initiation.

"My apologies, Mooriah," he said gravely. He bowed deeply and held out a hand to her.

"It is nothing. I am unharmed." Her voice was like the gentle rhythm of a drum. It soothed whatever remained of his disquiet. She blinked up at him then extended her hand in return. He held his breath.

His calloused hand enveloped her soft skin. He gripped her gently, swallowing down the fireflies that had taken flight within him. Her weight was light, and she was back on her feet in no time. She blinked rapidly, staring at their joined hands for a moment before slipping out of his grasp.

Though he had known her all his life, never before had he touched her skin. Its rich shade was a deep contrast to his—to all of the Folk, who shared similar features. But she had been born Outside, the daughter of sorcerers, and brought to the live in the caves as a baby. The two of them did not run in the same circles, and since she was as yet unclanned, their interaction was prohibited.

She caught sight of something behind him and scowled. He turned to find Divot leering at them from his position across the circle.

"Ember," Mooriah whispered. He spun back to face her. "Show that beast what the Night Snow clan is made of." She flashed him a smile that hit him harder than any fist ever had. He nearly stumbled backward but managed to nod.

He had enough time to towel off and rinse his mouth with water before the break between rounds was over. Then he cracked his neck and fingers, trying to concentrate on his opponent and ignore the scent of cinderberry that had clung to her skin. He flushed, willing away the feeling of fluttering wings the interaction with Mooriah had left inside him and reached for his focus.

The chime rang, and the fighters circled one another. "Your discourtesy to women shows what manner of vermin you and Iron Water are," Ember taunted.

Divot shrugged. "What courtesy do the low-ranked and unclanned deserve? Unlike Night Snow, we do not offer clan membership to Outsiders."

"And your clan's inferiority is well known throughout the mountain." He lowered his head and charged.

Ember did not generally use anger to fuel him as his brother and father did. Though his temper was not a vicious fire like theirs, it still scared him sometimes. But he did use it to focus himself, to home in on his opponent's weaknesses and exploit them.

Divot was a skilled fighter indeed, but Ember had much more to lose than just a bout. Expectation and the future of the clan were bound up in what was, on the surface, a simple game. He could not afford a loss today, and with Mooriah's whispered words spurring him on, he fought with renewed vigor and drive. He was fully in the zone, blind to the rest of the world, and emerged minutes later to the ringing of the final gong.

Cheers went up, and the official stepped forward to drape him with ribbons and declare him the victor. The shaman of Night Snow, an ancient man called Oval, stood next to the chieftain of the clan, Ember's father Crimson, both looking just as morose as always, as though the match had ended in defeat.

Crimson's voice rose to echo against the cave walls. "Once again, Night Snow shows its superiority. Let all the clans be on alert, we will take on all challengers and prove to them that we cannot be bested!"

Cheers from Night Snow were joined by grumbles and jeers from the other clans gathered. Divot stood with the Iron Water chieftain, head lowered, no doubt being chastised for losing the match. Ember felt a twinge of sympathy for him. With the First Frost Festival coming up in just a week, this match was the pre-qualifier for the largest competition of the year for each clan.

Tensions between Night Snow and Iron Water, the two largest clans, were high and these nonlethal games were meant to diffuse it, though Ember wasn't certain it was working. He'd certainly rather show his proficiency in the circle than have their people embroiled in a deadly war. He could only hope that his performance, and the opportunity these games gave for the chieftains to work out their differences, would be the key to peace.

As Crimson and Oval left the center of the circle, his father motioned for him to follow. Ember shot a glance at the section of the audience he'd fallen into but couldn't glimpse Mooriah through the crowd.

Once ensconced in the side cavern that Crimson had at his disposal, his father whirled on him. "Your victory was solid, but how in the Mother's name did he manage to roll you out of bounds? You lost your focus, and it could have cost you the match! Do not let it happen again."

"Of course not, Father." Ember dropped his head. The scent of blood still lingered in his nose, and he waged a constant battle to ignore it.

The echo of heavy footsteps entered the small cavern. That particular stomp could only belong to one person. "Well done, brother," Rumble said, insincerity dripping from his voice. "It looks like it will be you and me facing one another in the festival."

Ember met his brother's cool gaze. Eyes of pale gold regarded him with barely concealed hatred. They were the same age, born in the same month to two different mothers. As the son of the Lady of the Clan, Crimson's first wife, by tradition

Ember should have been the heir, but Rumble's mother effectively lobbied for consideration for her son. Had Ember's mother been alive, she might have objected, but as it was, Crimson had kept the two in competition all their lives, holding the promise of heir to the chieftain's seat over them.

"I look forward to besting you in battle," Ember said.

Rumble raised a brow. "I do as well."

Crimson grunted. "Come, we have matters requiring our attention. Try not embarrass me or the clan." Rumble smirked before following their father out.

Ember grit his teeth. A match against his brother was what he'd expected, and victory would offer more than just bragging rights. Both men suspected that this, their twenty-fifth year, would be the year Crimson made his choice between them.

Ember needed to win, not for his own sake, but for the sake of the clan. The Mother only knew what horrors a chieftain such as his brother would bring down upon them.

# CHAPTER TWO

Sanctification of Amity: To ensure a good rapport between rivals.

Combine generous pinches of star root and funeral bane along with a dram of natalus ichor. Do not inhale the fumes. In the case of reluctant participants, sprinkle ash of mercy.

— WISDOM OF THE FOLK

Mooriah only got a glimpse of Ember through the throngs of people after the match concluded. She still couldn't believe that the chieftain's son had helped her up after he'd crashed into her. It had taken quite a while to slow the beating of her heart, only to have it start racing again—this time with annoyance—when Glister's grating voice sounded behind her.

"Oval has summoned us."

Composing her face into a brittle smile, Mooriah turned to face the other young woman. "Of course," she said through gritted teeth. "I'll be right there." Glister narrowed her eyes, then turned on her heel and left. With a last, longing look at the circle but no further sight of the victorious warrior, Mooriah grabbed her satchel and followed.

They wended their way through the crowds to find the Night Snow shaman waiting at the entrance to a narrow tunnel. He was an ancient man, his skin leeched of all hue in the way of elderly Cavefolk, the effects of many generations spent inside the Mother Mountain with little access to the rays of the sun. Not just pale, like the younger Folk, but edging toward translucent, the bluish-green veins already easily visible all over.

Oval stood with Murmur, the clan prophet. Murmur was younger, still an elder, but his often dreamy gaze, which saw so much, gave him a more cheerful manner. Oval called his two apprentices over, and Mooriah and Glister hurried to the men's side and away from the crush of bodies.

"I hope you both enjoyed the festivities. To close out these events, and as a show of good faith between clans, we will join with Iron Water in the Sanctification of Amity." Oval's voice was low and creaked with advanced age. "We will seek the blessing of the Breath Father for continued peace between us and mutual advancement."

Anticipation grew within Mooriah at the pronouncement. For the past three years, she had worked diligently as apprentice shaman, studying hard and completing the duties she'd been tasked without complaint. At the end of her training, if she were promoted to assistant, then her place in Night Snow would be assured. She would no longer be unclanned, an Outsider, and though she would still be recognizably different in appearance, the slights and snubs that came with her current status would plague her no more. This chance to seal the peace with their old adversary was another opportunity to prove herself.

The elders led the way through the narrow tunnels to the

location where they would complete the ritual. Firerocks embedded in the walls lit the way, shining with the bright blue cast shared by the glow worms living in the innermost caves.

She was surprised when the path led them to the Origin, the holiest place for the Folk. It was neutral ground, though not a place where ceremonies were generally done. However, they did not enter the sacred cavern, but stopped just outside of it in a chamber where a large, flat altar rock lay, its height reaching her knees. It was oblong and of a size to fit a dozen people seated around it.

Footsteps sounded from one of the other entrances to the chamber, and the Iron Water contingent appeared. Their shaman was a younger man, perhaps only in his thirties. His chest, bare like all men's, was decorated in the black painted markings of his clan, his head bald and gleaming. Two male apprentices followed him, looking to be in their early twenties —of an age with Mooriah and Glister. The shaman bowed at Oval, who returned the gesture.

Beyond that no one moved, but Mooriah knew enough not to question it. Her apprenticeship had been composed of much waiting, listening, and figuring things out on her own. Murmur was helpful in private, away from Oval's piercing intensity, but the elder shaman's style of instruction consisted mostly of allowing his apprentices to shadow him, observe, and work things out for themselves.

Now, they waited in silence. Several minutes later, the Iron Water clan chief arrived with his daughter. Moments afterward, Crimson stepped into the chamber, followed by Ember and Rumble.

Many of the rituals required a chieftain's presence, though only the most sacred required that of his or her blood kin. In the years of her apprenticeship, she had never witnessed one. She called to mind the steps and requirements for the Sanctification of Amity. It was, indeed, strengthened by the blood of the chieftain's descendants.

As the eldest present, Oval began the proceedings. He led them in a prayer to the Mountain Mother and the Breath Father. All lifted their heads to the sky in reverence as he spoke.

"Hallowed Mother and Divine Father, givers of blood and life. We come to you in humility, grateful for all you have bestowed. Cleanse our spirits and anoint us with your care. Sustain us with your power and absolve us with your shadow and your light. Hear the pleas of your servants and accept our honor and praise. We revere you with the blood of our bodies, *umlah*."

After a few moments of silence to allow the words to penetrate the air and rock, Oval turned to his apprentices. "Let us begin the ritual. I will require the activating agents for the invocation."

Mooriah swallowed, running through the list in her mind. Funeral bane, star root, ash of mercy, natalus ichor. She reached into the hessian satchel strapped around her, which she carried for this very purpose. Glister did the same, though her bag was made of fine lizard skin from one of the master crafters. They raced one another to provide the necessary ingredients enclosed in tiny vials and leather packets.

A stricken look crossed Glister's face. She'd hurriedly produced everything but the natalus ichor, a foul-smelling substance that was difficult to procure. Obtaining the materials necessary for the spells and rituals was another of the apprentices' duties. Mooriah had spent three sleepless nights tracking a colony of bats and didn't want to dwell on what it had taken to retrieve this particular animal secretion now stored in the tiny vial she retrieved from her bag.

She set it on the altar next to the others. Murmur winked at her. Glister's stormy expression was its own reward.

Mooriah couldn't imagine the girl going to the same lengths to acquire such a substance. Oval merely nodded, not letting on whether he'd noticed which apprentice had contributed which item.

The Iron Water shaman spoke up, his tone thin and high-pitched. "Since we are all gathered, I humbly request we also complete the Binding of the Wretched."

Murmur frowned. "That is quite an arcane rite. I cannot recall it having been done for generations."

The young shaman nodded. "It is my belief that it has been too long. In these trying times, it would be wise to revisit it. If you agree."

Mooriah scanned her memory for the ritual in question. She had studied everything, no matter how old or rarely used.

Glister hailed from a high-ranking family, well-connected with the clan elite. She was talented and ambitious and offered strong competition. But unlike the pretty and popular young woman, Mooriah had no family commitments, no social engagements, nothing but the drive that propelled her.

Glister's dejection was evident on her face. She had no idea what the binding entailed. When Oval nodded his agreement to include the ritual and looked to his apprentices expectantly, Glister swallowed nervously.

Mooriah quickly produced the powdered featherblade and bitterleaf packets from her satchel and placed them on the altar. Oval's hairless brows rose slightly, the only indication that he was impressed. Her heart thumped a stalwart rhythm. It wasn't proper to smile, but light wanted to pour from her.

Then she glimpsed Ember, standing just a few paces from her. He appeared troubled. The Binding of the Wretched was also strengthened with the blood of the chieftain's kin, specifically his heir. Since one had not yet been chosen for Night Snow, both Rumble's and Ember's would be used—though he probably had no knowledge of that. It was unlikely he spent much time studying obscure customs.

Murmur lit the censer of incense, and fragrant smoke soon filled the space. Oval freed the white bone knife from its sheath at his side. He also loosed the simple clay bowl which hung from its handle on a loop on the belt around his waistcloth. The bowl spanned two hand-widths and was unadorned with decoration or markings. It was said to have been made from the same red clay and water with which the Breath Father initially made his own physical form.

The Iron Water shaman looked upon it longingly. No other clan had such a treasure and Night Snow's possession of it had been the cause of more than one war over the generations. But now they were invoking peace. Hopefully lasting peace, though a glimpse of Crimson's and Rumble's faces was not encouraging. As Murmur expertly measured out the various ingredients into the bowl and intoned the opening words of the chant, the chieftain and his son appeared bored. Was this ceremony all for show?

Crimson's hot temper was legendary. Mooriah's youth had been marked with the protracted war he had led against two smaller clans. Eventually, those people had been absorbed into Night Snow. First as unclanned, which some still were, but others had been accepted and initiated.

Oval's voice rose and fell with Murmur's, vocalizing the various chants and obsecrations required. Then it was time to seal the ceremony with blood. The Iron Water shaman gripped his own bone knife in a long-fingered hand. Oval set the clay bowl before him on the altar and motioned for them all to kneel. On the Night Snow side, Murmur was to the right of the shaman, then Glister, Mooriah, Ember, Crimson, and Rumble.

Oval made a shallow cut into his palm and allowed his blood to drip into the clay bowl. He whispered the words of the blood magic spell to close his wound then passed the bowl and knife to Murmur, who repeated the practice as they all would.

Glister followed, then Mooriah. When she passed the bowl and knife to Ember, his hands shook slightly upon accepting, before his grip firmed. He hunched over the altar to make his cut and then passed everything on to his father.

Mooriah noticed that Ember didn't mutter the healing spell. But perhaps such a small cut on such a strong warrior was of little matter. Mages needed to preserve their blood, but fighters spilled it all the time.

Once the bowl had made its way around the altar and was once again with Oval, he spoke the words of completion—another spell, this one transformed the contents of the bowl. The mixture of ingredients congealed and hardened into a small, jewel-like stone the color of blood. It rose into the air, hovering above the altar for pregnant moments.

Oval and the other shamans chanted, their voices harmonizing and growing louder and louder. The red stone—a caldera, or holder of magic—shimmered with a glittering shine and then continued to rise far above them, out of sight of the firerocks lining the walls, to the roof of the chamber, invisible in the darkness overhead.

Mooriah sagged with relief. Though she had not been leading the ceremony, as one of the blood mages the spell pulled energy from her for its efficacy. For some reason, the others never seemed as affected by the magic as she did. She supposed, being an Outsider, she was just weaker—or it could be because of the other thing that made her different from the Folk. The reason that she had been sent to live with them in the first place.

Not wanting to dwell on that, she took a deep breath and pulled herself together. Fortunately, the Binding of the Wretched was a simpler undertaking. Similar, but with different chants and ingredients designed to protect those who had left the safety of the Mother and sought lives Outside. With each generation, the population of the Cavefolk became more and more depleted, the lure of the Outside increasingly enticing. It did not tempt Mooriah, for life Outside was notoriously dangerous.

Oval surprised her by calling her name.

"Yes, Exemplar?"

"Lead us in the binding."

Shock did not begin to describe her reaction. But she held it all inside and merely nodded her assent. "Certainly, Exemplar."

She cleared her throat and took the clay bowl that Glister passed her, not missing the fact that the other woman's hands vibrated with barely leashed anger.

Mooriah mixed pinches of the powders together and retrieved her own bone instrument for use in the ceremony. Unlike the sanctification, the binding required only a drop of blood from those gathered, taken from the fourth finger of the left hand, the one that, according to belief, held the artery which led to the heart. As all shamans were blood mages, they carried a variety of utensils for piercing the skin; Mooriah pulled out a sliver of bone as long as her index finger, its tip needle-sharp.

Chanting the words of the ceremony, she pricked her fourth finger and allowed just one drop of blood to fall into the clay bowl. She passed the bowl and needle to the left, back to Glister. As each person contributed their blood, their voice joined the chant. Soon a chorus had risen with power vibrating the air.

Last in the circle was Ember. He took the bowl and needle from his father, placed the bowl on the altar, and held his left hand over it. His hand was definitely shaking. So was the hand holding the pin.

He brought the sharp edge to the pad of his finger and paused. The shaking intensified. Around the circle the chants went on. Ember's face was rigid, his eyes wide. He was terrified.

She checked on the others, but most had their eyes closed and hadn't noticed.

Ember's gaze met hers. He blinked rapidly, looking paler than normal. She didn't understand what was happening. His hands went to his waistcloth and fumbled at his belt. A small bladder hung hidden there, too small to be a canteen. He opened the stopper and a splash of blood leaked onto his hand; he visibly flinched. Then his body hardened, each muscle practically turning to stone.

Did Ember carry blood with him so he would not have to pierce his flesh? Mooriah nearly lost the rhythm of the chant in her surprise.

Whatever his reasoning, that technique would not work. This old ritual was specific, only a drop must be used, and he would not be able to get such an amount onto the point of the pin, not without piercing the bladder and leaving blood streaming down his leg.

She forced her face to remain calm and realized that now attention was on him. The Iron Water assistants as well as their chief's daughter had their eyes open. This ritual could not be corrupted—it was Mooriah's chance to show Oval and the others her true worth. Her opportunity to advance and prove herself. Plus, she had no desire to show weakness in front of Iron Water.

She made the decision in a split second. Raising her voice, she began to practically shout the chant, startling several around the circle. Now the attention was on her instead of Ember. In the breath between repetitions, she invoked a blood spell to conceal her movements for the next few seconds. Even Oval would not be able to see what she did. Those watching would only see her as she'd been the moment she'd uttered the spell.

She grabbed Ember's hand, wiping the blood away and grabbing the pin. She pricked his finger and, ignoring his flinch, added a drop of his blood to the bowl. Then she took the bowl from him.

The brief concealment spell petered out, and she finished the ritual like nothing had happened. The new caldera rose into the air like the others, an offering to the Breath Father and Mountain Mother. Beside her, Ember looked dazed, but held his peace.

After a few minutes of forced pleasantries between clan chiefs, Iron Water retreated. Ember and his family left as well. Mooriah glimpsed him trying to catch her eye, but she studiously ignored him.

Once the others had left, Oval turned to her, face stony as ever. "A thorough, if enthusiastic performance, Mooriah."

She lowered her head. "Many of the old rituals mention that additional fervency in our pleas gratifies the Breath Father."

"Hmm," was his only utterance before he turned away with Glister on his heels. The other apprentice hadn't looked directly at Mooriah since Oval had made his choice.

Murmur eyed her strangely as she cleaned up, putting away her materials.

"Do you think I will get marked down for too much exuberance?" she whispered.

He considered Oval's retreating form. "You could have gotten through it faster and perhaps quieter, but given the Exemplar's penchant for a snail-like pace, I would not worry overmuch." He smiled kindly and patted her shoulder.

Her triumph was somewhat dimmed by the oddness with Ember, and she hoped that helping him had not hurt her chances of joining the clan.

# CHAPTER THREE

Charm of Entanglement: To confirm an agreement between non-rivals to work together for mutual benefit.

Mix sapphire basil and crushed mammoth bone until well blended. Phantom rosemary may be substituted if the basil is overly fragrant but be mindful of its tendency to cause hiccups.

— WISDOM OF THE FOLK

For two days, Ember searched the city for Mooriah. When he wasn't training or studying, he was finding reasons to be near the shaman's cave. He caught glimpses of the old man coming and going, but never the woman he sought. And he couldn't just ask one of the elders because they would doubtless want to know why he was looking for her, and he couldn't really lie to them. It was said that elder blood mages could suss out truth without even piercing your skin.

Having no idea where she lived, he wandered the crisscrossing paths which stretched across the open cavern of the city, hoping to run into her. Silly, since such a thing had never happened before.

There were so many levels and tunnels and honeycombed chambers within the Night Snow mountain home. Endless staircases and bridges led to dwellings and businesses tucked away in caverns cut out of the rock. Moriah was not in the farming grottos on the bottom level, where firerocks shined bright as the moon and stooped farmers tended their plots. She was not with the fishers in the streams which circumnavigated the city or with the tanners or the masons.

He entered the teeming marketplace, wincing at the cacophony of voices echoing on the stone. Vendors shouted from stalls sectioned off with colored rope. The scents of stews and skewered meat wafted over, but did not entice Ember, preoccupied as he was. He was despairing of ever finding her as he turned a corner and ran, nearly headfirst, into Glister.

"Ember," she said, smiling brilliantly. "You nearly mowed me down." Her shaved head was painted with delicate artistry in the clan colors of white and gold. The nightworm silk chestcloth and waistcloth she wore were more expensive than all his possessions combined. Her family cultivated the creatures and harvested the fiber and even the chieftain only had a few bits of clothing made of the valuable fabric.

"Forgive me." He bowed in apology. "I was not paying attention. I hope you are well."

"Better now." She stepped closer until they were nearly chest to chest. "Where are you going in such a hurry?"

"I'm looking for someone. Actually, it's Mooriah. Have you seen her?"

Her flirtatious grin turned into a scowl. "Why would you be looking for *her*?"

"Clan business," he said brusquely. She flinched, narrowing

her eyes. Ember wasn't certain what sort of clan business he could manufacture if she questioned him further, but fortunately, she did not.

"Well, I haven't any idea where she is. You could, of course, summon her."

She pulled out a pin from her pocket and pierced her finger before Ember could do anything to stop it. He doubled over in a fake coughing fit to hide his horrified reaction. What must it be like to shed your own blood with so little care?

Glister muttered a summoning spell. Ember vaguely heard her mentioning his name but was using every faculty he had to keep the contents of his stomach in place. During a match or a ritual, he was prepared for the sight of blood, but this took him completely by surprise. He straightened, still fake coughing, and a nearby vendor handed him a cup of herb water, which he accepted gratefully. After drinking down the cool, sweet liquid, he faced Glister again.

"She should be here in a few moments."

"Thank you."

"You're welcome. I'm always here for you, for anything you may need." Her fingers grazed his arm. He wasn't sure if she hadn't closed her wound, or just hadn't bothered to wipe off the blood, for a trace of it lingered on his skin.

Two of her friends, whom he recognized from their days in school, waited for her a few steps away. She sauntered toward them, looking back at him saucily, while his arm burned. Logic told him a trace of blood couldn't possibly sear his skin, but such was the nature of his affliction. It was not logical, and he could not control it. Neither could he control the shame it brought him.

He stared at his arm, unsure of what to do. Beside him, someone cleared their throat.

When he didn't respond, they did it again. "Ember? You required my presence?" Mooriah sounded annoyed.

He shook himself and wiped his forearm on his hip, transferring the stain to the side of his waistcloth. "Thank you for coming."

"I didn't have much of a choice. Your summoning spell made me feel an all over itch until I complied."

His gaze shot to her, surprise lifting his brows. "I'm sorry. It wasn't my spell. I ran into Glister and apparently made the mistake of telling her I was looking for you."

Mooriah snorted. "Well, that explains it. I'm not her favorite person."

"Is this one bothering you, sir?" the vendor asked, stepping out from his stall. His wares included boots and clothing made of some kind of animal hide, one of the small rodents that made the caves their home. Mooriah's eyes narrowed, and she took a step away from Ember.

"No, she's not. Thank you for your concern." He gazed around the nearby crowd to find many eyes upon them. "We should speak elsewhere," he said in a low voice. "Will you come with me?"

She sighed, looking resigned and not at all pleased about it. A weight settled upon his heart. On top of the burden of the peoples' attitudes regarding the unclanned, he was adding an additional load, something he hadn't considered.

He led her away from the market and onto a wide avenue. "Were you busy? I didn't even ask Glister to do the summoning. I definitely wouldn't have if I knew it would be so forceful."

"Not busy, not really. Just studying. Practicing. That's mostly all I do." Her voice was matter of fact, but the statement was sad. Ember could relate. Fight training, strategy, and history lessons took up almost all of his day. If he became chieftain, he wanted to be a better one than his father. And even if he didn't, he would become an advisor to Rumble—not that he expected his brother to take any of his advice.

They headed to one of the upper tiers of the city, crossing a series of angled bridges, which took them higher into the domain of the upper classes of the clan. However, some levels were entirely abandoned as more and more had left the mountain for the Outside.

One of Ember's suggestions to his father had been to consolidate living quarters so that everyone was closer together and more defensible. Crimson had taken umbrage to the suggestion, seeing little cause to live so near to those he felt were beneath him.

After a few minutes of silent walking, they arrived at an empty chamber, one he knew quite well as it had once belonged to his nanny. The woman had passed on to become one with the Mother, but he had never found more comfort than he had between these walls. He kept the place clean and stocked with food since he often came to clear his head or just to be alone. The chambers all around were also vacant, so there was little fear of being overheard or discovered.

He invited Mooriah to sit on the mat while he stoked a small fire in the pit. The upper caves were cooler, especially now that winter was upon them. Smoke disappeared into the vent in the ceiling once the fire caught hold.

"Can I offer you some tea? I have jerky."

"No, I'm fine. Thank you."

She was patient as he settled himself and ordered the words in his mind. "I wanted to thank you for your help the other day at the ceremony. I... I don't know what I would have done without it."

Mooriah swallowed. "Of course. It was the first time for you, and the ancient rituals are a bit unusual. I understand the nerves, I felt them too."

He smiled sadly, both touched and shamed by her kindness. "We both know it wasn't nerves. I... I have never been able to, that is..." He took a deep breath. "I hate the blood."

She tilted her head in surprise.

"I've never been able to stand the sight of it. It makes me queasy. And the idea of cutting myself on purpose." He shivered. "I can't bring myself to do it."

Mooriah frowned. He could practically see the wheels turning in her head. "But how?"

He shrugged. "The chieftain's son has servants. They do the spells, charge the firerocks, put protection wards on everything."

"But your own personal protection." She looked at him wide-eyed. "Against danger. Against the sorcerers. Against me." She spoke the last words in a hush.

From the time they reached adolescence, all the Folk set yearly wards on their person against magic and curses. Parents did so for their smaller children. The wards also protected against the natural magic so many of the Outsiders were born with.

"You know what I am, right? Why my father brought me to be raised here?" she asked.

"The Outsider sorcerers' magic is called Earthsong—it's fueled by life energy. Your magic is different, right? You control death."

She nodded, her expression grave. "My father is a powerful Earthsinger. Apparently, my mother was too. But I was born different. I can't turn a seed into a plant in an instant, I can't control the weather or heal with a thought, the way they do, but I can kill with one. It's only safe for me to live in Night Snow because of the wards in place to protect the Folk."

Ember firmed his lips. He had not been warded since he was a youth. His shoulders sagged under her scrutiny.

"Does no one know about your... problem?"

He shook his head. "What do you think my father would do? Or my brother?" He snorted. "I've hidden my affliction for my entire life. Mother knew, and she told me I would grow out of it. But I'm grown now, and it's still here. It's paralyzing—I've tried so many things to get over it. In battle or in a match, blood is often drawn. It bothers me, but I can hide my reaction to it. However, my body shuts down when I try to spill my own blood."

She leaned forward. "What if you become chief? How will you...?"

Their eyes met. So much of Cavefolk society and culture revolved around blood magic. While the shamans were true mages, all the Folk used the magic for a variety of everyday tasks: a snick here to call a child back home for dinner, a scratch there to ensure a fair price at the market. But the chief used the blood for more important tasks—rituals to protect the harvest, for the health of the people, for their security and welfare.

"I need your help, Mooriah. Everyone knows how skilled a blood mage you are. Glister got her apprenticeship through favors and family ties, but you earned yours—unheard of for the unclanned. You can teach me, find some way to help me get over this disability. If I succeed my father as chieftain, the future of the clan will be in my hands."

Mooriah ran her hands over her face. "Forgive me for saying this, but perhaps you should not be chief then, given this... issue."

He stood and began to pace. "Believe me, I've thought of that. But what do you think life under Rumble's leadership would be like? He is more bellicose than even Father. The only way for the Folk to survive is to eventually combine the clans.

Otherwise we will continue losing more and more each year to the Outside until we are too weak to go on. But all Crimson and Rumble are concerned with are war and supremacy. Our people have fought enough. Another war would decimate us. We need peace. We need to get the people on board with the idea of uniting the clans under one banner, in one city. Share resources and survive for as long as possible."

She sat back, staring up at him. He stopped his pacing and stood straighter under her perusal. "It is your desire to become clan?" he asked.

She nodded. "This is my home. For all its flaws, I love it here. I want to be shaman, and I want to be clan."

Her earnestness and straightforwardness were endearing. "And do I speak false?"

Her eyes were heavy. She shook her head. "We lose craftsmen and farmers year after year. And soldiers, too. Another war would be devastating. Uniting the Folk is sensible." She stood and crossed over to him. "Very well, I will try my best to help you overcome this difficulty. I suspect you will have to work very hard."

"I am no stranger to hard work," he replied gruffly.

"No, you are not. I am not certain that you will succeed, but I vow to try. For the sake of the clan."

"For Night Snow," he replied, thumping his chest.

Mooriah bowed respectfully. "We can start tomorrow after my studies. Would you like to meet here?"

"Yes. This place is safe from prying eyes."

Her eyes roamed him up and down, an assessing gaze so different from Glister's possessive one which had left him feeling like a slab of meat. Mooriah's held worry. For her or him, he wasn't sure. But he was drawn to her face over and over again. Her cheeks were round and her eyes slightly slanted. They were so dark, the color of shadows and mystery. He felt that he could disappear in their depths and never be found again.

She blinked and looked away. "All right. We will meet here tomorrow after the dinner hour."

"Thank you, Mooriah."

She shook her head. "Don't thank me yet."

# CHAPTER FOUR

Binding of the Wretched: A protection to those who have sought their fortunes beyond the reach of the Mountain Mother.

Half a handful each of featherblade and bitterleaf. When seeking to strengthen, add no more than a bead of the blood of the chieftain and his or her heir, else participants may be struck with a cold plague.

— WISDOM OF THE FOLK

Mooriah sat in the cave that had been assigned to her for practice, far away from the business of the city. It was not located on the upper levels, like Ember's hidden place, but in the depths, muggy and warm where no one would want to go. Here, none could unintentionally stumble upon her while she trained with her unique ability.

Though the Folk were warded against her, and she would

not be able to kill any of them accidentally, she could still cause harm. The power she wielded was mighty and required a tight rein. Which was why, when she wasn't attending to her apprentice duties or studying, she was here practicing. Learning the fine-tuned control she needed to keep the others safe.

Often Murmur helped her, for while the Cavefolk had no inborn magic, they had long ago mastered the magic of the blood. Nethersong was death and spirit combined, and as such, shared properties with blood. She'd often wondered if she'd taken to wielding blood magic so easily because of her Nethersong abilities. Death was the power Mooriah controlled, one she was born with and would die with, but was determined not to kill others with.

On the Outside, she would have been murdered at birth, even a baby Nethersinger was deadly. But her father had sought to spare her and so had brought her here, to be raised under the watchful eye of the shamans who could control her if needed, and the prophet who would guide her in how to use her birthright.

Her thoughts turned to Ember, to his unique problem. She did not know if one could ward another adult—children were easy and pliable, but someone of his mental strength would be difficult. There was a reason why adolescents had to learn how to protect themselves. She would have to research the matter when she was done here.

She released thoughts of the chieftain's son to focus on the task at hand. Allowing her gaze to go soft, she relaxed enough to accept the embrace of the Mother. Her sense of her own body left her, freeing her consciousness. Her power awakened inside her, and she found herself in the heart of the Mother—another plane of existence where she could practice her deadly skills without fear.

She stood in a dark place where she was lit from within. An

obstacle course of sorts manifested before her. Focusing her will and intention, she felt for the death energy all around. She sensed the decay from insects and organisms and life-forms too tiny to ever see—things that lived and died in the blink of an eye.

Her inner Song unfurled with a dancer's agility and grace. She controlled it tightly as it always seemed like it wanted to escape her grip, to fly free like a bird soaring overhead.

She stretched her senses through the mountain, seeking death energy farther and farther away. Her awareness traveled through the veins of stone. To the freshly dead bodies in the morgue—elders who'd passed on in their sleep, to the blood flowing from a butcher's kill.

Echoes resonated from the ancient blood of the Folk from generations past, ones who had performed the human sacrifices that were far rarer now. Blood had coated the walls to create protection spells from Outsiders—from people like Mooriah's parents. But she was of the Folk now. She knew nothing of Outside and had dedicated herself to the future of the clan. She would be one of them.

A curious sensation reached for her, something new and different—not quite definable. She was just beginning to investigate it when a message reached her. This spell was a summons, not nearly as harsh as the one Glister had used the day before. A simple message from Oval to meet him at the detention chambers.

Her mind and spirit left the liminal space and returned to her body, then she hurried to follow the Exemplar's instructions. When she arrived at the prison area, she found Oval speaking with the guards.

They quickly left, and he turned to her. "An Outsider was found trespassing. He tried to steal a piece of the Mother and suffered Her wrath."

Mooriah gasped and peeked into the darkened cave behind him. On the ground lay a prone man, but all she could see of him was that he was covered in blood. "What happened to him?"

"The Mother has safeguards in place. An avalanche of rocks kept him from escaping. It took some time for our patrol to find him and dig him out. It seems he'd been there for several days."

She shook her head in disbelief and reached into her satchel. "I'll gather the healing supplies." But Oval held out a hand to stop her.

"This is part of his punishment."

She peered back at the prisoner whose head was turned away from her. His chest rose and fell with labored breath. It certainly appeared as though some of his bones were crushed, and he must be bleeding internally. Everything she could see was battered and bloody. He was gravely injured.

Still attuned to Nethersong, she felt it pulling at her. His death energy was potent. Without healing, this man would surely die.

"He will be interrogated shortly," Oval said. "Prepare the necessary elements for the Binding of Truth." She nodded obediently.

Oval went to confer with the guards again, and Mooriah knelt and dug through her satchel, organizing its contents so that she had easy access to everything she needed. As she did so, keeping Oval in view in the corner of her eye, she mentally scanned the death energy ravaging the prisoner's body.

Certainly he had committed a crime, but he was an Outsider and had no knowledge of the Mother's rules. Whatever he'd done, he could be punished for, but not like this. Not with a slow, agonizing death. With her Song, she pulled Nethersong from the man's body, taking the energy into herself. It invigorated her, filling her with vitality and staving off the man's death.

But it put him into a kind of limbo; he was not dead, but neither would he get better. She could not heal the way her father and the other Earthsingers could. Her Song could prevent death or give it. That was all.

However, she was also blood mage. Once Oval and the guards moved off down the hall, she crept into the darkened cave, approaching the prisoner's body. Since so much of his blood was present, she could use it for the spell. Softly, so no one would hear, she began the incantation that would set his bones.

It was a difficult working, forbidden for use by all but the shaman. If done incorrectly, it would do more harm than good. But having done little else but study and practice for years, she was confident in her abilities and focused all her will and intent on saving the man's life.

The blood allowed her to knit his bones back together and inflate his collapsed lung. It stopped the bleeding inside of him. She could not afford to heal him too much, else she would be discovered, but at least now he was no longer on the cusp. He would live—at least until his interrogation.

She sat back on her haunches and took a closer look at him. He shifted, his head rolling toward her, giving her a good look at his face. High cheekbones and skin a shade somewhere between the coloring of the Cavefolk and her own hue. His hair was coiled in thick, dark locks, and his eyes fluttered and slowly opened.

She sucked in a shocked breath. Gold and copper swirls moved inside his irises. She'd never seen eyes like that. They transfixed her so that she couldn't look away.

"Who are you?" he asked, his voice a rich honey. He spoke the language of her father, not the tongue of the Folk.

"My name is Mooriah, who are you?"

"I am Fenix." He looked around, then tried to sit up only to groan in pain and lay back down. "Where am I?"

"You trespassed in the mountain and disturbed a stone from the sacred Mother. Our guards found you and brought you here to await sentence by the chieftain."

A strange look crossed his face. "Another prison." He huffed a humorless laugh. "You are one of them? You don't look like the others."

Her back straightened. As if she hadn't heard that enough. "I was not born of the Folk, but they are my people. I have lived here my entire life." She stood and prepared to leave.

"Wait—I, I'm sorry. I didn't mean to offend you."

She froze at the sincerity in his voice. She was being over-sensitive. He wasn't from here, and it was a perfectly reasonable question.

Vibrations shook the floor. "Someone's coming. Please don't tell anyone I helped you."

He frowned. "You weren't supposed to. Why did you then?"

These were her people, but she still didn't understand or agree with some of the rules. She turned away, stepping to the entrance to the chamber. "The penalty for your crime is death. I probably shouldn't have bothered, but it should be swift, not slow and full of suffering."

The footsteps drew nearer. When the guards arrived again, she was pulling out the ingredients that Oval would need to aid in the man's questioning. The guards loaded Fenix onto a litter and carried him away. As he passed, he looked upon her with his golden swirling eyes, making Mooriah's breath catch.

They were so strange—he was so strange. She followed behind him, hoping once again that her impulsiveness would not come back to bite her.

318

# CHAPTER FIVE

Binding of Truth: To aid in determining lie from truth.

Best enhanced with doe herb and the scent of funeral bane. To be undertaken only by those well versed in communing with the Mother. The strength of the blood of the recipient will determine the spell's efficacy.

— WISDOM OF THE FOLK

"Who are you?" Coal, the clan's Protector, asked, his voice thunderous. Mooriah stifled a wince. She'd never liked the man who used his fists liberally for even the most benign of offenses. Crimson, Ember, and Rumble stood in a line next to him, standing over Fenix. The chieftain had included both of his potential heirs in this interrogation, probably to evaluate their leadership styles.

Mooriah and Glister were seated next the prisoner who lay upon the ground in the justice chamber, unable to sit upright.

Mooriah held the censer of incense and a fan, wafting the smoke over to him, Glister sprinkled him with herb water every few minutes. Both were used to keep the prisoner calm, as the Binding of Truth often agitated people.

Oval sat cross-legged at Fenix's head, deep in meditation with the Mother to monitor the man's answers. An incision made just above his lip was part of a spell that had transferred the knowledge of the speech of the Folk to Fenix so that he could speak and understand them.

"I am a visitor," Fenix replied. Fortunately, his eyes were closed, and Mooriah did not have to worry about becoming distracted by their odd shade.

"A visitor from where?" Coal questioned.

"Far away." He sounded wistful.

Crimson grunted and crossed well-muscled arms. "Were you sent here to steal from us? To plunder our valuables and take them back with you? Speak, Outsider!"

"I was sent to observe. I found myself in a cave and saw the jewels embedded in the wall. I did not realize it would be considered stealing to take one."

"Hmph." Crimson was not satisfied in the least.

"What were you sent to observe?" Ember asked, voice soft.

Fenix rolled over and groaned. Mooriah suspected he was acting a bit, playing up his pain and injuries. She appreciated the performance. "Why does my power not work in these caves? I should be able to heal myself, but I cannot."

"So you are a sorcerer?" Coal's voice rose. "We are protected from your magic here."

If he was an Earthsinger, he was an unusual one. Though Mooriah had only ever seen her father on his rare visits, she knew that the Singers bore similar features—quite different to Fenix's. She wished he'd answered Ember's question, what *was* he supposed to be observing?

Crimson let out an annoyed sigh. "This interloper from the Outside has nothing of interest to relay. He is sentenced to death. We will have no one desecrating the Mother in such a manner, ignorant or not."

Next to him, Rumble smiled while Ember's expression stayed carefully blank. But his gaze flashed to hers for a moment, and she recognized sorrow there. She pressed her lips, keeping her own emotions in check. Why did either of them care what happened to a stranger? She could do nothing to stop it. She just hoped his death would be speedy and painless.

Swift footsteps raced down the tunnel towards the chamber. A messenger stopped there, bowing low. "Forgive me, Chieftain, but the sorcerer has arrived." The young boy's gaze flitted to Mooriah, and her breath caught. "He wouldn't wait, he said he needs to speak with you immediately."

Emerging from the darkness behind him was a hooded figure. His brown cloak hid his features, but Mooriah recognized the walk. He stepped into the chamber, moving past the messenger and bowing before the chieftain, before removing his hood.

"I'm sorry to interrupt, but this is urgent," he said, voice gravelly. "I must speak with my daughter."

She swallowed the lump in her throat. "Hello, Father."

Seated across the fire from him in the chieftain's quarters, Mooriah studied her father, Yllis. It had been close to eight years since she'd last seen him. His hair was coiled in thick, silver locs, which cascaded down his back. The coloring was that of an old man, but he was only in his mid-forties. His face was still unlined, but stress and strain had changed his hair color too early.

Over the years, he had visited to check in on her at seemingly at random intervals. Always he asked how her studies were progressing, how her control of her Song had improved. He showed a detached sort of interest in her life but nothing of the love and care she saw between other fathers and daughters. He did not hug her or murmur endearments. Once he'd stroked her face and looked at her mournfully before leaving.

Now, seated next to Crimson, he sipped tea. Oval and Murmur were there as well, both remaining quiet. Ember and Rumble sat just behind their father, not included exactly, but observing. Soaking up knowledge for the day one of them would become chief.

"Why have you come, sorcerer?" Crimson asked gruffly.

Yllis was solemn. "I bring news of the war to you."

Crimson waved an arm. "We care nothing for your war. Whether you Outsiders annihilate yourselves or not means little to us."

"Even if many of those killed are your kin?"

Crimson sniffed and sipped from his drinking bowl.

"We are all kin when it comes down to it," Yllis said softly, staring into the fire. Ember frowned, but no one else acknowledged his statement.

"Father, what of the war? I thought there was peace now because of the Mantle. Why are you here?"

Yllis's eyes had deep circles beneath them. He looked haggard, as if he'd gone many nights without proper rest. He took a deep breath. "I came for you."

All the breath left her body. She tensed, childish hopes living entire lives within her.

"I need your help."

She struggled to keep the disappointment at bay. Of course he had not come to take her away with him, to be a real father. She was far too old for that anyway—she was a woman grown.

What need did she have for a father? Ember's gaze upon her was like a physical touch, but she kept her attention on her father's face. His skin was so like hers. Familiar, but foreign.

"You need my help with what?" she croaked out.

"The Mantle separates the two lands and has paused the conflict between the Earthsingers and the Silent—those with magic and those without. This is true. It protects us from one another, but in the east, on the side with the Singers, there is still strife. The fighting has changed, it's now more clandestine. The man who caused the war, who calls himself the True Father, has an uncontrollable lust for power. He steals it from the people, draining their Songs and taking them for himself. The Mantle keeps him trapped, locked in a land full of Earthsingers who fall victim to him."

Misery suffused his face. "There are those in the east who oppose him and who are willing to fight. I am helping them, but the True Father has begun looking for ways to destroy the Mantle and unleash himself upon the world. The barrier is strong but could be stronger. I have been endeavoring to reinforce it at its most vulnerable point, its cornerstone, but the working requires something I do not have."

Understanding dawned and Mooriah's eyes widened. "Nethersong?"

He nodded, grave. "Yes, daughter. I know the strife of the Outside means little to you all down here. The Folk exist beyond the complications of what we go through, but this is still important. The True Father is trapped in a web of his own making, but I fear what it would mean if he were freed to roam the world with his stolen Songs. It could very well impact the Folk."

"But how could Nethersong help?"

"I have long studied ways to combine the magics. We have successfully mixed Earthsong and blood magic and caused it to do things impossible with just one or the other. I have discovered that adding Nethersong can be quite potent. It can help form an additional layer of protection, one which I hope will not be necessary—my goal is still to defeat him—but I want to ensure there is a failsafe."

Mooriah chewed on her lip. "I will help if I can."

"It must not interfere with her studies," Oval spoke up. "When you brought her to us all those years ago, it was for good reason. We accepted her on certain conditions."

Mooriah bristled, her face growing hot.

"It is vital for her to master control of her Song, for the good of all, I know," Yllis replied evenly. "This task will only aid in her study. It will give her hands-on application, not mere practice."

Murmur swayed in his seat, eyes closed. His breathing was shaky, like it was when he received a vision. After a moment, he held up a hand and opened his eyes. "Something is coming, but I cannot see it yet." He sighed heavily. "It will come in its time, but your father is right. Your control is admirable, but you must better understand the use of your Song."

Oval huffed. "True, but that work is of a lifetime. She has also made a commitment to her apprenticeship that cannot be shirked."

"I'm quite certain I can do both, Exemplar."

His heavy-lidded eyes displayed some skepticism, but he merely nodded. "See that you do, else your position will be forfeited." Along with her hopes of becoming a clan member.

She should tell her father no, reject him the way he had always rejected her, but she could not bring herself to do it. Silently cursing her weakness, she grit her teeth.

Murmur peered at Yllis and stroked his chin. "Your work on the Mantle's cornerstone, would it benefit from the help of another Earthsinger?"

Yllis frowned. "Certainly, but none can cross the Mantle save me. All the others are locked in the east."

"Not all," Murmur said, looking at Oval significantly.

The elder shaman shook his head. "You speak of the Outsider? He has desecrated the Mother and must be punished."

"His work on this would benefit the Mother, protecting Her from a scourge of sorcerers from the Outside descending upon Her. It would offer restitution for his crime that his mere death would not."

Oval shrugged. "It is for the chieftain to decide."

Mooriah held her breath as everyone looked to Crimson. The chieftain turned to his sons, seeking their input. Rumble spoke up first.

"The penalty for his action is death, we must hold fast to justice." He crossed his arms, eyes flashing.

Ember tilted his head. "I believe that the prisoner's blood would sully the Mother. Better he offer a redress and benefit Her in some way and then be exiled with the knowledge that if he ever returns, he will be killed."

Crimson tapped his chin, considering. "Impure blood such as his should not be further spilled inside the sacred Mother. I will leave him in your custody, sorcerer. And you," he motioned to Ember, "ensure that he never returns."

Mooriah held back the sigh of relief. She shot Ember a grateful look. He gave an almost imperceptible nod. Though she was taking on this new task, she still had to find the time to meet with him and help him. It was more obvious than ever that he would be the far better choice for chieftain.

She turned to her father. "When should we begin?"

"As quickly as possible."

# CHAPTER SIX

Ritual of Banishment: Prevents the unwanted from entering protected ground.

The blood of the banished is sufficient. Attempting to use any other activating agents is unwise. The focus of sincere intention will prevent unwanted consequences, but any distraction or confusion may exile those you do not intend.

— WISDOM OF THE FOLK

Years had passed since Mooriah had been outside of the Mountain Mother. The only sunlight she saw usually came from far overhead from the vents and airholes in various caves. The streaming light up ahead at the end of the tunnel through which she followed her father was beginning to give her a headache. She used the bone needle in her pocket to pierce her finger, then murmured the words of a blood spell to help her adjust to the brightness.

Behind them, two guards carried Fenix on his litter. Ember brought up the rear of the party to carry out his father's command and ensure the Outsider was properly exiled and forbidden from returning.

They emerged on a plateau, with paths leading down either side of the peak on which they stood. She shivered as a sharp wind blew across her skin. Though there were no seasons inside the Mother, evidence of the weather still reached them. They celebrated the upcoming First Frost Festival every year, along with the Celebration of the First Bud, when the plants in the farming caves sprouted in the spring.

Once on the plateau, Yllis set down his pack and retrieved a heavy cloak from within, as well as a pair of boots then handed them to Mooriah. She accepted them gratefully, for her teeth were chattering. The boots were a bit too large but served to protect her bare feet from the weather.

The guards set Fenix's pallet on the ground, but he stood up at once, flexing his arms and legs. Out of the reach of the wards embedded within the rock walls, he had healed himself almost instantly. The bruises were gone, and the blood still encrusted on his limbs disappeared. His tunic and trousers were still stained, but the rest of him was whole and hale.

Holding their arms at their sides, the guards retreated without another word. That left Ember alone in the entrance to the tunnel, squinting at the land beyond. His eyes were also unused to the brightness of day, though, with a warrior's stoicism, he showed no sign of the effects of the cold on his bare chest and legs.

He turned to Mooriah, his eyes still narrowed against the light. "The Ritual of Banishment," he said, speaking low. She nodded. She would not need anything from her satchel, just her knife and the blood.

Ember eyed her warily but stood his ground. The wind

ruffled his waistcloth, revealing more of his well-muscled thigh. A shiver raced through him, uncontrollably, and she rushed to perform the ritual so that he could return to the warmth.

"Your hand," she said to Fenix. He looked at her curiously then extended his hand.

She sliced a shallow cut in his palm and allowed his blood to spill into her clay bowl. She did the same to her own palm before looking to Ember whose jaw was clenched. "This is the first lesson," she whispered to him. "Close your eyes."

He did so and held out his hand. She made the tiniest cut she could. His muscles were rigid as stone as she collected drops of blood into the bowl. Then with a whisper, she bound hers and Ember's wounds. Fenix's healed on its own a moment after she'd sliced him.

Mooriah closed her eyes and invoked the spell, banishing Fenix from entering the Mother again. To her surprise, Ember added to it, including words to banish all his kind. Her eyes opened in shock. Would that mean her father could not enter as well? He was an Earthsinger, too. But Ember spoke the words of closing and the blood in the bowl shimmered and hardened, forming a caldera which floated up and then back toward the tunnel entrance. It would embed itself in the rock there and become a permanent part of the mountain.

"It is done," she said.

Ember nodded and turned to Fenix. "Safe travels to you." He bowed.

Fenix raised a brow, a smile playing at his lips. He seemed amused by Ember's stiff formality.

Ember nodded at Yllis before turning to Mooriah. "I will see you later?"

"Yes, I will find you when I return."

His gaze held hers for a long moment as if he was trying to communicate something, though she wasn't sure what. Then he turned and walked back to the tunnel. She watched him until he disappeared into the darkness, then found Fenix looking at her, his golden eyes swirling. His skin also had taken on more than just a healthy glow. It seemed to be shining with some kind of inner light.

It was such a strange effect that she stared for several moments. "Did you know that you are..." She motioned to his body. "...radiating?"

He looked down and smiled ruefully. His skin dimmed somewhat but was still oddly luminous. "I still have not grown used to holding this form."

She blinked rapidly. "What form do you usually hold?"

He grinned before his body practically exploded into light. She stumbled backward and her father caught her as Fenix transformed. He was like a star come to life. He bobbed and weaved and then took on a human form again. This time, the tunic and trousers he wore were spotless. She noticed now they were of a material she'd never seen before. Had he manifested them with his power?

"You are not an Earthsinger," she said, awe in her voice.

"I use Earthsong, but I am not a Singer in the way that those born here are."

Yllis still had his arm around her. He peered at Fenix, tilting his head. "You are an observer? Sent from the remnant of the Founders' people?"

Fenix nodded.

"The Founders?" Mooriah asked.

"Do you recall the stories I told you of the origin of the Earthsingers?" Yllis asked.

She had listened to every word her father had ever spoken on his rare visits, committing them to memory. "A magical Lord and Lady from a distant land arrived here. They had great power and transformed the desert into farmland. They had nine children who found husbands and wives among the first of the Folk who left the Mother."

"My great-grandmother was one of those nine."

His family tree—hers as well—was of great interest to her. The children of the unions between the nine children of the Founders and the Cavefolk were born either Singers or Silent— one sibling could have magic while another would not. And these differences were the root cause of the war that had raged before her birth.

She could understand the jealousy of those who could not wield Earthsong. Any of them could learn to use blood magic if they chose, but after the Folk left the Mother to become Outsiders, they lost the old ways for the most part. And so they fought the sorcerers—sometimes their own brothers and sisters. Meanwhile, inside the mountain, clans fought for far pettier reasons.

"What were you sent here to observe?" Mooriah asked. "You never said."

Fenix spread his arms. "This land. Your ancestors settled here from my world and found safety and hospitality. There are those where I'm from who keep track of such things in case a need for another exodus comes to pass. Our world was destroyed, and our people scattered. If any of us find ourselves displaced once again, victims of another calamity, it is helpful to know where we might find refuge."

"Another calamity? What happened?"

His all over glow dimmed even further. "That is a long, sad story. One for another time."

Mooriah nodded. Curious as she was, she had no desire for a sad tale. The wind picked up again, ruffling her braid. She turned to her father who was pensive.

"How long will you be here?" Yllis asked.

"I am not certain," he said, gazing at Mooriah speculatively. "Until my task is complete, I suppose."

She didn't know how long observing took or if there were special requirements or perhaps a report he had to compile, and she sensed Fenix was being vague on purpose. They had explained what Yllis was planning on the trip out of the mountain, when Fenix was still playing at being gravely injured. "Well, will you help us?" she asked.

"Certainly. It seems I owe you a debt for saving my life from those vile, pale creatures in the caves."

She set her jaw. "You are lucky that some of those vile, pale creatures are kind and generous."

Fenix quirked his lip, which only served to stoke her ire. He took very little seriously. "I consider myself lucky, indeed." His tone edged toward flirtatious, which flustered Mooriah, but also had the effect of cooling her anger. He gazed so directly at her with eyes of liquid gold. They were almost hypnotizing.

"We have a long walk to the cornerstone," Yllis announced, breaking the strange effect she'd been under. "I will explain more on the way."

As they trekked across the mountain paths, Mooriah slowly grew used to the cold. The cloak her father had given her was lined with fur and provided adequate warmth, and she could always do a blood spell to further warm herself but decided to hold off. Part of her wanted to feel such a foreign sensation. The slight stinging of the wind on her cheeks was something new, something she wanted to investigate.

Yllis told Fenix of the war between Singer and Silent, of how the man who called himself the True Father was slowly draining the Earthsingers of their magic and how the Mantle kept him hemmed into his side of the mountain.

"So this Mantle, it's only above the mountains correct?" Fenix asked.

"Yes, you can pass through the mountain if you know the way," Mooriah said. "However, several million kilometers of tunnels and thousands of angry Cavefolk make that a nearly impossible proposition."

"Could they not be bribed to help?"

She laughed. "Doubtful. And even if you found someone brave or foolish or desperate enough, they would be discovered by others. Superstitions are intense among the Folk, and Outsiders are not welcome. As you've experienced."

"Hmm. So why do you live there?" Fenix asked. "Are you not a Singer?"

Mooriah fell silent, an old ache taking hold of her throat.

"Are you familiar with Nethersong?" Yllis replied.

Fenix stumbled and caught himself on a boulder. She wanted to laugh, but it really wasn't funny. He looked at her apprehensively for the first time. She swallowed her disappointment.

"My daughter was born a Nethersinger and would have been killed, or killed many people, had she not been properly trained. However, there was no one to train her except the blood mages. I had little choice but to allow her to grow up there."

She had always understood this reality, but it didn't make the sting of his rejection burn any less. She stared defiantly at Fenix, who now looked apologetic.

"Those with death magic are quite rare where I come from as well," he said. "Though as far as I know, in all the places settled by the refugees, the power has not manifested. I wonder why here?" His gaze was now alight with curiosity. "Are you proficient?"

"Yes."

A grin took over his face. "You are a rare creature indeed. Kind and powerful."

She felt flushed and looked away.

"We're close now," Yllis announced. "Watch your step." They

had crested a high ridge and were about to descend a steep incline. The cornerstone was well hidden in this section of the range. She questioned whether she would be able to find it again without her father's help.

"Perhaps we should create some sort of map," she mused, stepping carefully down the path.

"The whole point is for it to remain hidden, dear."

"Yes, but there may be cases in which someone will need to find it in the future. You are reinforcing it now. Such a thing might once again be necessary. We should be ready for all eventualities."

Yllis shook his head. "A paper map is too dangerous. Too easy to copy and distribute. And if it fell into the wrong hands..."

"No, not paper. I was thinking of something more substantial. But you're right, the cornerstone itself needs strong protections. The True Father knows it's here, does he not?"

"He does, though for now it's safe on this side of the Mantle, where he can't access it."

A caldera could be created holding the memory of the route to the cornerstone. It would serve as a map for those who would one day need to find this place. Her mind raced, considering what would be needed to create both the map and some kind of protection spell.

She was so focused on her thoughts that she barely noticed they had arrived until she nearly ran into a stone pillar. She backed up to find a ring of such pillars, towering high in the air —each one must be as tall as five levels of steps back in the cave city. They were spaced about ten paces apart. In the center of the ring of stone was a caldera, an enormous one in the shape of an obelisk. It was blood red in color and rose even higher than the columns surrounding it.

"It's magnificent," she whispered, her head tilted up.

"How is it made?" Fenix asked, staring in awe.

"Blood magic and Earthsong. I built this here so that the Mantle could stretch the entire length of the mountain range. It is my life's work." Yllis placed his hand on one of the outer pillars. "I know of no other spell like it."

"I have not heard of its like." Fenix's voice was hushed.

Blood magic and Earthsong. Her father had combined the magic in some way. The sheer size of the obelisk was beyond impressive—how much blood had it taken to create? She shivered, but not from the cold. A spell of this magnitude, one that could create a barrier so strong, it must have taken quite a lot of power. If Earthsong had not been present, she would have estimated this caldera would have required the blood of thousands, maybe more.

She tore her gaze away from the remarkable stone to view her father's face. The Mantle had stood since before she was born and she was afraid to ask how many people had sacrificed their blood to create this. Plus, the most powerful calderas required death to activate. Did she even want to know?

Yllis caught her eye, noticing her fearful expression. His face softened. "We were at war. There was quite enough blood to use without my having to shed a drop from anyone. The erection of the Mantle changed the war. Now the True Father can only terrorize those on his side of it."

Fenix had his eyes closed, both palms on the nearest stone pillar. "This is a clever spell. It fuels itself with Earthsong from all around, reaching deep into the earth and from the surrounding region."

Yllis nodded approvingly.

"So what will Nethersong do?" Mooriah asked.

"Nethersong, Earthsong, and blood magic are needed for a defensive spell. Something to protect the cornerstone and reinforce it. Though creating this was a singular achievement, it is not infallible. And I have no illusions that it cannot be destroyed. I will tell you my theory on combining the magics, and then we will find a way to protect this place. The Mantle has stood for twenty-three years. I don't know how much longer it will be needed, but it must not fall."

"I understand, Father. I will do all I can."

He smiled at her and her heart broke a little. He looked so tired, so worn. She had no idea of the burdens he'd taken on. When he'd built the Mantle all those years ago, he'd inadvertently become the only Singer left to the west of the mountains. He felt responsible for the actions of the True Father for reasons she never quite understood. But if this was the only way she could spend time with him, get to know him, she would do it. And protect his world in the process.

She just hoped it would not also serve to disconnect her from her own. Pulled in two different directions—family versus community, the man who'd abandoned her versus the people who never quite accepted her. She settled down to work wishing that her life could be easier. Wishing for something that could never be.

# CHAPTER SEVEN

Fortitude Seals: A series of wards against true death by various means.

Absolute precision is needed, else failure is assured. The spell may be enhanced by the consumption of water blossoms or blister seeds—but only by those well acquainted with their side effects.

— WISDOM OF THE FOLK

Ember paced the floor of his hideaway. The dinner hour had long ended and Mooriah had still not arrived. He had so much to tell her and beyond that, he just wanted to see her again.

Something about how she'd looked outside the walls of the Mother had made his heart stutter. Her hair blowing in the raw wind, her skin glowing in the light of the overhead sun, it made him wonder if she would ever return to the Folk at all, when she could take her place Outside where she had been born.

The prisoner had also given him pause. Ember had not thought the man's life should be forfeit for the mistake he had made. Yet on that ledge he had gazed upon Mooriah in a proprietary way. He was also a powerful sorcerer like her father. Though his skin and eyes were strange, perhaps they were more alike than they were different. Perhaps she would not come back at all.

Ember shivered and knelt to stoke the fire in the pit. His thoughts had grown maudlin and worse: fearful. But he had so much pent up energy within, he didn't know what to do with it.

He didn't hear any soft footsteps but all the same he became aware of her presence just as she slipped through the entrance. She looked tired.

He rose, worried. "Are you all right?"

"Yes, I'm fine. Just wanted to make sure no one saw me."

He winced, although he knew what she did was appropriate. "I made food, I wasn't sure if you would have eaten."

Her stomach growled then, and she smiled ruefully. "Thank you, I haven't."

He opened the pot of stew warming over the fire pit and she moaned at the aroma wafting from it. Turning away from her to hide his suddenly flushed face, he scooped some of the steaming vegetables into a bowl and handed it to her. Their fingers brushed; hers were cold. She still wore the voluminous, fur-lined cloak her father had given her, but shrugged it off seating herself on the cushion before the fire.

"This should warm you," he said, grateful as she dug into the meal.

He could not tear his eyes away from her as she wolfed down her food. When her bowl was empty, he gave her some more.

"Sorry to eat like such a beast," she said, grimacing. "The work my father has me doing, it triggers my appetite."

"The mage work?"

She nodded. "For some reason working a blood spell affects me more than it does Oval or Murmur or even Glister. I think it's because of my…" she waved a hand around, "…differences."

It seemed she was uncomfortable talking about her sorcery. Which made sense. The Folk hated sorcerers of any kind. Most here had probably forgotten that she held strange natural magic, since she was so adept with the blood.

"Anyway," she said, putting her bowl down at last. "I've been thinking about where we should begin."

"Before we start, I should tell you that something has happened."

She looked at him warily, her brow lowered. Ember took a deep breath. "Crimson has made it official. The victor in the match at the Frost Festival will be the heir to the chieftaincy."

Her frown deepened. "That's ridiculous. How can he base such a decision on the outcome of a game? What about leadership? Honor? Good sense?"

He smiled, pleased by her disgust. "For him, it is only the strongest who matters. Brute force is weighed far more heavily on his scales than any other quality. Only one who embodies the quality of victory may lead Night Snow."

"What a foolish man." She looked up suddenly, chagrined. "I'm sorry. He's your father and I shouldn't have—"

"No, it's fine. In this, we agree. He and I don't see eye to eye on many things." The apprehension which had filled his heart when Crimson had first shared the news came back full force. Ember was capable in the ring. He was more than a match for Rumble—if the fighting was fair.

"Well, the only good news is that Crimson's choice won't be based on you completing a ritual or ceremony." Her hopeful expression slayed him.

"The bout will be to the short death."

Her warm skin grew ashen, and her jaw dropped.

"We are to use wards to protect against a killing strike. But to win, we must land a death blow. Rumble is already warded against death by knife blade and strangulation. I must do so as well to survive."

His stomach had turned into a bottomless pit. Warding against danger, curses, and sorcery was part of Cavefolk life. Generations ago, fights to the short death were more common as a way to raise the stakes, entertain the audience, and truly practice for real battle. However, such practices had fallen out of favor.

"The festival is in one week's time," Mooriah said. "You will have to learn the Fortitude Seals by then?" Her voice evoked her disbelief that such a thing was possible. "This type of spell is difficult and layered. That is one of the reasons why brawlers do not do it any longer. One mistake and the spell will not work."

"I know." His body felt like it was made of lead. "My father has said that a chief should be able to do it. He is right."

She firmed her lips and nodded. "All right. That is our goal then. I will do my best to help you."

"I know you will."

She studied him for a long moment before pivoting to face him directly. He did the same, so they sat cross-legged, knees nearly touching.

"Give me your hands," she said.

His throat tightened as he considered her long, elegant fingers extending toward him. He rested his palms atop hers lightly, shivering at the contact.

She closed her eyes, giving him the opportunity to study her. Lit by firelight, her skin was smooth and unmarred. Her full lips formed perfect bows, and her lashes grazed her cheeks. He tried to clamp down his body's response to her closeness, to the feel of her skin but he could not. Then she stroked his palms gently, and it was as if the rod holding up his spine had been removed. He nearly collapsed like an empty balloon.

She smiled. "That's it. Release the tension you carry, Ember. You need to relax. Now, can you tell me what it's like when you try to pierce your skin?"

A shiver went through him and the tension returned, but he focused on the softness of her palms. All his awareness was on the place where they touched. It was innocent, but sensual. Her scent came to him, incense mixed with lavender today— fragrant and lovely, just as she was.

She'd asked him a question, what was it? Oh yes, his bane. He swallowed before answering. "I'm just paralyzed. It's not the pain, that is negligible. But to cut into myself... The blade against my skin..." He shivered. "I cannot make my hands move. My mind is telling my body to act, but it will not."

He clamped his lips shut, embarrassed that he'd revealed so much.

"It's all right. It sounds like you cannot control it. Some people have these things."

"Weakness."

Her eyes snapped open. "Not weakness. Your strength is within. You've bested every challenger in the circle. You show compassion and wisdom and good leadership. You are not weak, Ember."

Her glare was fierce. She believed every word. "Repeat it."

He lifted his brows. She stared at him until he complied. "I am not weak."

"Again. Louder."

He smiled. "I am not weak."

"Good." She squeezed his hands then released him. "I'd like to see you try to just prick yourself with this pin."

She held out a bone shard in her hand, the thinnest, tiniest one he'd ever seen. He took it from her, the thing was almost too small and delicate to hold in his thick fingers. He might just snap it in two.

"Try to pierce the meaty part of your palm," she said, her voice low and comforting.

He placed the edge of the pin against his skin until it indented the pale flesh of his palm. All he had to do was apply the slightest amount of pressure. She was asking for just a single drop of blood.

He held the pin there, willing himself to do it. But he couldn't.

He exhaled, realizing he'd been holding his breath. "I'm sorry, I can't."

"What happens when you try?"

He shook his head. "I'm not sure. My muscles lock up. They refuse to obey me. I feel like I'm not in control of my body any longer. It's... impossible." The weight of reality set upon him, and he wanted to give up. He would never be chief, and Night Snow would be embroiled in constant war.

"Nothing is impossible," she hissed, her voice steely. "I think we need to take another tack." She rummaged in her sack and pulled out a packet, which she opened and sprinkled over the fire.

"Lie down, close your eyes," she commanded. He did as she asked, lying across several cushions with his head at her knees.

She placed her hands on either side of his head, and his eyes popped open. She smiled down at him. "Keep them closed."

He did and she began massaging his temples. Whatever she'd sprinkled on the fire smelled sweet and a little cloying. He was going to fall asleep at this rate. Her fingers gently kneading his head was more delightful than he could have imagined. He focused on that sensation until everything else dropped away.

Ember's eyes opened and he was standing, not in his old nanny's dwelling, but in a dark place. Apprehension sparked, but then Mooriah flickered in place next to him.

"We are in the heart of the Mother," she said in a calming tone. "This is where I go to practice with my power. Your form here is not real, or I should say it exists only in your mind. Your body is still in front of the fire."

She held out the tiny bone shard. "Try again."

He swallowed and took it, surprised at how substantial she looked and felt when their fingers brushed again. He placed the pin against his palm again.

This time when his mind told his body to pierce his skin, it did so. A single drop of red welled against his skin.

His gaze shot to her, wide-eyed. Her smile broadened, illuminating the dark, ethereal cave in which they stood.

"That's the first step. You can get over this, Ember. I know you can."

He nodded slowly, trying to wrap his mind around what had just happened. He stared at the dot of red on his palm and wanted to cry with joy.

# CHAPTER EIGHT

Effusion of Hardiness: Reinforces sturdy good health and robustness of body.

Two parts wolf fungus, one part jade bite, and three drams of salamander ink. Excessive yawning and a loss of taste may occur in some cases. The recipient should avoid ingesting fish or sea fowl for at least three moons.

— WISDOM OF THE FOLK

Mooriah stood with her hands pressed against the red surface of the cornerstone caldera, searching for something—anything —within.

"What are you hoping to find?"

She startled at Fenix's voice behind her and spun around. "I'm not sure." She shook her head. "It's foolish."

He tilted his head, those eyes peering deep inside her. "I doubt that."

"Both of my parents were powerful Earthsingers—but my Song calls to death instead. Shouldn't there be something of them inside of me?"

He frowned then looked up at the obelisk's great height. "Unfortunately, that's not how it works. Would you rather be an Earthsinger?"

"I don't know. Sometimes. It would be easier for Father. I wouldn't have been sent away." The pain of the admission settled across her fiercely. She knew that Yllis had done it to save her life, but still...

"Do you enjoy living inside those dreary caverns?"

"They're not dreary," she protested. "They're beautiful. I wish you could see them as I do. Each wall is embedded with generations of history going back to the very beginning of the mountain. You can walk for days and learn the tales of people who lived long before you. And the firerocks illuminate the patterns hidden in the stone, they tell their own story in images—you just have to know what you're looking for. The Mother is truly wondrous."

She smiled, thinking of her home. "There are gardens with plants that only bloom under the firerocks, with flowers more colorful and impressive than anything above ground, I'm sure of it. And the lakes—all around the city there are lakes, places where you can go and meditate and be at peace."

"And swim?" His brows were raised, and his mouth quirked in a smile. *That* was what he had focused on?

"Well, yes, you can swim." She frowned.

"That, at least, sounds like fun." A grin ate up his face, and she sighed.

Fenix seemed good natured, but he also lacked the ability to take anything seriously. His constant smirk was beginning to grate her nerves. "We had better get back to work. I'd like to finish today, if possible."

He sucked in a deep breath of frigid air. "Helping your father is a great deal easier than what I was sent here to do. Observe the people, make reports, take a census. Boring." He rolled his eyes.

She stiffened. "But that's the assignment you signed up for, isn't it? Don't your people need the reports?"

He shrugged. "Need is a strong word. They desire them, but they'll just send someone else along if I don't complete the job. I only took this on because I wanted to travel. And I had old debts to repay. But what they don't know won't hurt them. I'd much rather be here with you." His smile was bright and charming, enhanced perhaps by his natural glow which he no longer bothered to dampen.

Looking at him was almost painful—he was beautiful, to be sure, and so different to anyone else she'd ever met. But his carefree nature and indifference to duty rubbed her the wrong way.

"Well, the faster you're done here, the faster you can leave and continue your travels," she said.

"Oh, but I like it here."

"On the top of this cold mountain?" She raised her brows.

"There are very pleasing things to look at."

Mooriah turned away, flushing at the compliment he obviously intended. "Well, I need to finish. So I can go back."

She had brought a large pot with her today and used it to combine the ingredients for the spell she was working on. Blood magic could, of course, be done without all the additional elements stored in her satchel, blood and intent were all that were needed, but generations of shamans had come up with formulas to focus and amplify the spells. The ingredients, properly used, brought a level of refinement to the magic, which it did not have on its own.

She'd added star root for longevity, featherblade to measure a person's heart, salt bronze as a calming agent for those who would trigger the spell. She was finally doing something she'd been longing to for her whole apprenticeship—creating a new spell. Putting her years of studying to the test was oddly gratifying, and it somewhat made up for the fact that her father was just as distant as ever.

An hour ago, he'd pronounced his Song drained and had gone off to his campsite nearby to rest. An Earthsinger's power needed to regenerate after heavy usage. Mooriah wasn't sure if hers did as well or if she'd just never used her Song for long enough to exhaust it.

She'd tried telling Yllis about her spell, explaining how novel and original it was. But he'd just smiled absently and given the verbal equivalent of a pat on the head. She willed herself to not let it bother her. Later, when she returned to Night Snow, she would tell Murmur and he would be appropriately impressed.

As her thoughts veered back to her working of blood magic, Fenix interrupted again. "Pretty lighting and calm lakes can't be the only reason you stay locked away down there. They have all that and more out here."

She shook her head, focusing on her work—the mixture had to be right or it would not work as intended. "It's my home. I like it there."

"Even though the people barely accept you. They consider you an Outsider, isn't that right?"

She pursed her lips. "For now. But once I'm initiated into the clan, things will change."

"Just like that?" She looked up to find his gaze intense. For once, the smirk gone from his lips. "Do you truly think you'll ever be one of them? That they'll ever really accept you for who you are?"

That gave her pause. But the other unclanned who had become full members enjoyed all the rights and privileges that every other Night Snow member did. No cutting remarks or stares. That would be her too, she was sure of it.

"I realize that you were eager to leave your home, Fenix, but not everyone is like you."

He shrugged. "Home is tedious. You should come with me and explore. See what this world has to offer."

She grit her teeth. "Have you forgotten why my father brought me there in the first place? My Song is dangerous to those not warded against it."

He scoffed and her temper rose at the sound. He wasn't listening to her. Not only was he irresponsible, he was self-centered.

He opened his mouth to reply and then froze, tilting his head. Then he jumped to his feet. "Your father is in trouble."

"What?" She leapt up as well.

"Follow me."

They raced down the trail leading to the plateau where Yllis had set up his camp. He had not yet had enough time for his Song to restore itself. If there was some danger, he would not be able to defend himself.

Fenix raced ahead of her and stopped. She reached his side and her heart froze. Yllis stood with his back to them as a mountain lion prowled just a dozen steps away. It was a male, and the biggest one she'd ever seen, easily twice her father's weight. Cool green eyes never left Yllis's still form.

A long dagger lay on the ground just out of her father's reach. The cat paused, sniffing, then bent its forelegs and haunches, settling into a pounce position, its gaze narrowing.

Mooriah clenched her fist and reached for her Song. Her power arrowed around her father and settled on the cat—a strong and healthy specimen with little Nethersong to latch onto. Little, but enough. With pinpoint accuracy, she multiplied the Nether, increasing the death energy until it spread throughout the creature's entire body.

"Mooriah, no!" she vaguely heard her father say, but it was too late. She manipulated the energy of the animal until it seized and fell over, its large green pupils filling with black.

When it was done, she released her Song and breathed heavily. Unlike when she practiced within the Mother, she now felt exhilarated by the use of her power. The exhaustion that had chased her for the past months as she studied for longer and worked harder, melted away. It was as if she was always supposed to use this ability.

But her father and Fenix both rushed to kneel beside the mountain lion. Yllis turned back to her. "What did you do?"

She blinked in confusion. "I saved your life. What do you mean?"

He sighed deeply, looking down, his hand on the animal's hide. "To take a life is a great burden, Mooriah. Even an animal's life."

She crossed her arms. "Do you not hunt for food?"

"Is that what you were doing?"

Disbelief made her blink rapidly. "You would have rather I let it attack you? Let it maul you to death?"

He shook his head and her frustration grew. Was she supposed to feel bad for protecting him? She took a step backward, pain filling her—not for what she did, but for how her father was reacting to her. His gaze was wary as he stared up at her.

"You've never seen me use my power before," she whispered. "Is that it?" Oh, he always asked how her control was progressing on his rare visits, but in all her years he'd never actually witnessed it. "Is it as awful as you imagined?"

"You should not use it in such a way."

Anger spiked. "So it's all right when I use it to help you, but any other usage is off limits?"

"I don't want you to become..." He searched for a word but couldn't find it. "I don't want you to live with regrets about what you've done."

She was speechless with rage and pain. Fenix's eyes were closed, his hands on the cougar's fur. They began to glow even brighter than anything she'd seen from him before. In a moment, the animal was breathing again, softly.

"It's asleep," he said, brushing off his palms and sitting back on his haunches. "We should move it away from your camp."

"You can bring life back to the dead?" Her voice was low and a little fearful.

He nodded gravely and stood. "The newly dead, at least."

"You are far more powerful than an Earthsinger," Yllis said, appearing thoughtful.

"My power overlaps in some ways but is different." He looked at Mooriah, some question in his eyes that she didn't have time to parse.

A weight had settled on her chest and was crushing her air. Stealing her ability to breathe. She could not help the power that she had been born with. She could not help her skin or her skill or her parentage. And even her father could not accept what she was.

She spun around and started back up the path.

"Mooriah!" Fenix called.

"Let her go," Yllis said.

Tears welled in her eyes, and she did not turn around.

# CHAPTER NINE

Appeal of Discovery: To find a path to one whom you pursue.

One drop each of hairy viper venom and nightworm pigment. The mixture is quite potent and may bubble or smoke. Avoid touching it as a blister may occur. Follow the tingling of your feet until you find the one you seek.

— WISDOM OF THE FOLK

Ember had watched Mooriah stir the food in her bowl for five full minutes before he couldn't take it any longer. In their short acquaintance, he'd never seen her avoid a meal. "What is wrong?"

They had been practicing in the trance state for an hour before breaking for a late dinner. He had successfully pierced his skin with the pin twice more and was working with larger and larger pins, hoping he'd get to a knife soon. It was progress, though it was slow, and they still hadn't tried it outside of the

Mother's meditative illusion. However, Mooriah had seemed out of sorts ever since she'd arrived. Something was obviously bothering her.

She took a deep breath and set her bowl down. "Are you afraid of my power? The Nethersong?"

He frowned. "No? Why?"

"Because I command death. Because I can kill with a thought. It's inside me—this thing that responds to what most people fear." Her hands were clenched tight in her lap, and he wanted to soothe them.

"Death is a part of life, the largest part in fact." He gave into the urge and reached for her hand, uncurling her fist to intertwine their fingers. She didn't pull away, so he continued.

"I remember crying when my mother was chosen in the lottery to be the Sacred Sacrifice. She was the last one, after her, my father insisted the shamans move away from the practice. Some of the elders protested abandoning tradition, but he truly loved her—in his way. Something inside him broke when she died. But she was proud to have been chosen. Proud to serve her community by giving her blood to the Mother. Her life reinforced our protections, and her sacrifice will go on until the Folk are no more. So, as much as I miss her and wish she was here, all life ends in death. I would have lost her eventually. We should not fear it, we must accept it for it comes regardless."

He squeezed their joined hands. "There is little point in fearing you because you wield death. You also are a powerful blood mage. I fear that more than anything." He smiled and her expression lightened.

"My father fears me," she whispered. She relayed what had happened on the mountain top with the cougar, her voice dripping with sorrow. Tears filled her eyes and overflowed.

"I don't know why I'm so upset about this. It's not as if he even knows me at all. He says he loves me, says he only wants to protect me, but he doesn't understand how his judgment is painful." She scrubbed at her cheeks.

"By not accepting your power, he's not accepting you."

Her eyes widened. "Exactly. And even Fenix had the nerve to look at me like I was made of ants after I killed that cougar."

"Fenix was there?" Ember stiffened at the mention of the sorcerer's name.

Mooriah sniffed. "Yes, he brought the cat back to life. His power is..." She shook her head.

Ember was glad that the man was banished. That sort of magic went against the will of the Mother and the Breath Father. "He should not have interfered with life and death matters."

"I did."

"You did not interfere. You defended your father. Should we not protect ourselves and those we love? If anyone, man or beast, came for someone I cared about, then their death would be assured. Bringing them back is unnatural magic. You should be careful of that sorcerer."

He wanted to tell her to be careful of Fenix for other reasons —the glint in the man's eye had shown that he admired Mooriah—but he stayed quiet on that.

She sighed deeply. "If I become clan, do you think I will ever be truly accepted? Will I ever be one of you and have my own place here—my own family?"

"When you become clan, you will need to fend off the men with one of Glister's itching spells."

She huffed a laugh. "Doubtful."

"Would you like me to do it for you?"

"Scare away all my imaginary suitors? No thank you. If I have even one, then it will be a miracle."

Her voice was light, but he froze. "Why do you say that?"

"I am not such a prize as all that. So far, the only man to

show interest in me is an Outsider, an arrogant thoughtless one at that."

She tried to pull her hand from his, but he tightened his hold. "Are you certain he's the only one?" His voice had lowered without him realizing.

She stared at their hands before meeting his gaze. Their faces were very close together all of a sudden. He wasn't sure how that had happened. She swallowed, bringing his attention to her elegant neck.

Her breath brushed across his lips; she was staring at them, blinking slowly. He held his breath. Then she shook herself and sat back. Disappointment was a mallet against his chest.

"You're going to be the chief, the Mother willing. You cannot..." She scooted farther away, forcing their hands apart. "You are not even supposed to speak to the unclanned."

"You are going to be our shaman," he said, longing for the feel of her skin on his once more. But she was focusing on her bowl again, still not eating, but not looking him in the eye either.

"That's not assured."

"Oval is not a fool, Mooriah. Anyone can see that you are better, more prepared, and take your tasks more seriously than Glister does."

She shook her head but was smiling softly. He would count that as a win. However, the moment, whatever it had been, was gone, and she still had a sad air about her that Ember wanted desperately to dispel. If nothing else, he could do that for her.

He stood and held a hand out. "I know what will cheer you. Let's take a break."

"We're already taking a break," she said wryly.

"Well a slightly longer break. I'd like to show you something."

She looked at his outstretched hand and instead of taking it, stood on her own. He fisted his hand at his side, ignoring the mallet that continued hammering away at him.

They exited his hiding place and walked along the abandoned corridors of this section of the city. Some of the staircases here were already falling into disrepair; he made a mental note to have them attended to. Anything to keep his mind off what had almost happened.

"Were you raised in the orphans' home?" he asked, realizing he knew little about her life.

"At first, though when I was around six, I went to live with Murmur and his family group. He'd had a vision and was convinced to take me in."

"What does he have again, four wives? Five?"

She shook her head. "Only three—Sparkle passed on to become one with the Mother two years ago. And they added another husband, Yaw, when I was fifteen."

"The old ways seem very complicated," Ember said. "How can someone keep up with so many spouses?"

"They have their way of doing things. Though I admit, I have no desire for more than one partner in my life."

Most of the Folk under one hundred years of age or so eschewed the polyamorous lifestyle that so many of the elders participated in. There just weren't as many people around any longer.

"I agree. I'd rather focus my attention on one person. Jealousy is a poison that infects too many hearts." His mother had never shown outward jealousy of his father's other wives, but had she merely hidden it from him?

"Where are you taking me?" Mooriah asked, looking around.

"We're almost there."

She huffed irritably, and he held back a smile. It was obvious that she liked to be in control. He wisely kept to himself how adorable he found her lack of patience. They climbed up a staircase and down another, then snaked through a warren of empty halls until they finally reached the destination.

This place was high in the city, located beneath one of the Mother's taller peaks. A narrow, dark tunnel, unlit by firerocks, led to a wide cavern. Mooriah gasped as they entered the much brighter space, and Ember tried to recall what it was like to see it for the first time.

The ceiling rose high above them, nearly as tall as Night Snow's entire city. Here, the Mother's ragged walls were not smooth like they were in so much else of the territory. This stone was unblemished by the spells which embedded memories or protections in the walls. It was just raw mountain, and on the far wall, an enormous waterfall fed a lake below. Rocks jutted up from the surface of the water, forming a rough path leading to the waterfall. The unexpectedness and majesty of the sight took Mooriah's breath away.

"Do you want to get closer?" he asked.

Her head tilted up, staring at the grand falls, she nodded mutely. With sure steps from years of practice, he showed her how to leap from rock to rock, crossing the lake in no time.

They stood on a ledge a dozen paces from the water's thunderous fall. The spray misted them as they drew closer.

"How did I not know this was here?" she said, voice raised to compete with the falling water.

"It was once a retreat for the elite who lived on the upper levels. Now no one really comes here anymore."

"You do."

He grinned as they approached the falls and stuck his hand in the spray.

"It's warm?" She laughed, splashing a little.

"There's a hot spring in a hidden mountain oasis up there somewhere. At least that's what they think. No one has ever been there, it's too high." He craned his neck to try to see the origination of the water but could not. He didn't even catch a glimpse of daylight up above. Firerocks were the only thing illuminating this cavern.

"How could there be a hot spring on the top of a mountain?"

He shrugged. "One of the many mysteries of the Mother. My own mother brought me here when I was young. It was her favorite place. I'm almost glad I don't have to share it with others anymore." He flushed and turned toward her. "I mean, I'm happy to share it with you."

She grinned, still enthralled with the feeling of the water streaming through her fingers. Her whole face was transformed with joy as she laughed, waving her arms. She accidentally splashed him, then laughed at his reaction of mock affront.

He splashed her back, and soon they were in an all-out water fight. Her solemnity of before was forgotten, and Ember was overjoyed to have put a smile on her face.

When they finally left, they were both soaked through. The fabric of Mooriah's chestcloth clung to her breasts, and her waistcloth made the curve of her wide hips impossible to ignore. Ember struggled not to stare. She didn't seem to notice though, still riding high—this place had that effect on people. In the days after his mother's death, it had been a great comfort. He didn't want to do anything to diminish her shine, and so with great force of will, he endeavored to look only at her face.

"Thank you for bringing me here," she said, still smiling as they entered the tunnel which was the only exit. At the other end she stopped, half hidden in darkness. "You truly don't care about my Song?"

"I don't."

Her gaze lowered to his chest, and he found himself holding his breath as she looked her fill. The only light was from the chamber they were about to enter. The air became charged between them, almost sizzling with a heat he was sure would dry them off in no time. When her gaze finished roaming and met his again, her eyes were heavy lidded.

She reached up to cup his cheeks and draw him down closer to her height. "I have something to tell you," she whispered.

He bent lower and lower, not resisting her pull. "What?" He wasn't certain when he'd last taken a breath, his attention was on her skin touching his, the intensity in her eyes.

"I've always wanted to do this."

This time neither of them backed away. They erased the space between them and met in the middle, pressing their lips together. The contact was like a spark on dry kindling. Ember ignited, the kiss moving from innocent and chaste to blazing in the fraction of an eye-blink.

His hands encircled her waist, and he picked her up. She wrapped her legs around him, pressing the heat of her core against his abdomen. He shuddered and broke the kiss, spinning her and bringing her back against the wall. Her arms came around his neck, and he pressed against her, causing her to gasp.

He sought her lips again, the kiss a fiery inferno of need pent up between the two of them. Her admission had surprised him. How long had she felt the pull toward him? As long as he'd felt it for her?

Their tongues danced together as she pressed tighter against him. If he could open himself up and bring her inside, he would. He settled for tumbling into the kiss, becoming consumed by it. He hitched her higher and enjoyed the feeling of her body clinging to his. The score of her nails against his back and neck. Her heat singed his stomach; he slid a hand up her thigh to explore and possibly get burned, when footsteps sounded.

Their mouths tore apart; Mooriah was wild-eyed, breathing heavily. They were at the edge of a hub where a half-dozen hallways converged. This place was obviously not as abandoned as it looked.

Ember set her down, and they swiftly straightened their drenched clothing before turning to face the person exiting a tunnel across from them. When Glister appeared, Mooriah stiffened and moved further into the darkness behind them.

"There you are," Glister said with a smile before she took note of Mooriah. Her welcoming expression turned harsh. "What are *you* doing here?"

Ember wrangled his expression, hoping he didn't look guilty or flushed or aroused or any of the other myriad things he was feeling.

Mooriah stepped to his side, though quite a distance away. "I've been looking for a new source of rubia honey. I had reason to believe a hive of cave bees was near here."

Glister frowned then turned back to Ember. "Your father is looking for you."

"Ah, okay."

"Why didn't you just summon him?" Mooriah asked, eyes narrowed.

Glister tilted her head coquettishly. "I could have, but I wanted to find him for myself." Ember's face heated, much to his dismay. She must have used some sort of locating spell. If he could ward himself, he could prevent being found—all the more reason to train harder.

Shooting another look of disdain Mooriah's way, Glister seemed to finally notice that both of them were wet. "What happened to you?"

"The ceiling of a tunnel back there caved in," he said, quickly. "Water started pouring down. I'm going to have one of the maintainers see to it." He cleared his throat. "Could be dangerous."

Glister's smile was brilliant. "And that's why you're going to make a great chieftain. Come along, we don't want to keep

Crimson waiting." She held out a hand as though she wanted him to take it.

When he did not reach for her, she grabbed him. Unlike Mooriah's, her palm felt clammy and sickeningly boneless. As Glister led him away, he looked over his shoulder back to where Mooriah stood with her arms crossed, watching them.

Her expression was shuttered, offering no clue to her feelings. Then she turned away.

This wasn't how he wanted to walk away from her—in fact, he didn't want to walk away from her. Not now or ever.

But he would go now to appease his father. He didn't want anything to make Crimson disqualify him before the match with Rumble. After that though, all bets were off. Ember would win—somehow—and then the whole clan would know how he felt about Mooriah.

# CHAPTER TEN

Inception of Illusion: To pass a memory on to another.

A liberal mixture of salt bronze, shadow nightshade, cinderberry, and ash of mercy may be optionally used to focus those new to working this spell. The true activator must be chosen by the mage and imbued with their intention. Light-headedness and fainting are common.

— WISDOM OF THE FOLK

Mooriah returned to the cornerstone the next day, confident she could complete her spell. Though after a fitful night tossing and turning in her bed—reliving the kiss with Ember, the way he'd felt pressed against her, and her body's reaction—she wasn't as bright and chipper as she could be.

She desperately wanted to know what would have happened if Glister hadn't interrupted them. His hand had been so close to where she longed for it to be. What would it have felt like if he'd reached his destination? Her face heated, along with other parts of her body.

She still couldn't believe Ember had taken her to a place that held so much sentimental value to him. And she had loved it. Adored being there amidst the beauty and majesty of the largest waterfall she'd ever seen or conceived of. Its strangely warm water had been comforting, and even walking back to her quarters through the tunnels soaking wet had not been a hardship.

Around Ember she felt peaceful. He wasn't judgmental. He'd never looked down on her for any reason. And though they had never been in each other's orbits before, she'd witnessed his kindness, compassion, and strength for years.

Something inside her had cracked open when their lips touched. The force of the feelings rushing out shocked her. She was so used to hiding everything, keeping everything tucked away so it wouldn't be cause for criticism, that now she felt raw and without protection. Her heart was at serious risk.

*Finish, and then you can see him tonight,* she told herself. Of course this day would last forever until she did.

"What has you smiling so mysteriously?" Fenix asked, cutting into her thoughts.

She startled, then with great effort, blanked her face. She'd forgotten he was there. "Nothing."

"Ah, I was hoping you'd share what put such an expression on your face. Could it be because you're here again with me?" He grinned, his lambent eyes seeking to hypnotize her. She blinked and shook her head.

"Not everything is about you, you know."

He chuckled. "No? If you say so."

She groaned at his arrogance and got back to work. Amazingly enough, Fenix did as well.

She was still feeling her way around the process of integrating Nethersong into her father's spell using the complicated weaving technique he'd described to her. Speaking of Yllis, he was nowhere to be found this morning. She squashed the pang of disappointment until it was so tiny as to almost not exist.

Mooriah flowed back into a meditative state, directing death energy around Yllis's existing spell. She could not affect the Earthsong, she could not even truly sense it, aside from a sort of emptiness where nothing else was. But that was the key to the technique, to braid a chain of energy that wrapped around what she could not see.

It was difficult but invigorating work. She was at it for half the day before falling back into her physical senses, excitement thrumming through her.

"I think I've done it!" She opened her eyes, surprised to find Fenix seated right next to her. She grinned at him. "I've finished and it's... Oh it's magnificent. I can't believe such a thing is possible. It's just—" His expression gave her pause. "Why are you looking at me like that?"

For the duration of their short acquaintance, he had generally been cheery and full of mirth. Not taking anything too seriously, except for the incident with the cougar. But now all traces of his signature smirk were missing. He reached up and touched her braided hair, freezing her in place. "It's wonderful to see such joy is all. You're so beautiful and even more so when you smile."

She swallowed and backed out of his reach. Though his face was almost grave, his body began shining bright.

"You cannot really want to stay here," he said. "Now you've completed your father's task, why would you want to retreat back into the darkness?"

"It's not all darkness. There's beauty there too." Like the waterfall and kissing Ember. Neither of which she'd share with him.

She stood and turned her back to him, her feelings a jumble.

There was something intoxicating about Fenix that made it hard to concentrate with all that brightness in her eyes. She didn't want to be addled, she needed to think clearly. Which was also hard to do when he stared at her like she was some sort of jewel.

She felt him at her back and stiffened. "What do you want?"

"I want you to come with me. Leave the darkness and come out into the air and the sunshine. Explore this world and live under the blue skies every day. Maybe even..."

She looked to the side, sighting him in her periphery. "Maybe what?"

"Maybe I could even take you to my world."

Shock stole her voice.

"I'm not sure if it's possible—we'd have to find a way for you to survive the portals, but I'm willing to try."

She spun around to face him, squaring her shoulders. "Why? Why do you want me to go so badly with you? You hardly know me at all."

"Because you're a diamond trapped in a bed of coal. You deserve to shine and let the world see your light. Don't you know that you're blinding?" He glowed even brighter as he said this, making her squint. One shining hand rose to stroke her cheek, and the touch was like sparks of energy on her skin.

He leaned in farther like he was going to kiss her, but she slid away from him.

He dimmed somewhat. "I'm not imagining that there is something between us. The way you look at me sometimes."

Her stomach churned as if cave bees had taken residence within. "You are very interesting to look at."

He leveled a gaze at her, and she shook her head. "I find you intriguing. You're different to anyone I've ever known. But I don't want what you want. I want—"

"A people who will only accept you once you reach a set of criteria? Who will never truly see you as one of them?"

"And you think out here would be different for me?" she said with a dry laugh.

"Out here is real; in there is not."

Once again, his arrogance got her hackles up. "In there is just as real as anywhere else. It's my home."

But an ugly thought raised its head. Yesterday, Ember had walked away from her with hope in his eyes. But even if he became chieftain, wouldn't a woman like Glister be better for him? Someone with a good family with resources and connections?

If Mooriah succeeded in becoming clan shaman, she would have respect and a place in Cavefolk society, but it was not the same as what Glister offered.

As if he saw the doubts in her mind, Fenix came closer. "I know you are thinking about it. I'm not giving up. I will be here, waiting. I know you will change your mind."

Some of the smugness was back, but underneath she sensed real emotion. She wasn't sure how much was bravado and how much was sincerity, but her heart hurt for him.

"I don't want to hurt you Fenix. I will not be here."

She spun around and headed back down the path that led her home. As her footsteps traipsed across the trail, a voice in her head wondered if she should accept his offer. But she shook it off.

Soon she was out of the cold and back inside the warmth of the Mother. Where she belonged.

# CHAPTER ELEVEN

Barrier of Rivals: Forbidden, except by the elder shaman. Blocks the spells of others for short periods of time. Can cause temporary blindness or double vision. Punishment for unauthorized usage is banishment.

— WISDOM OF THE FOLK

Mooriah held her breath as Ember sliced into his palm. His whole body was rigid, muscles carved from stone, but he managed it. A tiny trickle of blood trailed the route of the thin blade. His eyes were pressed closed so he didn't see it.

"Now the incantation," she breathed, afraid too much sound would startle him.

He intoned the words of the first Fortitude Seal, the one to bind him against death by blade. His voice was strong, though it cracked a few times before picking up again. And then the deed was done.

He opened one eye and looked at her. She nodded encouragingly. She'd already closed his wound so by the time he opened his other eye there was no trace of blood left.

"I did it?" His voice was hushed.

It was the weakest ward she'd ever seen, but the fact that he'd actually accomplished it made her heart burst. She grinned and leaned over to wrap her arms around him. "You did it!"

He hooted and tightened his embrace rocking her back and forth until they fell back on the seating mats, his deep laugh filling the space and warming her. He'd taken the brunt of the fall; she lay sprawled on top of him looking down into his pale eyes.

"I'm really warded?" he asked.

She grinned up at him. "Yes." It wasn't a lie; he was protected a little. But she didn't want to dim his joy.

He rolled them over until he was on top and smiled the brightest smile she'd ever seen on him. "I can't thank you enough."

"You worked hard. I know it's still really difficult, but you can build on this."

He sobered somewhat. "Is it enough for today?"

"It will have to be."

The match began in under an hour, so there was no time for more. The ward was weak, however, Mooriah would be in the audience watching him carefully. While he may not be protected from the worst Rumble had to give, she would make sure that whatever happened, he would survive. While Ember had spent the past few days practicing basic children's spells, Mooriah had been studying the forbidden workings for mending flesh and bones. The ones that could restore him if his own wards did not protect him.

But she did not tell him. He would need confidence to face his brother, not doubts. "You have everything you need to defeat him. Never doubt that you will win and usher our clan into an era of lasting peace and unity."

He blinked, visibly moved by her statement. "You truly believe that?"

"Of course."

"You are amazing, Mooriah."

Given their position, she thought he might kiss her again. Her breath caught and her gaze dropped to his lips.

"If I was not already nearly late for the match..." The look he gave her made her want to clench her thighs together. He was already between them. All he needed was to—

"But there isn't time for what I want to do."

"Then you'd best get off me," she said with a laugh.

He groaned and rolled away, leaving her cold without his weight on top of her. She swallowed and sat up, then took his outstretched hand and rose.

"We'll have to hurry," she said.

They raced through the pathways and down several levels to the arena. Since each clan celebrated the First Frost Festival on their own, the crowd that had gathered around the brawling circle was smaller than at Ember's last match—but still represented just about all able-bodied Night Snow members, plus the unclanned who desired to attend.

A troupe of dancers was performing the Winter Totter, a graceful interpretation of the season. It was one of Mooriah's favorites to watch every year, perhaps if she became clan she could join the dancers one day. But today, nerves about Ember's performance kept her distracted.

They stood at the entrance to the arena, hidden in the shadows. He was so close his breath tickled her ear. "A kiss for luck?" he whispered.

She smiled, her nerves dissolved for the moment. She looked

around—everyone was already inside the arena watching the dancers. No one to see their stolen kiss.

She'd intended only a peck on the cheek, but he turned his head at the last minute and their lips met. It would be so easy to shut out the rest of the world, the beating of the drums, the plucking of strings, the pounding of feet against the ground. But she knew they had to keep it short and pulled away before she fell under. Even still, she was left breathless, blinking up into his slow smile.

"Now there is no way I can lose. After the match, I need to talk to you about something."

And with that mysterious statement, he was off, jogging into the arena to prepare. Leaving her wide-eyed with a heart that had already missed several beats.

She turned around, intending to enter through another passageway and find a seat. No one was paying attention to her, but for prudence's sake it shouldn't look like they arrived at the same time. But her plans were dashed when she discovered Glister standing behind her.

A scowl marred the woman's beauty. Rage fizzed from her like steam. Her icy gaze shifted from Mooriah to the crowd beyond, where Ember had gone.

"You harlot," she spat through gritted teeth. Then she grabbed Mooriah's arm and, with her free hand, stabbed her with something small and sharp, muttering the words of a spell that made Mooriah's bones feel like they were melting. She could not resist as Glister dragged her off and away from the arena.

"You think a dalliance with him will get you anywhere?" Glister seethed. "The next chieftain will be mine. I will be Lady of the Clan."

Mooriah's mouth would not even work to protest, her tongue was heavy inside her mouth. The music from the dancers pealed and the drumbeats thrummed underfoot— they had not traveled far—when Glister stopped in an alcove cut into the stone. With her foot, she nudged at something embedded in the ground. The covering for an old maintainer's hatch. The clay lid was thick and round and protected the hatches that the maintainers used to service the plumbing lines and renew the firerocks.

Mooriah had never before been inside the warren of passageways used by the diminutive men and women who served the clan in that way. But now, Glister shifted the covering aside with her foot and then shoved Mooriah into the darkened pit.

She felt no pain when she landed, her body was still boneless and unresponsive to her commands. The shaft was as about three times her height and must have outlets, but she couldn't control her body yet to investigate. She'd landed on her back and looked up at Glister replacing the cover and leaving her in darkness before disappearing.

A few minutes later, the paralyzing spell wore off and Mooriah climbed to her feet.

"Glister! Glister! Help!"

The music from the dancers still overwhelmed all other sounds. Soon the crowd would be roaring, all keyed up for the brawl. No one could hear her. And she would not be there to protect Ember.

She slammed her hand against the rock wall and screamed in frustration. But there was no one to hear her cries.

Ember wiped the sweat from his brow, never once turning from his brother's glare. Taking his eyes off his opponent would be folly. Especially when that opponent was as ruthless as Rumble.

The two were well matched in height and weight, but Rumble had one advantage—sheer meanness. He also had access to a well of ferocious fury that Ember had never been able to tap into, and it made him brutal.

The last days spent practicing blood magery instead of training did Ember no favors either, though he'd been disciplined with his exercises for two decades—a few days here or there should make little difference.

Still, the blow Rumble had just landed on Ember's jaw made his teeth rattle. He prodded one with his tongue to see if it was loose and tasted blood. He swallowed it down, imagining his stomach lined with stone. He heard Mooriah's calming words in his mind, which helped him seal away his disgust.

He longed to find her location in the crowd but was almost glad he hadn't yet—he'd want to watch her, and that was a distraction he could not afford.

The chime signaling the end of the first round sounded, and he retreated to the sidelines to swish his mouth with water. He took the time then to search for her, surprised when he couldn't spot her immediately. His gaze had always been drawn to her like a magnet, and because of her coloring and hair, she usually stood out.

Movement across the circle drew his attention from the audience. Glister was there whispering in Rumble's ear. Ember had had the feeling that she was attempting to ingratiate herself with both brothers, hedging her bets to ensure that she found favor with whomever would be the next chieftain.

Still, whatever she told him made Rumble's gaze zero in on Ember and harden. A chill went through him.

The match had already been brutal, but he got the sense his brother had been holding back. This was confirmed when Rumble spoke briefly to an assistant, who then retrieved a dagger.

In fights to the short death, the second round was when the stakes were raised. Weapons were not allowed in round one because longer matches kept the crowd more entertained. But now the blades would be drawn.

Ember sucked in a deep breath and searched for Mooriah again. Somehow, he'd expected her to be in the front row. But being unclanned, she'd probably been pushed to the back by someone eager for a better view.

As long as he won, he could ensure that she never had to face such indignities again. He palmed his own dagger, his resolve hardening as the gong sounded.

Back in the circle, they fought hard, both drawing from their long experience. Ember had been battling his brother all his life and knew his tricks. He managed to nick Rumble's shoulder, which made the man growl and retreat.

"I hear you've been spending time with the little sorceress," Rumble said as they circled one another, crouching low. "Wonder where she is now?"

Ember faked right but Rumble anticipated and was there to meet him, lashing out with the blade, but Ember was too quick and avoided the strike.

"After I win, I'll make sure she's never initiated," Rumble continued. "She'll be wandering the peaks with the nomads, reduced to eating guano before she's ever a member of Night Snow."

Ember grit his teeth, refusing to take the bait and lose focus. "You won't touch her because you'll never be chief. And she *will* be clan. She will be my wife."

Rumble snorted. "Wife? She's not good enough to even be our servant. When I'm chief there will be none of these unclanned parasites hanging around. They'll all be kicked out, left to fend for themselves in the darklands or on the Outside."

Ember shook his head and took advantage Rumble's

unguarded side. In a calculated move, he slashed out and retreated, but Rumble caught his leg and flipped him. As he fell, he reached out and embedded his blade in his brother's side, just under the ribs.

His bones rattled as he hit the ground, hard, and Rumble howled in pain.

Blinking up at the ceiling high overhead, Ember's jaw dropped. He'd landed a killing blow. He had won.

Rumble was on his knees, holding the knife sticking out of him. Ember sat up, beginning to rise, when Rumble attacked and struck his own blade into Ember's belly. The move was illegal, the match was already over, but worse, the burning in his abdomen made it feel like the blade was made of pure fire.

He sputtered looking down at the blood pouring from him. It bubbled and frothed unnaturally.

Poison. He stared wide-eyed at his brother.

Ember's ward against blades would do nothing against one with a poisoned tip.

He fell back to the ground in disbelief and stared at the ceiling until the darkness welcomed him.

# CHAPTER TWELVE

Tempest of Enmity: Inflame tensions between opponents.

A fistful of ground blue ginger, two pinches star root, sweetened with rubia honey. Blood from five incisions corresponding to the Five Doorways of Breath.

— WISDOM OF THE FOLK

The sounds of the crowd rose and fell as the fight went on. Mooriah had tried everything she could think of to get herself out of this pit. She'd tried climbing, but the walls were smooth and slick. The maintainers used ropes and pulleys to get in and out, and she had none. She had beaten her hands against the rock walls until they were numb, to no avail.

She found no outlets from her dark prison. No holes to crawl through or other passages leading from where she was. Blood spells had not helped either. There was none she could think of that could make her fly or climb smooth walls. She tried to summon Oval or Murmur or one of Murmur's family group—but nothing. Could Glister have blocked her summoning in some way? Though Mooriah was the better mage, Glister was no slouch—it was certainly possible.

Everything she tried fizzled, but it was not until the crowd grew hushed that she truly became afraid. It was as if the entire audience took a collective gasp. One of the warriors had fallen, Rumble or Ember?

She cried out again, screaming in rage and pain, when light flared overhead. She looked up to find Murmur's face peering down at her. "Thank the Mother!" she cried. "Can you get me out of here?"

The elder waved a hand and murmured an incantation too softly for her to hear. The smooth stone of the walls changed and morphed into stairs which she used to climb out. She had no idea such a spell was possible and cursed her ignorance.

"Mooriah, I've been searching for you. I've had a vision—"

"I must check on Ember," she said racing past him back to the arena. She sped down the aisle to the brawling circle then stopped short.

Ember lay on his back in the center, a knife protruding from his belly. The wound was putrid, the blood foamed and was tinged with a bluish tint. She approached and dropped to her knees, horror making her movements jerky. The crowd was quiet.

This was poison. Even had Ember's wards been at normal strength, he would not have been protected from such.

Across the circle, Rumble stood with Glister. The match official had not yet awarded Rumble the winner's ribbons, but the warrior's expression was smug. Glister appeared flustered, her gaze returning again and again to Ember's motionless body and his bubbling wound.

Crimson stood at the edge of the circle, his gaze stormy.

Mooriah had no idea what the chieftain was thinking or feeling as he watched his son succumb to what was obviously poison, but at the moment it didn't matter. She sank into the embrace of her Song and reached for Ember with her power.

He was nearly gone but not quite. Wanting to cry with joy, she drew away the Nethersong filling him, pulling him back from death's door. Vaguely she heard the rising voices of an argument between the match official and Rumble, and Crimson's voice intervening, but her only focus was on keeping Ember from dying.

He was no longer on the cusp, but neither was he healing. She fumbled for the blade at her waist and sliced both her palm and Ember's, mingling their blood and working a forbidden spell. The damage to his organs from the blade she could patch, but she didn't know what kind of poison Rumble had used, and it was wreaking havoc on him.

She removed the Nethersong from the substance, making it inert, but it had already worked so quickly, affecting Ember's blood. Rumble had planned well, choosing something to kill his brother that a shaman would find nearly impossible to fix. Their magic required the patient's blood, and Ember's was tainted.

She looked around wildly and found Murmur only a few steps away. She pleaded with her gaze, but he shook his head.

"I'm sorry, child. This is not something I can undo. His blood is toxic, the blood cannot save him."

"Can we purify it?" Her mind raced for a spell that would do such, but Murmur's expression was her answer.

Her breathing became stuttered and a ringing jangled inside her head. Connected to her Song, she pulled away the Nether as it formed around Ember, but his chest had ceased to rise and fall.

Rumble's laugh drew her attention to him. Apparently tired

of the arguing, he wrenched the ribbons away from the official's hand. "Enough! What does it matter what the rules say? I am alive; he is dead. I am the chieftain's heir."

He lifted a hand in the air, seeking a cheer from the crowd. A low murmur rose, but not the exuberance he seemed to want. Next to him, Glister shook with fear. Had she somehow found the blood poison and shared it with him? She seemed to be afraid of him now, but Mooriah wouldn't put it past the woman to get in deeper than she'd expected with such a character.

"Did you hear me? I am the chieftain's heir!" Both of his arms shot into the air, and the audience caught hold of his mood. More enthusiastic cheers rose all around, though the people still seemed confused.

Mooriah stood and faced him. "You will *never* be chief."

She unleashed her Song from its tether and struck Rumble down where he stood. The cheering of the crowd echoed in her ears. How dare they applaud Rumble's fraud? How dare they support this pretender?

Grief and rage took flight, and her Song swooped outward on wings of pain. Was this the clan she wanted so badly to join? One who would encourage this charlatan?

A lifetime's worth of slights and judgment exploded from her, and her Song rode this wave. It took down everyone in its path; the roar of the masses was silenced.

Everyone around her fell to the ground, taken out by her power. Even Murmur was silent and still, laying prone beside her.

She swallowed, once again leashing her Song. Tears streamed down her face, and her heart hurt. All here were warded against her, they would awaken.

But Ember, her Ember.

Nethersong could not heal him. Blood magic could not save him. He needed Earthsong.

She raced to a cart used by one of the food vendors and emptied it, then levered Ember's body into it. He was so heavy that she wasn't certain she would even accomplish it, but pure force of will drove her forward.

She pushed the cart along the pathways and toward the only person who could help her now.

She found Fenix at the small plateau outside the tunnel. He faced away from her, staring out at the darkness beyond. Grateful that she would not have to drag Ember all the way to the cornerstone, she stopped, trying to catch her breath. Night had fallen, and a bright moon illuminated the frost, which covered not only the mountain but the farmland beyond.

"Your father has gone. He told me to tell you goodbye. You see, I knew you'd come. I..." He turned and caught sight of Ember in the cart, and the smile he wore dissolved.

She was breathing heavily and sweating from the effort of maneuvering the cart through passages that had not been designed for such. Ember was solid and probably weighed twice what she did. But she'd done it. Now she just needed Fenix to help.

She pointed to him. "He's gone. I won't allow death to take him, but he's in a sort of limbo. I need for you to bring him back."

Fenix frowned, staring down at Ember whose blood coated his abdomen and legs as well as the inside of the cart. It was becoming harder and harder to draw the Nethersong away from him without something else to fill it. But she would do it for as long as she could.

"Help him," she pleaded. Whatever force had held back her emotions up until now shattered, and she bent over the cart, tears streaming down her face. Sobs heaved themselves up from deep within. She fell to her knees, fingers gripping the edge of the cart. "Please."

Fenix's feet came into her vision; he kneeled next to her and tilted her chin up. "Of course." He gazed at her with tenderness and sorrow as she tried to stop her breath from hiccupping.

Fenix stood, then lifted Ember easily and lay him on the ground. Mooriah had forgotten her cloak, but even the bitterness of the cold or the frost at her knees didn't penetrate. Grief, hope, desperation—the emotions were like quicksand seeking to pull her under.

With a wave of his hand, the frost melted and the ground beneath her warmed. She looked up, surprised. But of course, she knew little of the extent of Fenix's power.

He knelt at Ember's head, hands at his temples. Very quickly, a bright light enveloped Ember's body and the knife she had been too afraid to remove, pushed its way out. The blood congealing on his skin disappeared, even his stained waistcloth was now clean.

When Fenix pulled his hands away, Ember's chest rose and fell as if he was in a peaceful, deep sleep.

Mooriah gaped and sat back in a daze. "I— I—" She shook her head trying to clear it.

"He'll need to sleep for a while. When he awakens, he will be perfectly fine."

She reached for Fenix, grabbing his hand in hers and squeezing. "I don't know how to thank you. I owe you such a debt."

His smile was sad. "You owe me nothing." His gaze returned to Ember. "Is he why you will not leave?"

She swallowed, eyes drawn to the warrior's sleeping form. She stroked his cheek. "He is one reason." She set her shoulders and faced Fenix again.

She owed him a truth. "I have to admit that there is a part of me that wants to go with you. To... explore this world. I am... drawn to you. But I don't want to hurt you. Because my heart belongs to another."

Fenix sat back and looked out across the moonlit vista again. "He is a lucky man."

She shifted, tucking her legs under her. "Perhaps in another lifetime things would have been different. Between us."

His gaze returned to her, intense, as his skin took on its signature glow. "In another lifetime, there still can be."

She tilted her head in question.

"I'm not giving up on you, Mooriah. I will return here. I will come back every ten years, at midnight on the day of the Frost Festival. I will wait for you."

Her heart clenched, and she shook her head. "Please don't. It would be a waste."

"No, it will be a hope. And sometimes hope is all you need to keep moving." He pierced her with sharp eyes that made her chest ache. She did not want him to suffer, but there was no way she could give him what he wanted.

He began to glow even brighter, shifting into his other form, the one made of light.

"Fenix?"

"Yes?" His voice came from a luminescence too bright to meet head on.

"Thank you again."

The light bobbed in acknowledgment and then raced away into the night.

# CHAPTER THIRTEEN

Elevation of Cheer: Raises sunken spirits and provides warmth when cold.

Combine three pinches salt bronze and half a palm's worth of crushed water blossom petals. To avoid overheating, use only fresh blossoms, not dried.

— WISDOM OF THE FOLK

Ember rolled over, pulled out of sleep by a sound he couldn't place. Memories rushed back, flooding him with vivid images and recollections of intense pain. He sat straight up with a gasp and clutched his stomach.

Only to find it whole. He ran a hand over his chest and abdomen, but the skin was perfect, unmarred. Even old scars had disappeared. His coloring was also higher, he was nearly glowing with health. A sense of wonder settled upon him.

He lay before the firepit in his nanny's old dwelling. Movement behind made him tense, but he turned to find Mooriah, pouring steaming water into two drinking bowls. She beamed at him.

"Welcome back." She brought the bowls to him and sat beside him. "Here, drink this," she said, passing him the fragrant tea. Its scent was comforting, reminding him of his mother and being taken care of when he was sick as a child.

The bowl warmed his hands, and he focused on that as he gathered his thoughts. "What happened?"

"What is the last thing you remember?"

"The match. I struck Rumble—a killing blow. That should have been the end but... He stabbed me. There was... poison." The memory of pain assaulted him, but he pushed it back. Did he feel disappointment over his brother's betrayal? He wasn't sure, but he certainly was not surprised. He should have expected as much from him.

She nodded solemnly, blowing on her own small bowl. "The wards could not have held up against poison. Especially not a poison of the blood. There is no protection for such."

"So how am I alive?"

Instead of looking at him, it seemed that she was looking anywhere else. Why was she avoiding his gaze? He leaned closer to find tears welling in her eyes.

"I'm sorry that I failed you." She shook her head, staring at her tea. "And my chance at becoming clan is gone."

His chest tightened with disbelief. "Why would you think that?"

She swallowed and shakily told him of what Glister had done. How Mooriah had arrived in the arena to find him near death and had lashed out with her power, knocking out the entire clan.

"After this," she said, sniffing, "I am certain none will feel safe around me."

Ember set his tea down and put an arm around her, pulling her close. She buried her head against his chest, wetting it with her tears.

"You have not been back there?"

"I brought you here once Fenix healed you. I didn't want to return until you'd awakened."

At the mention of Fenix, his mouth grew dry. "The sorcerer healed me?"

"I could not let you die, Ember. I know you don't think much of his manipulating life and death, but you should not have died. It was not your time, and your blood was not in service to the Mother. I will not apologize for saving you." She pulled back to glare at him, her jaw set.

He fought a smile at her mulish expression. "I will never ask you to. I'm grateful to you. Thank you. I suppose I owe the sorcerer a debt as well." He would have to release the wariness and jealousy of the man who had saved him.

"He is gone. You owe him nothing." Her voice was carefully blank, but she'd stiffened.

"Are you... upset about him leaving?" He held his breath, unsure if he really wanted to hear her response.

Her head whipped around until she was frowning at him. "What? No. I—" She shook her head. "No."

She set her mug down and stroked his face. "I only wanted for you to be all right. My father is gone too, apparently. Without even saying goodbye." She smiled sadly. "We were lucky that Fenix was still there. Without an Earthsinger, you would not be alive."

He felt his silent debt to the Singer in question grow. But was glad the man was gone.

Mooriah leaned against him, placing a hand on his chest.

Ember stilled, not wanting her to move. "I don't know where I will go," she said. "I doubt I will be able to stay in Night Snow now."

"We shall see," he murmured and lifted her hand to kiss the back of it.

"I would do it again though," she whispered, voice grave. "A thousand times over, no matter the consequence."

"We are not sure of the consequence yet. Not until we return and face the clan. How long has it been?"

"Half a day. But I don't want to go back yet."

The sooner they returned the sooner he could see about setting this right and ensuring her place in the clan. Maybe they would redo the match or maybe, since Ember had rightfully won, the officials or Crimson would rule in his favor.

"We should—"

She silenced him by pressing her lips against his. Her kiss was desperate, seeking. It ignited a strange energy that had been thrumming through his veins since he'd awakened. He felt more alive, more energetic than he ever had before. He deepened their kiss until he swore he could feel it in his spine and ankles and wrists. Mooriah was everywhere; infused into every cell of his being.

As if to reinforce that thought, she shifted to straddle him. He was vaguely aware of the drinking bowls tipping over and tea pouring down into the firepit. But if Ember was feeling more animated, Mooriah apparently was too.

She pushed him down until he lay on his back with her atop him. Her hands explored his chest, running across his pectorals, down the ridges of his abdomen, and back up again.

She lowered her head and trailed kisses across him, laving him with her tongue and gently nibbling his skin. Her teeth grazed his nipple and he hissed, hardening to stone. She ground against him, the heat between her legs inflaming his already needy erection.

He took control, rolling them until he was on top of her. She spread her legs wide to accommodate him. Starting at her jaw, he kissed his way down her neck and shoulder. The fabric of her chestcloth was in the way; he tugged at its tie to loosen it. Mooriah rose and removed the offending clothing, presenting her bared breasts to him.

Firelight made her skin glisten. He palmed her breasts, testing their weight and running the pad of his thumb across one, dark nipple. The urge to taste was too strong to ignore. His tongue ran circles around first one then the other, and he grazed her with his teeth, satisfied when she bucked in response.

Then he delved lower, kissing across the gentle curve of her belly, gauging her reaction. His hands cupped generous hips, and he nuzzled their apex through her waistcloth.

Her fingers trembled as she undid her belt and slid out of her remaining clothing. Then she was bare before him, and he could feast.

Mooriah writhed and squirmed as Ember's tongue attacked her core. He lapped at her with a fervency she would never have guessed possible. She squeezed her eyes tight under the assault and whimpered.

Her legs were mobile, kicking at the air when he placed his large hands on her thighs to still her. Then he resumed his attack with even more urgency.

She clutched the mats beside her as the pleasure rose and crested and she breathed out her emotions, chanting his name over and over again.

All was still for a moment. She no longer held control of her body, it belonged to Ember. He crawled up her body in order to claim it.

If her fingers worked, she would have undone his waistcloth, but she was lucky that he attended to the task himself, very efficient. She did manage to lift her arm to stroke the thick length of him. The action made him still, his eyes glittering in the firelight.

This brought back more of her fine motor skills. She stroked him again, squeezing her fist around him. He sucked in a breath in response and removed her hand, lowering his weight onto her.

He licked the shell of her ear and kissed her jaw as she wriggled beneath him, eager to rub against his solid hardness. "Mooriah," he said, voice husky.

"Yes?"

"I am yours now. Whatever happens."

She couldn't respond to that and was grateful when he guided himself into her. The slow push inside made her eyes roll back into her head with relief. It felt like he was coming home inside her body.

She gripped him tight, their breathing deepening. He found her mouth, and they kissed messily, then he retreated from her body to enter again.

She wrapped her legs around him and tilted her pelvis to meet his thrusts, urging him onward silently. He met the challenge and soon was pistoning into her. The mats beneath them slid across the ground with each thrust. She planted her heels on the backs of his thighs and gave herself over to the sensations overtaking her.

When she went over the massive crest this time, he was with her. Spilling his seed inside her and shouting his release.

They lay there afterward, clinging to each other. The fire in the pit had cooled to nothing but embers. Ember—the man—shifted his weight, but she squeezed him tighter, not wanting him to go yet. Not wanting him to ever leave her.

Wishing that when he said he belonged to her, it could somehow be true.

# CHAPTER FOURTEEN

Enhancement of Vision: Increases patience; nourishes foresight.

Crush phantom rosemary and add two drops of rubia honey. Meditate and await the Breath Father's voice. Only by his will may the spell be completed.

— WISDOM OF THE FOLK

It didn't take long for Ember to convince Mooriah to head back to the arena. She knew she had to face her fate, and Ember's optimism was endearing but she couldn't stand false hope. She would pay the consequences of her actions, whatever they might be.

The pathways and tunnels of Night Snow were oddly quiet. They encountered no one on the journey to the arena, which she found strange. This was a heavily trafficked part of the territory, and there would normally be dozens around at this time of day tending to their various duties.

But once they entered the arena, the reason became clear. None of the audience had yet awoken. They were all as they'd been over half a day ago, collapsed where they'd fallen when Mooriah unleashed her Song upon them. Their chests rose and fell with their breaths, but they were all still unconscious.

She reached out with her Song and found that virtually everyone present had the amount of Nethersong they should. Whatever she'd done to them had not harmed them in any way. It was just taking quite a bit longer than she'd assumed for the effects to wear off.

In fact, as she and Ember stood there slack jawed and staring, people began to stir, making soft movements and groans of waking.

"Come with me," Ember said, grabbing her hand and pulling her into the sparring circle.

They approached the place where his blood still stained the ground, a congealed pool of it which had dried to an unnatural purple hue, due to the poison.

Ember kneeled, tugging on her arm for her to join him.

"What are you doing?" she asked.

"No one will know what's happened. They can't blame you if this affected you too, can they?" His tone was urgent. Bewildered by this logic, she nonetheless followed his lead.

"Now collapse on top of me like you were mourning me."

It wasn't a stretch. This was the exact position she'd been in before Rumble had angered her. She lay across him, resting on his chest. His scent filled her nostrils as she settled and feigned unconsciousness.

All around them, people slowly awoke and began to chatter in low voices. Murmur begin to stir from his spot not far away.

Once the noise grew, she then blinked her eyes open, and sat up hesitantly.

Still monitoring the Nethersong of the crowd, she stilled at the sight of a motionless figure across the circle. Rumble lay there unstirring. Not breathing. His body was full of the Nethersong of true death. It filled him completely. Mooriah wondered if the whites of his eyes had turned black—the mark of death via pure Nethersong.

She took in a shaky breath.

The only thing she'd ever truly killed before was the cougar. Had his wards not worked properly for some reason or had her unadulterated vitriol against him pierced the protective spells?

She searched her feelings to find no remorse. He had fully intended to kill Ember, and had he lived he would no doubt have tried again. Though it was not her place to deliver punishment, had justice prevailed he would have died anyway, and deserved it. Still, if what she'd done was discovered then she would have difficult questions to answer.

As the people shook off their grogginess, the arena soon became abuzz with confusion and whispered theories of what had occurred. No one had any recollection of what had happened before they passed out. And all were shocked to discover how much time had passed. None felt that it had been so long.

Mooriah listened to it all silently, immobile as a boulder in the midst of a rushing river. Ember rose and approached his father who stood over Rumble's body. Glister was there too, staring in confusion at Rumble, and soon a medic was called to verify what Mooriah already knew.

She held her breath and moved no closer, though she desperately wanted to stay near to Ember while she could. But soon, Murmur beckoned her over to where he stood with Oval.

"It seems that no one recalls anything after Rumble stabbed Ember with the poisoned blade," Murmur said.

"Neither of you do either?" she asked.

Oval shook his head. He wore a thoughtful expression which creased his heavily wrinkled brow. "This is a great mystery," he said, voice low and gravelly.

Mooriah swallowed. "Some are saying Iron Water must be to blame. That they poisoned the air."

"That is unlikely but gather what's needed for the Trial of Purity."

She froze, she did not have her satchel, having left it in Ember's hiding place. It was quite unlike her, but the day had been full of the unexpected, and her mind was frayed and at loose ends.

Murmur noted her wide-eyed expression and nudged his own satchel toward her, which lay at his feet. She knelt, shooting him a grateful expression as the two men continued to talk.

"I suspect that this is a message from the Mother," Oval said. "It has been many years since She has sent us communication so clear."

"Or so inscrutable," Murmur added.

"Hmm." Oval strolled over to the chieftain and Murmur crouched down.

"What do you think? Is this one of the mysteries of the Mother?" he asked.

Her fingers shook under his perusal of her. She dropped the packet she had grabbed and scrabbled to pick it up again. "H-her ways are often beyond our understanding."

"True, they are. However, if something like this happens again, certain suspicions may arise." He looked at her significantly. The man who'd raised her and instructed her in the use of her Song was canny, and he suspected something.

She did not want to lie to him but feared his censure. "I—I..." She had no idea what she wanted to say. Fortunately, he glanced away toward the chieftain and his dead son. She finally settled on, "No one was seriously harmed, other than Rumble?"

"No. A few bruises and bumped heads, but nothing major."

She exhaled slowly still searching for the words to admit to him what she'd done. "I'm sorry, I—"

"Perhaps some things should remain a mystery," he said, drawing a line in the dirt with a finger.

Her mouth fell open and her breathing grew even shakier.

"Everyone will have their theories. Some will, no doubt, grow more popular than others over time. So long as this never happens again." His piercing gaze cut through her, and she nodded.

"I'm sure it never will."

"Good." He continued drawing in the dirt—another line and then three circles, separated by the two lines.

"Why?" He was effectively telling her not to tell him or anyone else what she'd done. Murmur knew more about her power than anyone, but apparently did not want to have any more information to verify his suspicions. He was trusting her to control herself better in the future—which she fully intended to do. She would train and practice even more until not even strong emotion would push her to where she'd been yesterday. But she didn't understand why he would bother to protect her.

"I had another vision." He looked around at the chaos unfolding around them. "I will tell you about it later, but it concerns your future. The path ahead is rocky for you, my dear. It holds happiness—" His gaze moved to Ember. "But also many trials. And your road is longer than you probably expect. You will be needed in the days to come. You must continue to prepare and study."

She nodded, her shoulders releasing the tension she didn't realize they held. "I will. And thank you."

He pursed his lips, his eyes seeing something far away. Maybe recalling his vision. "Don't thank me yet. By the time all is done, you may feel quite differently."

He looked down at his simple drawing. Three globes divided. She didn't know what it meant, and he wiped it away before standing and dusting his palms.

Part of her wondered what his vision would mean for her. But the other part was deeply grateful for the reprieve he'd given.

The official placed the ribbons of victory on Ember's shoulders and stepped away. A chill went through him, and his father stepped up beside him. No one in the audience was paying attention, still chattering away with one another, no doubt about the strange circumstances of their collective comas.

Ember sought out Mooriah and found her standing alone, expression plaintive. He motioned for her to come over, but she shook her head and crossed her arms over herself.

Crimson held his hands up over his head and waited for the crowd to settle and hush. Quiet descended as the clan awaited the words of their chieftain. The energy bubbling around was cautious and curious.

"I know that we all want answers as to the strange occurrences of today. One thing is clear, I have lost a son during the brawl. What the Mountain Mother and the Breath Father give unto us, they also take away."

"*Umlah*," the crowd repeated as one.

Rumble's body was still there laying at their feet. It was not the Cavefolk way to hide the dead with covers as if afraid to look upon them. Ember glanced at his brother's lifeless face. The medic had been shocked to discover that Rumble's eyes were completely blackened but posited that he might have accidentally ingested some of the poison he'd tried to kill Ember with. It was a decent explanation as no one knew what poison it was.

Crimson continued. "The Mother showed favor to my son Ember, saving him from the poisoned blade. And the prophet Murmur and our shaman, Oval, believe that while She delivered Ember from harm, She blessed the rest of us with sleep so as to keep Her mysteries intact."

Gasps sounded in the audience as this news penetrated.

"It was the Mother's will!" someone shouted.

"We are truly blessed by Her!" cried another. Exclamations of praise and gratitude rose until Crimson hushed them all again.

He gazed at Ember, solemnly. "My heir and your future chieftain is one consecrated by the Mother. Sanctified by the Breath Father who poured breath back into his lungs. Night Snow will be led by a warrior embraced by both our divine parents, and he will lead our clan to heights heretofore unseen!"

The crowd exploded into cheers. People cried out, chanting his name. "Ember! Ember!" He had no idea when Crimson had decided to spin the mystery into some divine selection, and as much as it made him uncomfortable, he had to admit it was brilliantly done.

The mass fainting of the entire clan could make them look weak, both to others and among themselves. It could deplete morale and give an opening to other clans to sow seeds of dissent. But if their chieftain was chosen by the divine parents— then Night Snow maintained its superiority, one touched by sacred hands.

And while to Crimson, this might be fertile ground on which

to start another war, to Ember this was the planting ground for lasting peace. This tale could help his quest to eventually unite the clans under one banner and preserve their true strength for as along as possible against the threat of dying out.

As the crowd continued to cheer, he acknowledged their praise with a bow. When he rose, he was pleased to see Mooriah approaching Oval. There was no doubt some type of ritual necessary now that he had been chosen as heir.

He looked around them and found Glister slowly retreating. She was sliding backward through the group of highly ranked clan members that usually flanked Crimson, trying to remain inconspicuous.

He motioned to Coal, the clan Protector, who approached. "Have Glister taken to the detention chamber. She has displeased me." Coal bowed and motioned to a guard who went to apprehend the woman. She had much to answer for.

Ember turned back as the crowd's chanting began to subside and lifted his arms to quiet them. Now that he was the heir, his commands were second only to Crimson's. And there was one thing he needed to take care of immediately.

He stepped forward to address his clan. "I am honored to be chosen as the heir and future chieftain. To serve Night Snow has long been my dream. I would also like to thank the Mountain Mother and Breath Father for their gracious blessings. I also owe a debt to the ancestors for their wisdom, to my mother, Raven, whose sacrifice has served the clan and my father, Crimson, who has led us with distinction for so long."

Applause and hurrahs rang out. But Ember was not done.

"Before the ritual begins, I would also like to show appreciation to our prophet, Murmur, for the gift of his visions and our shaman, Oval, for his protection of our home, our persons, and our spirits. Their work is essential to the clan. And to our future shaman, Mooriah—she has my deepest gratitude."

A hush settled over everyone as he called out a woman as yet unclanned. He turned to her, noting her shocked expression. "And beyond my gratitude, she holds my heart. If she will have me, I would make her my wife."

Mooriah's eyes widened and she blinked rapidly. She didn't appear to be breathing.

Beside him, Crimson hissed, "She is unclanned, son."

Ember smiled. "The chieftain's wife is by definition clan. Once we wed, she will be Lady of the Clan." He approached her, holding out his hands, waiting for her to accept them.

She looked around the silent arena. It was as if everyone was holding their collective breaths, awaiting her next move.

She extended shaking hands to him and grabbed hold. He squeezed her, and a band around his heart loosened.

"Will you have me? Will you be my wife, Mooriah?"

She was quivering, and it took her a moment to speak. "Yes, of course I will." He grinned and pulled her toward him.

Then the crowd began to cheer, more raucous and livelier than ever before. Chants went up of, "Ember! Ember! Mooriah! Mooriah!" They echoed through the stone walls of the arena all the way to the ceiling high above.

Holding her tight in his embrace, he whispered in her ear, "I am yours alone for as long as you'll have me."

"Well, you have me for life," she said, burying her face in his chest.

He was not sure that was long enough. But he would be happy to find out.

Fenix & Mooriah return in *Requiem of Silence* (Earthsinger Chronicles book 4).

# ABOUT THE AUTHOR

Leslye Penelope has been writing since she could hold a pen and loves getting lost in the worlds in her head. She is an award-winning author of fantasy and paranormal romance. Her novel *Song of Blood & Stone* was chosen as one of *TIME* Magazine's 100 Best Fantasy Books of All Time.

She started a web development studio in 2003 and is also an award-winning independent filmmaker, co-founded a literary magazine, and sometimes dreams in HTML. Her podcast, *My Imaginary Friends*, is a weekly journal of her publishing life, perfect for readers and writers alike. She lives in Maryland with her husband and their furry dependents. Visit her website to learn more: http://www.lpenelope.com.

Heartspell Media, LLC

ISBN Ebook: 978-1-944744-23-6

ISBN Print: 978-1-944744-22-9

Front cover illustration: Joel Pigou

Back cover illustration: Silents

Map illustration: S. E. Davidson www.thesketchdragon.com

CPSIA information can be obtained
at www.ICGtesting.com
Printed in the USA
LVHW100448070922
727708LV00003B/613

9 781944 744229